My
Magnolia
Summer

My Magnolia Summer

A Novel

Victoria Benton Frank

HARPER LARGE PRINT

An Imprint of **HarperCollins***Publishers*

MY MAGNOLIA SUMMER. Copyright © 2023 by New Low Country Tales Inc. All rights reserved. Printed in the United States of America. No part of this book may be used or reproduced in any manner whatsoever without written permission except in the case of brief quotations embodied in critical articles and reviews. For information, address HarperCollins Publishers, 195 Broadway, New York, NY 10007.

HarperCollins books may be purchased for educational, business, or sales promotional use. For information, please email the Special Markets Department at SPsales@harpercollins.com.

FIRST HARPER LARGE PRINT EDITION

ISBN: 978-0-06-332293-6

Library of Congress Cataloging-in-Publication Data is available upon request.

23 24 25 26 27 LBC 5 4 3 2 1

FOR MOMMA,
WHO TOLD ME I COULD DO IT.
FOR DADDY,
FOR MAKING SURE I DID.

My
Magnolia
Summer

Chapter 1
Magnolia

Last night I dreamed of Charleston, as I do almost every night. Far away from my beloved land by day, at night I am there. I dreamed of the marsh grass, the coral sunsets, the smell of plough mud, and the sound of the breeze rustling through the fronds of the palmetto trees. If you were to cut me open, you'd find the water of the Atlantic instead of blood, driftwood instead of bones, and seashells in place of everything else. When I was a little girl, and I couldn't sleep, my grandmother used to tell me to pretend that my breaths were the ocean waves rolling in and pulling away from the shore. I belong to Charleston. I belong to the island. Sullivan's Island, where I grew up, calls me home every night.

This is my story about how I returned to the island and found my wings.

My dreams are so realistic and vivid that sometimes I wake up with one foot still in the dream world. On an unseasonably cold morning in April, my alarm clock jolted me off my grandmother's porch. I quickly slapped the snooze bar to stop its blaring, shut my eyes, and went back to being eight years old.

It was Easter Sunday and we had just finished cleaning up brunch. The women in my family had prepared all the traditional food: ham, collards, red rice, and dozens of deviled eggs. We were sitting outside on Gran's rocking chairs. Sand dollars that I had collected from the beach were heaped on my lap. I had left them outside overnight and the morning sun had bleached them white. I could hear the music of the beach and the tide rolling in. My world smelled like salt from the ocean and sweet lavender from my grandmother's perfume. She picked up a couple of sand dollars and gently rattled the shells.

"Hear that, Magnolia, all that noise they are making?"

"Yes, Gran."

"Do you know what that is?"

"No, what is it?"

"It's the doves. Trying to escape!"

"Gran, those are seashells, not birds!"

"No, Doodle, there are doves trapped inside the dollars!"

"Really?"

I leaned toward her, readying myself for a story. But instead, she cracked one of the sand dollars in half, and out came white fragments that looked like little doves in flight, five of them.

"Oh, my gosh! Gran!"

"Isn't that something, Miss Maggie? That shell on its own is beautiful, with the five-pointed star in the middle and the five slits on the edge, but inside it is something even more lovely."

I was hugging her then, telling her I loved her. She was laughing at the shocked expression on my face from seeing the tiny birds fall out of the shell. We had wind chimes on our porch that were made of sand dollars. Each dollar was decorated for one of us. They were painted with a flower, representing all our names. Mine was a big magnolia, my grandmother's a rose, my mother's a lily, and my sister's a bright-purple violet. Violet had dipped hers in silver glitter and the sunshine always caught it, sometimes blinding me for a moment.

Then Gran, my mother, and I were on the beach. My mother, Lily, who had wanted to be a dancer, was entertaining us with some choreography from an old ballet class. Her bathing suit was red with white polka dots, and she danced along the sand, leaping and turning with amazing grace. Gran and I applauded and hooted loudly as she pirouetted across the hard-packed nickel-colored sand of the beach.

Gran and I were on a blanket eating one of her famous baguette sandwiches, something with ham and butter and little cornichon pickles. Gran was telling me how to pronounce "jambon aux beurre," the French name for a ham and butter sandwich.

The sound of my alarm was now so intense, I could not ignore it again. With a longing for that exact sandwich, I rubbed my eyes and stretched my stiff, sore body. The old radiator in the bedroom of the Manhattan apartment sounded like twenty hammers pounding away, struggling to keep up with the chill in the air. I sat up, turned off the blaring alarm, and looked at it. Five thirty a.m.

"Ugh."

I put my bare feet on the parquet floor and instantly I pulled them up like a crab. The floor was as cold as ice. A glance out the window confirmed what I suspected—it was snowing again, in April, the same month that it had been in my dream. In South Carolina, it was an entirely different climate. If I was on Sullivan's Island, I would have had a suntan. I groaned and searched my pale-skinned legs through the tangle of sheets for my socks, which I had kicked off in my sleep. I slowly padded my way to the bathroom, hoping not to slip or wake up my roommate, Jim. I caught one of the more pleasant scents in New York City, the smell of fresh coffee brewing. I silently thanked myself for remembering to program the coffee maker last night to wake up with me this morning.

I jumped into the shower, craning my neck so I wouldn't get my hair wet. I couldn't go outside into the tundra with wet hair and risk getting sick, and I didn't have time to dry it. I couldn't be late for work. For the past two years, I had been working as a tourant, basically a floating or relief chef who helps out wherever needed, at Bar JP, one of New York City's most popular restaurants. I was currently the only female cook on the line, and that alone was a huge accomplishment. However, now there was an opportunity to move up to a sous-chef position. I wanted that promotion because it would help me achieve my next big goal, which was to work at the company's flagship restaurant, Jean Paul's. I'd never be considered for a position in that prestigious kitchen unless I rose through the ranks at Bar JP, and not until the head chef, Jamie, deemed me ready.

Wishing I could linger under the warm spray of the shower, I turned off the water and toweled off my copper-red hair. It felt good to let the cool air hit my warm skin, but I could feel how puffy my sea-glass-green eyes were, and no doubt they were ringed with dark purple. My eyes are the same rare color as my grandmother's. Gran is the original Martha Stewart, and my personal champion. Looking into my own eyes, knowing they looked so much like Gran's, sometimes gave me strength to get through whatever I was struggling with. Gran never backed down from a challenge, so whenever anyone said I resembled her, it was a reminder to me to toughen up and put out the fire, so to speak. I felt too old for twenty-nine. This job was wearing me down.

I sighed deeply. It was going to be another long day of unpredictable hours and having to prove myself against all odds. In my mind, I heard Chef Jamie say, "You're only as good as your last plate." I nodded at myself in the mirror. I was ready to prove myself again. I couldn't cave now, not when there was an opportunity to be promoted.

Sometimes all this seemed futile. Why did I want to work at a Michelin-star-rated French restaurant in

New York City where I made a laughable minimum wage of twelve dollars an hour with no health insurance, working an average of eighty-five hours a week with no overtime pay? Why did I put up with this when I could work at any of New York's unionized hotels, where hours were normal and you earned a salary you could actually live on? Plus, the terrible weather. No one at Bar JP quit, because if you did, you'd never chop onions in a kitchen of any importance again. Anywhere. You accepted all the indignities along with the excellent training you received with a *Yes, Chef.*

Or I could have stayed on Sullivan's Island and worked in my family's restaurant, the Magic Lantern, which my great-grandmother Daisy had opened in 1942 and which my grandmother Rose still ran to this day. The patrons considered it a second home, a restaurant built on love and passion. It was about good food, good service, and fun. My grandpa Eddie used to play the horn and jam with a few of his musician friends on the front porch during dinner service. It wasn't about getting good reviews (although it did), winning awards (although it did), or featuring the next James Beard chef. As much as I loved the Magic Lantern, I'd decided to forge my own path. I'd felt that if I stayed in the South, working for my family, I'd never grow, never realize who I really was as a chef or a woman. And let's be honest, Charleston was nothing compared to New York. My life in New York, living with my best friend, Jim, was blissful. Even though he was obsessively neat and I wasn't, we hardly ever fought. We lived in his aunt's apartment, so it was inexpensive. We both loved to cook and watch old movies together. It was sort of the perfect marriage.

I worked all the time, so any potential real marriage wasn't in the cards. I had been involved for two years in an on-again, off-again relationship—if you could really call it that—with a chef I worked with named Ronny. Nothing had ever been made official, but the feelings were there. One day he'd tell me he loved me, and the next he wouldn't even look at me. Sometimes I felt like the cat and mouse game we played was part of the attraction. Deep down, I really wanted him, and I wanted to be his in more rooms than the bedroom. It was complicated. He was smart, funny, talented, and one of the best cooks I'd ever met. He seemed to know everyone in the city's food world. He was so connected. When we went out, we could get a great table anywhere. He was also incredibly sexy, in that unattainable way.

Everyone knew restaurants were pools of incest. All that close time together in a hot kitchen, either you were going to fight with each other or flirt. My two buddies at work, B-Rad and BJ, knew the mess Ronny and I were in and tried to be supportive every time I found him in the walk-in with a waitress. Kitchen crews were dysfunctional families, and Ronny was a bad habit I couldn't seem to kick.

Recently, a sous-chef had announced he was moving to Miami, and the rumor was that Chef was considering me, Ronny, and one other line cook for the job. I was surprised that the job didn't just go to Ronny, but I suppose Chef wanted to consider his options, or make us sweat. Possibly he wanted to diversify the management team and consider a, gasp, woman for the job? Either way we would all work extra hard for the shot; we all wanted to move up. Now, my on-again, off-again flame and I were competitors.

I hurriedly brushed my shoulder-length hair into a bun, stuffed it into a beanie hat, and started to pull on my layers of clothes—a navy ribbed tank top, a long-sleeved T-shirt from my high school track team, a fuzzy gray sweater, leggings, two pairs of socks, and my Uggs. Looking for my scarf, I turned around to find Jim holding my coffee in a to-go cup and wearing my long, chunky, bright-blue scarf, knitted by my grandmother. He almost scared me to death.

"Here you go, dah-ling!"

"Jim! I didn't see you there! What are you doing up?"

"Girl, it's Sunday! I haven't gone to bed yet!"

Upon further inspection of Jim's face, I noticed some lingering glitter around his eyes.

"Of course! What was I thinking?"

"I was almost surprised when I heard you get into the shower. I guess for a micro moment I forgot what you do, who you work for, and what city you work in. This city really doesn't sleep. How many orders of eggs Benedict do you expect to bang out today?"

"I have no idea. Given this weather there's no telling. I haven't heard anything from Chef, so I guess the restaurant is still open."

"I just looked at the news and the weatherman says to expect at least a foot of snow by noon! How is it possible for that many people to brunch in this weather?" Jim said.

At the same moment, we locked eyes and said, "Bacon and bloodies!"

New York City never took a vacation, and it held one important ritual every Sunday. Brunch. Even in a blizzard. I unwound my scarf from his neck, rewound it around mine, struggled into my puffer coat, the one that goes to my ankles, and kissed him on his cheek. I checked my phone. No messages from the restaurant, but I saw eight missed calls last night from my mother, Lily. She's really more like my sister than my mother. My real sister and I were raised almost totally by my grandmother.

"Please tell me that wasn't him stalking you," Jim said, referring to Ronny.

"Nope, just Lily. All calls post one a.m., so you know what that means." I put the phone in my coat pocket.

"Maggie, you don't know that she's drinking again. Maybe something is the matter," Jim said.

"With my mom, there is *always* something the matter. I'll call her on my next day off. Or shoot her a text later. I have real problems to attend to. Gotta run, I'm late."

It wasn't that I didn't care about my mother, it was just that there was constantly something "wrong," and over the years I had learned that eight phone calls didn't necessarily mean a real crisis. Sometimes she called me over and over just to see if I would pick up. I always felt a pang of guilt for not responding to her right away because even though we didn't get along, she was still my mom. I'd just . . . learned along the way to protect my daily life from her daily distractions.

I would call her later.

Stepping into the lobby of our apartment building I took one look at the outside and realized I would be walking to work. The buses and taxis were not an option. Even in April, sometimes it felt like winter would not give up to springtime easily, and we'd get a bizarre blizzard. It looked like the inside of a snow globe, and I couldn't see more than a few feet in front of me. It was bitter cold today, but I also knew that by Easter, this would all be cleared up and I'd be staring at tulips instead of snowdrifts soon enough. The drifts reminded me of the sand dunes on Sullivan's Island. I tried to visualize the beaches of my hometown as I started my journey to work.

On my walk I pondered how life in New York was a daily assault. Yes, it was the center of the universe, and yes, I was working at one of the best restaurants in America, but sometimes I wondered if it was worth it.

I was then pretty sure that had Gran ever heard me complain like that, she'd choke me with her pearls, slap me in some seersucker, and give me the world's longest lecture on decorum and being a Southern lady. She'd remind me that you get more flies with sugar than vinegar, and to be thankful for my chance. And as always, even in my mind, she was right. But, some days, like today, when I was freezing in the middle of the city's madness, I missed her. I was barely able to visit. I was always so caught up in work, so busy chasing my dreams. It had been a little more than a year since I had been back to the Lowcountry, and let's not forget COVID. I never felt like risking the lives of my loved ones for a hug around the neck.

I knew in my heart that I needed to be in New York in order to make it in the food world. This is where I had to build a reputation.

Chapter 2
Magnolia

Making my way downstairs to the kitchen basement, I punched in. I was thirty minutes late, which didn't seem unreasonable to me, considering the weather. I opened my little gray locker, peeled off my layers, and put on my chef's coat, apron, chef's pants, and clogs. As I brushed my hair up underneath a skullcap, I briefly looked at my reflection in the mirror on the wall. I looked severe and unfeminine. Couldn't they at least give us baseball hats to wear? When I exited the changing room and went down the long, dimly lit hallway into the main kitchen, I saw BJ, who looked like he had been there all night.

"Hey, BJ. Morning! Sorry I'm late."

"Hey, hey! It's all right, guess what? Service was canceled."

"What? Why? Why didn't anyone call me? BJ, did you get any sleep? You look worn out! Did you go home last night?"

"Nah, I figured I should just sleep here on the flour sacks."

"Oh, my God! BJ!" Even though he was short and skinny, I wondered how he'd managed to sleep on those sacks.

"What? I was here so late, and I knew the trains wouldn't be running anywhere close to normal, so I figured I'd just stay here. I didn't know they would cancel service, it's brunch!"

"I sure would have appreciated a phone call."

"Oh, you think your personal life matters now?"

I saw a long list taped over our prep area.

"What's that?"

"Oh, yeah. That's from Chef Jamie. Left us a mighty list. I guess he thinks the weather will chill out and expects a busy dinner shift."

"Amazing," I said, thinking it was anything but amazing. "Even in COVID, our orders were crazy with takeout. When is dinner ever slow?"

"Maggie, brace yourself, Chef Jamie has been calling every five minutes to see if you came in. He sounded pissed."

"Are you freaking kidding me?"

"I know. It's ridiculous, let's just crush this list and get through it! Allez!"

"Oui. Guess so," I responded with the French we used in the kitchen. There was never a good reason to not be on time. Being late to work was considered abandonment. It was also not okay to be sick or have a family emergency. You had to be there on time every day. Actually, on time was late. There was just so much to do, it was never ending. If you were late, you were behind, and then so was everyone else. Last week, a kid came in fifteen minutes late and he was invited to clean the grease traps, which was the most disgusting job.

Please, God, don't make me do the grease traps!

I took a look at the list. It had over fifty items.

"Okay. What's first?"

"Well, I started the beets. Why don't you start breaking down the squash?"

"Sounds good."

BJ made a huge pot of coffee, which helped us get through the enormous prep list. As soon as I was immersed in my work, cutting up the kabocha squash for the winter butternut squash soup, dicing the carrots to braise in orange juice, and starting another giant vat of chicken stock, I allowed the aromas and natural muscle rhythms of the kitchen to sweep me up in what I loved.

I calmed down and experienced—as corny as it might sound—the joy of cooking.

I was in love with food, obsessed with it. Food wasn't just fuel; it could heal a broken heart, it could entertain, it could bring you home. Magic happened when a perfectly balanced dish came together. A beautiful symphony of flavors. Salty, sweet, acidic, crunchy, colorful, soft, hard, warm, cold. It should take you on a journey. Once I had an Italian dish called Genovese, consisting of braised rabbit over thick noodles with a carrot and pea sauce. It was so beautiful, earthy, clever, and delicious, and it warmed you from the inside. It was what I liked to call a "circle of life plate."

Even though it was crazy, I also loved restaurant life. The rush of service and the satisfaction of a successful evening. The combination of the excitement and the pressure of knowing that you are only as good as your last plate. The bar is set to impossibly high standards, and when you reach that bar there is nothing more gratifying in the world. How do you grill a perfect steak in six minutes, in addition to taking care of forty-six other tickets? How do you keep going? Well, you just do, and maybe that makes us cooks adrenaline junkies.

One by one the other cooks trickled in. Ronny had called, saying something about being stuck in Queens.

Why was he in Queens when he lived in Brooklyn? I thought it odd for him not to tell me, but then I'm sure there was a reason . . . I tried not to think about it. He would be late. That meant I might have to work through dinner service. Great. A double shift. Actually, it would be more like a triple. Not only were the days crazy long and tiring, but I worried about accidents and hurting myself. Anyone would get squirrelly after ten hours in a hot kitchen. It was hard not to make mistakes.

Even on a good day, there were real setbacks to your health. Your knees would swell, your feet would throb, your back got stiff, not to mention the inevitable cuts and burns. If you played with flames and knives, you were going to get hurt. Also, it was hot, very hot, scorching hot, and there was no relief from it until you left the kitchen. To make matters worse, I was expecting Chef to come in and really give it to me for being late.

At four o'clock, we stopped, as usual, for family meal. I dreaded and loved family meal at the same time. It was important for morale for us to get together and take a break before service. Also, it guaranteed that we had something in our stomachs before service began, but at the same time it was hard to stop our enormous prep list to make family meal for the entire staff of the restaurant. Everyone ate together, both the front and the back of the house. Each station prepared part of the meal. The garde-manger (the salad cook) made the salad, the rotisseur (the meat cook) made the protein, and the entremetier (the vegetable cook) did the side dish. Sometimes, if we were lucky, the pastry department would even pitch in. I loved when they had cake scraps or extra cookies. We set up a buffet down the line and we all ate, sitting on the floor in the hallway outside the kitchen. Right as we were finishing the meal, Ronny came in. That was a blessing because it meant I wouldn't have to do a double shift and could go home right after dinner service slowed down, probably around nine. He walked right past everyone, gave me a "hello" nod, and sailed into Chef's office. I must have been so busy I didn't notice Chef's arrival. I wondered if it was a good or bad sign that he hadn't immediately reprimanded me for being late. While Ronny was in there, I started to prep out his station. I got all his mise en place ready, portioned out some of the meats, and counted six orders of garnish for his fish dish. I figured I might as well. I hadn't been given the green light on an early departure yet. After about a half hour I started to worry about him. What could Chef be saying to Ronny that was taking so long? Maybe Ronny was in trouble. I'd seen how his arrogance and strong opinions about the menu could irk Chef. Or maybe he was getting the promotion. *That* would only further complicate things between us because we both wanted that promotion so badly, we could taste it. Who knew with Chef Jamie? I was so deep in thought about Ronny and Chef Jamie that I didn't notice Ronny walking right up to me.

"Hey, Red."

"Hi."

"Chef wants you."

"I didn't even see him come in," I said.

"He's sneaky like that."

"Okay, thanks."

I was about to take a verbal beating. I decided that it was best for me to just *Yes, Chef* it. If I had any hope of leaving early, I'd have to make this short and sweet. Chef Jamie's style of punishment was giving you more side work to do.

I pushed open the door to his office, which was ajar. He was sitting at his desk, his eyes glued to his computer. There were already several empty cups of coffee around him. I looked around his office, waiting for him to acknowledge me. The walls were decorated with newspaper reviews, framed certificates, and a huge picture of Rachael Ray's head with darts in her face. I remembered him telling me how much he hated her and everything she stood for. I secretly loved

Rachael Ray. I thought she was fabulous. I loved her bubbly personality. She had the back of every mom in America or anyone with just thirty minutes to cook. Some of her technique was off, but who cared? I never understood what restaurant cooks had against Food Network cooks. Maybe they were just bitter about the Food Network paychecks.

I cleared my throat in case Chef Jamie hadn't noticed that I was standing in his office.

He broke his glare at the computer screen and asked me to sit down. I sat down and immediately started to sweat. I always got nervous talking to him because he was so unpredictable. I gave him a nervous smile. Whenever anything went wrong, I smiled, because maybe if I did, he wouldn't yell. The worst thing I could do was cry.

"Maggie, you have a phone message."

"A message, Chef?"

"Yes. Here."

He handed me a small blue piece of paper with some handwriting on it that I couldn't make out.

"Chef, this message is urgent!"

"Yes. It's from last night."

"Why didn't you give it to me *right away*?"

"Maggie, have you ever seen me take personal calls during service? Or, for that matter, *any* personal calls?"

"No, Chef."

"Who is this message from, Maggie?"

I took another look at the message, scrutinizing it. I saw "Violet" at the bottom of the page. Then I could make out another word, "urgent."

"Chef, it's from my sister, and it says *urgent!*"

I saw a creepy smile cross his face. He took a deep breath, and in a very calm voice said, "Maggie. I don't give a *fuck* about messages for you or what they have to say. When you are here, you are at work. This is not *your* kitchen. We are not *your* secretaries. No one, under any circumstances, should be calling you at work. Unless your sister is impaired, and I don't recall you saying that she was. In fact, I remember you telling me she is a photographer in North Carolina or something . . ."

"South Carolina, Chef."

"Are you correcting me, Maggie?"

"No, Chef! I'm sorry."

He stared at me for a moment, took a deep breath, and looked up at the ceiling.

"Maggie, you can't teach someone dedication, or how to be a team player. I can teach you how to cook, and I have. I can teach you how to cook on a line, and I have. But you cannot teach someone the value of loyalty. You either take your job here seriously or you don't. First, you are allowing personal calls during work hours, and then you are arriving wildly late to work. Next thing I know you'll be taking personal days, or I'll find you with your cell phone!"

"Chef, I would never—"

"I don't want to hear it, Maggie. You've disappointed me. There are things I like about you. You cook very well. Your dishes are always executed exactly how I showed you. I respect that. However, you are a bit of a drama queen."

I felt my face turn red and my neck get hot.

"Oh, don't get upset, Maggie. This is exactly what I mean. If you are upset, don't let me know it. I don't care for emotions; this is not how we behave in my kitchen. It is unacceptable. Are you going to cry? Ugh. Please get yourself together, this is so unprofessional."

Through the mix of concerns I felt about a message from my sister labeled "urgent" and the various attacks he was making not only on my character, but my work ethic, I could feel myself losing my composure. I couldn't believe what he was saying. Pulling myself together, and fighting back tears, I got angry.

"Chef, I am not being overly emotional. What you are saying is upsetting me. It is unfair. I was late today. It is not a reoccurring offense, it was a onetime thing, and it won't happen again—"

"Stop! Once is enough. When you work here you are on a team. One minute late is late. We rely on you. Your fellow cooks are depending on your presence to do your job so they can do their own jobs later. We are links in a chain, Maggie. If one link breaks down, then the entire chain is broken, and useless."

"Chef, I can't read this handwriting. What does the rest of this message say?"

He sighed, grabbed the note from my hand, rolled his eyes, and read it as if it were a grocery list. "'Maggie, please call home as soon as you can. Gran is unconscious in the hospital. Mom and her were in a car accident. This is urgent.' Seems like drama runs in your family, doesn't it?"

I was stunned. What had happened? It seemed that all the noise was sucked out of the room and time stood still. I couldn't breathe for a minute, then I realized I was holding my breath, as if I were bracing myself to be hit.

Chapter 3
Magnolia

Less than an hour later, I was seated next to Jim in a cab. He had packed my bags for me and secured us two seats on the last flight to Charleston. We were lucky United had a direct flight. He opened up his coat pocket and pulled out a silver flask.

"Here, sweetheart, you look like you need this," Jim said.

"Can you bring this on a plane?" I said and took a swig, admiring the beautiful monogram on the front.

"Nope, so drink it down." He shot me a smirk. "You okay, girl?"

"Are you? You're flying commercial with all the other peasants!" I teased. Jim usually flew with his aunt Belle on her jet.

"Yes, it isn't a private jet as I am spoiled rottenly used to, but this is an emergency!" Jim said.

"Must be nice, sir," I said and handed him back the flask.

"Well, it certainly is easier than going through that god-awful security!" He pursed his lips.

"Thanks for getting down in the dirt for me," I said and gave his arm a pinch.

I felt thankful in that moment for our sarcastic back-and-forth. The humor gave my imagination a distracted beat before it started to spin again. I was inches away from spiraling, and it wouldn't end until I laid my eyes on Gran. I felt my palms get sweaty and clammy, as they did before I started to panic. I took a deep breath and jiggled my leg.

"Easy, Fred Flintstone, the cab drives itself," Jim said as he grabbed my knee to stop it from bouncing up and down.

"Sorry, I know, I'm just . . ."

"Worried, baby girl, we both are. Right now we are doing all that we can," Jim said.

"I just . . ." My eyes started to spill out tears again. "Jim? What if I lose her? I haven't seen her in so long! What would my life be like without Gran? How could I ever do anything if I didn't have her? I'd always dreamed of opening my own restaurant. And in all those dreams

Gran was there by my side, and this stupid COVID has kept me from my family and I . . ." I was speaking so fast I could hardly hear myself. My eyes were getting teary.

"Let's not pay the toll twice, Maggie. Let's save the tears for the Lowcountry, when we know exactly what we are dealing with." He was right.

"Okay," I said in a small voice. "Let me have a little more of that." He handed over the silver container of liquid strength.

The next hour was a blur of going through security and finding our gate, and before long we were on the plane. My seat was by the window, and Jim settled into the seat on the aisle. He had a black cashmere eye mask over his forehead and a matching neck pillow around his neck. Before long, the plane was ascending, and I peered out at the millions of twinkling city lights. New York really was a dazzling city. When we reached cruising altitude, the flight attendant took our drink orders. Jim bought us three mini bottles of red wine, which we downed the way we'd done behind the bleachers at prom when we were teenagers. The wine helped me to begin to relax. I grabbed a blanket and kicked off my boots. I went through my tote bag, which Jim had packed for me, and found a pair of fuzzy socks that he'd knitted for me during one of his domestic phases.

It was the small things, like his remembering my feet turned to ice on planes, that made me love him.

"Jim, you're so good to me, you always have my back," I said.

"Well, you have always had mine, lady." Jim and I both raised our glasses. "Cheers to Gran, and her recovery." We both drank to that. Then he added, "And to a smooth homecoming, for both of us. We can do this, Maggie—together."

"But what if . . ." I started.

"Manifest a recovery, honey, and it will be," he said. "Now, let's get a little beauty rest."

He put down his drink and pulled down his eye mask. I was too wound up to sleep. Buzzing through me was an odd combination of feelings—anxiety about Gran's condition, but also excitement about returning to Sullivan's Island, the place I loved most in the world, and a bit of trepidation about how I'd be received by my mother and sister. Deep down, I knew we all loved each other, but my relationships with them were strained. My mother was a broken bird who kept trying to fly and kept failing. She spent most of my childhood either in rehab or trying to escape Charleston. She battled anorexia and alcohol, and we battled each other. She was complicated. Despite her addictions, she could be self-righteous and prissy. I thought that maybe she behaved that way so no one would ever guess she struggled with any sort of weakness.

As a child my mother was a talented ballet dancer. She'd had an opportunity to train in New York City, but at the age of seventeen she got pregnant by her high school boyfriend, Scott Parker. All her dreams were shattered. My mom blamed me. She married my father right before I was born because his parents insisted. For two and a half years they had a rocky marriage, but when they found out she was pregnant with Violet, everything changed. They decided to really give the marriage a try, and for a while it worked. They were happy. My dad was around more when Violet came along. He took us everywhere with him, showing us off to his friends. Violet was born out of love, whereas I was born out of carelessness and teenage heat. Her birth brought sunshine into my mother's life. But the storm clouds returned the summer after my sister's fourth birthday, when our dad was injured in a motorcycle accident. Life took a wrong turn then, he became addicted to pain meds, and that was when my mom started drinking.

Suddenly, my father wasn't around anymore. He took off. We never heard from him again, because a few months later, my mom got word that he'd been killed in another motorcycle accident, out West; I think it was Montana. My father's parents were devastated by his death, but perhaps ashamed of his behavior, and they felt awkward with us. They wound up moving to California. We got Christmas and birthday cards with five-dollar bills from them for a few years, but as time went by they seemed to forget about me, Violet, and Mom.

Thank God for Gran and Grandpa Eddie, who swooped in and took the child-rearing reins. They gave me and Violet the stability and security that our parents had never provided. But three years later, tragedy befell us again when Grandpa Eddie died of a heart attack. Mom fell apart again, but not Gran. Despite her heartbreak, she took charge, raising her daughter's children and improving her family's restaurant business. There was nothing she couldn't do. She loved her family and provided a life for her girls. She made a home for my mother, me, and Violet. She made sure we got up on time, got to school, did our homework, bathed, and all sat down for family dinner. She gave us everything we were proud of, even her name. She convinced Mom to have our names legally changed to Adams.

Even so, my mother and I fought a lot when I was growing up, mainly because I could never forgive her for her erratic behavior, and the nasty words and her drinking. How many birthdays, how many holidays, how many regular nights had been spoiled? Violet always forgave her; I let the scar tissue build up.

Gran always looked for the best in everyone. I heard her voice.

"You must find some compassion in your heart for your mother. I know it's difficult, but people make mistakes. You make mistakes, too. We all do. Magnolia, one day you may have children and then you'll understand. You will want them to thrive. You will want to help them launch themselves into a satisfying, happy life in any way that you can. Let go of this anger you have for her. You need to cut your mother some slack."

My eyelids were heavy under the weight of the drama of the day. I closed them, thinking that Gran always gave good advice. I vowed to cut my mother some slack when I got to Charleston. I fell asleep under the soft blanket. Soon I was in my grandmother's garden, sitting in the middle of a soft patch of grass. I could feel the warm sun on my shoulders. Peeking out from underneath a sun hat, Gran winked at me. She was knee deep in romaine lettuce plants. Around me, dark-purple eggplants, bright-yellow squash, and long, slim green cucumbers decorated the edges of the white fence. I walked toward her, letting the soft, cool soil squish between my toes and running my hand along the leaves of the tomato plants, hoping to pick up their scent.

There was a birdbath in the center of her garden, covered with tiny mirrors. It glistened in the sunlight. A cardinal swooped in and perched on the edge. The color of his feathers against all the green around him made me reach for him.

"You're so beautiful, Mr. Cardinal!"

He looked at me, seeming to size me up. After turning around in circles, he plopped himself in the middle of the bath. The reflection of his feathers in the water made the whole bath turn a bright crimson. I looked over at Gran, who was humming a song I recognized. I joined her, and we sang the verses for a few minutes. Before long, the cardinal joined us. Then the cardinal turned into a dove and flew off.

Jim shook me to wake me up.

"Maggie! Lord, you were singing in your sleep!"

Whenever Jim was in Charleston, he slipped into his Charleston drawl, adding an extra syllable to "Lord."

"Yeah, I'm fine. Are we there yet?"

I already knew the answer. The plane's door was open, and I could feel the humidity. Even in the beginning of spring, the Lowcountry was humid. I could smell the salt air and inhaled deeply as I stood up. I wondered if I would have to face my mother right away or if I could postpone that until morning.

After we disembarked and walked to the taxi stand,

I called my sister to see if she was at the hospital. She picked up on the second ring.

"Hey, Violet, it's me, we just got here. What's going on?"

"I'm at the hospital and Gran's still unconscious. You should go home and sleep, that's okay. You can come by in the morning. I'm not leaving, though."

My sister dealt out truth the same way she drank her coffee, dark and strong. But as blunt as she could be, sometimes she triggered me. She had just made clear that she was the more devoted granddaughter.

"Vi, I just flew all the way from New York. I'm coming to the hospital if that's where everyone is. I'm a part of the family, too."

"Well, thank God you could tear yourself away," Violet said.

"Violet, don't be like that, please. Aren't things bad enough? I'll be there soon." Then I hung up.

"What was *that* all about?" Jim asked, arching an eyebrow.

"You know Violet. We're going to the hospital," I said.

"Okay. Do you want to go by Gran's first and pick up her car or have a taxi take us directly to the hospital?" Jim asked.

"You know what? Violet said there was no change in

Gran's condition, so let's drop off our bags at the house and pick up the truck if it's there."

"Sounds good." Jim signaled a taxi driver, and he and the driver stowed our bags in the trunk.

We rode side by side in silence, inhaling the salt air blowing through the lowered windows as our taxi turned onto the illuminated Arthur Ravenel Bridge, which crossed the Cooper River, connecting the Charleston peninsula to Mount Pleasant. Looking south, I could see Charleston Harbor, at the confluence of the Ashley and Cooper Rivers, sprinkled with huge container ships.

We pulled up to Gran's house on Sullivan's Island. It was so quiet and still. Faded yellow clapboard, with a wide wraparound porch that hosted some of my favorite childhood memories, from birthday parties to my first kiss right at the big front door. The lights on the porch illuminated her hanging plants and her sleeping camellias. The house looked welcoming even at night. It made me feel that everything would be all right. I believe that space has memory, and this space hadn't forgotten me.

While Jim paid the driver, I got out of the car. The salt air seemed to push me toward Gran's front door. The red door needed a fresh coat of paint, but the brass octopus door knocker shone even in the soft porchlight.

I ran my hand over the top of the doorframe, found the key, unlocked the door, and went inside. Instantly I felt the warmth of home. I took a deep breath, trying to take in all the smells of my childhood. I could smell the gardenia candle Gran always had out and a faint touch of her lavender perfume. I put my bags down and walked around the living room. Not a thing had changed since I'd last been there. I peeked into the dining room and on the mahogany table saw a foil-covered dish with a note on top of it. I walked over and picked it up.

Dear Maggie May—Left you something decent to put in your stomach, not the haute cuisine you're used to, but tasty nonetheless. When you've finished eating, go straight to bed. It's going to be a big day tomorrow. —Violet

Jim noticed the foil-covered plate. "Looks like Violet knew you were coming even without a return phone call."

I smiled. "I'll share it with you after we put our stuff away."

Jim went upstairs to drop off his bags in the guest bedroom. Another mark of an old friendship, he knew exactly which room was temporarily his.

I crossed the living room to get my bags. The old

house sure did feel empty without Gran. Since COVID hit, this was the first time that I'd come home, and she wasn't there to greet me with a hug. Still, just being home was comforting; it always made me hit the pause button on everything else in my life. The *real me* lived here, in this kitchen, among the worn-out cookbooks like *Charleston Receipts* and the huge book from Cypress, a fab restaurant on Broad Street that no longer stood, and the mismatched plates and lingering aromas of Gran's baking. I could feel my skin prickle. I knew that the house was trying to tell me something. It was like my fourth mother: Gran; Lily; Gran's best friend, Alice; and this house. Everyone on the island said the house was haunted, and why shouldn't it be? It was over a hundred years old and had housed generations of my family. When I was little, though, I would swear that I could hear whispers whenever I passed the wall of portraits of long-dead family members. Every square inch of this property had a story. From the pictures to the floorboards (long planks of wood that were part of my great-great-grandfather's barn) to the garden, where Gran grew heirloom vegetables from special seeds that only a few people had. If you asked me, that's why the food was so good here. It had something to say.

The South is different from anywhere else on earth. Every time I returned, it seemed it was the beginning of my greatest story, like something was about to happen, the kind of something music was written about. There was a touch of magic in the air, and the Lowcountry was extra special. It must have something to do with the region's history, or maybe it was just the weather, but I felt more alive here. Even the sky was different. The sunrises were more jubilant, the stars brighter in the evenings, and the flowers more fragrant. It was easy to lose touch with nature in New York City, but just like a love that got away, you never knew how much you'd miss it until it was gone. In the evening when the sun would set, the horizon looked as if it were in flames. Alice said that it was God playing his finale for the day. During a summer storm, giant blue-gray clouds pregnant with heat lightning rolled across the sky, making you run indoors filled with terror.

Early springtime in the Lowcountry hosted the most unpredictable temperatures. It could be seventy degrees during the day and forty-five degrees at night. But the air was crisp, the sky was blue, and the sun was still warm. In general, people were nicer here, which I attributed to the sunshine. In New York City it was gray until May. No wonder the people there were so pushy, they didn't have enough vitamin D.

I climbed the stairs, passing the whispering wall of family portraits. I paused at the framed photo of

Great-Grandmother Daisy, which was askew. She was standing on the front porch of the Magic Lantern the day it opened, with her hands on her hips and a wide grin on her face. Her red hair, the same shade as mine, was wild and curly, no doubt due to a strong ocean breeze. I straightened the photo and moved on to my bedroom's pink door with magnolias painted all over it. I opened it and my eyes immediately went to the colorful quilt on the bed that Gran and Alice had made for me. Part of me wanted to lie down, pull the quilt over my head, and pretend the car accident hadn't happened. But what I wanted even more was to see Gran.

After Jim and I devoured the delicious pot roast Violet had left us, we found the keys for the truck in the small Charleston sweetgrass basket by the front door and left. It was close to 11:00 p.m., and even though I was tired, my mind was racing about what we were going to encounter at the hospital. Jim went to sleep as soon as we got moving. He was snoring softly, letting out little puffs of air every few seconds. I rolled down the window a bit on my side and let in the smell of the plough mud. I was so tired I didn't realize I'd closed my eyes until I felt the jolt and heard the crash as I collided with the pickup in front of me.

I followed the pickup, which had swerved onto the

shoulder of the road. I put Gran's truck in park and started sweating, as I always did when I got nervous. The driver was getting out of his vehicle.

"Oh, my God, Maggie! What happened?" Jim said.

"I hit that pickup. I think I fell asleep! I'm so sorry! Are you okay?" I said, horrified.

"Yeah, girl, I'm totally fine," Jim said after doing a body check.

"I'm okay, too, I think," I said.

I wondered if the driver would totally flip on us. It was the worst time for something like this to happen, but then that's when bad things *always* seemed to happen. I was out of practice from all my days in NYC. I almost never drove anymore! My headlights illuminated the driver, a tall, sandy-blond-haired man, as he moved around to look at his rear bumper. The right taillight was hanging off it.

Great, I thought. *I had pissed off a hot guy.* I looked over at Jim, who had noticed the sandy-haired dream, too.

"Well, well, well. What do we have here? I've always been a sucker for long-haired men," Jim said, pursing his lips.

"Probably not gonna ask us out, Jimmy," I said. "You know guys down here love their trucks more than their mothers. We just messed up his rear bumper."

"We? Honey, that was all you!"

"Please," I said, rolling my eyes and trying to prepare myself for a bad encounter.

Should I cry? I thought. That had always worked well for me with cops.

Think, Maggie. What do you need to do?

I pulled the truck's registration card out of the glove compartment, grabbed my cell phone, and got out of the truck.

"Behave. I'll be right back," I said to Jim then walked over to the driver.

"Hey. I'm so sorry! I didn't see you brake," I managed to squeak out. Where was my voice?

I locked eyes with the handsome driver as he towered over me. The guy had golden eyes. Not pale brown. Golden, almost the color of his hair. Lord Almighty.

"Hey, lady, I didn't brake. You rear-ended me."

His voice was as deep as the thunder I heard rumbling in the distance. He took a step closer to me. I noticed he was wearing cowboy boots.

"What's the problem? Too much to drink, or did you just feel like playing bumper cars?" Now he was scowling at me.

"Of course not!" I gasped. "I only had one drink on the flight down here." I saw his scowl deepen, so I quickly added, "Uh, well, that was hours ago. I should have been paying closer attention. I'm so sorry. It's just that I'm on my way to the hospital. My gran got into a . . . car accident—"

"Oh, so reckless driving runs in the family?" He narrowed his eyes.

"No! That was a serious accident, this happened not because I'm reckless but because I'm tired and was distracted. Please let me cover the damage! I'm Magnolia Adams. But everyone calls me Maggie." I stuck my hand out. His golden eyes raked over me for a few seconds—longer than was polite—before he took my hand. I was startled by how warm his hand was as he shook mine.

"Adams? Any relation to Rose Adams?" he asked.

"Yeah, she's my grandmother," I answered.

"Oh, man. She was a friend of my late grandfather's. She gets her tomatoes from us. I'm Sam Smart. My family's farm is on Johns Island, she's one of our best customers."

"Hey, listen, please take my number and please call me. I will pay you to fix my mistake."

"You think I don't know how to replace a taillight?" He sounded offended.

"No, I'm sure you know a lot about trucks and fixing them. Again, I'm so sorry."

"What's your number? Do you have a card?" he asked.

"No, but I have a Sharpie," I said, pulling one out of my back pocket.

Sam Smart rolled up the sleeve of his flannel shirt and extended his forearm, motioning for me to write my number on it.

"Are you sure? This isn't going to come off easily," I said.

"Something tells me I'll need to remember it," he said.

He didn't sound like he was joking, so I started writing.

"Six-four-six? Is that a New York number? You're a Yankee? Oh, man, no wonder you don't know how to drive."

I couldn't help rolling my eyes at his good-ole-boy joke. "Yes, it is a New York number. But I'm Southern born and bred, I just live in New York now. I have dual residency. I say 'y'all' *and* 'schlep.'"

He let out a laugh. I was relieved he was lightening up a little.

"Okay, better get to your grandmother. I'll take care of my taillight." He turned, and I thought I heard him laughing as he walked back to his truck.

I quickly scrambled back to Gran's truck, put on my seat belt, carefully pulled back onto the road, even though I was still shaking, and let out a hysterical giggle when I exhaled.

"Giggling after an accident? Was he as good looking up close as he was from my vantage point? Did you really write your number on his arm? How big did you make the numbers?" Jim asked, wiggling his eyebrows.

"Too big," I said. "I wish I'd written them in disappearing ink. Ronny. I feel guilty," I mumbled.

"Magnolia Adams, I hope it was a permanent marker! You need that bad boy out of your life! He's nothing but a headache," Jim said, rolling his eyes.

Before I could think about a defense for Ronny, the sky opened up and poured gallons of water, drenching the world. *Great,* I thought, *just what I need—more hazardous driving conditions.*

Chapter 4
Magnolia

The rain had stopped by the time I pulled Gran's now a-little-more-dented truck into a parking space in the hospital's visitor lot. I sat there with my hands gripping the wheel, rubbing the pads of my thumbs back and forth into the steering wheel cover. I took a deep breath, inhaling strength. I had seen enough episodes of *Grey's Anatomy* to know that what I was going to walk into wouldn't be easy to see. I choked back a tightness in my throat. I would hold it together for Violet, my mother, and Jim. I would be strong for Gran. I would be the woman she raised me to be. God, but what if Gran never got better?

"Maggie, you okay?" Jim asked. "It's okay if you're not fine, ya know. It's just you and me in this vehicle. I won't tell anyone if you're not. You know, *fine*."

I looked through the window at the illuminated hospital entrance. I wanted someone to come outside and tell me that Gran was being discharged, and this was all for nothing.

"I'm scared, Jimmy. I don't know how bad it is, and I know that I have to see Gran to find out, but I'm also afraid of moving because it's . . ."

"Real, and so then you can't tell yourself it's probably nothing," Jim said, finishing my sentence.

"Yup. Thanks for being here with me," I said, grabbing my bag and turning the engine off.

"Of course, darling. Let's go see what we shall see," Jim said.

I shivered as the air-conditioning hit my damp clothes and we entered the hospital and headed to the information desk.

"Hey. I'm Magnolia Adams, and I'm visiting my grandmother, Rose Adams. Which room is she in?" The pretty girl behind the desk wore a name tag that read *Ashley*. I wondered how many Ashleys were in South Carolina. Probably about a million. People in the South liked to name their children after family members, and when we ran out, we chose places. Charles from Charleston, Ashley from the Ashley River, Caroline from South Carolina, and Charlotte from, well . . . if all else failed we swapped out maiden names for first names. Tradition was very important here, and so was location.

"Let me look, hold on," Ashley said. "Room 412."

"Thanks."

Hospitals make me nervous. Every inch smells like sickness and death to me. There's so much stress in the air. I don't know why I never think about happy things like babies being born. Gran calls them loading zones between heaven and hell.

"You got this, Maggie. Here we are," Jim said as we found the right room.

I pushed the door open in what seemed to be slow motion. Gran was lying in the bed, unconscious and so still. Her eyes were purple and swollen shut, and a white bandage with some dried blood on it was wrapped around her head. She had a thick tube down her throat, and lots of tiny clear tubes connected her to various pieces of medical equipment. Her hands were bound to the rails on her bed. Her elegant arms were bruised and scratched. Her long fingers were limp. She had such beautiful hands. I'd always thought she should have been a piano player. I heard the tiny beeps and sighs of the machines in the room.

Gran looked so awful, it startled me. If it wasn't for the sound of the machines next to her, I would have thought she had already left us. I felt a pull on my heartstrings. I stood there for a minute, taking it all in, feeling the moment weigh on my heart, forever storing this memory for future nightmares. I looked around the room. Violet was curled up on a small couch in the corner. She was small, like my mom. Her inky-dark hair had fallen over her face, and she looked like a rag doll who had been thrown there. She stirred awake and saw me.

"Maggie! Jimmy! What time is it? When did you get here?" she mumbled, sounding like a little girl, not a twenty-six-year-old woman.

"Hey, Vi. We just got here. You okay?" I said quietly.

"Hey, Violet, darlin'. It's dang late, but not a moment too soon, it seems," Jim whispered, going over to her as she moved her legs off the couch, sitting up and giving him space to sit. They hugged, then Violet immediately straightened out the creases in her perfect Lilly Pulitzer shift dress and bright-pink cardigan and rearranged her pearl necklace, so the clasp was in the back. I watched my sister twist her hair up into a clip, away from her face and neck.

"Maggie, I'm just so glad you came," Violet said, as her blue eyes filled with tears, which started to spill over. She came over and gave me a hug.

I wondered where Chris, her boyfriend, was, and

why she was here alone. "Of course. I'm sorry I couldn't get here sooner. Violet, what the hell happened?"

Violet took my hands in hers. She looked down at them and made a face at the state of my nails, which I had bitten down to an embarrassing length. I jerked my hands back. I didn't need criticism, and I didn't need steadying. I was fine. I could handle this.

"What happened, Violet?" I repeated.

"Maggie, before I give you all the details, I want you to promise not to blame Mom. Okay? I can't take a family blowout right now. It's too much. I swear she . . . it was an accident," Violet said all in one breath.

"Violet, who was driving?" I asked.

"Gran," she said. "She was picking up Mom from a bar, she needed a ride and they got into a fight and, well . . ."

I took a deep breath in and then slowly exhaled, tempering my anger. *I knew it.*

"I mean, what happened in the car was an accident . . ."

"Fine. Whatever. What *happened?*"

"Mom was downtown with Buster, her boyfriend. They were out for dinner, I guess. I thought everything was cool. I didn't think she was drinking. She had been going to all these meetings at a church, and was doing well . . . I mean, she was sober. At least for the seven or eight months she's been seeing Buster. It was the first time in a long time that I'd seen her happy. You know how miserable she can be."

"Yes, I do. What's Buster like?"

"He seems like a nice guy, a little rough around the edges, but something happened between him and Mom, a fight or whatever, and he broke up with her yesterday. So, I guess she fell off the wagon and ordered lots of drinks. She decided to drive herself home, but someone at the restaurant insisted she call someone to come get her. So she called Gran, and they got into an argument or something and Gran . . . she ran off the road. Somehow, by the grace of God, Momma made it out with just a twisted shoulder and a few cuts and scrapes, but Gran hit her head hard and was knocked out, unconscious. I'm so worried." Violet's eyes filled with tears, and she blinked them back. "I wish Mom had called me, not Gran. It should be me in the bed, not her! But she probably was embarrassed and didn't want me to see—"

"Her drunk again," I chimed in. Violet frowned at me. Before she could reprimand me for what she no doubt viewed as brutal honesty, I asked, "But what about Gran? What happened when she got to the hospital?"

"I'm going to go grab us some caffeination." Jim left the room to find a coffee machine.

"They did a CT scan and found some swelling in the brain from the crash, and some possible bleeding. This morning she had surgery to stop the bleeding, and so the doctors could find out more about where the bleeding was coming from."

"Oh, my God, she had brain surgery?" I gasped. "How did the surgery go? When do they expect her to wake up?" I asked.

"We'll know after the doctor examines her. We're hoping to begin to wake her up then. And if that goes well, they'll try to get her to sit up and maybe walk in the next few days. They are hopeful that if she responds well, she can move into the rehab wing," Violet said.

I walked over to Gran and leaned in to give her a kiss on her cheek. She was warm, but all the color had left her face. She looked like a mannequin. I noticed her fingernails were painted her signature red color, OPI Big Apple Red. She had a drawer full of the bottles in the vanity in her bedroom. She had been using that color for years. Gran always wore her pearl necklace, and it was unnerving to see her without it. All I wanted to do was grab one of her shirts from her closet, iron it, and dress her. I hated to see her in a hospital gown. It wasn't right. Gran was always so stylish. She never let anyone see her in her pajamas. She would be so angry if she knew we were seeing her like this.

I turned back to my sister. "Violet, where's Mom?"

"Well, you just missed her. But she'll be back. She needed to get out of the hospital for a while. She's really upset about Buster. You know, it's a blessing Mom wasn't hurt worse in the accident."

I shook my head in frustration. "Jesus. Have you caught her drinking or acting sneaky? I mean, was this like a onetime thing, or . . ."

"I should've known this would happen," my sister said, looking at the ceiling.

"Violet, you can't blame yourself. Mom is really good at hiding things. Has anyone heard from Buster?" I said.

"No, not a word. Mom left messages and he hasn't returned her calls. It's like he disappeared. Ugh. This is my fault." My sister shook her head. "I should have seen this coming. She wasn't ready to handle a relationship and manage the restaurant at the same time. It was just too much for her. Gran shouldn't have let her take over."

"Wait! Mom's in charge of the Magic Lantern?"

"Yes, Gran thought it would be good for her to have a project. Last year, after Gran fell and hurt her hip, Mom was basically doing the job anyway. When Gran got better, Mom asked her if she could take on the manager's job on a trial basis, and she did well, Maggie, she really did. Gran was able to relax a little, spend more time in her garden."

"Why didn't anyone tell me about this?" I asked indignantly. "I'm a member of this family, too!"

"Maggie, you were in New York, and you're always too busy to talk to us! Not to mention stupid COVID keeping us apart," Violet huffed. "Besides, everything was going fine. Gran was so proud of Mom, seeing her rise to the challenge. And I've been helping Mom occasionally, after I finish my photography jobs. Which is why I got so tired, I guess, and missed the signals that Mom was in over her head, dealing with both the restaurant *and* Buster."

Still bruised from Violet's comment about my being too busy to talk to them, which I admitted to myself might be warranted, I tamped down my anger at my mother and took on the role of the older sister. I had let a lot of excuses go by as to why I couldn't make time. The whole world was on lockdown, and even when the restaurant closed for two weeks because of COVID-19, I still didn't do a lot of FaceTime like I should have. "Listen, I'm glad Mom had a period of responsibility. But I'm here now, so you don't have to shoulder this alone."

"Okay. Thanks. Gosh, you're so strong, Maggie. How are you not falling apart?"

"Violet, I'll fall apart later. It doesn't help anyone to

cry and lose it. Fix your lipstick, hide your crazy, ya know? We're gonna get through this no matter what. Now, back to Gran. I'd really like to talk to one of the doctors and get an update on Gran's condition."

"Well, I don't know when the on-call doctors will come by, but there's a great, very smart ICU nurse. I'll go get her. She can tell us what all these signals and numbers on the machines mean."

I looked down at Gran, willing her to recover, willing her to wake up and talk to me. I turned when the door opened. Instinctively, I took a step back. In walked my mother, wearing a sling around her left shoulder and arm. Her dark-brown hair was cut in an attractive bob. I noticed how her hip bones jutted out from underneath her sweaterdress. She was rail thin, which was never a good sign. I felt myself choking up for some reason. "Hi, Mom, are you okay?" I asked softly.

My mother's gaze ran over me, from head to toe. I braced myself for criticism. "No. I am not okay, Maggie. I just lost the love of my life."

"Mom, she's not gone." I was touched that she was referring to Gran that way.

"No, not Gran, but yes, of course, this is deeply troubling. I meant Buster. He's left me and I can't get hold of him."

"Oh."

"Maggie, you can't possibly imagine the heartache I am feeling right now. One day when you find yourself in an adult relationship, you'll see things aren't so black and white. Don't try and make it sound like I don't care that my own mother is in a hospital bed. I can see that. It's just not the only problem I have."

I decided not to take her bait. "I'm sure you're right, Mom. Sorry."

"It's not like you even know what's going on around here, Maggie. How could you? But if you knew Buster you'd understand—"

Jim walked in, carrying a paper drink holder with three large coffees.

"Jimmy!" my mother said with a big smile. "How wonderful to see you! And you brought us coffee. So thoughtful of you." She reached out and took one.

"Lily, it's great to see you, but I'm sorry it's under these sad circumstances," Jim said politely, but I could sense his discomfort. He set the tray down and handed me a coffee cup. "Violet's," he murmured.

I shook my head, letting him know he should save it for Violet. My mother had grabbed my coffee.

Violet walked in with the nurse, a sturdy middle-aged woman with a kindly face. "Oh, Mom, you're back. Great! Maggie wanted to talk to Nurse Hallie, get an update on Gran. Hallie," Violet said, "this is my sister, Maggie. She just came in from New York, and this is our friend, Jim."

After we exchanged greetings, I asked, "How is my grandmother doing? I just found out she had surgery this morning. Is she going to be all right? Do you think she can hear us, knows we're here?"

Hallie went over to one of the beeping machines next to Gran, looked at the numbers on its screen, then straightened one of the tubes that was embedded in Gran's right hand. She turned back to us and smiled. "Your grandmother's vitals are just fine, right where we want them to be. I can't say for sure if she can hear us. She's in a medically induced coma so her body has time to recuperate after surgery."

"When will she come out of the coma?" I asked, noticing Violet and my mother sitting down on the sofa. Both looked bone tired.

"We'll know more tomorrow," Hallie said. "May I suggest you all go home and get a good night's sleep? Your grandmother's condition is unlikely to change tonight, and if it does, we'll call you." She was looking at Violet and my mother. I could see Jim nodding.

"As long as you promise to call us," Violet said, standing.

"I certainly will. Good night." The nurse left the room.

Violet and I walked over to Gran, one of us standing at each side of the bed. My mother joined us.

"Gran, we're all here for you," I said, gently rubbing my grandmother's elegant hand. "We love you."

Tears were running down Violet's cheeks. She nodded and added, "Gran, you just rest. Sweet dreams. We'll see you in the morning."

"You know, she can't hear you." My mother rolled her eyes and turned away from Gran. "Come on, kids, let's go home."

Chapter 5
Rose

I am here. Not dead. Not gone. I hear beeping noises. There is light somewhere, I can feel its warmth across my lap, on my hands, but I can't open my eyes. I can't move. I am trying to move my arms, wiggle my toes, roll to the side, turn my head, open my mouth to yell out . . . but nothing. Am I frozen? Am I paralyzed? What happened? Where am I?

I drift in and out of slumber. I am here, and in another world with palm trees, gardenia bushes, and the Confederate jasmine that climbs up the side of my porch. I hear the rattle of ice clinking against glass as my husband, Eddie, and I sit on the front porch drinking sweet sun tea with lemon. I can taste its bite, I can see his beautiful sea-glass eyes, and I hear my granddaughters shriek with laughter inside the house. Eddie shakes his head, smiles at me, and I hear his rumbling laughter and the sound of my sand dollar wind chime clacking in the ocean breeze.

My thoughts scatter. I must gather them, what is around me? I hear the beeps again, muffled sounds of a door opening, what sounds like shower curtain rings sliding across a rod. There are the smells of bleach and rubbing alcohol. I have something pretty uncomfortable in my mouth. A tube, I think.

Well, I'm either in a spaceship or a hospital. I am in a hospital. Must stop watching all that science fiction. I am in a hospital bed. Someone is talking. A few voices? My girls, my flowers, they are here! Magnolia, Violet, and Lily? One is crying, probably Violet. Maggie never cries unless she's mad. Woo-wee, that girl has a temper on her. I can only hear a word or two. Something about waking me up! I am awake, I just need help opening these darn eyes of mine! Then I hear Lily? Wait, Lily . . . we were in the car. I was driving. Oh, no. *What happened?* Think, Rose!

What *happened?*

Okay, I was in my car. Lily called for a ride, she drank too much. She was embarrassed, yes, I remember feeling sorry for her but relieved she called me for help. It doesn't matter how old you are, or how old your children are, you will always go to their rescue. I remember hearing her hiccup tears. She was crying so hard, she sounded the way she had when she was a small child, so helpless and scared. I had to go get my baby.

I got in my car. I remember throwing on an old plaid flannel shirt over my nightgown and slipping on my slide-on sneakers. Running down the porch steps, fumbling with my keys to get to her. I didn't even check my reflection. What happened next? Think!

Yes, when I arrived at the restaurant Lily was standing outside. She got in the car and was babbling about that Buster man she's been seeing. They broke up, or she thought they did? I don't remember, but I remember . . . Oh, yes, she was . . . she was pressuring me again about the restaurant. God, I hate to be pushed into things. She has been doing a good job with the restaurant, running it and keeping it open, despite the tacky alterations Buster has been making. Why does she listen to him? She just isn't ready . . . and as much as I love my daughter, I don't trust her. Not with her past, and not yet.

We started arguing and she brought up that old trouble. That's when a fury I hadn't felt in years took hold of me, but at the same time I felt guilty, regretful.

I wondered if Eddie and I had made a mistake. Lily is yelling at me and I am desperate to be anywhere but in the car with her and those bad old memories.

My heart starts to race. The beeps get louder, and an alarm goes off. No! That's not good, calm down! I hear some voices, and the rush of fabric. I am poked and moved around, and suddenly, I feel a warmth go through my veins. I am afraid. What if I am trapped and can't get out of this state? What if that old trouble resurfaces?

Chapter 6
Magnolia

If I live to be a hundred years old, I will always feel like a little girl in Gran's house. I sleep most soundly there. All the familiar smells and objects allow me to unload whatever seventy-pound monkey happens to be on my back and let me finally get some rest. Sleep therapy can be found at Gran's.

I rubbed my eyes and threw back the quilt. I stretched and inhaled the scent of the lavender that Gran put in the laundry. She said lavender soothed, and I would have to agree. It would always remind me of home. Outside, sunlight flashed through the fronds of the palmetto trees and into my bedroom. The birds were singing.

I swung my legs over the side of the bed, yawning and looking around my room. It was just as it had been before I'd moved to New York, as though I had never left. I glanced at the walls where I had hung about thirty different-sized gold picture frames. All of them contained recipes. One summer, I decided I wanted to start collecting recipes. I started with Gran's recipe box. Then, any time I ate a delicious meal, either at home, a friend's house, or a restaurant, I would ask whoever had made it to write out the recipe and sign it. Some of the recipes had been written on cocktail napkins, others on scraps of paper, but most were on index cards. My favorite was Great-Grandmother Daisy's recipe card for fried chicken. It was thin and yellowed from age, missing a corner, and creased from being folded in half and kept in pockets. That was the recipe that had started it all, becoming the Magic Lantern's signature dish. I cherished that recipe, as did my whole family. I wondered how many times each of us had used this card before committing its contents to memory. I knew it by heart but still liked to read it from time to time. It was our family's greatest treasure, a love letter from an extraordinary lady I'd never met but felt I knew.

After a quick shower, I opened my suitcase. Looking at all the clothes it contained, I realized that Jim had packed way more than I needed. There was more than a week's worth of clothes in there, including a chef's coat, clogs, and a little black cocktail dress covered in sequins. Wasn't it so like Jim to pack a sequined dress. There was no way I was going to be here long enough to wear all of these clothes. I smiled and chose a pair of jeans and a gray cashmere pullover sweater.

I went over to the dresser and opened the jewelry box to find my old pearl studs. This was where I'd kept my treasures when I was growing up. As I rummaged through the little jewelry boxes, figurines, ticket stubs, and photos, I saw the photo of me and my dad on my fifth birthday, when he and Mom had given me my first "big girl" bicycle. My father had taken off the training wheels and told me I didn't need them because I was big enough, smart enough, and brave enough to ride a two-wheeler. He held the back of the seat and ran behind me as I was learning how to ride. Then one day he let go and I was riding it by myself! I remembered how amazed I'd been to be riding it myself and how proud my father had looked when I'd circled back to him. I didn't know one day he would never be behind me again. I tucked the photo into a safe spot, found the pearl studs, and put them in my ears. I gave myself a squirt of the perfume sitting next to the jewelry box. Chanel No. 5. Gran gave me and my sister a small bottle for Christmas every year. I was about to grab my Uggs when I remembered how warm it was here. I dug through my closet and found a pair of red Converse sneakers.

Last night Violet had come home with me and Jim, saying she was too tired to drive home, and why go all the way back to her and Chris's house in West Ashley when she and I would be going right back to the hospital the next morning. As the visiting chef, I intended to make biscuits and eggs for her and Jim, but first, remembering one of Gran's rules, I made my bed.

As I passed my sister's room, I heard her light snoring; she sounded like a baby bear. She had never been a good sleeper. When she was little, she used to crawl into bed with me and curl up to snooze. Something about sleeping alone never worked for her until she pulled our dog Henry's bed into her room. Having another heartbeat in the room allowed her to finally get some nocturnal peace. I knew her sleep was precious, so I let her be. I'd call her downstairs silently with the aroma of bacon.

At the end of the hall was Gran's room. The door was open, and I couldn't resist. Dominating the room was Gran's giant canopy Charleston rice poster bed. I'd loved that bed since I was little, thinking it looked like it was made for a princess. The canopy was made of lace, which Gran's mother-in-law had tatted by hand. Southern homes were full of family history. I looked around her room, without her in it. It was like looking at a smile that was missing a tooth. The night tables at either side of her bed were loaded with mismatched picture frames filled with smiling faces and newspaper clippings. There was one from the *Post and Courier* lauding me for winning a cooking competition when I was seventeen. It was a chili contest, and I had beaten the previously undefeated fire department. It was just a little competition, but Gran had made such a big deal about my win. Another picture was of Gran, Grandpa Eddie, Violet, and me, covered in flour in the Magic Lantern's kitchen. It was Christmas Day and Grandpa Eddie was wearing a Santa hat. Violet had started a flour fight with me because I said I wished it were a white Christmas. Gran and Grandpa Eddie came in and were furious, but after witnessing our giggle fits, they decided to join in. Mom had taken that picture of the four of us, smiling like idiots, winded from all the laughter. Happier times.

I made my way downstairs, holding myself back from sliding down the banister. I decided to compromise and just run down as fast as I could, but halfway down I stopped. The picture of Great-Grandmother Daisy was askew again. I looked at the faded black-and-white photograph. Perfectly posed in front of the restaurant. I could feel the weather just by looking at it. Her red hair escaping her signature topknot. Her smile showed that she was all grit and good humor. I hoped she would approve of me. I'd straightened it yesterday when I'd arrived. Maybe one of us had brushed against it on our way upstairs last night? Whatever. Reaching the bottom of the stairs, I heard noises in the kitchen. Then the strong scent of the best thing in the world, orange cinnamon buns, hit me. Gran's best friend, Alice, was here! There in our kitchen she stood whisking and humming to herself. She was just like an angel. Seeing her made my heart clench. She was wearing a pink dress and a green apron tied tightly around her waist. She looked up at me and smiled, her giant silver earrings dangling against her neck.

I ran over and gave her a hug. "Alice, what are you doing here?"

"Came over to water Rose's garden before opening the shop and noticed she had some guests. Thought I'd make them breakfast."

"How did you know we were here?" Over the years, I'd observed that Alice somehow knew things that other people didn't or couldn't know.

"Nice to have you back, Magnolia. I knew you'd come when you heard about your grandmother's accident."

"Oh, Alice, I went to the hospital last night. Gran looks awful. I'm so worried about her. What if she doesn't recover? She had to have *brain surgery*!"

"And she came through it just fine. Your grandmother's a strong, determined woman. Give her time to heal. Why don't you make yourself useful and help me cook these pancakes? You know how to do that, right? Or have you forgotten up in that fancy New York kitchen?" Alice winked at me and tossed me an apron.

"How could I forget Alice's Fundamentals?" I washed my hands, getting ready to work.

Every summer as far back as I could remember, I cooked and baked alongside Gran in the restaurant. Alice, who was also a great cook, often came by in the early evening to lend a hand after she'd closed her shop. Alice and Gran had laid the foundation for my love of cooking. One summer Alice told me she would teach me everything she knew about cooking, calling our sessions "Alice's Fundamentals." She gave me a notebook that I still have, and in it I wrote down every recipe she taught me. Okay, maybe she didn't use the correct terminology for knife cuts or know how to make a foam, but she showed me how to hold a knife and how to season food to make it tasty. I got my palate from her. Every time I cooked a pot of pasta, I thought about her telling me that the water should taste like the ocean before you added the noodles. When I asked her why, she didn't explain, she just said, "'Cause it makes the noodles taste good, that's why!" Later, when I was in culinary school, I learned from one of my chef-instructors that you should salt the water because of all the starch in the noodles. The only chance noodles had to soak up any salt was when they cooked in the water. They didn't taste salty when they were done, just more flavorful. The same went for cooking green beans or any other fibrous food. Alice and Gran laid out the dots of cooking for me; culinary school and professional cooking connected them.

"Alice, I've been dreaming about your cooking," I said as I beat the eggs, flour, and baking powder.

"Trying to butter me up, Miss Magnolia?"

"Not I, said the goose!" That was the answer I'd given her when I was a little girl. Violet and I had loved the story "The Little Red Hen."

"Yes, Miss. Goose you is! Don't you know I notice when you don't call me?"

"I'm sorry, Alice. I work well past midnight and I

know you are sleeping. I don't want to wake you up!" I looked at her and pouted a little.

"Crazy hours they have you working up in New York City. I hope they're paying you well."

"Alice, it isn't about money . . ."

"Oh, yeah? What's working about, then? Hmm?" Alice rolled her eyes and stuck a finger in my pancake batter. "More sugar, and make sure when you add those blueberries, you don't stir too hard. Don't want purple pancakes, now."

"Yes, ma'am," I said. "But, Alice, it really isn't all about money, it's also about experience!" I heard myself, and I hoped I didn't sound whiny.

"Oh, yeah? Experience gonna pay your rent?"

"Alice!"

"I know, Miss Top Chef. I just miss you is all. We all do. I'll only say this once, but I do miss that carrot soup of yours! What's your secret ingredient?"

"Experience."

"Humph." She rolled her eyes and then giggled.

Alice always said you could get away with saying anything you wanted, even something downright rude, if you wrapped it up in funny, smart packaging; it's all about the delivery. As I took out the skillet for the bacon, I heard someone pounding on the front door.

Alice raised her eyebrows. "Entertaining gentlemen callers this early in the day?"

I gave her a saccharine smile. "Right, I'll go see who it is." Still in an apron and holding a long meat fork, I walked through the living room and opened the front door.

Chris looked surprised.

I was surprised. At first, I didn't recognize the handsome, well-groomed man in a business suit standing on the porch. The last time I'd seen Chris he was wearing jeans and a camo shirt, and his hair had been longer. His light-blue eyes still had that soulful glint and contrasted handsomely with his dark-brown hair. He'd been my high school sweetheart, the boy I'd thought was perfect. But as I'd contemplated my future when I was nineteen, I had big dreams. I wanted to go to culinary school, maybe become a famous chef in New York or Paris—I'd broken it off, no longer wanting a boyfriend or anything holding me in the South.

Now Chris was a lawyer at a big Charleston firm, having pursued big dreams of his own, and as fate would have it, he fell in love with my sister and was now living with her and her chip on the shoulder about being Chris's "second choice," which of course was ridiculous. I hadn't understood him or even guessed his ambitions, but she did.

"What—" we both said at the same time.

Embarrassed for having stared at him for so long, I said, "You go first," waving my hand, forgetting that I was holding a long, sharp fork.

Chris stepped back defensively. And we both started laughing, the way we'd laughed years ago when our fishing lines had gotten tangled together or when we'd fumbled with each other's clothing in the back of his truck. He rolled his lower lip into his mouth, and I felt my cheeks go red.

I stepped out onto the porch and cleared my throat. "Don't worry, I know how to handle a fork. I am a professional chef."

"Yes, a professional *New York* chef. And I bet you came down here because of your grandmother's accident."

"That's right. And I bet you're here to get Violet."

"Gee, we're both geniuses at deductive reasoning." He grinned. "I thought she probably was here or at the hospital. She's hardly left the place since the accident, she's so concerned. I'm sure you're worried, too. I'm sorry this happened, Maggie. It's good you're home. There's strength in numbers."

"What do you mean?"

"Three Adams women looking out for Gran is better than two." He gave me that shy half smile that used to melt my heart. My head and my heart started spinning from present to past, past to present, probably because I was still tired and anxious about Gran. It was time to get back into the kitchen with Alice.

"Why don't you come in and join us for breakfast?" I said. "Violet should be up soon."

"Pancakes on the menu, right?"

"How did you know?"

Chris moved closer to me and put his large hand on the side of my head—the way he used to do before he kissed me. "Flour in your hair." He brushed it off with his fingers.

"How nice that you're getting reacquainted!" Violet said sharply, stepping out on the porch, letting the front door slam behind her.

Chris and I practically jumped back from each other.

"Vi!" Chris went over to her and leaned in to give her a kiss. My sister slipped out of the way.

"Where have you been? I didn't get my usual goodnight text." She put her hands on her hips and pouted like a little girl, but I couldn't help noticing how chic she looked in slim red jeans and a close-fitting red-and-white-striped T-shirt—and pearls, of course. She had come into her own. How she got her hair so straight in this humidity I'd never know.

"I told you I'd be working late last night on the

Myrtle Beach case. I'm due back in the office now, but I wanted to find you first." I could see Chris was a little exasperated. "How's your grandmother?"

Violet's eyes filled with tears. "The same, no change."

Chris put his arms around her, and this time she leaned into him. "Come here, baby. Let's sit down and you can tell me about it." He led Violet over to the wicker sofa at the end of the porch.

"If y'all want breakfast, it should be ready in five minutes," I said before making a beeline for the kitchen. Alice was frying bacon.

"Where you been?" she asked.

"It was Violet's gentleman caller. She got prickly." I rolled my eyes.

"Don't be too hard on her, Maggie. Little sisters grow up in big sisters' shadows. Fact of life."

Before I could refute Alice's words of wisdom, the back door swung open. In came my mom and Jim, covered in dirt from the garden. Two surprises this morning, and it was only a quarter past nine. Gran always asked Mom to help her in the garden, but Mom had never really shown an interest. Clearly, today she needed to stay busy. It looked like Jim had been her partner in crime, and he was holding three beautiful golden-brown eggs.

"Hi, Mom. Jim, what are you doing up? I thought you were still in bed?"

"Well, good morning, sunshine!" Jim said, air-kissing me. "I slept like the proverbial baby and didn't want to waste a glorious Lowcountry morning, so I went for a walk. Then your momma drove up and I helped her in the henhouse. I had a farm-girl moment feeding them! I was worried those little jerks would peck my face off. Anyway, it paid off." He placed the eggs in a dish on the counter.

"Such a warm morning! I think I started to glisten!" Mom said. "Thank you for making us breakfast. How thoughtful."

"Alice has been cooking up a storm, and I've been helping her." I leaned over and gave Alice another hug. Now I knew how she had figured out we were here— Jim had beaten me out of bed, and she'd seen him prowling around the garden.

"Magnolia, your next job is to set the table," Alice said, untying her apron. "Time for me to go to work. And you better call Violet and Chris in before the food gets cold."

"Chris is here?" my mother said, her face lighting up. "I better go tidy up before I sit down."

"Don't wait on me," Jim said. "I need a shower after

all that farmwork. Thanks for breakfast, Alice!" he added before running upstairs.

Alice shook her head. "That boy is a whirlwind of energy!" She lowered her voice before adding, "And your mother must be feeling a little better if she stopped by. I bet she's happy you're home."

"You're assuming too much, Alice, I don't—"

"Stop right there. Don't start this morning, be patient with her. You're all going through a lot right now." Alice picked up her handbag and took out her car keys. "Anyhow, it's nice to see Rose's house filled with people again. And, Maggie, it's nice to see you in her kitchen. When you get to the hospital, you call me at the store, okay? Let me know how she is. I'll be visiting her after work, or sooner if you think she needs me."

"Will do. Thanks, Alice, for everything."

In minutes the table was set—pancakes piled on top of Gran's pastel milk-glass platter, freshly squeezed orange juice in the cut-crystal pitcher, coffee in the serving pot, and Alice's cinnamon buns displayed in all their glory on a serving plate.

"I desperately need coffee," my mother said, sitting down at the table. I noticed how worn out she looked, even though she was her normal radiant self. "The past few days have wearied me." After I poured her coffee, my mother looked up at me. "Maggie, you used the wrong napkins. But how would you know when you're never here?"

I inhaled sharply. "Which ones should I have—"

"Oh, Mom!" Violet walked into the kitchen and kissed my mother's cheek. "So sweet of you to come by. We can all go to the hospital together. How does your arm feel?"

"It still hurts. Where's Chris?" my mother asked. "Alice said he was here."

Violet sat at the table across from my mother and helped herself to a cinnamon bun. "He's working on an important case and had to get back to the office. But first he wanted to see me. He was worried when I didn't come home last night."

"Violet, how could you do that?" My mother set the pancake platter down on the table a little too forcefully. "I'm sure he wants you at home with him. That man adores you!" She stared at me purposefully.

Violet didn't say anything, she just delicately licked the bun's icing off her fingers.

I wished I didn't have to hear this conversation, so I concentrated on the pancakes. Perfect, light, and fluffy, and I hadn't mashed the blueberries.

My mother wasn't done yet. "Violet, look at me." She did. "It's time you had a ring on your finger.

You're living together already! That boy just needs a little push. You know how to push."

"Yes, Momma, I know, but—"

"Violet, you're a lovely, talented young woman. You shouldn't just be photographing other people's weddings, you should be having one yourself! Show your sister some of your photographs. They're brilliant. Bring her up to date."

"Momma, we're eating now," Violet gently protested.

"Doesn't matter. It's just the three of us. Show Maggie how good you are!"

My head was spinning. Poor Violet, getting such conflicting signals from our mother—you're talented and brilliant, but hurry up and get married! Violet went into the living room and got her laptop. She showed me her latest wedding shots. They were good, not just the standard bride-and-groom portraits and the wedding-party lineup, but vibrant candid shots that captured the couple's personality and joy.

"Vi, these are great!" I said.

"Here are the ones I'm really proud of." She showed me pictures of Gran's black-and-white chickens, bright-red tomatoes, and giant dark-purple eggplants. There were a few of Gran's hands, mostly covered in dirt. The last picture was of our mother, in a white dress, sitting on a bench in Gran's garden, holding a tiny bunch of violets. She looked so different from the tired, tense woman who sat across the table from me now. Our mother was beautiful. I always seemed to overlook her natural grace and poise. She was smiling gently at the camera, an expression I hadn't seen on her face in a long time. Violet was able to catch her essence in one single photograph—beautiful, mysterious, and sad all at the same time. It was spooky, but clearly a true mark of a talented photographer.

"Violet, I think you should show these to a professional photographer who does more than weddings, maybe someone at the local museum. You've got real talent. I think you should show someone who knows—" I heard fast, pounding footsteps on the stairs.

Jim burst into the kitchen, clutching his cell phone in the air like a baton. "Oh, my God, Magnolia! Destiny is calling! My agent called me and said the casting director for the soap opera *ICU New York* wants me to audition for a hot young intern role!"

I was speechless for a few seconds. "Wonderful! Amazing!" Violet and I jumped up from the table and hugged him.

"That's wonderful, Jimmy honey," my mother said. "I hope you get the part."

Jim was out of breath, so he had to inhale deeply before adding, "They want me to audition today at noon, but obviously I'm here, so I begged them to let me Skype in a cold reading, and they agreed. Oh, my gosh, I'm so excited!" His eyes widened with alarm. "How do I look?"

"Gorgeous!" the three of us answered in unison before we all started laughing.

"Thanks, but I need an ice pack for my eyes," Jim said.

After we prepared one for him, he went upstairs to get ready for the audition. He said he'd join us at the hospital later. My mother left. Violet answered emails from her clients in the living room while I washed the dishes and straightened up the kitchen. I got the impression that Violet was still annoyed at me for talking to Chris. There was enough tension between me and my mother, now I had to deal with Violet's frayed emotions, too?

Twenty minutes later, I got behind the wheel of Gran's old truck, and Violet rode copilot. I enjoyed driving—it sure beat the subway—despite the mishap the night before and the truck's making more noise than a marching band.

"You know, Violet, it was nice to see Chris, but we just exchanged a few words before you—"

"Look, Maggie, just forget it!" She turned on the radio and started to softly sing along to a Taylor Swift song. I knew the lyrics, too, so I joined in. That seemed to ease the tension between us, maybe because it felt like high school again, driving around in the truck, listening to music. We were only three years apart in age, but she really felt like the older sister sometimes.

My thoughts shifted to Gran. She was so frail. I felt the pang of guilt I always experienced when I realized how much of my family's lives I was missing because of living in New York. I hated that I hadn't been here the night of the accident. At a stoplight I checked my phone. I saw a missed call from Ronny. I decided to ignore it. I needed to chew something, so I asked Violet if she had any gum.

"No! Of course, I do not have any chewing gum! What am I, a cow chewing cud?" She looked at me in mock horror, then popped open the glove box. "What you want, girl, cinnamon or winter fresh?"

I let out a snort, chose cinnamon, and let myself gaze out over the cocoa-powder-colored marsh grass. I loved the marsh in April, with its brown grass and water that looked dark blue one minute, steel gray the next, depending on the light. White egrets dotted the landscape. I'd always preferred the Lowcountry in the early spring. The beaches were so gray, you couldn't tell where the water ended and the sky began.

You could keep New York's skyline; this place was the landscape of my soul.

"Mags," Violet said, "tell me about the city! Tell me about work, tell me about Ron. Are you still seeing him?"

I didn't want to get into the gory details of love or work, so I just said, "Yep, and work is still crazy and wild, busy all the time. New York is amazing, you know, being the center of the universe and everything. It's a kaleidoscopic carnival, twenty-four seven."

My mind drifted back to the beginning with Ronny.

When I first took the job at Bar JP, Ronny was working as a line cook. I wasn't allowed to touch anything for the first week I was there, not even to peel a carrot. Chef wanted me to observe how the cooks worked. He wanted me to absorb everything. "You can learn a lot by just watching," he said, so that's what I did. I stood in the corner every night, in a chef's coat three sizes too big for me, in pants that were not made for girls, with my little notebook. I wrote down everything I observed, from how the stations were set up to the procedures that every cook went through for each dish. It was then I noticed Ronny.

He was trouble in a chef's coat, but that didn't faze me. He had dark hair and piercing dark eyes, so brown they were almost black. When they looked at you, you felt like he could call out your secrets. It was unnerving, and the first time I made eye contact with him, I felt shivers all over my body. He could have been awkward being as lanky as he was, but instead he moved with an elegance and a refinement. He always appeared cool under pressure, almost comfortable in the kitchen chaos.

I watched Ronny add garnish to a salmon dish with tweezers. He moved so fast but with the precise timing of a synchronized swimmer moving through water, except he did it with fire. One night, Ronny saw me watching him, and I'll admit I was totally staring at him, so he called me over.

"Hey, new girl, wanna come sauce this plate?"

I had been there for a week; I was champing at the bit to do something. Now a line cook was offering to let me sauce his plate. Even though he terrified me, I wanted to help.

"Yes, please!"

Ronny looked me dead in the eye.

"Yes, Chef?"

"Umm, yes. Chef."

The line cooks burst into laughter, and I felt the back of my neck get hot. What was so funny? He wasn't a chef; well, he wasn't *the* chef, or even a sous-chef. But I guess he was ahead of me in the pecking order, so . . .

"I'm sorry, Chef."

"Don't apologize, just don't do it again. I'm Ronny."

"Yes, Chef."

"I'm just a line cook, kid, don't call me Chef."

"Oh."

"Get over here, I'm gonna show you how it's done. Although I'm pretty sure you wrote down my every move. That's a good girl. Watching the big boys do it. Maybe one day you'll be in my shoes."

He then showed me how to dip a spoon into sauce, tip first, picking up a dab of sauce about the size of a quarter. Then he gracefully circled the plate, letting the sauce slide off the tip, so it sprinkled dots of sauce.

"You move around the plate with the tip, letting it determine where the sauce drips. Gives you more control. That's a pretty plate," he said, flashing a smile that melted my insides.

"Thank you . . . *Chef*," I couldn't resist adding as I smiled back at him.

Suddenly, I felt the heat of the kitchen, and I was sure it wasn't from the stoves.

After service, Ronny invited me to go out with him and all the line cooks. He said he would buy me a beer for teasing me so badly. I went, eager to fit in. I changed clothes quickly, ditching my whites and donning all my layers, wrapping my chunky scarf around my neck, pulling on my hat, and zipping up my puffer coat. Before I reached the exit, I caught a glimpse of myself in the mirror: I looked like Frosty the damn Snowman.

I threw my knife roll around my back and felt like Robin Hood with his bow and arrows. I always felt tough wearing all those knives. But not really, because if I was ever in a dangerous situation, it would take me a solid five minutes to pull them out of the roll and their respective cases. In Manhattan, you could be dead by then. But still . . .

"All right, Spark Plug. Ready? Jesus, look at you! It's not *that* cold outside!"

"Ronny, I'm from South Carolina, where right now it's like sixty degrees. So, to me, I'm basically in Antarctica!"

"What was that? I couldn't hear you through your layers."

I pulled the scarf from my mouth and let my hood fall, exposing my bright-red sparkly hat. "I said, it's cold."

"New name. Sparkle."

"Perfect. I'll answer to Chef Sparkle." It was prettier than Spark Plug.

Ronny laughed, threw his arm around me, and led me outside into freshly fallen snow. It looked like we were walking into an exquisite dreamland. That's how New York City was, though. Once you had written it off as impossibly harsh or aggressive, the snow would fall, and suddenly the unforgiving hard city was softened and quieted by blankets of pure powdered sugar. The Big Apple took a total one-eighty.

Ronny and I stopped and watched the snowflakes dancing across the frozen cityscape for a moment, his arm still on my shoulders. I caught a whiff of him. At that precise moment, I knew I was in trouble. I didn't just smell kitchen. I smelled *him*. Even through all my layers of unsexy clothing, which at that moment, I regretted, as all those advertisements for winter clothes with girls in long sweaters, headbands, tall boots, and short peacoats flashed through my mind. You never saw someone in a puffer coat on the cover of *Vogue*. Puffers weren't sexy, but catching a cold and blowing your nose was worse. I was glad my sense of smell was as sharp as ever as I inhaled deeply again, and yeah, there was definitely a strong aroma of pine or something manly. I didn't know what it was, but, Lord Almighty, it was delicious.

We walked about three blocks and took a flight of stairs down to an underground dive bar with cement walls and dim lighting from neon signs advertising adult beverages. It smelled like beer and bad decisions. The bartender delivered shots to us the moment we walked in. It was some dark-brown liquid that I knew would warm my insides and lubricate my social awkwardness. I spied two pool tables and a sprinkling of booths.

We went to a booth in the corner with BJ, B-Rad, and a pile of coats and knife rolls. Ronny informed me that this booth was ours. It was basically reserved for our kitchen crew no matter what. I snapped off my coat and added it to the pile, turned around, and threw back a shot. I could feel Ronny's eyes on me.

"What?"

"Well, who knew you had a body under your whites?"

"Thanks?"

"Yeah. That was absolutely a compliment. *George?* Another round of shots, but bring bourbon for my little Southern Magnolia."

"Normally I don't do shots of bourbon, but I am Southern, and I want to be polite. I take it in a glass with two cubes of ice, if you're buying."

"I am buying. *George?* Rocks glass. Mister Jim Beam, light on the rocks. And Maggie, please don't be polite with me. Nothing interesting will ever happen if we behave."

I pulled off my hat and yanked my hair out of its ponytail holder, remembering that Gran said a woman's hair is fifty percent of her looks. It had been up in a bun, so I was counting on waves.

"Maybe your nickname should be Red!"

"Why are you so concerned with giving me a nickname, Ronny?"

"Because, once you name something, it's yours."

That's when the air changed, and I knew he wanted me, and I wanted him, too. I looked directly into his black eyes and sized him up. I noticed a tattoo creeping out from the sides of his V-neck.

"What kind of tattoo do you have?"

Ronny maintained eye contact and pulled his T-shirt up over his head from the back, revealing a maze of tattoos on his upper chest and shoulders. I saw the most beautifully colored pair of koi fish swimming in a pool with water lilies and a lotus flower. I noticed several words written in different languages and lyrics to a Led Zeppelin song.

"Which one?"

"The one on your collarbone? Isn't that Tibetan?"

"Yeah. How'd you know that?"

"My mom was into yoga. I think she has that written on her fridge, too. Reminds her not to go totally crazy or something. I wish she'd read it more often."

"Well, it says *Learn from yesterday, live for today, hope for tomorrow.*"

"And Ronny? What are you hoping for?"

Ronny smiled wide and looked me up and down. I felt my cheeks turning red and I was slightly embarrassed to be looked at so brazenly. But to be honest, I liked it, too. It was all too forward, and too fast . . . but I didn't care. I felt powerful and attractive and as if I belonged to someone. I knew that it was dangerous, but I liked to play with fire.

"Hey, Ron! Put some damn clothes on! You're making us look bad!" one of the guys called out, breaking the tension.

The other guys laughed and pulled me into the booth with them. The night went on like that for a while. We compared battle wounds from the kitchen. They showed me burns and scars and tattoos and told the stories about their origins. We laughed and drank so much, I was happy that I had the next day off. I was going to need some recovery time.

My relationship with Ronny was exciting.

At first. Two years ago.

And I have been chasing that high ever since.

How could I ever explain my messy relationship, if you could even call it that, to my sister?

"Man, I'm jealous. I wish I could live in New York City! The light's so different there, imagine what I could photograph. So many unique people, because seems like here everyone looks the same," Violet said.

"Well, there's a whole lot of *unique* right here in the Lowcountry," I said.

"You can say that again. Momma sure keeps us entertained. She and that stupid Buster. I wonder what's going to happen if they stay broken up."

"I guess he made Mom feel special," I said. "She'll miss that and will have to look for a new boyfriend."

"On to the next as always, I guess. I just don't understand why he's poking around the Lantern like he is, calling all the shots and making changes," Violet said, chewing on a piece of her hair.

"What kind of changes?" I asked, feeling my loyalty shift from my mother to the restaurant.

"Mom didn't tell you?" Violet sounded a little worried.

"No," I said, trying to focus on the road.

"He's at the Magic Lantern, Mags. Running the place with Momma."

"Excuse me? Running it? What do you mean *running* it?" I cut my eyes at her.

"Oh, man. I can't believe . . . well, yes, I can. I thought at least Gran would have told you about some of the, umm, changes?" Violet said.

"Nope. No one told me about any changes. Why didn't *you* tell me?" I could feel myself getting angry. It was just like my mother and Violet to keep me out of things. It was a punishment for leaving.

"Maggie, Buster came into Mom's life when she jumped into the manager's job and he sort of convinced her to make it more tourist friendly . . ."

"Wow, well, that is certainly a left turn from the restaurant that Gran and Grandpa Eddie built. How tourist friendly are we talking?" I asked, readying myself for bad news.

"Well, to be fair, at first it did okay. A lot of the locals liked it. It's just . . . recently the quality of food has really changed, so the Lantern has lost some of its longtime clientele," Violet said.

"The quality? What do you mean?" I asked.

"I think you need to see it for yourself, but don't start a war, okay, Maggie? Please?"

"I'm not going to start a war, Vi, I just don't understand why we needed to change the Magic Lantern at all. It's an institution! Has been for the last fifty years," I said.

"Maggie, it wasn't making money. It needed updating. Gran was past it, so she let Mom make some changes. I mean, Gran changed it when she took over the restaurant from her mother!"

"Yeah, but for the better," I pointed out.

"Gran got in and completely changed Great-Grandmother Daisy's vision. This isn't totally different."

"She added a bakery! She elevated the place." Something told me I wasn't going to like the new Magic Lantern.

Chapter 7
Violet

We pulled into the large multilevel parking structure of MUSC in downtown Charleston. It always seemed out of place, that building, so modern in between historic Charleston single houses, which are, for those who don't know, the clapboard homes with two-story porches that run along the sides of them. Built to catch the breeze off the water. My big sister, Maggie, hopped out of the driver's seat of the truck. She had to slam the door twice to close it. I fished around in my purse for my sunglasses and my favorite Chanel lip gloss. I opened the visor and looked in the mirror to make sure it was perfect. I hopped out and looked over at Maggie, who was squinting in the sun as we walked down the pathway that led directly into the hospital.

"Seems you have forgotten what some good ole Southern sunshine feels like?" I said to her.

"I mean, it's just spring! Where I live these days, it's gray till almost June!" Maggie grumbled and held out her hand for another pair of sunglasses. She knew I'd have an extra. I dug around and handed her a pair that was bright yellow with daisies on them. She arched an eyebrow at me but put them on.

The sky was what we called Carolina blue. It was just gorgeous, despite the mood of the day. I looked over at Maggie's torn jeans. She could look better; she really was beautiful, even if she didn't know it. But along with the sunshine, she had forgotten how to dress Southern. Everything my sister wore was basically shades of black or gray. But we were in the middle of a crisis, and I decided I shouldn't pick at her.

We made our way to the hospital's automatic sliding doors and were greeted by the smell of bleach.

"Yuck!" Maggie said as she grimaced.

"Girl, get ahold of yourself, please?" I said.

"I know, I'm a baby. I'm thinking about blood and guts," she responded.

"What's wrong with you? You butcher animals at your restaurant but can't deal with a little blood here? By the way, where is all this blood? Do you see it?" I said, teasing her.

"No, gross, but I know it's here somewhere . . . lurking beneath every needle and scalpel."

"Hey, crazy, let's be adults . . . keep it up and they'll put you in the upstairs north wing for a psych evaluation. You want that? *American Horror Story* style?" I gave her a wicked grin.

"Get over yourself. I'm fine." I smiled at my normally brave sister's fears.

We took the elevator to the fourth floor, and after walking what seemed like a half mile, we arrived at the room. Maggie started to pace outside it.

"Maggie, you okay?" I asked.

"Yeah, yup, totally cool," she said to her feet. She reminded me of a spooked cat. She was jumpy.

"Maggie, we won't know anything till we get in there and speak with Dr. King. No sense paying the toll twice," I said and stopped her pacing by grabbing her hand, which she immediately pulled back.

"Sorry, you're right, of course. I'm just nervous, Vi."

"Yes, I know. This isn't easy, Maggie, but we have to try to hold it together."

"You have lipstick on your teeth," she said and pushed the door open.

"It's actually a *gloss*!" I said to her back.

I was anxious yet dreading to hear what the doctor had to say today. Until then I would try to think positively and keep a smile on my face no matter what I saw inside the room. I quickly checked my teeth in the monogrammed compact in my purse, and realized she was teasing me. I lowered my shoulders, took a deep breath, and followed her in.

Gran was lying in the bed, looking the same as she had last night, still except for the slight rise and fall of her chest. Momma was sitting beside the bed, and next to her, Buster. He was a stocky man, and his large presence was only amplified in contrast to my mother's small frame. His gray chest hair was poking out of the Hawaiian shirt he was wearing, which was unbuttoned one button too many. I could tell that Maggie disapproved of him, and I understood. I didn't care for his look, either. He appeared cartoonish, but she didn't know him like I did. He might have blinded us with the sunlight bouncing off the gold chain around his neck, but not a human on God's great earth loved like he did. He was shaking his head and holding my mother's hand between his meaty paws.

"Hello, Maggie, Violet," Mom said. She was always short when she was nervous.

"Hi, Magnolia. I'm Buster." He extended his hand, and she shook it. "Tough time to meet you. But I'm glad we finally are meeting." He offered her a smile.

"Yeah. Nice to meet you, too," she said, and I

could tell by her body language that she wanted to be alone with Mom and Gran and me. She turned and met my eyes, and I was correct; I could see she was aggravated.

"Hey, Maggie, I think I dropped my keys outside. Come help me look?" I asked her. She nodded and we went outside the room. I grabbed her arm.

"You need to keep it cool, Maggie. Everyone can feel your moods. This isn't the time for a showdown. Momma will only get defensive," I said urgently.

"Who does this guy think he is? He dumped Mom and was the reason she got drunk and put Gran in the hospital."

I looked at her blankly.

"Ugh. I know, he's not to blame. This isn't anyone's fault but Mom's." She sighed.

"Magnolia . . ." I started.

"Fine. Let's go back," she said, and we reentered the room.

"Buster, call me Maggie. Everyone does," she said, and I shot her a small smile when I caught her eye.

"Okay. Maggie, I just want to apologize to you and your family for being so *stupid*. I can't . . . I can't forgive myself for leaving your mother in that state the other night. I just . . . got scared. I've never been so in love before, and I let my baby go!" Buster's voice caught in his throat, and he started to sob. Huge, bulbous tears exploded from the sides of his eyes and his face turned red. He put a fist to his mouth and bit down, trying to catch his breath. Our mother was looking right at him, and I saw her tear up. Maggie's mouth hung open in horror, and I wanted this emotional outburst to end quietly, before Maggie's words caught up with her.

"Buster, it's okay. We forgive you! None of us blame you! It was an accident!" I said, quickly going to his side and hugging him. I felt bad for him.

"Thank you, princess," Buster choked out. "I'm just so thankful to God that I got my girl back!" He made the sign of the cross and kissed the top of my head.

"*Princess?*" Maggie said. "Man, I missed a lot. Y'all look like a little family."

"Maggie . . ." I said.

"We're gonna be okay, Maggie. I'm so sorry I let all of you down," Mom said as a tear slid down her cheek.

"How's *Gran?*" Maggie asked, annoyed.

I could sense the tension rising. Maggie was more concerned with Gran's state than getting an apology from Momma. I could see that Maggie thought that Momma was making this moment about herself and

Buster, when the real drama was with Gran. I bit the inside of my cheek to keep from scolding them. They always took their stress out on each other. We really needed to stay calm. Who knew how much Gran could hear or sense? I was having a hard time myself, and to be perfectly honest, that hug from Buster felt good, but I knew that if I didn't break away and stand next to my sister, Maggie would decide I'd chosen sides. I was well conditioned to be Switzerland.

The door opened and the doctor walked in, carrying a clipboard and breaking the tension. She was the kind of woman who made you straighten your posture and tuck loose hair behind your ears. She was stunningly beautiful. Her hair was pulled into a classic bun and her pearls shone against her dark-brown skin. How could a woman be this beautiful *and* a doctor? How was that fair?

"Good morning," she said with a warm smile, looking around the room. Her gaze rested on my sister. "You must be Maggie. Your sister and momma told me all about you. I'm Dr. King." She extended her hand, and Maggie shook it. "Violet, it's good to see you again." I shook her hand, appreciating her firm handshake. I'd always thought there was nothing worse than a weak handshake. Weak handshakes are like Velcro shoes, only appropriate for the very old or the very young.

"How nice that you were able to come down from New York to spend some time with your grandmother. She's quite a fighter," Dr. King said to Maggie.

"Well, thanks for all you're doing for her. How is she now? When do you expect her to wake up?"

Dr. King looked at Gran, then down at the chart in her hands. She wasn't smiling now. "Your grandmother came through the surgery fine. But her vitals weakened last night. Her heart rate is a little low—"

"Just do whatever you have to do to save her!" I burst out, gulping back a sob. It came out of nowhere. Seeing Dr. King's smile drop was all I needed to feel hopeless. Buster grabbed my hand and I gave it a thankful squeeze back.

Dr. King motioned for the two young men in white coats who were standing in the doorway to come in. One was pushing a cart that held a large machine. "I'd like to do a few tests. Why don't you take a coffee break or find some magazines in the waiting room? We'll talk again when I have more information."

On our way out of Gran's room, neither my mother nor Maggie nor I said a word.

"Girls, I'm so sorry. I'll *never* let Lily go again. Biggest mistake of my life." Buster sniffed loudly, looking more and more like one of those sad-puppy-dog velvet paintings.

"I'm so sorry, y'all. I'm just so . . . so . . . embarrassed," my mother said.

"Mom, we are just so relieved that you're okay. I thought I might lose you, too. I can't imagine a world without you," I said, wiping away tears.

"Jesus Christ," Maggie said under her breath and turned down the hallway.

Chapter 8
Magnolia

Outside the hospital room, there was something freezing up inside my chest, hardening against my heart. I clenched my fists. My mother's slip-up could have *killed* her, or another person. It could have been *so* much worse. I couldn't help but view my sister and Buster as enablers. At least my mom said she was embarrassed, that was a first. But the others were treating her like the victim when it was Gran lying in a hospital bed. I needed some air. I knew I had to step away.

I walked down the hallway in the opposite direction of the waiting room, not giving them a chance to respond. What was wrong with me that I couldn't just feel happy that Gran was alive? Had my childhood really been that damaging? God, sometimes I felt so twisted. I absolutely needed caffeine . . . or chocolate. I would keep walking until I found a vending machine.

I walked with purpose. With every step I took I could feel my heart beat harder. I was mad. I was mad at Buster, because who the *hell* did he think he was, walking in and out of my mom's life like that, deserting her when she could have done who knows what to herself, and now *poof*, he's back? I was mad at Violet, for not telling me about the restaurant and, also, for just being so dang weepy. Why was I the only one who saw how much bullshit this was? I was also mad at myself, for not being able to cry like a normal person, because at that moment all I wanted to do was cry.

I found a vending machine that sold coffee. I slid a dollar into its mouth and watched as a cup popped out and coffee streamed into it, steam billowing around it. This process had always amused me. This was exactly what I needed—wonderful liquid energy that would pull the Jesus right out of me and make me nicer.

The cup was full, and the machine sang a happy tune, letting me know it was finished. I picked up the cup, turned around, took a step, and slammed right into a doctor, spilling the scalding hot coffee all over my hand, down the front of my cashmere sweater, and on his white coat. The cup hit the floor.

"Watch it!" I said, shaking the hot liquid off my hands.

"Whoa! Not again!" he said.

"What? Oh, my God." I looked up at the doctor's face. Was he the same guy? He was! He was the guy whose truck I'd hit last night. *He was a doctor?* "Hey, nice to see you again . . . Sam, umm, Dr. Smart."

"Call me Sam. Did you burn your fingers? Here, let me have a look." He took my hands in his and looked at them closely. I didn't know what was burning hotter, the coffee or his touch.

"You would think I'd be used to this by now," I said.

Sam raised an eyebrow. "You mean running into me?"

"No, I mean the burns. Because I'm a *chef.* I work in a kitchen. Anyway, do you have any burn cream?" I asked, looking into his yellow-gold eyes and feeling dizzy.

"Maggie, this is a hospital. Yes, we have burn cream, come with me." He led the way down the hall.

Experiencing a fair amount of cognitive dissonance at the discovery that the farmer from last night was a medical doctor this morning, I kept glancing at him but didn't say anything. *What an unusual guy.* I took a look at my right hand. It stung a little, but it wasn't badly burned. Maybe I'd take a page from Violet's book and work this a little. Sam Smart looked even more handsome under fluorescent hospital lights.

We went into a small utility room. After he washed his hands, he motioned me over to the sink so I could do the same. "Okay, Miss Maggie, we're going to fix you right up. You have minor burns on the thumb, index finger, and palm of your right hand. They might sting for a couple of days."

Sam rubbed cream into my right hand, which instantly cooled my skin. It was ten times better than the stuff we had at work. Then he bandaged my hand with gauze and adhesive tape.

"I thought you worked on a farm," I said, confused.

Sam grinned at me. "I did in the past. Farming is in my blood—it's the family business—but my profession is medical doctor. I'm a pediatrician. How is your grandmother? You mentioned last night you were on your way to visit her here."

I shut my eyes for a moment, wishing I didn't have to say what I was about to say. "My grandmother is still in the ICU. Her doctor is examining her now."

"Who's her doctor?"

"Dr. King."

"Well, she's a total rock star. Rose is in good hands," Sam said, giving me a smile.

Something about his face, probably the surprising warmth of his smile, made me feel totally safe. There was nothing intimidating about him now. He put his hand on my shoulder and it felt as if the ice inside me was melting. My shoulders sagged and a huge tear rolled down my cheek. It was so sudden, it startled me. I rarely cried, and absolutely never cried in front of people I hardly knew.

I smiled, hoping he wouldn't notice the tear. "Thank you for not making another joke about bad driving running in my family, because the opportunity is totally there."

"Too easy," Sam said, shaking his head. "You okay?"

"Yes. Sorry, I'm not a crier, I don't know what's the matter with me." I tried to pull myself together as another tear escaped. But I did know—all the emotions I'd been bottling up were spilling out of me.

"You're just having a bad day," Sam said.

"Yeah, it sure has been a challenging one. Oh, God, I can't stop." Then I really started to sob.

"Hey, why don't you sit down for a few minutes," he said, leading me to a chair. "It's okay, let it all out. Sometimes you just need a good cry." He sat down next to me. "Hell, I need a good cry every once in a while. It's therapeutic."

That startled me enough to halt my sobbing. "I swear I'm not usually like this," I said, totally embarrassed.

"You know what you need?" Sam reached into the pocket of his white coat and produced a bite-size Snickers bar, my favorite candy.

"How'd you know?" I said.

"I'm a doctor," Sam said.

I was so touched by his kindness and relieved that he didn't pry that I could feel myself calming down. We sat there for a moment, and he handed me a Kleenex. Using my unbandaged hand, I blew my nose harder than Gran would have liked to see me do in front of a gentleman, but whatever.

"Thanks, Sam," I said before popping the candy into my mouth.

"All good?" he said.

"All good," I replied.

A moment or two passed and the conversation picked up again, as if I hadn't just had a breakdown.

"I know you live in New York. Where are you a chef?" he asked.

"At a restaurant in Manhattan, Bar JP," I said.

"Well, that's impressive. I'd imagine it's pretty tough working in the Big Apple," he said.

"You're a doctor! That's way more impressive. I bet

your job is a little harder than mine. You *save* people's lives. I just feed them," I said.

"I'm fresh out of my residency, so I haven't saved that many lives," he said.

"Are you happy to be back in Charleston?" I asked.

"Well, honestly, one of the reasons I moved back here was a girl. But it didn't work out," he said.

"Sorry to hear that." Really, I was anything but sorry to hear that.

"Yeah. We got along so well, and I thought she was perfect. It was long distance, mostly. We met online, and not long after I got here, we realized it wasn't right. But, of course, I had already accepted the job. It was complicated."

"Well," I said because I didn't know how to respond to that. He was providing me with personal information about himself, a novel experience for me with men. I should have felt uncomfortable with how open we were being with each other, but I wasn't.

"I guess it sort of just shocked me. I've always done everything by the book. I made good grades, got into a good college, got into med school, met a girl, and then I hoped that she would be the next step, but it didn't work out. I'm still sort of mad at myself . . . for hurting her. I'm a healer, for God's sake. You know?" he said, looking right into my eyes.

"Actually, no. I don't. I've never done anything by the book. But I'd say you did that girl a favor by being honest with her, and it's not necessarily a bad thing to surprise yourself," I said.

He smiled. "So, how long are you going to be in town?"

"A few days, probably. I have to get back to work," I said.

"Do you want to have a drink with me?" When I didn't immediately reply, he added, "I mean, you sort of owe me for totaling my truck."

"Total? I did not *total* your truck, mister," I said.

"I want to see you again . . . to check on your burns."

"Okay." I couldn't help but smile.

"I still have that tattoo you left on my arm, so I'll call you later, around six or so? I get off around five," he said.

"Perfect."

I sailed out of the room, not quite believing what had happened, and down the hallway toward Gran's room. I had been gone for about twenty minutes, and I was sure my family was wondering where I was. I pulled out my phone to check my messages and saw one from Ronny.

Red, we need to talk. I miss you.

I texted him back after taking into account that I'd

ignored the last few attempts he had made to contact me. I was well within the allotted time to return a text without appearing desperate. Plus, he'd said he missed me. I couldn't remember him *ever* saying that.

Ron, sorry. I've been with family. Everything okay?

I expected to have to wait another hour or so before hearing back from him. That was one of the rules he followed in the game we'd been playing for two years. But much to my surprise, my phone buzzed with a response.

Can I call you?

If the man wanted to talk on the phone, it must be serious.

Sure.

I found a bench and sat down, waiting for my phone to ring. But I waited and waited, and nothing happened. I decided to call him. Maybe there was bad reception in the hospital. The phone rang three times and then sent me to his voice mail. Was this another game? My mind started to race. Maybe he was with someone he couldn't get away from. Maybe he needed me to call him so his phone would ring, giving him an excuse to leave the room and call me back. He could say he had to return a work call. I wasn't a shady girlfriend, but after hanging around a shady boyfriend for so long, I could think like one.

My phone rang. I wished I hadn't been right. I didn't pick up until the fourth ring.

"Hey," I said.

"Hey, Red." Long pause. "How are you?" I could hear him breathing heavily.

"I'm fine. I'm in Charleston. Why are you out of breath?" I asked.

"I'm outside, and it's cold." I heard him take a drag of a cigarette.

"Are you smoking?" I asked.

"Yeah," he said.

"So, what's up, Ronny?" I asked.

"You tell me! You ran off to Charleston without telling anyone. Is everything okay? I mean, obviously everything isn't fine, but what's going on, Mags?" He sounded as if he were my devoted boyfriend.

"I'm fine. My mom and my grandmother were hurt in a car accident. Where are you?"

"Outside a friend's house," he said.

"Oh."

Here I was on the phone with the man who had pushed and pulled my heart for the last two years. When he asked me to jump, I was in the habit of asking, "How high?" In all that time, I'd never considered anyone else, yet I had just accepted a date with another man. Something in me had shifted.

At that moment, I was hell-bent on finding out, once and for all, all about the parts he kept secret from me. I was tired of my family's drama, I was tired of Ronny's games, and I was tired of who I had become with him. Where had all my strength gone? Where was my spine?

"Ronny, are you with someone else?"

"Umm . . . no. No, why would you ask me that?" He sounded nervous.

"Ronny, just be honest with me, please," I said, feeling my heart hammering in my chest.

"I'm outside Rebecca's apartment," he said.

"And who is Rebecca?"

Silence.

"Got it. Thank you for finally being honest with me, Ronny. I think we're done here." I ended the call.

I exhaled. Whoa. I had never been that direct or strong with him. I waited for another round of tears, but none came. I shook my head and actually felt . . . relieved. My phone rang again, and I hit the ignore button. It rang two more times and then stopped. I waited for the voice mail sound. After a minute or so, it pinged, and I listened to his voice mail.

"Come on, Maggie! I'm sorry, but you can't be mad at me. I don't get it. It's not like we're exclusive, and you ran off! You've been ignoring me. I don't know why you're always so needy. I called to tell you something,

but I guess you don't want to talk to me. Fine. Call me back if you want to talk. I'm going to work soon."

Needy. Wow. I stood up and shoved my phone back into my pocket.

"Maggie!" I heard a voice behind me. "Magnolia Olivia Adams!"

I turned around and saw Jim.

"What's the matter, Lovebug? Oh, God. Gran? Did she . . ." Jim said grabbing my shoulders.

"No! She's still in a coma and the doctor is running some tests," I said.

"Oh, thank the Lord. What in heaven's name happened to your hand?"

"I burned myself on coffee. How was your audition?" I asked.

"No, ma'am. First, tell me why you look like you just ran over a puppy." Jim tightened his grip on my shoulders.

"Gran's condition has not improved, and last night her vitals dropped, which is why they're doing the tests. And I met Buster, who gets under my skin and wiggles. Then I ran into the hot guy from last night. Turns out he's a doctor, and is quite nice. That's how I burned my hand, and oh, I think I'm done with Ronny forever, so . . ."

"Magnolia, that last part is fantastic news! Your hot cowboy-farmer is a doctor, and ding-dong, the douche is dead? Thank you, Jesus!" he said, smiling.

"Oh, I'm having a drink with Dr. Cowboy tonight," I said, feeling myself cheering up.

Jim grinned. "Oh, *are* you? Maybe I should leave you alone more often."

I rolled my eyes. "So, are you famous yet?"

"Don't know yet. They said they'd call me."

"Cool, cool. Well, maybe I'll marry a doctor and fulfill my Southern destiny and you'll become a famous movie star. Things are looking up, Jimmy," I said. That was true, but I'd taken a punch in the heart from Ronny, which hurt. I felt my resolve faltering a little.

"Yes, and I'll fund your restaurant with my buckets of Hollywood money," Jim said. "Okay, so tell me. How did it end with Ronny?" Bull's-eye.

I told him as we walked to Gran's room.

"Well, when one door closes another one opens. Time to open a door with Dr. Cowboy. I mean, the chef thing is hot, but cowboys? No contest." Jim gave me a side hug and smacked my butt.

The door to Gran's room was open. She lay in bed, the machines still beeping and humming around her. My mother was asleep on the small couch, and Violet was sitting in the chair next to her, looking at her phone. Buster was gone.

"Hey, y'all," I said softly. "Sorry I left, but I needed to get a cup of coffee and wound up burning the ever-living hell out of my hand. That's where I was, if anyone was wondering."

"Oh, no. Maggie, are you all right? Thank God we're in a hospital!" Violet said.

"Oh, Maggie's fine, so fine in fact that the doctor bandaging her up asked her out!" Jim said.

"Really?" Violet said, looking very interested.

Before she could say more, I asked, "How is Gran?"

My mother, apparently, wasn't sleeping, because she sat up and said, "She's not ready to be brought out of the coma. Dr. King said she will know more after they analyze the results of the tests. We have to be patient. Let's head home. We can come back later if you want."

"I don't want to go just yet," Violet said, standing up. "Whoa, my head is spinning."

"Are you okay, Violet? You don't look so good, your face has gone all pale," Jim said.

"Yeah, I'm good, I'm fine . . . maybe I need to eat something," Violet said.

"Vi, seriously, sit back down. You probably got up too fast or . . ." Before I could finish, Violet fainted.

"Oh, my gosh! Call a nurse!" Jim said.

"I'm on it!" I ran into the hallway and yelled, "Help!" After about five seconds two nurses in pink scrubs were coming around the corner, hurrying to our room. Violet was out cold, her head resting on Jim's lap as he fanned her with a magazine.

"What's going on?" one of the nurses asked.

"My sister just fainted," I said.

"Is she diabetic? How long since she had anything to eat or drink?" the other nurse asked.

"No, Violet has no medical issues," my mother said. "She had breakfast with us just a few hours ago."

The nurses put a cold compress on Violet's face and neck, and soon enough she came to.

"Wha . . . what happened?" Violet said.

"You fainted, Miss Drama," I said, happy to see the color returning to her cheeks.

"Oh, man, how long was I out?" Violet asked.

"Just long enough to scare us," Jim said.

"Violet, honey. I'd like to run a quick test on you if that's okay," the older of the two nurses said.

"What kind of test? Am I okay? I just fainted, right?" Violet said.

"Do you faint often?" asked the nurse.

"No, never, actually. I feel all jittery," Violet said.

The other nurse left the room and came back with a glass of juice.

"Sip this," she said, handing Violet the glass.

"Thanks," Violet said.

The older nurse leaned closer to Violet. "I need to ask you a personal question, and there are other people in the room."

"It's okay, this is my family, it's okay if they hear," Violet said.

"Okay. Is there a possibility of you being pregnant?" asked the nurse.

"No!" Violet said, taken aback. Then, after a pause: "Well, actually . . ."

"Violet!" all of us said at once.

I couldn't believe it. My super responsible little sister!

The nurse smiled. "Violet, can you stand? Follow me." Jim helped her up and she followed the nurse out of the room.

Twenty minutes later, Violet returned.

"Well, am I going to be a fairy godfather or what?" Jim asked.

"I'm pregnant, y'all," Violet said.

"Holy shit!" I exclaimed.

"Oh, my God!" Lily said.

"Don't any of you tell Chris!" Violet said with an expression on her face I had never seen before. "I need time. I've got a plan. I just need to work some things out."

"Yeah, like maybe telling the father of your child!" I said.

"Maggie, hush. This could really change things for Violet! I smell that big three-carat diamond, baby!" my mother said, and threw her arms around my sister.

For once, I was left speechless.

Chapter 9
Magnolia

Violet had calmed down by the time Jim was driving us back to Gran's house for lunch. She was no longer babbling about how excited she was to be pregnant and trying out baby names on us. The only thing she didn't chatter on about was Chris, the father-to-be. She had her hand on her tummy and a dazed smile on her face as she stared out the window. She seemed lost in her thoughts. I was so used to her being the noise that filled up our space that I found her silence deafening.

I sat sandwiched between Jim, who was chewing his gum, and my sister. I kept glancing at her, with rising concern. It had begun to rain again. The drops of water hit the windows sideways, and the swish-thump of the wipers matched the beats of my heart. Violet was still a baby herself; maybe I would always think of her that way. How was she going to be a mother? She had such a small frame, I had a hard time thinking about her belly becoming swollen with life. Pregnancy was a massive physical process. Was she prepared for that? She didn't even like it when her nails weren't perfect. How would she feel about her expanding waistline?

I was also unsettled by what she'd said at the hospital. Surely, this pregnancy was an accident? This wasn't her way of forcing Chris to propose to her, was it? With a sinking heart, I thought about the breakfast conversation between Violet and my mother—my mother's saying that it was time Violet had a ring on her finger and that Violet knew what to do. I wondered if history was repeating itself. A pregnancy forcing a young couple to the altar. I was the result of an unplanned pregnancy twenty-nine years earlier, and it hadn't worked out great for my parents. It would be wrong to push Chris, or any man, into marriage because a baby was on the way, and certainly in the modern world a marriage isn't a necessity, although in the South the alternative still isn't great. I knew my mother hadn't gotten pregnant to get my father to marry her; she'd been heartbroken that her pregnancy had ended her "dreams" of becoming a ballet dancer, one of her silly delusions. But I wasn't so sure about my sister. And how could I ask her, when this morning she was so touchy about my having been Chris's girlfriend eons ago? I couldn't. But I could assert myself as the responsible older sister and ask some practical questions.

"Vi, did that nice nurse at the hospital give you the name of an obstetrician?" I asked.

"Yes, Mags, she did. But I already know of a good obstetrician. All my friends who've had kids rave about her. I'm going to call and make an appointment when we get back to Gran's. I need those big pregnancy vitamins . . ."

Violet raised her hand to her mouth, and I immediately thought morning sickness—she was going to throw up! But she said, "I can't go to Dr. Vick right away. One of my friends might see me in the waiting room and say something to Chris."

"Violet, you have to tell Chris! You're going to tell him tonight, right?"

Violet snapped out of her dreamy daze. "Don't tell me what to do! And don't you dare interfere with Chris! He might have been your boyfriend once, but he loves *me* now!"

"Violet, I know. I didn't mean to—"

"Just leave me alone, Maggie!" My sister went back to staring out the window.

The tension in the truck was so thick you'd need a meat cleaver to cut it.

"Anyone want to listen to some music?" Jim asked.

"No," Violet and I said in unison.

By the time we reached the house, the rain was really coming down, and the gutters were pouring rivers of rainwater down the sides of the house into the driveway. Violet and I went into the kitchen. I saw that Alice had given us a bowl of boiled peanuts, a Lowcountry staple. Everyone has his or her own way of making them, but I always prefer Alice's. She boiled them in hot salted water, with red pepper flakes and a bay leaf. Boiled peanuts are an acquired taste. They're briny, and their slimy texture can turn people off . . . unless they're from these parts. Boiled peanuts are Lowcountry popcorn. I grabbed the large bowl of peanuts, and a small empty bowl for the shells, and nodded at Violet.

"Come on, Vi, let's go out on the porch and watch the storm."

"Okay, I'll get the Cokes," she said.

I heard a rumble of thunder. We walked out and I found two white rocking chairs that were not yet soaked by the rain. I pulled our long side table in front of them and sat down. I took off my soaked sneakers, rolled up the wet cuffs of my jeans, and put my feet up on the porch railing, letting them get misted. With the bowl of peanuts in my lap, I pushed myself back and forth. Vi joined me and we sat there eating peanuts and listening to the storm, something we had done all our lives.

"So," I said.

"So," Violet said.

"So, you're going to have a baby," I said.

"Looks like it." She took a swig of Coke.

"Well, here's to a new adventure then." I clinked my Coke bottle to hers.

Violet took a long gulp, then took a peanut, popped the shell, and sucked the nuts into her mouth. "I can't believe this is happening to me, Maggie. I don't feel any different."

"I can't believe it, either, Vi. How *did* this happen?"

She looked at me as if I were an idiot. "Obviously, I had unprotected sex."

I heard an edge in her voice, but at least she was talking to me. I had to tread gently. "Vi, I'm sorry, I guess I don't understand."

She looked out at the lawn where little ponds were forming. "Have you ever made a decision too quickly, in the moment, and then couldn't take it back? Well, that's what happened."

"Okay, but I still don't understand. Did you and

Chris make the decision together, or did you make it on your own?"

Quick as a cat, Violet jumped out of her chair and glared at me. "That's right, Maggie, you don't understand. I'm willing to do whatever I have to do to get the life I want. After Chris took that job at the big law firm, I was worried he was pulling away from me. Maybe he's just overworked and tired. I know he loves me. I might have behaved rashly, but I didn't think it would really happen. It was one time, I swear. I have married friends who have been trying *for years* and they can't get pregnant. Seriously, getting pregnant isn't as easy as sex ed would make you think."

"Well, evidently it is for us Adams girls! Look at Mom. She got pregnant just looking at Dad. Twice!" I said.

Violet laughed. "Yeah, I know. But my situation is different. Chris and I love each other and have talked about getting married someday. Now, it'll happen a little sooner. It's gonna be fine! I'm just ready for my next chapter."

I was glad she was so sure of everything. "I'm very happy for you, Violet, but this *is* the kind of news you want to share with the father-to-be as soon as possible. It's really unethical not to. You're not the only one who this is happening to."

"Okay, thanks for your opinion, but I'm not telling him yet, not when he comes home from work tired and irritable. I'll wait till the weekend when he's relaxed." Then she changed the subject. "So, when are you going back to New York?"

"I was thinking in a few days, but Gran isn't even awake yet," I said.

"No, you need to go back to your life in New York, Ronny and the restaurant."

"The restaurant, yes. Ronny, no. That's over," I said.

I told Violet about the phone conversation.

"Ugh," she said.

"No kidding. I hate men," I said.

"Except me, I hope?" Jim said as he came through the screen door onto the porch. He slid a rocker up next to ours. "But we all know I don't count. I'm a superior race of human. So, what did I miss, ladies? Man-hating party and all," Jim said.

"Nothing, really, just filling Vi in on the Ronny situation," I said.

"Oh, right. I hope our little Violet is telling you to head for the hills once and for all," Jim said.

"I haven't gotten there yet, but yeah," Violet said.

"Guys, now that I think about it, maybe I'm assuming the worst," I said.

"Oh, come on, Magnolia!" Jim said. "Let it go and it can all be over. *You're* driving the bus, honey, not him."

I thought about that for a moment and then said, "Is it bad that I just don't want to believe it?"

"*Yes!*" they both said at the same time.

"Maggie, you are the one who has always told me to trust my gut instinct about people, also not to settle for anything less than what I deserve. The same goes for you. Surely you deserve someone who loves you back. What's with you?" Violet said before draining her Coke.

"I don't know. I think I love him, and maybe we are meant to be together in the end. Maybe we just have to get through this," I said.

"Are you freaking kidding me?" Jim said. "Oh, yeah, because the man God sends to be with you messes with your head a little while and then gets his act together. Do you think that *God* wants you to drive yourself crazy? Do you think your soul mate is meant to emotionally terrorize you? I don't think so, missy. Enough."

That stung. "Ouch, but I know you are right. You are so right," I said.

"God, I hope you mean that," Jim said.

"I do mean it, I'm just having a hard time following through," I said.

We laughed at that and it lifted the mood. The storm was slowing down, and I was feeling stronger by the minute. Some kind of magic happens when you are surrounded by your tribe. My sister and Jim always brought me down to earth. When I was with the two of them, there was no running away from the truth. I knew what I had to do. I felt like an addict refusing her first drink or smoke.

My phone buzzed. I had a text from Chef. My stomach sank, but I opened it anyway.

We have come to a decision about filling the position of Sous-Chef. Ronny has showed dedication and perseverance, he has diligently served his time, and we feel he is the stronger candidate. When you return, you will resume your position as Tournant. I hope your personal business settles so you can return to work a.s.a.p. Let me know when to expect you.—Chef

"Wow," I said, punched in the gut.

"Let me guess, an apology text from Ron?" Jim said.

"Nope, a text from Chef."

"What did his viper ass say?" Jim asked.

"I lost the promotion . . . to Ronny."

"Oh, my God, no," Violet said.

"Yup, and that's probably what Ronny wanted to talk about on the phone," I said.

"Well, this sucks," Violet said.

"This is more juicy than the soap opera I auditioned for!" Jim said.

"My life is a soap opera," I said. "What now, y'all? This is such a weird situation. If I call Ronny he's going to think that I'm just jealous of him for getting promoted, which I admit I am, a little."

"Maybe this is a sign," Jim said.

"A sign of what?" I asked, trying to fight off a growing sense of despair.

"A sign that you should move on. I mean, it isn't like it's the best job in the world, Mags. They totally take advantage of you. I get it, it's a chic restaurant, but last time I checked, there is more than one chic restaurant in New York freaking City," Jim said.

"Yes, Maggie! Go in there when you get back and quit, or better yet, don't show up!" Violet said.

"She can't do that. She'll be blacklisted," Jim said.

"Yeah, Jim's right. If I don't show up, Chef will never give me a decent reference, and it will basically be like me throwing away the two years I've worked there. I can't do that," I said.

"How long till you can open up your own spot?" Violet asked.

"Violet, opening my own restaurant is like the impossible dream! Especially in New York City. First, I've got to get my name out there, and the only way to do that is to work for other people, build up my reputation as a chef, and get some experience in management. Then I'll need to attract investors. I don't think anyone, much less a bank, will throw me the huge sum I'll need if I haven't even been a sous-chef yet. It took me a few years to face the reality that this is a really difficult dream to try to achieve. I still want it, but it's kind of like winning an Oscar or being drafted in the NFL."

"All right, y'all. This is depressing. Maggie, you'll go back to work and crush it for a few months, and on the side, be looking for an opportunity at another restaurant. Take some time to think about where you might like to work next. Make an exit strategy. It's never good to leave on bad terms," Jim said.

I put on a brave face. "Again, Jimmy, you are one hundred percent correct. That's what I'm going to do. Thanks, y'all. I feel better," I said, lying a little.

"It's always better to have a plan," Violet said.

"Sometimes it's okay to have some surprises, too. Keeps it spicy," Jim said, looking at Violet's tummy.

I picked up the empty Coke bottles and looked at the two true loves of my life. "Come on, I need some heartbreak soup, and I noticed a pot on the stove."

Alice's heartbreak soup was one of my childhood favorites. She made it any time we broke up with a boyfriend or suffered a disappointment. She'd made it for Jim that awful night he came out and his family disowned him. It was a tomato-based Italian bread soup with tiny sausage meatballs, spinach, and tons of Parmesan cheese. It wasn't complicated, but it was delicious. Heartbreak soup healed a broken heart the way chicken noodle soup healed a head cold. It was magic, and of course, exactly what we all needed.

By the time we finished eating, the rain had stopped, and I felt calmer and stronger, capable of facing the challenges of the day and the ones that lay ahead of me in New York. The soup had worked its magic.

Jim leaned back in his chair. "Amazing! Alice makes the best soup. How are we going to top that tonight at dinner?"

"Hey, what do y'all think about having dinner at the Lantern tonight? I'd really like to see it, it's been so long. And Alice told me she's going to the hospital after work, so Gran will have company tonight. Alice said she's going to read her the new Dorothea Benton Frank novel," I said.

"Gran loves her! Maggie, don't you have a date with that doctor?" Jim said.

"I don't really feel like going on a date right now. I'm not in the mood. I'll reschedule," I said. "I'd rather just see the restaurant and hang out with y'all."

"Umm, Maggie, maybe another time. Today has been crazy enough," Violet said.

"I really want to go," I said.

"Well, then, let's go." Jim looked at Violet like she was crazy to not want to go to the Magic Lantern.

"Fine. You're going to see it sooner or later," Violet said.

"See, that's exactly why I want to go. I have to get the full story here. I mean, how bad can it be?"

Violet said nothing. Jim shot me a look, but I ignored it.

"We'll go around seven. Okay, everyone?"

"Yup. Fine," Violet said.

"Fine by me," Jim said. "I could use a steak from the Lantern. Miss it."

"Umm, that isn't on the menu anymore. Hope you like fish tacos," Violet said.

"Fish tacos! Funny. Okay, y'all, I'm going upstairs to change my clothes," I said, plucking my coffee-stained cashmere sweater away from my midriff, "and then I'll be ready to go back to the hospital."

As it turned out, I headed back to the hospital alone. Jim had heard from his agent; the *ICU New York* producers wanted him to do a second reading tomorrow morning, and he had to study the script. Violet desperately needed a nap, and she preferred her childhood bed.

When I got back to Gran's room, I saw Dr. King on her way out.

"Hello, Maggie," she said, smiling.

"Dr. King, hi! I'm so glad I didn't miss you. How's my grandmother? Did you get the results of the tests?"

"Yes, they were all negative, which is actually quite positive. We're giving her a new medication to stabilize her heart rate. She needs time to recover."

"How much time?" I asked, because Chef wanted to know when I'd be back. "Do you think she'll regain consciousness tomorrow or the next day?"

Dr. King shook her head. "I can't say for sure. Every patient responds to traumatic brain injury and surgery differently, but we are hopeful that it should be soon. We will start to wake her tomorrow."

"Thank you, Dr. King—for everything."

Disappointed that the doctor couldn't tell me when Gran would be awake and talking again, I went over to the bed and looked down at Gran's beautiful face. She looked a little better, not as pale now. Maybe I was just imagining it. I placed my hand over hers and spoke to her silently with heartfelt thoughts. *I'm here, Gran, and I love you. Please summon all your amazing strength and get better. Come back to us. We need you!*

I sat on the small sofa by the window and called Alice, to thank her for the soup and to apologize for not calling her earlier. "It was a crazy morning. Unfortunately, Gran's heart rate is too erratic for the doctor to bring her out of the coma. Dr. King gave her some new medication."

"Well, I'm not worried. Rose needs to rest. Surgery on the brain is a big deal. But I'm going over there tonight after I close up to take a look at her myself. Now, what else made your morning crazy?"

"I met Buster. He and my mother are back together."

Alice was silent for a moment. "I see . . . Keep in mind, Magnolia, this could be a good thing. The heart works in mysterious ways."

I thought about that after we ended the call, then turned back to my phone and found a text from Ronny. Great.

Hey, Red. Look, I think there has been a misunderstanding. Rebecca and I are just sort of friends, you know? I feel bad for her; she doesn't know anyone, and I think she might like me a little. I'm just trying to be nice to her. I swear there is nothing going on. Please don't be mad at me. I just want to let you know I'm thinking about you. Don't worry about things here. Take all the time you need to be with your family, okay? Talk to you soon.

That message frustrated me on a few levels. Why hadn't he broken the news of his promotion? Also, I knew that the kitchen staff was inconvenienced, to say the least, by my absence. It meant extra work for everyone. But should I trust Ronny? Where did we stand?

Sometimes when I went out with Ronny, I'd catch him texting someone under the table and I would do everything I could to stop myself from blurting out, "Who are you texting?" or "Who's that?" Sometimes I coolly asked, "Oh, is that work?" "Is that B-Rad about tonight's service? Does he need something? Maybe my phone isn't getting a signal here."

I needed to get a grip. When I was with Ronny, I felt we were in the center of a storm with my emotions whirling around me. Sometimes it was exciting, more often it was confusing.

I remembered forever ago, when we went out on a proper date, right around Christmas. We'd had an argument because I was upset that we so rarely went out on an actual date. We only ever spent time together, just the two of us, at the end of the night. Ronny liked to stay out late, remaining at a bar until it closed. He had to soak up every last ounce of nightlife and then we could go home. I was adamant about breaking that horrible pattern.

Ronny had a friend who was a chef at a little Italian restaurant downtown. It was a small place, with exposed brick walls and candlelight. Ronny wore a sport coat. He gallantly pulled my chair out for me and complimented me on my dress. He ordered for me, and everything was perfect. He held my hand in public. But the real cherry on the sundae was when his friend the chef came out from the kitchen to check on us and said, "Oh! You must be the famous Maggie!" as if Ronny had talked to him about me.

It was one of those perfect New York evenings, right out of a film. Ronny was cute, he was amusing, and he gave me his undivided attention. We went back to my apartment and made love with the windows open. It was snowing, but we were warm in each other's arms under the covers. In the morning when I woke up, he was gone.

The next time I spoke to him was at work. Which was strictly business. I felt embarrassed and empty.

I shook my head, trying to clear it, and picked up a magazine. The sun had come out and the afternoon light beaming into the room warmed me and made me drowsy. My eyes kept closing as I tried to read.

I was beside the ocean at dusk, and I had the urge to swim. Every islander in the world will tell you that it is never a good idea to swim when the sun is rising or setting because that's when the sharks feed. Even in my dream I was reminding myself that it wasn't a good idea. Ronny was about fifteen yards away from me, his body bobbing like a cork in the navy-blue water. I looked down at my toes. My nails were polished a bright red, and I let the tide rise and foam on me. He was waving at me to join him, but I was nervous. I looked up at the nearly full moon glowing in the darkening sky. The world was just so much bigger than my own tiny reality. Ronny dove deep beneath the waves, popping up every so often to wave me into the water. His body was luminous, the moonlight catching the beads of water on his tan skin, making his tattoo of the fish appear to be dancing.

I walked slowly into the waves but could feel my body being pulled down into the sand. I sank down to my ankles. I was trying to move toward Ronny, but the beach wouldn't let me. The island wouldn't let me swim to him, wouldn't let me move. The harder I tried to push forward, the harder it pulled me back. I was frightened that I would drown, but it seemed that some force of nature was trying to keep me on the beach, so I shifted my weight back on my heels and the sand let go of one of my ankles, letting me move only backward to the beach. I pulled my other foot out of the wet sand and ran back to the beach, feeling a sharp pain where the wet sand had grabbed me. I looked down and saw scarlet rings of blood around my ankles. Alarmed, I looked out into the ocean and saw Ronny dive down again, but this time I saw one dark, slimy charcoal fin on his back.

I woke up covered in sweat, my ankles still hurting. I looked down at them, almost expecting to find blood, but of course there was none. I took a deep breath and felt my heart rate settle down. I looked at Gran, who lay still and silent in her bed, the machines and monitors around her making the only noise in the room. A strange thought occurred to me—had she given me advice in that dream? *Beware of Ronny?* I poured a glass of water from the pitcher on the table and drank it almost in one gulp. Refreshed, back in the real world, I checked the clock on the wall. It was almost dinnertime. I gave Gran a gentle kiss on the cheek and headed home.

Chapter 10
Rose

Somewhere in a distant hallway I can hear the feet of children run down my cypress-wood plank floors. I see my mother run her fingers across her pearl necklace just below her collarbone. Her red lips part and she smiles. I hear my daughter shriek in laughter, and my granddaughters erupt into giggles. They must be young, under seven. There is a wind chime tinkling and a bee buzzing around a bright-orange rose. I come back, but then I drift again.

I'm young again, maybe twenty-six or twenty-seven? I can't tell. My hair is long, past my shoulder blades, and tied back with a pink ribbon. I'm wearing an apron, a sleeveless button-down denim blouse, and a breezy skirt. I am in the kitchen of the Magic Lantern making the only thing my mother, Daisy, trusts me to make for the customers, my peach cobbler. I have a large crate of peaches to my left where I can grab them, gently pressing their fuzzy skin to test for ripeness. Everyone thinks Georgia is the peach state, but it's really South Carolina. Our peaches are the best, and every peach we eat is from here. I inhale one, smelling the sunshine on it. My mouth salivates a little. My nails are painted a candy-apple red; my mother will disapprove, but ah, they look so classy!

I pull out my paring knife, anchoring my thumb at the bottom of the fruit, and gently but firmly peel back the fuzz, exposing the bright yellow-pink flesh of the peach. A bit of juice runs down my wrist and I instinctively bring it up to my mouth and suck it off. There, standing before me, is a tall, thin man with the bluest eyes and blackest hair I've ever seen. His suit jacket is hooked on his finger over his shoulder and he's wearing suspenders, something I would normally dismiss, but somehow he wears them well. He is shrugging slightly as if to apologize for his height. He is watching me. I feel a burst of shivers all over my body.

"Hiya! I'm Rose, can I help you?" I say.

"Well, hello there, Rose. I'm Eddie, and I'm looking for something to eat. I'm starving, and I hear this place has the best fried chicken in all of Charleston!"

he says as he pulls out a hankie and dabs the corner of my mouth.

"Oh, I'm sorry, was no one out there? Momma!" I call out, flustered by the handsome stranger's touch.

My mother bursts through the swinging saloon doors in the kitchen, carrying a stack of menus and breaking the dreamy mood.

"Yes, Rosie, what is it, dear?" Momma says and drops the menus.

Eddie right away picks up the menus, neatly stacks them back up, and hands them to her.

"Why, thank you! My, my, my, aren't you a nice tall glass of water? My name is Daisy, and you are?" my mother says, openly flirting with Eddie.

Eddie blushes and tips his hat. "Thank you, ma'am. Name's Edward Adams, but most call me Eddie." He smiles.

"Well, what can I do for you, handsome? You hungry?" she says, flashing her red-lipped smile.

"Enough to eat a whole horse!" he replies.

"How about a whole chicken?" Momma says, arching an eyebrow.

"Well, that's what drew me to this beautiful garden," Eddie says, referring to our flower names. I smile knowingly. "I hear it's the best."

"Sure is. Go on and take a seat in the dining room.

It's a little early for supper, but we can make an exception, and if you stay a spell, you can have some of my daughter's peach cobbler, best in the world."

"Well, now, that is an offer I surely can't refuse," Eddie says. He taps a folded newspaper. "Y'all take your time. I can wait. You know that Michelangelo didn't paint the Sistine Chapel in a day. You can't rush perfection." He leaves the kitchen as if he's walked through our doors a hundred times, whistling the tune of some song I can't remember the name of.

Before long, Momma carries out a plate of fried chicken with coleslaw and biscuits. I follow her with a pitcher of sweet tea so I can refill Eddie's glass. We learn he lives in the Midlands, about a hundred miles north of Charleston, and sells construction supplies for a company in Spartanburg. His territory was recently expanded to the Charleston area, and he opened a handful of new accounts in Mount Pleasant and the barrier islands, so he might be moving down here. After he pronounces the fried chicken and the peach cobbler the best he's ever had, he adds, "Glad to have another reason to return to Sullivan's Island." And he winks at me!

There's a spring in Momma's step whenever Eddie comes into the restaurant during that long, hot summer of 1970, when the world is going mad. Momma has seen a lot of changes in her lifetime, but she's never going to embrace bell-bottoms or bright nail polish. She goes into the office to comb her hair and freshen her lipstick before greeting him; she's still stuck in the days when women were naked without lipstick. I am a bundle of nerves whenever he looks or smiles at me, wishing I had Momma's easy charm. I let her do the talking, because I know Eddie has come for the fried chicken and my beautiful momma's warm welcome. But on his third or fourth visit that changes. At the end of August, a cold front moves in, and a heavy fog covers Sullivan's Island.

Eddie walks into the restaurant later than usual. "If you didn't have that lantern out front, I might not have found you!"

When Momma and I bring out his dinner, he asks us to join him, and we sit down with him because it's a slow night due to the weather. "So where did you get that lantern? It looks old with that ornate wrought-iron pole."

Momma folds her hands on the table and matter-of-factly says, "I didn't. I found it here when I came to work one afternoon in late July 1944. It was cemented into the patch of grass in front of the sign for Daisy's Chicken Shack, which is how my dining establishment was known in those days."

Eddie puts his fork down. "Who do you think put it there?"

"I suspect it was a few of the vagrants who slept on

the beach at night, men who couldn't find steady work and were too old for the draft. Some of them scavenged for scrap metal to sell. We were still feeling the effects of the Great Depression in the Lowcountry. Whenever they came to the back door at night asking for handouts, I gave them leftovers. No use wasting good food."

"Momma!" I pipe up. "Anna, your helper, told me you always made extra for those poor men. Tell Eddie about the note you found under a rock next to the lantern."

Eddie raises his eyebrows.

Momma frowns and for a second I wish I hadn't spoken up, but then she smiles. "The note read, 'With this magic lantern, may good luck always find you.'"

Eddie nods his head and is silent for a moment. Then he taps the table with his hand. "Well, doesn't that beat all. A gift to show their appreciation for your fine cooking and generosity. A magic lantern is a tough act to follow. I'm wondering how I can show my appreciation for the same." Eddie laughs.

Momma shakes her head. "I believe they did it because my husband was killed on Omaha Beach during the D-Day landings the month before and they wanted me and my restaurant to prosper. They knew I had little Rosie to raise. They never came back after that. Probably didn't feel right taking from a widow woman."

Eddie looks startled. The first thing he does is reach

across the table and take my hand. "Rose, I'm sorry you lost your daddy when you were so young." My heart melts and I am suddenly lost in the warm intensity of his blue eyes. I hear him say, "Daisy, you are a heroic woman to carry on so courageously after such a huge loss."

Before Momma can say anything, the front door opens and a group of four walks in. I push my chair back to get up to greet the customers, but Eddie is still holding my hand. Momma looks over at our hands and rises. "I'll take care of this, Rosie. You stay here and keep Eddie company."

And, so, I did.

Oh, how I miss my husband, Eddie. We had such fun together, despite weathering a few storms. We were married for what feels like a lifetime and a heartbeat.

I come back to the beeps and hisses of machines, and then I drift away.

I am older than eighteen, in my thirties maybe? I have Lily on my hip. Her blond pigtails on top of her head move as she wiggles to get free. I could never hold that girl still. I think she never got used to me holding her. After she was born, I hemorrhaged, and the only way the obstetrician could stop the bleeding was to perform a hysterectomy on me. I was cautioned against carrying anything heavy. I could not even hold my own baby! Eddie and Momma held Lily and fed her for over a month after I got home. Now Lily reaches for Eddie, who is next to me. He takes her, and she crawls to his shoulders, calm and cheerful again. I sigh and look ahead of me. I am staring at the front doors of the Magic Lantern. Momma gave us the restaurant, and it's opening night for the redecorated Magic Lantern and our new French menu! Eddie and I fell in love with French food on our honeymoon in France in 1972. The steak frites and escargot and onion soup we had in Paris, the *moules marinières* and Camembert cheese we had in Normandy, the crusty French bread we ate everywhere! Back home, I bought Julia Child's cookbooks. She was the master, and when we got home I set my mind to learning how to make our favorite dishes.

Eddie worked all winter adding a little bakery nook to the kitchen. I am almost always covered in white flour, busy testing the perfect crusty-bread recipe. I am tired, and sore, but proud and happy. I've never been more fulfilled in my life. I am making a lot more than cobbler these days. I quickly push away thoughts of how Lily has always preferred her father. I am so excited for this new chapter of our lives, but also nervous. What if our guests don't like the changes? Sullivan's Islanders like tradition, and this is a big, big change.

Lily, around three, sticks her tongue out at me.

Chapter 11
Magnolia

The familiarity of the landscape warmed me as I drove back to Sullivan's Island. This was home. The beauty of the place still excited me—the ocean, the rivers, the harbor, the marshland, all of which I could see for miles and miles from atop the several bridges I had to cross. It had been a mistake to stay away for so long.

Back in my bedroom, I twisted my hair up into a ballerina bun, put on a sleeveless cotton button-down tank, some black leggings, and my red flats. I added a pair of gold hoops, some red lipstick, and black eyeliner. With a squirt of Chanel No. 5, I was ready to go. I turned my phone back on to see a text from Sam; it was like he was reading my mind.

Hey, Miss Maggie, forgive me but looks like I'm at
work for the foreseeable future. If you decide to go

out downtown later, let me know. I hope to be out by ten. Sorry to cancel, I was really looking forward to seeing you. —Sam

I decided to text him back.

Actually I was about to text you to try and raincheck.

Totally ok, let's do it another time! See you soon!

I met Violet and Jim downstairs, but they were running late. They said to go on ahead and they would meet me there.

I decided to walk.

We lived on the corner of Goldbug Ave and Station Twenty-Three. On Sullivan's Island, some of the roads were named stations because they used to have a trolley system for getting around. The Magic Lantern was only a few blocks away from the house, on Middle Street, and I felt like moving after that crazy dream. I passed the houses that I'd seen every day when I was growing up, the same familiar gates and front porches. It was nice to see them just as they'd always been. Like the people who lived inside them, the houses were old friends. The Venas' house, which was next to Gran's, was empty. They spent half the year in Florida and would be returning in May for Spoleto—couldn't stand the Charleston chill. The Dursts, islanders who lived on the other side of Gran, were close friends of Gran's and were keeping in touch with Mom about Gran's condition. People in the neighborhood were turning on their porch lights for the evening, welcoming home family members from work or school. It took me a long time when I moved to New York to learn that you don't say *hey* to a stranger. God forbid you wish them a *good evening!* But I was in the South now and was reminded that people value things differently here. It's a kinder and gentler existence.

I turned the corner to Middle Street and stopped, wondering if I was on the right street. But, yes, there was Dunleavy's Pub, Taylor's Realty, Café Medley, and there on the corner sat a ghost of the Magic Lantern. I almost didn't recognize it. It looked dark and dull, as if the life had been sucked out of it. It had been painted navy blue. While the ornate old-fashioned lantern stood straight as a flagpole on the patch of grass in front of the restaurant, it was not illuminated, and there were no white Christmas lights on the porch, only two giant heat lamps. Where the window used to be was a giant cutout covered with a plastic tarp, which I guessed was supposed to keep the cold out. They had started a project to open the front, but it looked like the job was unfinished.

I realized my mouth was hanging open, because when I closed it, it was bone dry. I swallowed hard. I crossed the street, full of shock. I swallowed again and took a deep breath, remembering my mother's words. She was right, I hadn't been here in a couple of years, and things had changed. Maybe things have to change. Change can be good, right?

The Magic Lantern's original front door was made of thick wood that was weathered by the years of people using it. Heavy, and painted red over and over throughout the years. But it was gone. It had been replaced by a cheap glass one, which looked like it belonged on a Pizza Hut. I walked into the dining room expecting to see one of my favorite heirlooms, the long velvet bench, where patrons sat while they waited for a table, but in its place there was a huge fish tank filled with murky water. I could barely make out what, if anything, was swimming in it. The saltwater fish tank was a good idea, but it was in bad shape.

The smell that greeted me was bleach, not the familiar one of comfort food. I guessed that meant the restaurant was clean. I shuddered. I looked around and saw a woman behind the bar, leaning toward a male customer in a business suit, exposing her cleavage as she poured a shot out of a liquor bottle that looked sticky, even from where I was standing. The ornate old mirror was still behind the bar, but now a neon Pabst Blue Ribbon sign was right above it. My eyebrows rose to my hairline.

All the art that had hung on the walls—beautiful watercolors and oil paintings of Sullivan's Island's beaches, the countryside, and Parisian street scenes—

was missing, replaced by lifesavers, anchors, and a giant fake marlin. *Kill me.* There was nothing worse than clichéd restaurant décor. I was standing smack-dab in the middle of a Southern version of the Olive Garden. I felt like I had been punched in the stomach. I decided to take a little walk around.

With each step I took, my flats stuck to the floor. It hadn't been cleaned in days, maybe weeks, despite the smell of bleach. There were barely any customers in the dining room, and the ones there were shoveling fries in their mouths or holding up *plastic* mugs, asking for refills. They were not dressed for dinner; they were in hoodies, basketball shorts, baseball hats, and tank tops, and a small child was running around in a bathing suit. Who were these people?

I did not see one French word, like the ones my gran had painted on the walls so many years back. I did not see one lantern; there used to be fifty or so hung around the restaurant. What was really missing was the welcoming smell of freshly baked bread. It was soberingly absent. Standing at the center of the restaurant, I saw a waitress dressed in a pirate costume carrying a platter of various fried foods. Everything everyone was eating was golden brown.

"Maggie, honey?" My mother's voice sailed across the restaurant. "Why don't you come to the bar and have a drink while you wait for Jim and Violet? She told me y'all were coming by tonight."

"I'm gonna check out the kitchen, say hi to everyone," I called back.

"Maggie, honey, they are busy in there. Come over here, baby!"

That was two "honeys" and one "baby." She was being too nice. My mother was hiding something, and whatever it was, I was sure it was in the kitchen. Not good. I unclenched my jaw, weighing my options. I knew I wouldn't like what I saw in the kitchen, and I didn't want my mother to start a fight with me in front of the customers. I needed to relax. I could use a glass of wine.

"Linda, this is Maggie, my eldest daughter," my mother said to the sexy bartender as I hopped onto one of the old red leather stools. "Please get her whatever she's in the mood for." She gave me a nervous smile. "Honey, I have to get back to the reservations desk. It's gonna be busy tonight."

"Pleased to meet ya. What would ya like?" Linda asked.

"Not sure. I need a few minutes to decide," I said. "Have you worked here long?"

"No, just filling in for a few days. Now that Buster's back, I'll go back to hair."

I grabbed the menu lying on the bar. It wasn't the

leather-covered menu that had presented our family's classic dishes for so long, it was a few sheets of printer paper encased in plastic sleeves strung together loose-leaf style. The menu was written in Comic Sans font. Something about that font always made me cringe. It was like whatever was written in it was a joke. The menu pages had stains on them, despite the plastic sleeves and their smelling of Windex or some other cleaning product. If you have to "wipe down" the menus at night, what does that say about a restaurant's atmosphere . . . or clientele?

I scanned the first page of the menu. Appetizers included fried mozzarella sticks, fried fish sticks, fried shrimp, a fried appetizer sampler platter, clam chowder, and garden salad. Let me tell you, nothing says *no soul in this place* louder than *garden salad*. I could imagine the pale-pink, mealy tomato slices, the large chunks of iceberg lettuce, and the too-thick-to-eat slices of red onion.

Salads are the kind of menu item that reveal a lot about a restaurant. A good Caesar salad is really satisfying, but it requires crisp, fresh romaine lettuce, crunchy garlic croutons, and maybe a poached egg on top, all tied together with just the right amount of creamy Parmesan cheese dressing. It's simple and wonderful, and you *have* to have it on a menu. It's what people in the restaurant business call an "approachable item." Not everyone is down with duck confit or a Brussels sprout salad. I once worked with a chef who liked to talk to me about menu building. He said you always had to have a Caesar salad, a burger, a cheesecake, and a pinot grigio on the menu because that's what most people wanted. Some items were for the foodie, and some were for the everyday customer. You had to offer both because first and foremost restaurants were service businesses, and if your food was too unusual, you wouldn't attract a large and loyal clientele. But a garden salad? All that says to me is *I've given up.*

I ran through the main courses: ten types of burgers, sixteen subs, grilled chicken, and fried chicken. I was glad that the fried chicken was still on the menu, but I wondered if it was still prepared according to our family's classic recipe. There were about a dozen or so ways you could eat chicken and burgers. This mix-and-match menu was about convenience and making easy money while catering to the open mouths and wallets of tourists. Gone were the distinctive French dishes and the restaurant's unique ambiance. Now it was a gimmicky seafood shack that desperately needed to be reunited with a mop.

"Maggie? The place looks different, right? Fun!" Mom said through a forced smile. "You like the changes?"

"It sure has changed a lot," I said.

"Well, not the lantern out front."

That made me feel better. My mother had retained the longtime symbol of our family's restaurant. Maybe she'd retained other important traditions, too.

"I wanted the contractors to take it out—it looks so old-fashioned—but that wrought-iron pole that holds the lantern is cemented in so deep, it will cost a fortune to remove."

My eyes widened. There are moments in adult life when in the face of controversy, you know you ought to hide your emotions and behave maturely, but sometimes when you're around your mother emotional maturity flies out the window. For whatever reason, fighting with my mother could unleash my inner teenager, and I always wound up saying things that my adult self would never dare say normally. Luckily, a family of five entered the restaurant and my mother glided away to greet them.

A few minutes later, Violet and Jim walked in. Jim's eyes were the size of dinner plates, and Violet kept her eyes on her feet. Jim was looking around with his mouth hanging open, not hiding one ounce of emotion. He clapped his hand over his mouth when he saw me. They came over and stood on either side of me.

"Maggie, what in this ever-loving world . . . ?" Jim said, barely able to speak.

"Jim, we have a situation here," I said, not making eye contact.

"How mad are you?" Violet asked. "Like on a scale from one to ten."

"About a hundred and fifty-seven," I said, nodding.

"I think it's time for a drink," Jim suggested.

"Or four," Violet added.

"It's past time for a drink. It's time to start abusing drugs," I said.

"Let's start with a red wine, and we can move to meth later?" Jim said, and I laughed.

"Sorry we're late, I had to get my eyeliner wings to match," Violet said.

My mom saw that Violet and Jim had arrived and came over to take us to our table. The way she walked over reminded me of a cat. Light as a feather, swishing her tail behind her. Even with her arm in a sling, my mother looked graceful.

"Well, hey, there, Mr. Jim! Violet, you look wonderful! How are y'all doing?" my mother purred.

"Hey, Lily! Nice to see you! The place sure does look *different*. Much more *casual*," Jim said, trying to be polite, but at the same time showing the faintest whiff of disapproval, as only he could.

"Yeah, well, our customers got what they asked for. Cheap and easy," Lily said through a smile so tight I thought her face would split in two.

Mom led us to our table. When we sat down, the table leaned to the left; one of the legs was uneven in length. Jim took a business card from his wallet, folded it in fourths, and stuck it under the leg, fixing the problem. A waitress came over, pirate costume and all.

"Hey, y'all. My name is Frankie and I'll be taking care of y'all tonight. Can I get you a drink or interest you in one of our specials?" Frankie smacked the gum she was chewing.

Jim, who was staring at her as if she were holding a bloody knife over his head, managed to say, "What kind of specials?"

"Well, we have a Pirate's Booty special tonight that's fried seafood with a side of fries and a garden salad with your choice of dressing. Ranch, Italian, French, or raspberry vinaigrette. That's twelve ninety-nine. Or you can get Blackbeard's Bounty, which is a blue-cheese burger with a side of onion rings and fried shrimp. That's thirteen ninety-nine. We also have a build-your-own pasta, which is my favorite. Choose your noodle and choose your sauce. Fettuccini, spaghetti, ziti, and you can have red sauce, meat sauce, or white sauce. Any of that sound good?"

We all stared at her for a minute, our mouths open long enough to catch flies. A $12.99 special?! What was this, Subway with the $5 footlong? So tacky. And why was the special called the Pirate's Booty? Because everything on the plate was golden brown? I was dying.

"Y'all okay?" Frankie asked.

I was fuming. A fury was building inside of me that was going to explode at any minute. I'd managed to hold it down when I was in front of my mother, but I could feel the waves of my hot temper growing into an imminent tsunami.

"Hi. Frankie, was it? I'm Magnolia, the restaurant owner's granddaughter. This restaurant has been in my family for three generations," I said, feeling my veins fill with lava.

"Oh, yeah? Your momma did say this was a VIP table!" Frankie said, the fake parrot on her shoulder shaking with every word she spoke.

"I know this isn't your fault, because I am sure no one has ever told you how to describe a sauce before. But the meat sauce is called Bolognese, the white sauce is Alfredo, and the red sauce is marinara. Please do me a favor and write that down," I said.

"Umm, I just think it's easier to describe it the way I did. Sorry," Frankie said, looking at me as if I were crazy and asking her to do something ridiculous. I wasn't done with her.

"Easier? Frankie, what do the chefs in the kitchen

call the sauces they make? Do they refer to one of them as a *red sauce*?" I asked, nearly rising out of my chair. "Those guys back there make that sauce fresh every day and work really hard. Yeah, it's red, but it has a name. Do you like it when people call you *waitress*?" I was almost spitting.

"Maggie." Jim put his hand on my arm, trying to reel me back in. I was about to lose it.

"They don't make it fresh. They just call it by the name that's on the can—red tomato sauce," Frankie said, embarrassed as she looked at Violet, who was nodding and smiling.

"The *can*?" I was almost yelling now, and the family with the kid in the bathing suit were turning their heads toward our table. I was gathering unwanted attention, but I didn't care.

"Umm, can we just get some peel-and-eat shrimp and a round of sweet teas? Can I look at a wine list?" Violet said, trying to keep me from committing a murder and causing an even larger scene.

"We don't have a list. I can just tell y'all. We have house white or house red. The house white is a pinot grigio and the red is a merlot. By the glass it's five dollars or you can get the upgraded wine. We have a zinfandel by the glass for six dollars or by the bottle for thirteen. We also have a chardonnay for five ninety-nine on special, bottle's twenty. We have beer and a full bar as well," Frankie added, smelling of Bubblicious.

"We'll take a bottle of your chardonnay," Jim said quickly, trying to get her away from me.

Gran used to have a deal with this amazing guy named Drew Harris who had a cute spot across the street called Café Medley, which also sold wine. He used to curate the Lantern's wine list. I wondered what had happened to him. I was wondering about a lot of things.

Just then Buster walked in. To say he walked in was a huge understatement. He sort of burst in.

"Why, hellooooo, Sullivan's Island!" Buster roared.

Violet turned to me and put both of her hands on my shoulders. "Maggie, calm down. That girl doesn't know any better. It isn't her fault. You are getting a little out of line. Seriously, dial it back. You're turning red."

Violet knew I was too far gone. I had crossed the edge; I was over the line. I was about to give anyone who was there a piece of my mind. Jim went up to the bar to get the wine, telling Frankie not to worry about serving it herself. I guess he wanted to get a drink in my hand ASAP, thinking it would distract me. He placed the glass in front of me. I picked it up, tossed it back, and poured myself another. I was pounding a glass of wine. This wasn't good.

Jim sighed and poured himself one, and Violet

sipped her sweet tea. They knew there was no helping this. The train had left the station. I swung around to face Buster, who was greeting everyone as if he were the mayor. He was in a bowling shirt, Bermuda shorts, a gold necklace, matching bracelet, and flip-flops. An unlit cigar was in his hand. I could smell it and a whiff of his potent aftershave from where I was sitting.

"There's my queen!" Buster moved toward my mother and planted a huge kiss right on her mouth. He dipped her backward and kissed her again, making a huge scene. To my surprise, my mother blushed.

"Stop it, Buster! I'm working here!" my mother said through a giggle.

"Wow, Lils, you almost hurt me with that giant rock on your hand! Someone must love you very much!" Buster said, winking to a guy drinking at the bar.

"Oh! Someone does!" I saw an expression on my mother's face that I'd never seen before. It was close to how she looked when she saw a cute puppy.

"I'm a lucky man, ain't I?" Buster said, loud enough for everyone to hear, and pinched my mother's butt, sending her a few inches into the air.

"Buster, you're so bad!" my mom squealed.

Everyone at the bar laughed. The people at the table next to us were now watching them, instead of me.

I could taste bile at the back of my throat. Holy God.

What was happening? Was I watching an episode of *Jersey Shore*? And Buster gave Mom a ring?! I hadn't noticed it until he announced it to the whole restaurant.

I must have said that aloud, because Violet said, "I didn't, either. I guess he really loves her. We'll be going to their wedding before we go to mine."

Jim was frowning. "It's big, looks like three carats. He can afford three carats?"

Just then Frankie placed an enormous platter of boiled shrimp in front of us, along with a dish of runny red cocktail sauce. "Y'all want carrots? I don't think they're on the menu. I'll ask the cook!"

I rolled my eyes and turned my attention to what *was* on the menu. The little shrimp were so tightly coiled that I wondered how I would peel them. That meant they were overcooked. I picked one up, wrestled off its shell, and popped it into my mouth. Just as I expected, it had the texture of a spongy piece of bubble gum. I spat it into my napkin. "This is gross, y'all," I said.

"Maggie, I knew this wasn't a good idea, but just look at how happy Mom is!" Violet said, also spitting a shrimp into her napkin.

I looked at my mother. She was making cooing noises to Buster. This woman, this tightly wound, prissy mother of mine, was cooing! Could she be . . . happy? Suddenly, I felt awful. I was being a brat and I knew it. I'm the one who left. I owed it to my mother to give this a chance, and I owed Frankie an apology. This wasn't New York, it was Sullivan's Island, and my mom knew the customer base better than I did. I hadn't lived here in ten years. Maybe Mom was right, maybe things needed to change.

"Maggie, dear heart, you are right. This is gross, but Lily is practically glowing!" Jim said.

"Yeah, she really is." I felt my temperature cooling.

"Mags, the sauce isn't all that bad," Violet said.

I dipped a spoon into the sauce to taste it. It was watery, meaning it hadn't been fully cooked down, but the flavor wasn't terrible. The garlic was actually pretty nice.

"It's just so much change to absorb," I said.

"A lot of change. But the Lantern is still open. I never wanted to work it, but it's okay," Violet said, shrugging.

"I could do without the costumes, though," said Jim.

"I do not appreciate theme restaurants," I added.

Just then Frankie appeared and dropped a basket of biscuits on the table.

"Here y'all go. Just thought I'd drop something off for the VIPs. Sorry about the way I described the sauces. I really didn't know . . ."

"Frankie, I'm sorry, too. I shouldn't have corrected you on that. I'm a chef, and we really shouldn't socialize outside of a kitchen. Sometimes I forget my manners," I said.

"Oh, my gosh! That's so true! My ex was a chef! Couldn't take him anywhere. Dropped the F-bomb like every other word!" Frankie said, laughing. She turned on her heel and went over to the table next to ours.

"She probably spit in your biscuit, Magnolia," Jim whispered before picking one up. "I will serve as your taster." I watched him closely as he took a tiny bite and chewed and chewed. I reached out to take one. "Don't, Maggie!" He shoved the basket to the edge of the table, almost knocking it to the floor. "They're nowhere near as good as yours."

Violet sighed dramatically. "I admit it, Maggie makes the best biscuits."

She and I laughed because, growing up, we'd competed to see who could make better biscuits, and everyone in the family, even my mother, had preferred mine.

It was hard sometimes to divorce myself from my job. Bar JP wasn't run according to the standards of most restaurants. Its standards were crazy high. I needed to remember that and not be so critical. Except this wasn't just any old restaurant, it was my family's restaurant, where the food used to be delicious. I wondered if I ran my own restaurant, what would my priorities be? What would I focus on?

"What I don't understand is how Louie, a fairly so-phisticated chef, can prepare food of this caliber."

Violet's eyes widened. "No one told you? Louie left last year after Gran had the hip problem and Mom and Buster took over. He said he was relocating to Florida. But I ran into him in Charleston. He's working at one of the big hotels. I think he didn't want to hurt Gran's feelings, but he just couldn't go along with Mom and Buster's menu changes."

"Of course, he couldn't! And no, no one told me. Why didn't you tell me? Oh, never mind! So, who's the new head cook?"

"A guy named Nate."

"Should I order the fried chicken for my entrée?"

Violet shook her head. "How about a burger?"

The rest of the dinner went okay. The burgers we ordered weren't bad. I watched the other people, mostly families, at the surrounding tables. They were talking, eating with gusto, and giggling over their kids. They seemed satisfied with the food. The moms and dads were not that much older than I was. It oc-curred to me that I could have been married with chil-dren of my own if I hadn't pursued a career in New York. And here I was, struggling to come up with a reason to keep Ronny in my life. Maybe I was getting it all wrong.

"Violet, I still can't believe you're having a child. Congrats, Momma!" Jim said, planting a kiss on her cheek.

"Shh! Jim! It's still so early. But y'all could always move back here and lend a hand!" Violet said. "The way Chris's work takes him out of town for weeks at a time, I could be a single mother."

"Not a lot of acting opportunities down here, princess, otherwise I would," Jim said.

"You don't think parenting is acting? Keeping a smile on your face? Having children means you constantly have an audience. You could be the kid's manny!" Violet said, laughing.

"Oh, you don't want me as a manny. I'd sugar the tyke up and let him or her have anything they want!" Jim said.

"Well, if the cooking thing doesn't work out, I'll make a beeline for my niece or nephew," I said.

"Ha, ha, Maggie," Violet said. "I'm juggling so much with decorating the new house, my photography work, watching out for Mom and helping with the restaurant, worrying about Gran, and now a baby? Sometimes I feel like I am a plate spinner. You know what I mean? I learned that phrase from a novel I read by my favorite author, Dorothea Benton Frank," Violet said.

"DBF? L-o-v-e her!" Jim said.

"Book groupies! Violet, you'll figure it out, and

you'll always have us to offer expert advice from afar," I teased. Turning more serious, I said, "We should call Alice for an update on Gran. She said she's going to the hospital tonight. But before we go, I want to say good-bye to Mom."

I looked around the restaurant, thinking that maybe if I just shifted my perspective and found this "fun," I could support my mom's "vision." If she wanted to run a theme restaurant, I guessed that was her little red wagon. I didn't see my mother anywhere. She was probably in the kitchen.

As I headed in that direction, I heard Violet say, "Maggie, don't!"

When I pushed my way through the swinging doors, I realized one thing—the kitchen was dirty. No, it was *filthy*. The long line that had once been a beautiful pol-ished stainless steel fortress was now covered in a layer of grease, topped with a thin film of dust. Three of the burners were missing, and there was a stove that clearly was being used for storage. The pots and pans were piled in no particular order, and I could see from where I was standing that they were also covered in grease.

"Mom?" I called out.

No response, so I went farther. None of the cooks were in the kitchen, which was strange. It was only ten thirty, shouldn't they be here cleaning or prepping for tomorrow's service? I looked at the sectioned area of the line that was usually loaded with cut-up vegetables or garnishes, what we professionals call mise en place, and I saw that it now held pens, chewing gum, and cigarette butts. Oh, my God. I decided to be brave and look into a lowboy, a small refrigeration unit underneath the pass. It was loaded with old quart containers of God knows what. Everything seemed to be old, like more than a month old. A moldy odor was coming out of one of the half hotel pans covered in tinfoil. I gagged and put it back. If the health department ever got a whiff of this, we'd be shut down in no time. It was clear to me then that no one was actually cooking, they were assembling.

In the kitchen there were two large walk-in refrigerators, one for meat and one for vegetables, and a smaller walk-in freezer. I couldn't even imagine what condition they were in, but I couldn't contain my curiosity. I opened the veg walk-in and was hit in the face with a smell so putrid that I gasped for air. Pulling over a milk crate containing something heavy, I propped the door open and went inside. The vegetables were past their prime, to say the least. I don't know why, but I pulled out a large hotel pan. I must have pulled too hard, because it slipped right off the shelf, splashing red lumps, formerly known, I think, as red peppers, and vile brown water on my legs, my shoes, and the floor.

"*Gross!*" I yelled.

It was obvious that no one had been in here recently except to grab one of the dozens of heads of iceberg lettuce. If this was the state of the vegetable walk-in, what were we dealing with in the freezer and the meat walk-in? Even though I was gagging, I needed to see it all.

The freezer was a different story. It was *packed.* Every single shelf was crammed with frozen food. Frozen seafood, frozen vegetables, frozen everything! No wonder the kitchen was empty, and no one was cooking! There were large bags of frozen hamburger patties that someone had ripped open. Then I found the worst thing, a huge box of prebreaded, ready-to-fry chicken parts. So much for my great-grandmother Daisy's fried chicken recipe.

My heart broke.

I stepped outside the freezer, closing the door behind me. I needed to find a mop to clean up the mess I had made in the veg walk-in. I probably should have just lit a match and walked away. That would have left the kitchen cleaner. A familiar scent was sailing through the air. It wasn't garbage, although the smell was sweet. It wasn't any cooking aroma, but it was a little herbal . . . oh, my God! It was pot! Someone was smoking pot in the kitchen!

I could hear someone talking, but I didn't recognize the voice at first.

"Oh, man, baby, when we sell this hellhole we can live wherever we want!"

"Oh, honey bunny, I can't wait! I've been here too long. These people make me sick! The tourists, the washed-up islanders! My stupid family! What would I do without you?" My mother's voice.

I made my way over to the meat walk-in, opened the door, and there, sitting on a stack of milk crates, were my mother and Buster, lighting up.

"Busted!" they said in unison before dissolving into fits of laughter.

"Oh. My. God. Mom?" I said, equally shocked and grossed out. "Are y'all getting high?" I could hear my voice go shrill.

"Who, us?" Buster said, making my mom almost fall off the milk crate and gasp for air, she was laughing so hard.

"What's going on here?"

"We're just winding down, Maggie. *Relax!*" my mother said.

Quick note: if you ever want to really piss someone

off when they are on the verge of getting angry, tell them to relax.

"Mom, I'm going home. Thanks for dinner," I said, deciding not to behave like the child I used to be.

"Oh, Maggie, don't be so uptight. Who cares?" Buster said.

"Who cares? I care!" I said, taking the bait and reversing the decision I'd made seconds ago. "This is our family's restaurant! What do y'all think you're doing? You want to *sell* the building?"

"Excuse me, little girl, this is *my* restaurant, and don't you talk to Buster like that. If it wasn't for him, we'd be closed!" my mom said, glaring at me.

"Oh, I'm sorry. Yeah. Thanks, Buster. Did a real nice job here! Go look at the freaking disaster in the vegetable walk-in and the mess in the kitchen. Great job! Zagat will be here any minute now," I said.

"Don't be such a little bitch, Maggie. No one here gives a shit about Zagat," Mom said.

"That was really rude, Mom. Please don't talk to me that way, it hurts me when you use language like th—"

"Oh, don't give me that therapy bullshit language. I'm not a mental patient," my mother yelled.

"Yeah. Not today," I said under my breath.

"What was that?"

"Lils, let's just go, okay? This isn't worth it. I don't

want to see you ladies fight," said Buster, clearly un-comfortable with me messing up his buzz. "Let's just go back to my place and watch some *Planet Earth*."

"I'm so sick of your self-righteousness, Maggie! You think you know everything about restaurants! I've been in the business since before you were born!" my mother said. "Don't you dare insult what we are doing here! This is *my* show, *my* restaurant, and *my* ticket out of this hellhole!"

"Well, it's only a hellhole because you've made it one! It used to be a great restaurant and now it's a joke! How could you let everything slip through your fingers? Don't you care about anyone besides your-self?" I responded, my voice louder than it should have been.

"Oh, you wanna go there? Okay, Maggie. Just where the hell have you been for the past ten years? If you care so much about your family and this restaurant, why has it been so long since you've visited? Little Miss New York City! Oh, so important. So, are you a top chef yet? Don't come in here all of a sudden pretending to be a concerned family member, Magnolia!"

"You have no right to talk to me like that. I've been trying to achieve something with my life. Much more than any of us can say about you."

Before I could process what was happening, my

mother leaped from the milk crate, and I felt a hard smack right across my cheek.

"I'm your mother. All you've ever done is criticize and critique everything I've ever done. This is *my* time now. You've only ever had everything easy in your life. Well, guess what? I'm selling this piece-of-shit restaurant and I'm going to finally have the life I deserve and want. Buster. Let's go. Maggie, get out of my way."

Buster, refusing to make eye contact with me, grabbed my mother by the waist, pushed past me, and shut the refrigerator door hard behind him. I was left alone, staring at boxes of meat, holding my throbbing cheek. I felt hot tears running down my cold skin.

I was so full of emotion that, despite the wine I'd had at dinner, I felt sober. It hurt me more that she wanted to sell the restaurant than anything she said about me. I knew her opinion about me, but I thought she loved the restaurant. Was she *really* going to sell the Magic Lantern? If she did, it would not only change my and my family's lives but those of the people who lived on the Lowcountry islands. The Magic Lantern had been around for so long, it was as much a historic landmark as the forts on the islands! So many people's happy memories had been made at the Magic Lantern. It was considered a local gem . . . or had been.

I was shocked that Gran had let the Lantern fall

apart like this. She couldn't have known, or maybe she had known and had simply let go of the reins. I wished I could talk to Gran to find out what was going on. I hated the world without her in it to guide me. It also would have been so different if she or I were actually here. I never would have let this happen. *Oh, Gran! Please wake up and be all right!*

I wiped my tears and went into the kitchen. After finding some paper towels and wiping off my leg, I grabbed a mop and cleaned up the red-peppers mess, because even though obviously no one else cared about this place, I did. I cared a lot. I grabbed a large trash can and started to pitch in every rotten tomato, every bag of soggy herbs, that biology project that had spilled all over me. I got rid of it all. Then I got mad—at my mother, my grandmother, and everyone else who worked here.

Violet and Jim found me ranting out loud to no one as I threw out rotten vegetables left and right.

"Maggie?" Jim said, dodging a flying carrot.

"I just can't believe how gross it is in here! Do you see all of this?" I said, not turning around or stopping my purge.

"Oh, God, it smells horrible!" Violet was holding her nose. "This is too much for me to take!"

"Girl, stop. This isn't your job, you don't have to do this!" Jim said.

"Yeah, I do, for Gran. Lily's let it all go to hell. The health department could come at any minute and shut us down!" I turned to face them.

"Maggie, Mom's never really liked this restaurant, and you can't force someone to like or love something . . . or someone. It would take more than one night to fix this. More time than you have," Violet said.

More time than I had . . . She was right. This was too big a job to handle in my limited time here. The restaurant that was the heart and soul of my family's history was now a dump. It had gone from being my great-grandmother's miracle to my Gran's passion to my mother's burden. I was the one who had walked away.

"Violet, does Mom own the restaurant now? Did Gran sign it over to her, or did she and Buster buy it from Gran?" I asked.

She looked startled. "I'm not sure. Mom said something about it being hers, but I'm not sure if it is legally."

"Mom said she wants to sell it," I said, looking at my feet.

"What? No!" Jim said.

"Can she do that?" Violet said.

"Well, that's what I want to find out. If she's planning on selling it, Gran must have given her the restaurant. But if she isn't the legal owner of the property, she can't do it without Gran's consent," I said.

"You can't let her do that, Magnolia," Jim said.

"What time is it?" I asked.

"Late. Time to go home." Jim pointed at his watch. "Like Violet said, this is an enormous mess. Wow, that is one dirty stove!" Jim said, looking around.

He was right. It was too big a mess for one person to clean up. I put the mop down.

We put out the trash, and after Violet found an extra set of keys in the office, we locked up. Outside in the parking lot, I looked back at the Magic Lantern. The building looked tired, just like my mother.

I wasn't surprised that my mother and I had had a fight, and I really wasn't all that surprised that she'd smacked me. She wasn't stable, never had been, even though she wanted everyone to believe she was. She'd been through a lot. I was angry at my mother, but I also felt sorry for her. Actually, I was more worried than angry. Smoking pot, violent behavior, irresponsibility . . . this could mean only one thing. My mom was drinking again. I'd been there with her before . . . I knew the signs.

Chapter 12
Magnolia

"**M**aggie, are you going to call Alice, or should I?" Violet asked.

I clicked on my phone and saw a voice mail from Alice that had come in ten minutes ago and a text from Ronny. I played the voice mail on speaker so Vi and Jim could hear it: "Maggie, I'm about to leave the hospital. Your gran is still resting, no change in her condition. Your mother just called me. I'm going to stop by the house on my way home. We need to talk."

I saw Violet and Jim exchange a look of concern. Word travels fast on this island. I wouldn't mind talking to Alice. Maybe she could explain why Gran had entrusted the restaurant to my mother, which led it to go downhill. Without reading Ronny's text, I deleted it, feeling powerful and in control of at least one part of my life.

"I'm glad Gran isn't any worse," Violet said. "I'm going home tonight. Want me to drop y'all off at Gran's?"

"No, thanks. I need a walk tonight. See you tomorrow," I said.

"You want company?" Jim asked me. I shook my head, and he hopped in with Violet.

I decided to take the long way home with the salty breeze from the ocean sailing through the air.

I saw Alice's car in the driveway. I pushed open the familiar gate and walked through Gran's garden, taking an inventory of the new growth, a habit I had developed when I was a little girl. Finding a new vegetable or a new bloom was almost as much fun as finding a Christmas present, and I couldn't wait to tell Gran what I had spotted. Now, looking at the tomato plants, which grew even in the winter, producing plump tomatoes that looked purple in the moonlight, I couldn't help thinking of all those sad tomatoes I'd found in the walk-in refrigerator at the restaurant.

Once I got inside, I was greeted by Alice and Jim, who were in the living room. Alice was knitting something that looked as soft as a cloud.

"There you are!" Alice said, putting aside the fluffy poof that was starting to look like a sweater.

"Hey, Alice," I said.

"Well, it's been a long evening, ladies, and I need my beauty rest. Good night," Jim said, excusing himself before running up the stairs.

"What's going on, Maggie? Your mother just called, quite upset," Alice said.

"I could ask you the same question. What happened to the restaurant?"

"Maggie, sit down," Alice said. I knew I was in trouble. "Why are you so determined to fight with your mother? What has gotten into you?"

"How can you ask me that? The restaurant is terrible, and Gran's let it happen! How could she let my mother do this to the Lantern? Or to our family, or to me?" I said, suddenly fighting back tears. I'd been more emotional in the past twenty-four hours than I'd been in the last year.

"What do you mean to *you*? Maggie, this isn't about you. Look, your mother has made some choices that maybe I wouldn't have made, but the place is making money! Sometimes you have to let others take over when you can't do it all yourself. Rose is no spring chicken, you know, and Lily needed something to do with her life. For as hard as she's worked and for as far as she's come, she needed to have something to be proud of, hard work that produced results. You of all people should understand that," Alice said.

"But, Alice, the Magic Lantern isn't the way it used to be! I feel like the soul has gone out of the place, and you can't tell me my mother wants that job, or even respects it! She's changed everything!" I said, almost whining.

"Maggie, let it go. Your momma is finally doing something productive and good with her life. Sure, it may not be up to your New York standards, but this isn't New York, and the restaurant has been around a long time. Maybe it needed a change. It was time for your grandmother to take a step back and let your mom rise to the occasion. Did you think Rose would be in that kitchen forever?"

"No, of course not . . . I just always thought . . . that things would always be the same," I said, but realized how childish that sounded.

"Look, Maggie, your momma isn't you . . . she can't boil an egg, and she could give a damn about a culinary degree or a Michelin star. You do, I do, and your grandmother does, and you are living that dream in New York, right? I understand what Lily is doing on Sullivan's Island, so does Rose, and you should try, too."

"Alice, I overheard Mom say she was planning on selling the restaurant," I almost whispered to her.

"She said *what?* Maggie, you must have misheard her. It isn't hers to sell," Alice said.

"Alice, I heard her and Buster talking. They were calling the Magic Lantern a dump and she said she can't wait to sell it!"

"Well, last I heard, your grandmother still owns it. Lily may have made some changes, and I know Rose is grateful for that, because for a while there the restaurant was barely breaking even. Business is business, even with those dang pirate costumes, and I'm sure Rose would rather let it become something else than sell it to someone else! That property would be sold in a flash, and the restaurant knocked down and replaced by some brand-new joint. Everything is changing on this island," Alice said with a sigh. "I'm sorry your mother isn't happier with her lot in life, but she can't be serious about selling the Lantern." Alice started to pack up her knitting.

"I don't know. Maybe now that she has Buster, she thinks her life can change or something. She wants out of South Carolina, that I *do* know," I said.

"That girl has been running away for forty-six years. She never fit in, and that's okay, but I'm sure Rose won't let her take everything down with her.

You should have more faith in your grandmother, Magnolia," Alice said.

I took a beat to think about that.

"Y'all can be two cats in a bag sometimes. More like sisters than mother and daughter! But, Maggie, honey, you know better. You shouldn't let her get under your skin! You have a beautiful, full life in New York. Don't worry about us here," Alice said, patting my knee.

"Alice?" I squeaked, feeling my throat tighten.

"Yes, baby?" Alice said, automatically registering my emotional shift.

"I don't think New York is working out," I said.

"What do you mean?" Alice said.

"For me, I mean. My life isn't so beautiful there. I just don't really . . . I'm still struggling after almost ten years. I haven't really accomplished anything yet, I'm barely making any money, my boss is a jerk, and I didn't get the promotion I was hoping for. I hate saying this, but maybe New York isn't for me." I sighed heavily.

"Maggie, you *have* accomplished a whole lot to be proud of. You have grown into a woman! First of all, you've studied at a prestigious culinary institute and worked in some of the world's most famous kitchens, even if not higher than a line cook. At least you can put that on your résumé, which at this point is golden!

And just because you missed out on one promotion, it doesn't mean you won't get another. Second, you have a boyfriend! I know it's complicated, but you . . ." She was trying to convince me, but I cut her off.

"He isn't my boyfriend." Saying that to Alice made it official in my heart. Ronny wasn't and would never be my boyfriend because I wasn't enough for him, and that was no longer enough for me.

"Maggie, I'm sorry, honey. I know you're feeling overwhelmed right now with Gran getting hurt and the Magic Lantern changing, but what's really going on here? I've never seen you like this. When did we teach you not to be proud of yourself?" Alice said with a smile.

I nodded. I needed to be alone. But I wasn't ready for bed.

I hugged her good night and listened to the gravel crunch under her car's tires as she drove away. I grabbed my gran's oversized zip-up cardigan. It was lime green, but it was cozy. I took a pair of flip-flops from the hall closet and walked to the beach. Inhaling the smell of home, I looked up at the stars. They were so clear. Without all the light pollution of New York, I could make out familiar constellations.

I crossed the street and made my way down a path over the dunes. There was something about the sea and its roaring, thunderous power that humbled and in-spired me. I knew that feeling small beside something so large would make my problems seem smaller.

I thought about what I really wanted as I listened to the waves roll in and crash against the sand. The truth was that deep inside my heart, I belonged on this island. But that didn't mean I couldn't belong somewhere else, too, right? I really wanted to be a great chef. I had wanted to succeed in New York, work among the most sophis-ticated, skilled chefs and become their equal, one of the best. But was that still my dream? I'd had the courage to venture into the tempestuous waters of the New York culinary scene, now did I have the grit to stay on course and not be deterred by a lost job, a surly boss, and a fickle boyfriend? I could return to Bar JP and quietly look for a sous-chef position at another starred restau-rant where I wouldn't have to work alongside Ronny. Alice was right, my résumé was golden, and I didn't have to give up on everything to improve my quality of life in the Big Apple. I just needed to refocus and remember why I cooked in the first place. There were plenty of restaurants in New York, and I could find one less stressful and not as high volume as Bar JP.

I felt my phone buzz and was going to ignore it, but then I saw it was Sam calling, and we hadn't spoken since he postponed our date.

"Hey, there, beautiful," Sam said.

"Hey, yourself, Sam."

"What are you up to?"

"Nothing, just . . . I'm taking a little night beach walk."

"Very romantic . . . I hope you're not entertaining another gentleman," he said, and I smiled at his playful jealousy.

"Just me and the fish," I said.

"You, okay? You sound a little . . ."

"Rough night."

"Oh?"

Usually I would dismiss this and just get off the phone, but he had a way about him that made me want to tell him everything.

"At the risk of getting too personal . . ."

"Oh, I'm fine with getting personal, Maggie, please continue. The doctor is in."

I felt my frown pull into a smirk. He was flirting with me and being corny at the same time. I took the bait.

"Well, my restaurant isn't what I remembered it to be," I said, trying to hide my amusement.

"Ah, yes. Nothing is when we leave it alone for a while."

"I guess, but this place . . ."

"Was your constant. It's what didn't change ever, so sure, you feel a little off kilter."

"Yeah, exactly. It's almost like I'm lost without its familiar shape."

"You need a lighthouse."

"What?"

"A lighthouse to bring you to shore. Something or someone to make you recognize your surroundings."

"Yeah, that would be Gran."

"I see."

"Actually, if I really think about it, Alice is also a lighthouse of mine. She's my grandmother's best friend, and she basically just told me to lean in a little to the new Magic Lantern."

"How do you feel about that?"

"Itchy," I said and let out a laugh. "It makes me feel jumpy and uncomfortable."

"Sounds like you'd do some things differently than whoever chose the changes."

"Yeah, it's not the direction I would have taken."

"Sounds like a character builder to me. The art of letting go what you cannot control."

"Very Zen of you," I grumbled.

"Oh, us doctors are onto lots of different ways to heal the body, mind, and spirit."

"Good grief," I said, but laughed.

"You're gonna figure this out, Maggie," he said, and somehow I felt like I could.

"I know," I said.

"Did I help?"

"Just what I needed. I'm feeling better already. Thank you." I smiled and hung up.

The wind was chilly, and it was getting late, so I headed home, still feeling confused. I needed a good night's sleep to let my unconscious work this out a little.

Climbing the stairs to my bedroom, I flopped down on my bed. Sam was right, there are some things that you just need to let go of. I thought of that song, "You gotta know when to hold 'em, know when to fold 'em." This was a "fold 'em" moment as far as Ronny was concerned. This problem was in my control.

Ronny—Thanks for your concern about my grandmother. Chef sent me the news about your promotion, congratulations! I know this is something you've wanted for a long time and I'm proud of you. Being at home has made me think a lot about everything back in the city, and I've decided to make some changes. The first being with us. I think we both know this isn't anything real, and I want a real relationship. I know that is something you can't give me. So, I'm letting you off the hook. Friends?—Maggie.

I knew that was a lot to put in a text, but I was

confident Ronny, who lived half of his life on his phone, could handle it. I clicked send and turned off my phone.

After brushing my teeth and changing into pajamas, I was exhausted, but I said a prayer for Gran before falling asleep.

The next morning came quickly. It seemed like no sooner had I drifted off than Alice was shaking me awake. "Maggie? Maggie, wake up."

"Alice? What are you doing here? What time is it?" I asked, blinking a few times.

"A little after seven. Maggie, something's happened. Buster, your momma's man, had a heart attack last night."

My mind started to race. "Is she okay? Where are they now?" I asked.

"She lost him," Alice said.

"What about Mom, where is she?" I asked, hearing my voice crack.

"She went to the hospital with Buster. And called Violet, who went to the hospital about an hour ago," Alice said.

My mother would be out of her mind.

I thought about our fight last night and felt awful. Despite everything, she was still a human being and would be beside herself and hurting.

"We can't find her," said Alice.

"What do you mean? You just said she was at the hospital," I said.

"Yes, she was, but she disappeared after he passed and after your sister showed up. She just took off and didn't tell anyone where she was going," said Alice.

"What do you mean, she took off?" I asked.

"Maggie, your momma is a hurt bird. She loved that man, you know, very much," Alice said.

"Yes, I realized that when I saw them together. Where's Violet now?" I asked.

"She's still at the hospital, trying to contact Buster's family," Alice said.

My mind was all over the place. Where did my mom go? Wherever she was, it wasn't good. This could lead to her spiraling. And of course she had left it to Violet to clean up the mess, as she'd so often done in the past.

"Oh, Maggie, I know what you're thinking. Your mother's come a long way . . . she'll surface," Alice said.

"But what if she doesn't?" I asked.

Alice stared at me, both of us running movies behind our eyelids of past benders. I could see Alice pushing them into the back of her mind. She always thought the best of everyone and always gave people second chances, and thirds, and fourths. I wasn't as forgiving. I'd always held it against my mother when she indulged herself, leaving me, a small girl, wondering why my mom was a little too friendly with every man who crossed her path, or where she was for days at a time. I understood that she wrestled with darkness.

"Alice, let's go to her apartment. Maybe she's there," I suggested.

"Well, I called her up on her landline, but there was no answer. Hmm, you're right. We don't need an invitation. Let's just go on over there. I'll cut some roses from the garden and bring them to her." Alice was on it.

"Okay. Let me throw on some clothes and I'll meet you at the car in a few," I said, getting out of bed.

I went downstairs and got in Alice's car, where I spotted a bouquet of pink roses on the back seat. We were in for another crazy day.

Chapter 13
Magnolia

We drove to my mother's apartment in silence. I thought about how much death and sadness my mother had dealt with in her life. The two of us had coexisted side by side for so many years in the same house, living very different realities. Her estranged husband, my father, Scott, died in a motorcycle accident when she was twenty-five and I was seven. Her own father died a couple years later of a heart attack. While I had felt angry and abandoned when my father left us, I had gotten used to life without him by the time I learned he'd died, and at the age of seven, I hadn't fully comprehended that I'd never see him again. Grandpa Eddie's death had been more somber, Gran had been so shaken, and the whole community had mourned his passing. After the funeral, ordinary life had pretty much resumed for me with school, swimming lessons, and birthday parties, and of course Gran taking charge of our family despite her heartbreak. My mother hadn't had a similar routine to anchor her through those searing losses. And years earlier, my mother had buried her grandmother, my great-grandmother Daisy, the only woman who my mother felt had understood her. Now here she was having to bury the love of her life. Her black dress was worn out. Why hadn't I thought of all this before? My mother wasn't a victim. She was a survivor.

I looked over at Alice, who was humming a sad hymn. I remembered it from my childhood but couldn't recall the words. I rolled down the window and let the breeze into the car. Our mood was similar to that of the audience at a live performance before the curtain goes up. Everyone is quiet, so they can pay attention to what's about to happen.

Alice pulled into my mother's apartment complex, a group of well-maintained red-brick two-story buildings. Holding the pink roses, Alice led the way up the stairs to an outdoor covered hallway and to the door of my mother's apartment, 7H. I knocked. No answer. I knocked again. Still nothing. Alice knocked louder, and still nada. I looked over the railing into the parking lot for my mother's old yellow car. It was there. Before

I knew it, Alice pulled out of her purse the largest set of keys I'd ever seen. They looked like something a janitor would carry.

"Alice, what in the . . ."

"Lots of people need to give someone a spare key. In case they lock themselves out. I'm a lot cheaper than a locksmith," she said as she searched for Mom's key. "Here it is." She inserted it into the lock.

Alice pushed the door open with a shove, hitting something behind it. On further inspection, and with me using the weight of my body, I was able to push the obstruction out of the way. It was a chair, which indicated that my mom knew someone would come looking for her, and she didn't want to be bothered.

"Mom?" I called out.

No answer.

"Lily?" Alice called.

No answer.

"Is anybody home?" I realized immediately it was a stupid thing to say. How else would the chair have gotten there?

I was stunned by what I saw. The apartment was immaculate. I don't know why I was expecting it to be otherwise, but it was like something out of *Elle Décor*. Dove-gray walls with crown moldings, giant, beautiful gold-framed prints on the walls, and dozens of pictures of my mother and Buster sprinkled across the mantel above the fireplace. Her snow globe collection was displayed on a side table. Six ghost-clear chairs surrounded a dining room table that was a midcentury treasure, and there were fresh flowers at the center of the table. I walked on a teal rug over polished hardwood floors and went into the kitchen. It was clean. Like, super clean. Like see-your-reflection clean. The stainless steel appliances were mirrors.

"Mom?" I called once my shock subsided. Alice was behind me, also taking in the view. "Alice, can you believe this place? *So* clean."

"Humph, everything this girl knows about clean she learned from me," Alice said almost under her breath.

A noise emerged from what I guessed to be the bedroom. We went down the small hallway and opened the door to find my mother lying in bed under the covers, still as a stone.

"Mom?" I said so quietly I could barely hear myself.

"Please go away," my mother said, her voice muffled by a pillow.

"Mom, we're just checking on you. You disappeared from the hospital, we've been calling you," I said.

"Magnolia, my life has just fallen apart. Go. Away," Mom said.

"Mom, come on. Please let us stay with you. We

brought you some roses," I said, putting the bouquet on the bed. "Can we get you something else?"

My mother sat up. "Yes. Yes, you can. You can bring back Buster. If you can't do that, please just go. I need to be alone right now!" A glass rolled off the mattress, shattering on the floor. Alice made eye contact with me. The stench of bourbon was in the air.

"Lily, don't you worry. I'll get a broom and clean it all up. You stay right there," Alice said as she left the room.

I just stood there and looked at my mother. I wasn't totally surprised that she was drunk. I mean, if anything would throw an alcoholic into relapse, losing your partner sure would. My mother was so thin she was almost skeletal. She clearly wasn't eating these days. She looked so small in her huge bed. Her hair was pulled up into a topknot. She almost looked like a teenager. Her eyeliner and mascara, which were always perfect, were now smeared around her eyes and all over the stark white monogrammed pillowcase. She pulled her legs up under her chin and stared at me.

"Don't look at me like that. I had a drink, so what?" My mother's eyes locked onto mine, challenging me.

"I'm so sorry Buster died. I'm not judging you. Can I help you?" I asked.

"Can you *help* me? Yeah, you can go back to New

York City and live your own life. Leave, Magnolia. Go live the life I should have had."

"Mom, you have a great life here," I said too quickly, wanting to comfort her.

"*Great life?* Ha! Yeah, okay. My life was *going* to be great, but then Buster . . ." My mother's words broke off and tears began to stream from her eyes. She wiped them away and stared out the bedroom window for a few moments.

"You don't get it, Maggie. You never have. My life isn't like yours. I didn't have chances like you did. I had one chance, and I blew it. I could have been something and instead I'm stuck here on Sullivan's Island in the exact same spot I've always been. I met Buster and thought my life could change. I thought I could finally get out of South Carolina."

My mom then looked at me. "I know you know I resent you. There's nothing I can do about that. You are a grown woman, and I don't think I need to lie to you anymore. Don't feign shock with me, kid. I never wanted a child, and I never wanted to stay here. Buster was my only way out, and now I don't know what I'm gonna do. I guess wait for Mom to die and then sell the restaurant, but by then I'll be so old." My mother started sobbing, and I felt my heart break.

Alice returned with the broom and silently swept up

the shards of glass, threw them into the garbage can, and came to stand by me.

"Lily? I know you don't mean those nasty words. You'll regret them someday, so I would take them back if I were you," Alice said softly.

My mom just sobbed. She didn't apologize. I stood there frozen by her cruelty. She had said out loud all the words that kept me up at night, made me feel I was never good enough. *My mother never wanted me.* My whole existence was a mistake. I mean, I *had* always known it, she was right. I wondered if her emotional abandonment of me had made Gran love me more, enough for both of them. I'd always felt that my mother considered her love a privilege, one that I didn't deserve. I felt tears stinging my eyes, but I couldn't blink them back.

My mom sat up to blow her nose. She looked over at me and saw me crying. I realized I had made a mistake showing my emotions. My tears were blood in the water, and once again I was her prey. She narrowed her eyes like a hungry tiger who'd just found a wounded animal, and cocked her head to the side, as if she was trying to read my thoughts. She slid off the bed. Her sweatpants sagged off her impossibly small waist, and she tightened the strings to keep them up. Her collarbones poked through her thin T-shirt. She had always reminded me of a fragile bird, but now she was full of rage. Suddenly, I was a terrified little girl again.

"Mom, I . . ." I started to choke out something, but it sounded like I was begging her not to hurt me. I sounded as small as I felt.

"Oh, shut up, Maggie. I'm sure you're going to make this all about you, as you always do. Make me the bad guy, and you the helpless child. Go run off to Gran and tell her how I'm drinking again, a mess, irresponsible, crazy . . . go ahead. Maybe she'll be able to hear you in her coma. Make it the Maggie show. You think I can't hear the wheels turning inside your head? You think I don't know your plan?" she said.

"Mom, what are you talking about?"

She pushed past me, grabbed the bottle of bourbon, and poured a large amount into a glass on Buster's side of the bed. She paused to look at the glass, tracing the rim with her fingers, then pressed it to her lips and closed her eyes. She threw her head back and emptied the glass. She wiped her mouth with the back of her hand and turned to face me and Alice.

"I know you want the restaurant. I know you want to come home. I know that you want to rat me out to my mother and take away the last thing I have. That's what you've always done, Maggie. You have always taken from me. But you know what's so upsetting? I let you. I drink, I smoke weed, I do all of it, giving you the ammo to fire at me. I can't face my own life anymore, Maggie. Go. Get out of my house. You can take the restaurant. See how you do. But just you wait and see how awful it really is here." She turned away from us.

"Mom, I'm going to assume everything you've just said is words of anger. I get it. I forgive you. You're sad," I said, inhaling and trying to put up the emotional shield I'd gotten in the habit of using with her.

Alice put her hand on my shoulder then, as if to say, "That's enough now."

My mom started to laugh. "*Sad?* Maggie, don't you get it? I'm not *sad*, I'm defeated."

"Mom . . ." I said, trailing off into silence. I didn't know what to say. Reality set in as I watched my mom pour another drink.

"Mom, I love you! I'm going to stay here a few more days and fill in for you at the Lantern. We can talk later. I hope you feel better. I'm sorry . . . for your loss." I looked at Alice, who was shaking her head.

"Oh, fuck off, Maggie," my mom said, spinning around.

"That is *enough!*" Alice said in a louder voice than I'd ever heard her use. "Lillian Grace, you listen to me. We know you are sad, but sadness can't be a weapon you use against your own family. Maggie is your child! You can't drag the world down with you because you have a broken heart. Those things you said . . . she might *never* forget them! You are being selfish and foolish, and I *know* your momma taught you better than this. You lay yourself down and I'll be back to check on you in a few hours. You think long and hard about what you said. You owe your daughter an apology, because what you said is just not true. Come on, Maggie."

"I'm not a child, Alice," my mom said.

"That so? Then grow up," Alice said.

Mom started crying again but turned away from us and got back into bed.

Fine, I thought, *let her sleep off her evil mood.* As Alice and I were about to leave the apartment, I saw on the table by the door a small framed photograph of me and my mother dancing on the beach. I was so little, and she was laughing. I didn't remember that photograph being taken, but it captured a happy moment. I slipped it into my pocket. Alice saw me take it and said nothing.

We got into the car and drove back to Gran's house, and Alice sighed the whole way. Whenever I fought with my mom, I always felt torn to pieces. Chefs could scream in my face, and I would be fine, but when my own mother did it . . . *I should go back to New York*

City and leave all this bullshit, I thought, as we drove down Coleman Boulevard. I could just go back to my life in New York and ignore all of this. But, of course, I couldn't. Gran was still in the hospital, the restaurant was failing, Violet was pregnant and wasn't all that anxious to share the news with her boyfriend for some reason, and now my mother was going off the deep end.

Back at the house, we found Jim in the kitchen.

"Did you find your mother? Violet told me. Is she okay?" he asked.

"Well, we found her at her apartment," I said, feeling weary even though it was only nine o'clock.

"Let's leave it at that for now," Alice said, giving Jim a long look.

He immediately poured us cups of coffee and brought them over to the table. "I didn't go to the hospital because Vi was on her way home to get dressed properly for what she said was going to be a very busy day. She notified Buster's daughters and she's going to meet them at the hospital in a little while."

"Maggie, why don't you do the same while I make breakfast," Alice said, opening the refrigerator. "After a good breakfast you'll be ready to face the day."

Of course, Alice was right. Fortified by scrambled eggs and two cups of coffee, I called Violet on the way to the hospital. She couldn't talk long because she was in Gran's room with Dr. King. When we arrived, my sister was standing by Gran's bed, stroking her hand.

"What did Dr. King say?" I asked.

There were tears in Violet's eyes. "She said the medication is working. Gran's heart rate is stabilizing, but there was a spike in the middle of the night. She doesn't know why that happened. She said there's no reason for concern, Gran just needs more recovery time." Violet shrugged and sat on the sofa. She looked exhausted.

Alice nodded sagely. "Rose isn't ready to come back yet."

"Did you find Mom?" Violet asked.

"She's at her apartment. And not in fine form," I said, revealing nothing about our mother's emotional assault on me. "I'll stand in for her at the Magic Lantern tonight."

Alice smiled proudly at me, then turned to my sister. "Violet, honey, I think your mother would benefit from your company right now. She's hurtin' bad."

"What happened with Buster's family?" I asked.

"Once his two daughters arrived—I'd never met them before—they took over making the arrangements with the hospital," Violet said. "I gave them the names of two local funeral homes. They're pretty broken up—and a little angry that Mom just disappeared."

"They mustn't know our mother very well," I murmured, before saying, "Violet, I'll stay with Gran, and you can go over to Mom's. Jim, don't you have a video audition this morning?"

"Sure do!" he said. He slipped his arm around Violet. "Come on, little momma, I'll buy you breakfast, then you can give me a ride back to Gran's."

Violet turned to me. "See you at the Lantern at three o'clock, Mags. Service starts at five. That's enough time for you to meet the staff and familiarize yourself with the procedures, right? I can bring you up to speed on a few, um, operational issues."

"Thanks, Vi, I'd appreciate that," I said, feeling a little less anxious about my debut at the "updated" Magic Lantern.

As soon as Violet, Jim, and Alice left, I went over to my grandmother. "Now, Gran, in case you heard any of that conversation, I don't want you to worry. Violet and I have everything under control. You just rest and regain your strength." I leaned down and kissed her cheek.

I spent the next couple of hours agonizing over an email to Chef, writing and rewriting it, striving for the right tone. I wanted him to give me a week's early vacation so I could stay with Gran and help at the Magic Lantern without losing my job. I also politely expressed my disappointment at not getting the sous-chef job and my hope that he was still considering me for the job at Jean Paul's. Once I hit send, I treated myself to a cup of coffee at the vending machine down the hall. There was no collision with Sam Smart today. I wondered if I'd ever see him again.

I settled down in a chair next to Gran's bed and chatted away, recounting old times, and telling her about some of my favorite dishes I'd been cooking at Bar JP. I also had a chance to get to know the day nurses who came in to check her vitals. They were truly impressive health-care professionals—smart, kind, and caring. After talking with them, I felt better about leaving Gran when I noticed it was already close to three o'clock. I needed to get to the restaurant to learn more about the menu, even though I disapproved of it.

With no time to go home and change, I looked down at my outfit, black jeans and a floral-patterned blouse. I could work in what I was wearing, I'd just throw on some lipstick. Laura Mercier's Portofino Red made anyone look like a movie star. It had been a while since I had done any sort of front-of-house work, but I was sure it would be like riding a bike. Witnessing a dinner service firsthand would give me a better idea of what was going on at the Lantern.

When I reached the restaurant, the dining room was

empty. I looked around for members of the bus and wait staffs, expecting to find them tidying up and setting the tables, but I didn't see anyone. I went into the kitchen and found three cooks smoking cigarettes, two busboys picking at a plate of French fries, one female server talking to a male server in a conversation that looked as if it should be taking place in a bedroom, and Frankie in the corner on her phone. Dishes were piled up in the sink and everyone had a beverage in their hand. They seemed to be having a good time.

"Umm, hey, y'all, has anyone seen my sister?" I asked.

Frankie looked at me, rolled her eyes, and responded, "Yeah, she's in the office, but nobody has seen Lily or Buster." She was chewing gum again.

I took a deep breath and walked across the sticky floor to the small hallway where the office and the back door were located. Violet was sitting at the desk, which was covered with paperwork, open files, and a calculator.

"Hey, Violet."

"Hey, Maggie. I haven't been in this office in months. It's a real mess," my sister said.

"What do you mean you haven't been in here in months? Last night you told me you've been helping Mom."

"Yeah, I've been helping a little here and there, but

not looking at the books after Buster got involved. He wouldn't allow it. He used to lock the office door," Violet said as she picked up a file filled with receipts.

"So, how'd you get in?" I asked.

"Duh, remember I found the keys last night after they stormed out? They were in such a hurry, Buster forgot to lock the door. I think we're in some trouble here," she said.

"What kind of trouble?" I asked.

"Money trouble. This is a mess, Maggie. Looks like Mom and Buster made some seriously bad financial decisions in just about every department. Also, I can't seem to find any proof of payment for payroll." Violet threw the file back down on the desk, looking exasperated. "Now this, on top of Mom's meltdown, Buster dying, and Gran's accident!"

"I just want to help out tonight, and for the next couple of days while she figures things out." I was trying to focus on dinner service, not on our mother, the emotional terrorist.

"Maggie, I'm sorry Momma is so full of anger, but her heart is broken. I felt bad about leaving her alone. I need to go back and check up on her. But before I do that, I need to bring you up to speed so you can help. I can come back later. Let me get Frankie in here and I'll have her show you the new system. I'm calling the shots now," Violet said. She got up and opened the door to the kitchen.

I wondered if Violet's newfound authority was pregnancy related, or if it was a direct reaction to whatever she'd found on that messy desk. Either way, my sister was enraged, and I couldn't remember the last time I'd seen her take charge like this.

"Are those cigarettes I smell? Just what in the hell is going on here?"

I jumped out of my chair at the sound of Violet's voice and went into the hallway, where I had a view of the kitchen.

"I can't believe what I'm seeing in my kitchen! Are those French fries? Why are these dishes in the sink and not in the dishwasher? What about prepping for dinner? Y'all think it's okay to behave this way because my mom isn't here? Are you serious? Get to work. Now. Frankie? Get in my office." My sister's face was red. She obviously hadn't checked on the staff and seen what I had witnessed on my way to the office. Hearing her refer to the kitchen and the office as hers surprised me. Gone was the fragile younger sister from the other night, and in her place was my oldest partner in crime snapping into gear.

Before I went back into the office, I saw Frankie spit out her gum. Seconds later Violet returned and sat behind the desk, followed by Frankie, who was tightening her ponytail. I sensed that Violet was about to dish out some old-school-chef attitude. I was a little nervous for Frankie.

"Frankie, what is going on in that kitchen? Smoking? Eating French fries?" Violet asked.

"Well, that was family meal," Frankie said.

"*Family meal?*" I said, unable to help myself. "We have never used French fries in family meal! First of all, it doesn't meet requirements, and second, we don't eat like pigs! We have always made a protein, a starch, and a vegetable! Who authorized this change?"

"Nate has been running the kitchen ever since Louie left," Frankie said.

"Please go get him. I'd like to speak with him," Violet said in an eerily calm voice.

Frankie left, and Violet wouldn't make eye contact with me. She was furious. She started to pace. Nate came in wearing one of the dirtiest aprons I'd ever seen.

"You wanted to see me?" Nate said.

"Nate, would you like to tell me why you see it fit to serve the staff a bin of French fries? You are a cook, you went to culinary school. So, cook. This is unacceptable, and frankly embarrassing," Violet said.

"Violet, I have to accommodate the new budget and

also the timing. There isn't enough time between three and five for me to cook family meal," Nate said, his face turning red.

"What new budget? And why no time? How many cooks do you have working for you, Nate?" I asked, trying to help my sister get to the bottom of the money problem.

"Well, Lily said we have a ten-dollar budget for family meal every day, and I only have Ben and two part-timers, Leo and Miller, working for me since Louie left and Lily let Eduardo go," Nate said.

"Ten dollars? Why aren't you using extra product or pasta? Wait. We're only running with three cooks? We do a hundred covers a night. How many days are you working a week, Nate?" Violet said.

"Six days, usually, and so do the guys. Lily and Buster wouldn't let me use any pasta. The cheapest things we have are French fries and chicken fingers. I just put out what we have excess of. We always have French fries. I suggested doing away with family meal altogether, but the staff didn't like that," Nate said.

"Not anymore. From now on, you cook. Maggie, how many cooks do you have on your line and how many covers do you do in a day?" Violet asked.

"We have seven cooks, and around five hundred

covers. We do usually one hundred and fifty for lunch, and about three hundred to four hundred for dinner. Sometimes more on the weekends."

"And you are able to do family meal?" she asked, clearly using me as an example.

"Yes," I said.

"Yeah, well, this isn't New York City, and we don't even have produce to work with, aside from iceberg lettuce and tomatoes," Nate said, a little louder than necessary.

"What do you mean? Of course you have produce! Sunflower Farms ships to us directly! Has for years!" I said.

"Not that I know of. I think that stopped a while ago," Nate said.

"Who's head chef, Nate?" I asked.

"We don't have one. I mean, I kind of run the line a little, I do some of the ordering, but ever since Louie left . . . Lily does most of the ordering with Buster."

"So, you're telling me there's no head chef, there's no fresh produce, and family meal comes out of a bag from the freezer?" Violet asked.

"Yes, ma'am," Nate said, clearly embarrassed but with an edge in his voice.

"Thank you, Nate. Get the kitchen cleaned up and ready for service," Violet said, dismissing him.

She turned to Frankie. "How many are on the books tonight?"

"We only have about forty-five, but usually we have a bunch of walk-ins. So, I'm expecting about eighty by the end of the night."

"I can see that we have a big job ahead of us. Okay, change of plans. Maggie, you're in the kitchen tonight. Tie up that hair. I want you on that line. Frankie, do you think you could give us a rundown of the new system up front?" Violet said.

"Yeah, I could do that."

"Good. I'd also like you to hostess until I get back. I need to check in with my mom, who won't be coming in today. I want you to manage the reservations and seat guests. Okay?" Violet said.

"Sure thing. I'll go roll some silverware in the meantime," Frankie said as she left.

"You do that. Thank you, Frankie. I'll see you in a few," Violet said.

"Violet, how could you have not known what's been going on here?"

"Maggie, I have my photography, the new house, Chris. Just recently, I've come back to fill in when a staff member calls in sick or to help Mom order food and supplies. Honestly, I wasn't paying close attention. I was too wrapped up in my own life. I love shooting weddings, and things are really picking up! I am learning so much and enjoying it. It really is such an honor to capture someone's best day ever," she said.

"I would love to get you back to a place where you could focus on that, Vi. I'll help. The best I can, anyways. This is a huge job," I said.

"You can say that again," Violet said. "I'm so worried about Gran and Mom, and I . . . Can you believe Buster is dead?"

"No. I mean, can we pause on *that* for a moment? Does anyone here know that Buster died?" I asked.

"Nope, no one knows," Violet said. "I just don't feel up to answering any questions about his death right now. I'm still sort of in shock. I mean, the man behaved like a clown, but he was lovable, too. I'm sorry you never got to see that side of him. He could be so sweet and helpful."

"Yeah, helpful in running our restaurant into the ground and causing our mother to relapse. Excuse my candor," I said.

"Maggie."

"I know. Okay, so to help Mom we're doing this? You and me? We're going to run the Lantern? A sister act?"

"Yes. I mean, if not us, who else?" she said. "Call Jim."

"Oh, my gosh, that's right. I want to find out how

his audition went." I dialed his number and he picked up on the second ring.

"Hey, sugar. Oh, my gosh, what a day! You okay? How's Lily? How's Gran? How's the restaurant?" Jim said in one breath.

"They're all pretty much the same as the last time we spoke. But tell me, how did your second audition go?"

"I need a facial, maybe an eye lift, too. The producer is flying to New York to meet me in person on Monday! I'm thinking of heading back to the city on Friday or Saturday. You'll come with me, right?"

"That's fabulous! I'm so happy for you, Jimmy! My schedule is still up in the air. Can we talk about that later? In the meantime, I need a huge favor," I said.

Violet grabbed the phone out of my hand.

"Jim, lovebug, this is a 911. I need help tonight at the restaurant. Do you have any interest in making some good tips with that sparkling personality of yours? Want to put your genetic mixology abilities to good use? We need someone to man the bar," Violet said, switching the call to speakerphone.

"I will happily do anything you ladies need. You know my aunt Belle makes the best cocktails in the world. I feel some inspiration already! When do you want me?" Jim said.

"Yesterday. Get here ASAP! Thanks, Jim, you are a star!"

Jim arrived forty-five minutes later with a big smile on his face and a grocery bag, which he set down on the bar. He was dressed in perfectly tailored khaki slacks, chef's clogs, a pale-blue button-down denim shirt, and a red apron tied around his waist. He was the only person I knew who could throw together an entirely new identity in only forty-five minutes. He looked as if he had worked in a restaurant his entire life. I knew the front of the house was in good hands with Jim. I silently thanked the theater business for creating great servers. Everyone knows that every great server in New York is also an actor.

"Hey, Jim! Thanks again for helping us tonight. You're a man of many talents. What do you have in here?" I asked, peering into the tall paper grocery bag.

"Oh, a little of this, a little of that. I'm going to make a signature cocktail for the guests. I thought why not have a little fun while I'm here?" Jim pulled oranges, red sugar, and some fresh mint out of the bag.

"Jim, it sounds great. Thanks for being such a trouper. Are those blood oranges?" I asked, slightly starved for fresh produce.

"You're welcome, and yes, right from your grandmother's garden," Jim said.

"Well, at least our guests will enjoy *something* fresh. Great idea to do a special cocktail, Jim," I said.

I made my way back to the kitchen and bumped into Frankie.

"Hey, Frankie. I want to apologize for the other night. I was being a real jerk," I said.

Frankie took a long look at me and pursed her lips. Then smiled. "That's okay, girl. We're in the trenches together tonight! Water under the bridge, as they say. At least you tipped well," Frankie said and gave me a hug.

This would never happen back in New York. I would never have apologized and she would never have hugged me. New Yorkers were so wrapped up in their egos and professional status. I didn't know how I felt about having become a stranger to hugs.

Chapter 14
Magnolia

In the next two hours Nate filled me in on how the kitchen was run. It was a chop-and-plop operation, just as I'd suspected. You opened a bag of something frozen (fish, burger patties, shrimp, even sauces) and you either heated it up or chopped it up and *then* heated it up. It was something a trained poodle could do. Even though it tore out my soul, I went along with it because, technically, it wasn't my kitchen, and we had no time to do a different menu.

Cooking at the Magic Lantern had turned into a hack job. I had so many happy memories of Gran rolling out fresh dough and asking my opinion of a new recipe. I remembered inhaling the scent of fresh basil in her tomato sauce or onions with fresh garlic cooking in olive oil as I awaited something delicious. Personally? I have always thought that the sizzle of onion, garlic, and olive oil beats the smell of fresh-baked cookies any day. But the only smells circulating in this kitchen were those of fryer oil and defrosting meat.

Nate walked me over to the small refrigeration spaces under the prep areas. He kept referring to them as "mini fridges," which I guess they were, but I wondered how many hours he had actually spent in a professional kitchen, because an experienced cook would have called them lowboys. He pulled out a few very large vacuum-sealed plastic bags, which contained what appeared to be sauce.

"All right, so here's how we do it. You grab a pot, turn on the stove, cut open this bag, pour whatever sauce is inside it, and heat it up. Stir it every so often, make sure it doesn't burn, and boom, you got yourself house-made red sauce," Nate said.

"Nate, that isn't *house made*, it's from a bag," I said.

"Well, if you don't like that, we also have sauce in cans, but I think the frozen stuff is better. Maggie, it's a lot cheaper to buy it ready-made than to pay some-body to cook it. Ten bucks an hour plus ingredients is more than the five bucks you pay for a gallon of this red stuff," Nate said.

"Nate, by red stuff, I'm assuming you mean marinara sauce? It's not expensive to make it from scratch, and it tastes better," I said.

"Oh, you think you can just whip it up two hours before service? We have other things to take care of, Maggie," Nate replied.

"Nate, it takes no time at all. Let me make some sauce, and you'll see. If you like it better, we'll use it. If not, we can rip open another bag or can." I knew I was challenging him, but I couldn't help myself.

"Fine. I guess we could use some of those chopped onions," Nate suggested.

"Wait, you have prechopped onions?" I said.

"Yeah, check the mini fridge to the left," he said.

I opened the lowboy and was stunned to see piles of plastic bags that contained prechopped onions, carrots, and celery. How much did this cost? Did my mom really think this was economical? Were any of these cooks actually cooking? *Yikes*, I thought, as I closed the door.

"Nate, do you have any whole onions?" I asked.

"Umm, maybe a couple in the walk-in," he said.

"Onions get puffy when they're refrigerated. They should be kept in a drawer or someplace dark and dry," I said.

"Well, that's what we have, Maggie," Nate said. I could tell I was bugging him.

"Okay, look, I'm not trying to poke a bear here, I just think that . . . well, I know that we can do better. I know it seems like a lot at first, but with some time management and really good delegation we could be doing more from scratch. It would make the food so much more delicious."

I saw him shake his head.

"Fine." I sighed. "I'll make it work."

I had gotten myself into a tough spot here. I wanted to show the kitchen staff that there was a better option, and if I was going to prove a point, I needed fresh ingredients to work with. I needed to go to another source.

I walked out of the kitchen and grabbed Jim.

"Hey, love of my life, I need a favor," I purred and slipped him a shopping list.

"What do you need, baby doll?" Jim purred back.

"I need you to run to the Teeter just over the bridge. I'm having a marinara emergency."

"An emergency involving tomatoes and fresh basil? What's going on, Magnolia?" Jim said, arching a perfectly shaped brow.

"I'm making a point with the head cook. Please just do this for me?"

"You're lucky I took Gran's truck. Okay, I'll be back in a few," Jim said and was out the door.

I went back into the kitchen to find Alice, who was

being a good sport, but I knew her patience was limited. She was sighing a lot, raising her eyebrows, and
avoiding eye contact with me. There was only so much
this woman could take, and heat-and-eat food was
borderline blasphemy to her. To me it was cheap and
careless. It went against every scar and burn that lined
the insides of my arms. Everything I had learned at
culinary school and as a professional cook was being
thrown into the garbage with every plop of a chicken
tender into the fryer.

Jim returned not a moment too soon, with everything I had asked for.

"Go get 'em, kid," Jim said and left the kitchen to
get the party started at the bar.

I emptied the grocery bag, pulling out some of the
plumpest tomatoes I'd seen in a while. Good ole Harris
Teeter. I knew they carried local farms' fresh produce.
These tomatoes must have come from Johns Island,
which was famous for its tomatoes. Also in the bag, I
found fresh onions, basil, garlic, as well as a six-pack of
Diet Coke and a lemon. I smiled. There wasn't anything
better on God's green earth than a cold Diet Coke with a
slice of lemon. I cracked open a can, found a glass, filled
it with ice, sliced the lemon, and got to work.

I unrolled my knife bag and saw all my old friends

staring back at me. Some girls liked diamonds, some liked pearls, but just give me a good knife. Knives are sexy, that's all there is to it. Mine were sharp and strong and had been through a lot with me. I pulled out my trusty chef's knife and my small paring knife.

I filled a big pot with water, put it on the stove, turned the burner on full flame, and poured in the salt. Nate was watching me.

"That's a lot of salt, Maggie. Are you trying to kill us?" he said, trying to get the attention of the other cooks.

"No, Nate. It's just enough. You want the water to taste like the ocean if you're going to cook anything starchy like pasta," I replied as I used my paring knife to core the tomatoes, removing the stems and cutting small Xs into the bottom of their skins.

"What are you doing with the tomatoes?" Nate asked.

"I'm giving them a bath, Nate," I said and then decided to explain what I was doing. "I'm dropping them into boiling water for a few minutes. The hot water will cause the skin to pull away, making it a lot easier to peel them."

Alice caught wind of what I was doing and came over with a large bowl of ice water.

"What's that water for?" Nate asked.

"The ice bath will stop the hot tomatoes from cooking further," I said.

"Sounds like a lot of wasted time to me," Nate said as he ripped open another bag of frozen chicken tenders.

I rolled my eyes and focused on the sauce. I took the head of garlic and broke off the cloves. Then I found two small metal bowls and dropped the cloves inside one of the bowls, turned over the second bowl and put it on top of the first, creating a little dome, and shook them together.

"What are you doing? Making music? Shaking your maracas?" Nate said, making the other cooks burst into laughter.

I separated the bowls and showed them that the cloves had popped out of their paper skins. That shut them up. Next, I diced the onions. When the tomatoes were ready, I chopped them and put them in a bowl. I grabbed another large pot and heated some olive oil. When the oil started to ripple, I added the onions. I knew it was hot enough because when the onions hit the hard surface, they sang to me. That little sizzle they gave off let me know they were ready to be transformed. I turned away from the pot to slice the garlic. I let the onions cook undisturbed for a few minutes until they became translucent.

"You better stir your onions! You'll burn them!" Nate said.

"No, you don't want to stir them too much, just enough so they don't get colored. But a little browning is okay because it means the onions are caramelizing and that gives the sauce a little sweetness. Of course, if it winds up being too acidic you could always add a little sugar. Anyway, if you constantly stir, you are constantly lifting them off the heat, which will slow down the cooking process," I said, getting a little annoyed at all of Nate's second-guessing.

"Okay, Miss Smarty-Pants," Nate said.

I let the onions cook, turned them over a few times just to make sure they weren't burning, and once they were almost clear, I added the sliced garlic, which filled the room with one of the original perfumes of this restaurant. It might very well awaken my great-grandmother from her grave. I wished it would—I could use her help right now. I let the garlic do its magic and I added the tomatoes. I used a hand blender to puree the mixture into a sauce and let it cook. I brought it to a boil and then let it simmer. I stacked the basil leaves in a little pile, placing the largest on the bottom and the smallest on the top. Then I rolled them up like a cigarette and sliced them. I pushed it to the side because I wouldn't add it to the pot until the sauce had cooked down.

While my sauce cooked, the first few tickets came in. Fried chicken, fried potatoes, fried fish, even fried vegetables. A few pasta orders also came in, as well as a few for godforsaken garden salads. I watched as the cooks pushed out each plate as if they were sleepwalking. They weren't excited or in a hurry. They looked bored.

At around six thirty I checked on my sauce and lifted the lid. It smelled and looked perfect. I dunked in a spoon a few times to taste it, adding salt and freshly cracked pepper, seasoning it to perfection. I went back to my original pot of salted water and turned up the heat, bringing it back to a boil. I grabbed some pasta, cooked it for about seven minutes, to the point where it still had a slight bite but wouldn't take out a filling. I placed the drained pasta in a bowl, added the chopped basil to the sauce, and ladled some of the sauce onto the pasta. Twirling the pasta around a large serving fork, I turned it into a little tower of happiness.

"Sure smells good," Alice said.

"Here you go, Nate—family meal," I said, sounding a little too sassy.

Nate and the other cooks grabbed forks and dug in. Alice took a bite, too. I knew it was heaven, and I knew I had won the battle when I saw Nate's face.

"Yeah, okay, it's pretty good. Could use some bacon, though," Nate said.

I let out a little laugh.

"What couldn't use a little bacon?" Alice said.

"True enough," Nate said.

Over the next few hours I kept expecting a push. I kept expecting to hear the ticket machine screech with tons of tickets. But it never did. Business was slow, and I mean sloth's pace. We fed maybe thirty people by seven thirty. What was happening? I thought Mom had said they were busy. It had been the busiest at five, and then it had slowed down. That wasn't good. That meant we were feeding early birds and had no real draw come dinnertime. The cool crowd was eating dinner elsewhere.

At about eight o'clock, we were all just standing around. I looked for Alice and didn't see her anywhere.

"Hey, Nate, have you seen Alice?" I asked.

"She went off somewhere a while ago. I don't know, we're so dead, maybe she just went home." He shrugged.

"That's unlike her. She would have said goodbye," I said.

Just then, like a hot knife through butter, the unmistakable aroma of Alice's apple pie cut through the smell of grease in the kitchen. The scent of apples baking in butter, cinnamon, and sugar made our mouths water.

"What the hell is that?" Nate said in a trancelike voice.

"*That* is undoubtedly where Alice has been, making her mile-high apple pie, if I'm not mistaken," I said. Nate looked confused, so I pointed to the little room at the back of the kitchen. "In the bakery nook, which I guess you guys haven't been using since the restaurant no longer serves fresh bread, pies, and cobblers."

"Yes, that's where I've been," Alice said, joining us. "I decided something around here should be home-made. I found some apples in the office, and some flour and sugar, and whipped up something real. I'm sorry, Nate, I just couldn't look at another frozen chicken cutlet."

"Oh, you ladies think you can just go off and do whatever you like, do you?" said Nate.

Uh-oh, I thought. This wasn't good. Alice had gone off to do her own thing without asking Nate, and I had sort of done the same thing.

"Nate, I'm sorry. I just thought it might be nice for the customers to have something special," Alice said.

"Whatever . . ." Nate started to say something, but Frankie whisked through the swinging door of the kitchen holding two dinner plates. One was a fried fish something and the other was a half-eaten burger.

"What's wrong, Frankie?" I asked.

"Uh, sorry to do this, but the customers at table ten said that these weren't fully cooked, and the fries were cold," she said.

I took a look at the plate, and the food was indeed ice cold.

"Mile-high apple pie?" Violet sang as she walked in through the back door.

"You know it!" Alice said.

"Oh, I can't wait! Cut me a piece right now! It's medicinal, exactly what I need after this trying day," Violet said.

"Violet, you know I have to let it set up. You can have some tomorrow. You, and your customers!" Alice said.

"She can have a piece as soon as it's out of the oven! Hello, warm apple pie? You're going to tell me that's not the way it's done in New York or something?" Nate said.

"Actually, Nate, you do have to let the pie rest and cool completely before slicing into it," I said. "The pectin has to set. That's what creates that lovely jamlike consistency around the apples. If you slice it when it's hot out of the oven, the filling goes all over the place."

"Is that right? Okay, *Chef* Maggie," Nate said sarcastically.

"Nate? Is there a problem here?" Violet said.

"Uh, yeah, I've got a problem. How do these girls just walk into this kitchen, taking over, thinking they can do whatever they want? I mean, it's not my fault we use crap ingredients. I do what I'm told, and, honestly, I can't do this anymore. I'm done. I was done when Lily didn't hire anyone after Louie left. I was done when Lily told us we couldn't *cook* anymore. All we do is assemble, and now I'm done having these girls drop in and make me look bad for just doing my job! I'm out of here," Nate said as he took off his apron and threw it on the floor. He walked out the back door and we all just stood there, looking at each other.

Then one of the other two cooks did the same thing, following Nate out the door, leaving me, Violet, Alice, and a very worried Frankie, who was still holding the cold fish and half-eaten burger in the kitchen. I immediately switched into survival mode, and my years of training kicked in.

"Frankie, go tell Jim we have a problem with table ten. Ask him to send them a round of his special cocktail. If there are children at the table, give them chocolate milk. Tell the people we'll get them a new burger, a new order of fish, and fresh, warm fries in a few minutes. Alice, can you help me?"

"I'm on it," Alice said.

"Maggie, you sure you can do this?" Violet asked.

I rolled my eyes. "Yeah, I got this. It's Restaurant Cooking 101."

"I'll take over as hostess so Frankie can focus on the customers," Violet said, heading into the dining room.

I went over to the cook who hadn't said a word to me all night. He looked absolutely terrified. "What's your name?" I asked.

"B-B-B-Ben," he stammered.

"All right, Ben, let's get through this, okay? Where is the original ticket for table ten?"

Ben snapped into gear, grabbing the spike where all the tickets were stuck once the plates went out and finding it with no problem. He handed me the ticket. I saw exactly how they'd ordered the burger and the fish and noticed that they'd asked for mayo.

Violet came back into the kitchen. "Maggie, we just had a ten-top walk in. Are you ready for this?"

"Yes, I got it. Don't worry, it's all under control," I replied. "Alice, let's cut up the rest of that fresh basil, we are going to make an herb mayo. Ben, I need you to tell me where everything is."

The next few minutes were a bit of a blur. Ben gave me the ins and outs and Alice whipped up a yummy aioli. We decided to add it on the side of each burger or plate of fries going out. I looked around the kitchen and decided to make some homemade mac and cheese. We had all the ingredients: milk, cheese, flour, butter, and even some dried ground nutmeg and cayenne pepper. We threw the mac and cheese into little ramekins and crushed up some bread crumbs to put on top. At least I could contribute something new to the menu.

Once we got through the ten orders, which were mostly burgers and fried shrimp or chicken, we got a moment to come up for air. Ben, as it turned out, was pretty speedy, and really helped us by filling in where we couldn't. Even for experienced cooks like me and Alice, it was always a challenge to cook in a new kitchen. Before long it was nine thirty, and we closed at ten.

"All right! Well, y'all, we survived it!" I said to Alice and Ben.

"Maggie, I really liked that pasta. Could you show me how to do that sometime soon?" Ben asked.

"Of course! Okay, Ben, what's the breakdown routine?"

"What do you mean?" Ben asked.

"Oh, Lord. Where do y'all keep your cleaning supplies?" Alice said.

"Umm . . ." Ben looked at his feet.

Alice and I made eye contact, knowing well and good that there was no breakdown routine or schedule. We'd have to make it up. I needed to locate sanitizer solution and sponges and get some hot water. We could do the deep clean another night, but right now this place needed at least an hour's scrub-down. At least the teenage dishwasher my mom had hired had shown up after his school's band practice and was taking care of the pots, pans, and dishes.

"Okay, Ben, here's what I need from you. Could you mix me some sani solution and grab some sponges or metal scrubbies or even some side towels? If you've got bleach, that's good, too. We need to take apart the stove and give it a real clean," I said.

We all got to work. Ben scrubbed the ever-living you-know-what out of the prep station. I looked at the clock, and after about forty minutes I decided to check the books for tomorrow. Now that the Lantern was down two cooks, my help in the kitchen was needed.

I went into the dining room and saw Violet hugging Jim behind the bar.

"Maggie, Jim told me the bar was packed all night. We totally sold out of his special cocktail, and everyone was raving about the mac and cheese and that basil aioli!" Violet said.

"I've never received so much in tips!" Frankie said. "Wish we had food like that every night. Will you be here tomorrow, Maggie?"

"Yeah, I think I can stay a few more days. At least till a new head cook is hired," I said.

"Oh, my God, lifesaver!" Violet threw her arms around me.

Jim shot me a wink.

"Jim, I am not staying here forever!" I said.

"Of course not! But this sure was fun tonight. If she stays, I stay—for a couple more days. I'll whip up something wonderful for tomorrow night," Jim said.

"Violet, who knew you were El Capitán?" I said, pinching her butt.

"I know, right? I don't know what got into me. Sorry if I was bossy," she said.

"Girl, that was refreshing. It's nice to have some direction around here," Frankie said as she wiped down some tables.

"Well, let's hope it sticks, because I think Momma will be back pretty soon," Violet said.

"Is Miss Lily okay?" Frankie asked, making us all realize we still hadn't told anyone at the restaurant what was going on.

"Yes, girl, she's just a little under the weather is all. No worries. Why don't I help you finish those tables?" Jim said, grabbing a rag and giving table eight some elbow grease.

I went back into the kitchen to find Alice and Ben making a prep list for tomorrow's service.

"Hey, Alice, Violet is going over to Mom's. Ben,

thank you for everything tonight, as soon as y'all are done you are free to go home," I said.

"So, you're the chef now, Maggie?" Alice said, smirking.

"For the next few nights, that's what it looks like," I said.

"Awesome!" Ben said. "We could use a little fresh air in here."

"Fresh is absolutely the right word, Ben. Thanks," I said and smiled. "So you're doing your fried chicken, Alice?"

"No, ma'am, I'm doing *your* fried chicken. It's time to bring back the original recipe to the Lantern," Alice said.

"I love that idea," I said.

Tradition always markets well in the South. I started imagining menu planning, but my thoughts turned to Mom and Gran. Then the kitchen doors swung open and in walked Sam Smart.

Chapter 15
Magnolia

"Hey, there, Magnolia Adams."

"Sam?" I was disoriented for a moment seeing him in the Magic Lantern's kitchen. "Nice to see you. How'd you know I'd be here?"

He flashed a smile, tilting back his cowboy hat, and in his hands was a bunch of fat red beets. "Lucky guess. I thought you might still be in town, so I figured I'd check here," Sam said. "The guy at the bar told me you were back here. Hope I'm not intruding on anything."

"So, you're stalking me now?"

"Guess it looks that way, huh? Okay, I'm embarrassed. I just wanted to see you before you left."

"Well, good news, Dr. Cowboy, looks like I'm in town for a few more days," I said, putting my hands on my hips. Man, he looked good.

"Is that right?" Sam asked. "These are for you. Thought you'd appreciate them more than flowers."

"Yes, turns out bad things do come in threes," I said, taking a deep breath and fighting a smile over the beets. "My Gran still hasn't woken up after brain surgery, my mom's fiancé suddenly passed away, and I lost the promotion I was hoping to get back in New York to my ex-whatever," I said, spitting out all my cards at once.

"Ex-whatever," Sam said, raising an eyebrow. "Hmm. Sounds . . . complicated."

"You have no idea," I said, inspecting the beets. "These are gorgeous."

"Only the best for you, Magnolia." He smiled. "Can't say I'm sorry to hear you have an ex, but I'm sorry your grandmother's recovery isn't progressing more quickly. And that's terrible about your momma's beau. How's she doing?" All of a sudden Sam's demeanor shifted from magnetic to comforting.

"She's hurting pretty badly," I said. "It's sad."

"Nothing sadder than losing the one you love. Can I take you for a drink? Sounds like you could use one," he said.

I looked him up and down and decided to welcome a pleasant distraction into my life. "Let me take you for one, Sam. I know a good bar." I led Sam into the dining room and found Jim finishing up.

"Hey, Jim, you remember Sam, right?" I said.

"How could I forget? What an amazing first impression!" Jim said, widening his eyes.

"Saw you sitting in Maggie's truck, but we weren't properly introduced. I'm Sam Smart," Sam said, extending his hand.

"I'm Jimmy Williams. Pleased to make your acquaintance." The two men shook hands.

"Jimmy Williams? Sounds like the name of a movie star!" Sam said, causing Jim to fan himself. Sam was a charmer, which meant trouble. Oh, well, how bad could this really be? I mean, I was thinking of going back to New York next week, so why not have a little fun with the doctor?

"Well, nice to meet you. Y'all need anything? If no, I'm going on home. Got to get my beauty sleep," Jim said.

"No, I think I've got this, Jim. Thanks for everything. I'll see you back at the house," I said.

"Night, Maggie, Sam," Jim said. He hurried out the front door, pausing only to mouth the words "I won't wait up."

We had the restaurant to ourselves.

"All right, Miss Maggie May. What's your poison?" Sam said, sliding behind the bar. He took off his hat and rolled up his sleeves.

"Sam Smart, this is my bar. Please let me serve you," I said, loving the sight of him taking charge.

"No, I insist. Plus, maybe I can impress the lady with my mixology skills," he said.

"Oh, man, mixology skills? Okay, Sam. Hmm, I like bourbon," I said.

"Yeah, one summer I needed a change and I decided to take a bartending class. I used to bartend during med school to make a little money on the side. I've got just the thing," he said and helped himself to whatever the bar had.

I watched him in the dimly lit room, making himself at home in my family's restaurant. He looked so calm and at ease. Watching him move was hypnotizing. His shoulder muscles rolled under his plaid pearl-snap shirt. He was focused on what he was doing but was completely aware that he had my full attention. His sun-kissed forearms tightened as he cut up a lime, shook a cocktail shaker, and grabbed two glasses. I felt hot. When he looked at me with his golden eyes I felt, for a moment, like I would faint. It was like he knew that bar. It was as if he had been there before.

"Here you go, Miss Maggie. Something about your day inspired me," Sam said as he placed a tan drink in front of me.

I took a long sip and said, "A dark and stormy? Ha! That's funny."

"Yeah. Just seemed to fit today's forecast." He took a long sip of his own. "Not too bad. What do you think?"

I savored the drink but thought about whether to give him my honest opinion. Something told me Sam was used to compliments. It was a perfect drink, though. The bitterness of the ginger beer with the sweetness of the spiced dark rum was delicious. That bite of lime was so refreshing, it reminded me of a hot summer night.

"Pretty good, Sam. Pretty good," I said, smiling.

"Hey, if it got you to smile, I did my job," he said.

"I need to smile. I think my face forgot how these past few days," I said, looking at the bottom of my now almost-empty glass.

"Let me make another round. The first was medicinal, and I'm a doctor, so I should know," he said, smirking.

"Yeah, well, if it's doctor's orders," I said, draining my glass.

"It is." He got to work.

"Maybe make it a double batch, Sam," I said, half joking.

"Got it," Sam said with a chuckle.

I knew where this was going, and I had a choice. I could have two more drinks with Sam, flirt a little, and go home to bed. I knew that this could never really go anywhere. I had a life I was just not ready to give up on in New York. A life that eventually I'd have to go back to and face. But tonight I could linger. I could ask Sam about his life, tell him about mine, and perhaps find myself caught up in the moment.

I considered my options.

My mother often got caught up in the moment, my sister had obviously done the same with her boyfriend recently, but I never did. I always moved forward and pushed harder and climbed the ladder. I never let myself just indulge in something. I never took even a day off or a long vacation, or anything just for me, so maybe a little indulgence was not such a bad idea. Maybe my mother was right. Maybe I was horrible. But this guy didn't think so. He thought I was interesting enough to show up at my family's restaurant and make me a few drinks. He wanted to spend time with me. He was a professional doctor, for crying out loud! I was having late-night drinks with a *doctor.* Where were all the little debutantes I'd grown up with now, when I would have liked them to watch me digging into their holy grail?

I needed to have some fun, and this had all the signs of a good time. I pushed my chest out, took a deep breath, and exhaled, trying to relax.

"So, Sam, man of many talents, how's your day been?"

Sam set down two new drinks. He gave me a sideways glance as he slipped onto the barstool next to me. His proximity to me made me straighten my back and inhale the unmistakable smell of danger. The good kind. The kind that drew you in and made you beg for another dose.

"It just got a lot better, Maggie." He looked right at me, laughed a little, and drained his glass.

"Sam, you sure do make yourself easy to look at," I said, not sure where that came from. I guessed it was someplace I had never felt comfortable before.

"So do you, Maggie. God, you're beautiful," he said, unleashing the adjective Ronny had never used to describe me.

"Ha, come on, I'm still a mess from the kitchen," I said.

"I don't see anything messy. I smell dinner, and you're making me hungry," he said, moving closer.

God, this was heating up quickly. "You don't smell all the garlic, onions, and fryer oil?" I said, giggling and feeling shy.

"I love fried food, Maggie." He inhaled deeply, and we both laughed.

"What else do you love?" I asked.

"Well, I love a woman who isn't afraid to open her heart. I love a woman who says what she thinks and feels. I love a woman who is strong and has the drive to do something she loves and believes in," Sam said, reaching out and moving one of my stray curls behind my ear. I shivered.

"Yeah?" I said.

"Yeah, I do. Passionate people are rare. So many people are too afraid to feel something real, so concerned with cultivating the right image that they are afraid of being themselves. The heart's a powerful thing, and I love it when it obviously drives someone."

"Is that me? Do you see my heart driving me?"

"Yes. Right into the back of my truck. How could I ignore that?"

"Oh, God!" I threw my head back and laughed at myself. It felt good. All the stress lifted off my shoulders.

"Now, that's what I wanted to hear. Sound of music," Sam said. "So speaking of driving, what drives you?"

"My grandmother is my hero, so a lot of it is her. She's a role model for me. I really want my own restaurant one day. So I guess working toward that, but I just love to cook for other people. It's such a gift to be able to nourish someone else and entertain them at the same time. Being able to be creative with a different herb or spice, giving home recipes a little twist or refinement. It would be such an opportunity to do that for people on a larger scale. What about you? What made you become a doctor?" I asked.

"Well, my mother wanted it. But I fell in love with it on my own. Growing and taking care of the land was where I thought I'd spend my days, and turns out, taking care of people isn't that much different. I love making people feel whole and healthy. I love doing the same for my plants. It makes me feel connected to something bigger than myself. The earth's natural rhythms and people's, too," he said as he caught me diving deep into his eyes.

"Sam, I can't take it anymore, just kiss me already," I said.

Sam looked me right in the eye and sized me up. He looked like he was deciding how to do it. He didn't look scared, he looked determined to give me the best kiss of my life. He looked like he was deciding what to touch first. Like he was analyzing my face. Like he was looking for something. I felt the last bit of self-control slip away from me.

He lifted both of his large, warm hands up to my face, ran one around the back of my head, and gently slid his fingers through my hair, pulling my face toward his. He paused for a moment, locking his eyes to mine, then closed his own and kissed me. His lips pressed up against mine and I felt cold and hot at the same time. I hadn't realized I was still holding the cocktail glass in my hand, and my arm went limp. I dropped the glass and the drink spilled all over the floor as the glass shattered. We stopped and looked down at the mess, then at each other. He pulled my barstool closer, parted my legs, stood up, and put his body up against mine. I wrapped my legs around him and squeezed, pulling his face back where it belonged.

It felt like we were on fire. Everything got so hot, it was almost too much to stand. Kissing him, having his body close, I thought of how you feel when you're eating a meal and don't realize how hungry you are till you're three bites in. You start eating faster, savoring every bite. Now I couldn't stop, so I took another kiss, then another. I let his tongue slip into my mouth, and I shivered again. He smiled at my reaction and went in for more. The way his hands started to move over my body gave me the impression he had been there before. I could have stopped, I knew I should have stopped, but all the drama and emotional pain I'd experienced over the last few days made me recklessly ignore that thought. I tore his shirt off.

He gasped, which made me giggle. I covered my mouth, and he grabbed my hand and put it around his neck. He scooped me up and I tightened my thighs around his waist. He sat me down on the bar and peeled off my blouse. Any last ounce of Southern lady I had left in me exited the building. I unhooked my bra and threw it across the room. Screw it. If I was going to go ahead and make a mistake, I might as well take the fast lane. We watched it slingshot and land on a booth.

"Is the door locked?" he asked, gasping for air.

"Think so," I said, taking big gulping breaths. I was drowning and was totally fine with it.

"Good," he said.

He pulled me to the end of the bar and pulled my shoes off. I hopped off and helped him along by unbuttoning my jeans and wiggling out of them as sexily as I could. He did the same.

"Man, you look good enough to eat," he said.

"So do you. Take a bite," I said.

We were standing about four feet apart and our clothes were all over the floor. I stood there almost naked and drank in the sight of him. He took a few slow steps toward me, like a lion about to jump on his prey, and dug in.

Chapter 16
Magnolia

"Back in the halls of blood and guts!" I pretended to shiver with fear as my sister and I waited in front of the shiny silver elevator doors.

"Maggie!" Violet put her hand on her stomach and grimaced.

"I'm sorry, Vi. I was just kidding. Do you feel sick again?"

"I'm going to buy some peppermints to settle my stomach," Violet said, running off to the gift shop.

I pulled out my phone and started going through my emails. When the elevator doors opened, a group of doctors in white coats, talking loudly and laughing, walked out. I stepped back, out of the way, but not quickly enough, because one of them bumped into me.

Annoyed, I looked up from my phone and saw Sam's golden-brown eyes gazing down at me.

"Old habits die hard. You can't stop running into me, Magnolia," he said, shaking his head. And then he grinned.

He looked so handsome I thought I was going to melt—but not before I corrected him. "Actually, you ran into me this time, Dr. Smart!"

"Did I? We'll have to debate this over dinner. When can I take you to dinner?"

"I don't know," I said, feeling totally overwhelmed by his proximity and the memories of what we'd done last night. "No, I'd love to have dinner, but my grandmother still hasn't regained consciousness, and I don't know how long I'll be here."

He frowned. "Damn, I'm on my way to a seminar now. But I'll be out in a couple of hours." He looked over his shoulder. I saw Violet walking toward us. "Text me later so we can meet up for coffee and make a plan," Sam said quickly and walked off.

Violet fluttered her eyelashes at Sam and drawled, "Hello . . ." as she walked past him. He nodded at her. I rolled my eyes. My sister the Southern belle.

"Well, well, Maggie May," Violet said as she jabbed the elevator button, "how do you know that doctor, other than biblically?"

Leave it to Violet to guess right away who Sam was. She started laughing when we got on the elevator. "I have unerring intuition when it comes to sexual attraction. How did you meet him?"

I felt my cheeks turning crimson. "I rear-ended his truck the night I got here."

Violet's eyebrows rose. She obviously wanted to hear more.

"And then I ran into him here at the hospital at the machine where I spilled coffee all over us."

Violet slapped her hand over mouth to stifle her laughter. "Sounds like this was meant to be. And his name is . . ."

"Sam Smart," I said, grudgingly.

"Hmm, M-A-S. Nice ring to it," Violet said.

"Huh? What are you talking about, Violet?" I said, genuinely confused.

"Your monogram, silly!" Violet said.

"Oh, my God, Violet, stop it! I'll probably never see him again. I'm leaving in a few days."

"Do you think of yourself as a fall or spring bride? Oh, do it in October! Your red hair will be beautiful with . . . I'm thinking emerald green and gold as your colors! Wait till Mom hears you snagged a doctor! She'll be thrilled! She might even be nice to you!"

"So dramatic, Violet. Please stop," I said, thinking

MAS would make a cute monogram. As if that would make a relationship strong.

What is it with us Southern girls and our dang names? Why do we have to print them or our initials on every single item we own? Violet did this, and it was overkill. Everything, from her doormat to her glassware to her bath towels, had her monogram on it. I wondered if she'd have to throw everything out when she and Chris got married. They only thing I owned with my monogram on it was my knife roll, and that's because Violet gave it to me.

Violet pushed open the door to Gran's room, which felt cold and empty. I wouldn't have noticed that, except that it was so different from the warm, cozy atmosphere of any room Gran usually occupied. She lay motionlessly on the bed with all the machines beeping softly around her. Violet and I grabbed chairs and pulled them up to Gran's bedside. It was ten thirty. Dr. King would be here soon. I had brought a book, but I was too nervous to read.

Looking at Gran, I knew she would hate to see us sitting around waiting on her like this. She had been the invincible matriarch in our lives for so long that it was deeply disturbing to see her lying there helpless. The doctors said that she might be able to hear us. I tried to send her a silent prayer, just to cover my bases, and looked for a response. I would take anything at this point. I was starving for an eye flutter, a twitch of a finger. I longed to hear her voice.

She was losing weight quickly. The skin on her normally rosy cheeks was dull. Her body looked like a vacant shell. I thought that maybe she was already someplace else, begging us to end it for her. I pushed away that frightening thought and looked over at my sister. She popped a peppermint in her mouth.

"Do you feel okay, Vi?"

She nodded and held out the tin of peppermints. "Want one?"

I shook my head. "When are you going to the obstetrician? Maybe she can give you something to help with the morning sickness."

"I have an appointment tomorrow morning. But I've been thinking about what you said, that when you're a member of a family, you don't just belong to yourself. That's why I'm so nervous about becoming a mom, Maggie. I'll be responsible for a tiny human. But I didn't get forced into motherhood, I entered it willingly, even sort of asked for it. So, I have to step up and get all my crazy together so I can be better for this child. I will be his or her model for adulthood," Violet said, inhaled, exhaled, and took Gran's hand. "Thank God we had Gran to show us the way."

"Violet, you shouldn't worry, you're going to be a great mother. And, yes, we were so lucky to have Gran, especially considering our—"

"We all belong to one family," Violet said, cutting me off, "and it's time we all started acting like it, because it's growing."

Just then Gran's eyes fluttered open, and she looked right at me. I gasped as adrenaline raced through my body. Then her eyes closed again.

"Maggie, did you see that? She looked at you, right? Gran?" Violet leaned over her. "Can you hear us? It's me, Violet, and Maggie's here, too! All the way from New York!"

"Violet, I don't know if she can hear us, but yeah, she looked right at me. Gran? It's me, Maggie. Open your eyes again! Call a nurse, Violet!"

"How do I do that?" She started screaming, "Nurse! Nurse! Help!"

"Violet, this isn't a TV medical drama. Isn't there a button we press, or . . ."

"Yes, there is! Sorry, I forgot." She smiled. "It's right next to her IV over there."

I looked down at the side of the bed and saw a little blue button with a cross on it. I pressed it and it lit up.

We waited, our eyes glued to Gran, watching her chest rise and fall. There was hope in the air. It had to be a good thing that she had opened her eyes. I wondered if she could feel any pain. I was silently praying that the doctors had given her generous doses of painkillers. Violet got up and started to pace. I leaned over Gran and called her name over and over, hoping she could hear me. I silently wondered if Gran perked up to hear the tea. Maybe she *could* hear us.

"What's going on?" A nurse walked briskly into the room and went straight to Gran's respirator and heart monitor.

"She opened her eyes," Violet said excitedly.

"She looked right at me," I added.

After checking Gran's vitals, the nurse touched her hand. "Mrs. Adams, can you hear me?" No response. "Mrs. Adams?" Still nothing. "I'm going to check her blood sugar level." She extracted a small sample of blood from Gran's arm and put it in a small square machine. "It's fine," the nurse said.

"Is she waking up?" Violet asked. "What's happening?"

"I'm sorry, y'all, I can't say for sure. Last night we started weaning your grandmother off sedation and lowered the ventilator setting because the numbers indicated she's requiring less oxygen supplementation."

"That sounds good," I said, hopefully.

"It is," the nurse said. "But your grandmother's

opening her eyes could have been a reflexive muscular action. It's totally normal and happens sometimes when a patient is unconscious, but it's hard on the family members who see it, because I know y'all want her alert." The nurse gave us a little smile and I felt our hope shrivel. "Dr. King is running behind schedule, but she'll be here soon and can explain in more detail."

"Oh. Okay," Violet said.

We both took our seats again and I stroked Gran's hand. The back of her hand was soft and cool to the touch, but inside it was callused from years of gardening, cooking, and raising women. The sunlight picked up the tiny flecks of glitter in the red polish on her nails. I wondered if her toes were the same color. I carefully untucked the sheet at the foot of the bed.

"Maggie, what are you doing?" Vi said.

"Electric blue nail polish? Gran is a wild woman!" I said.

"Yeah, she's all about the crazy colors lately. I love it. I do them for her. It's a sweet little activity," Violet said.

"Hmm, maybe do mine next? You did a pretty good job," I joked.

The nail polish reminded me of one of Violet's birthday parties when we were growing up. She invited all these girls from school over for a nail-painting party. Gran had covered the dining room table with plastic and bought all the tools the girls would need for manicures. There was nail polish everywhere despite the plastic. It became a joke finding different flecks of orange, green, and pink all over the house. It charmed me that Gran never tried to remove the little colorful marks. Just this morning I had seen a light-blue streak in the bathroom that I had never noticed before.

"I can't wait for her to wake up," I said. "Do you think she can hear us?"

"I think Gran can hear us no matter where we are!" Violet said.

"God, that's the truth. My phone always rings at the spookiest times. It's like she knows when I need her."

"Who's going to tell her about Mom and about Buster?" I whispered to Violet.

"Who's going to tell her about the baby? I don't know if it's better coming from you or me, but I know Gran will be worried," Violet whispered back.

"I'll tell her about Mom," I said quietly.

"I have enough to tell her," Violet mumbled.

"This woman is waking up to a whole new world," I said.

"Truth. She is going to be thrilled about you being here, though. Especially working at the restaurant," Violet said.

"Well, it isn't forever," I said, not looking at her.

"If you say so. To be honest, I'm kind of excited to see you sink your teeth into this project, applying everything you've learned in New York to our family's—"

Gran squeezed my hand then.

"Gran? Oh, my gosh!" I said out loud and squeezed her hand back.

"Did she just do something, Maggie?" Violet asked.

"Yeah, she squeezed my hand! Call the nurse again! Gran?"

Gran opened her eyes, closed them, then opened them again. I gave her the biggest smile. "Vi, her eyes are open and she's blinking normally. She's awake!"

I didn't realize my sister had left the room until she returned seconds later with Dr. King, followed by the nurse who'd come in earlier and a male nurse.

"Hey, Rose, welcome back," the doctor said.

I stepped away from the bed and watched Dr. King examine Gran. Then she studied Gran's chart and checked each of the beeping machines. "This is the kind of progress I like to see. You don't need that breathing tube anymore, your lungs are doing a good job on their own. Nurses, let's prepare to extubate Mrs. Adams." Dr. King turned to me and Violet. "It's going to take a little while to remove the breathing tube and make sure your grandmother can breathe comfortably on her own. She might need an oxygen mask and she might not be able to speak clearly right away. Why don't you both get something to drink and come back in a half hour?"

I was elated. "Thank you, Dr. King!" I walked over to Gran and patted her hand. "We'll be back soon for a good, long chat with you."

"We love you, Gran!" Violet added.

Violet and I were so excited, we were beside ourselves.

"I don't want anything to drink. I want to stay right here with Gran," Violet said. "We have to call Momma." She pulled out her phone.

"Good idea. Let's go into the waiting room and give everyone the good news."

When we got to the waiting room, there was a funny look on Violet's face. "She's not picking up."

Violet slumped into the chair next to me. "What should we do? Gran will want to see Mom."

"I'll call Alice and ask her to check on Mom, and she can drive her over. Alice is going to want to come here anyway." I took out my phone and saw a text from Sam. I couldn't deal with it right now. I called Alice and felt better as soon as I heard her voice. She was thrilled that Gran had awakened and said she'd be happy to pick up Lily and come right over.

"Okay, Vi, Alice will bring Mom over. Let's see how Gran is doing."

I was glad we decided to hover outside Gran's room, because Dr. King stepped out. "The nurses still need a few more minutes with your grandmother. She's doing well, but keep in mind that sedatives are still in her system, and she will probably fall asleep soon, which is normal. She's breathing on her own now with a little help from an oxygen mask, so she's not going to do a lot of talking. But you can go in and talk to her." Dr. King smiled warmly. "I'll check on her again this evening."

Violet and I barged into Gran's room without further ado. The nurses had partially raised the top of Gran's bed and she was almost sitting up. While one of the nurses straightened the oxygen line, another was changing the bandage on Gran's head. I don't think she'd ever looked more beautiful to me. I was thankful the bruises around her eyes were fading.

Gran raised her hand, motioning for us to come over to her.

"Can we hug her?" Violet asked one of the nurses.

"Gently. Everything needs to go gently right now," the nurse said, giving both me and Vi a meaningful look, and then a smile, before she and the other nurse left. I got the message and hoped Vi had, too. This was no time to spring a lot of big news on Gran.

We both gave Gran a gentle hug and sat down at her bedside. She said something, but I couldn't hear her through the oxygen mask, so Vi and I leaned closer to her, and I heard her mumble, "My girls. Where's Lily?"

"Gran, she's on her way over," Violet said. "Don't worry. She didn't get hurt in the car accident, just a sore shoulder. But you scared the poop outta us! I'm so glad you're awake."

Gran reached for my hand and her eyes widened.

I guessed she was surprised to see me. "Gran, of course I'm here. God, I'm so glad you're awake. You had us so worried! No early checkouts, lady. We need you, okay?"

Gran nodded and then closed her eyes, as if that simple movement had tired her out.

"Maggie's going to help out at the Lantern for a few days," Violet said.

Gran opened her eyes and nodded again.

"And Violet's busy with her photography business," I said, redirecting the conversation away from anything related to Mom and Buster, but Gran started to say something. I leaned closer and heard her say, "Happy to see my girls together. Go get Lily."

"She's on her way, Gran." I wished my mother and Alice would hurry up and get here.

I knew Gran had a long road to full recovery ahead of her, but I was so excited that she was back. Relieved, too. When she got stronger, we could bring her up to date on family matters, and she would know exactly what to do about Mom and the restaurant, and she could offer good advice to Vi about her pregnancy and her reluctant groom. I wouldn't mind getting some advice and encouragement from her, too.

"I think she's sleeping," Violet said.

I nodded. "Dr. King said the sedation hasn't worn off yet." Vi and I sat there gazing at Gran. I didn't want to be anywhere else. She could wake up at any minute, and I wanted to make sure she saw family when she opened her eyes.

A nurse came in, checked Gran's oxygen levels, and gave us a thumbs-up. "She needs to rest. We might be able to remove the oxygen mask later today."

I stepped into the hallway to call Jim and saw Alice walking toward me. My mother wasn't with her. My heart sank.

"How's Rose?" Alice asked.

"She's sleeping. Where's Mom?"

"Thank the Lord. Go get your sister."

I waved at Vi to come out to the hallway and we huddled with Alice.

"Your momma is sleeping it off with a half-empty bottle of vodka on her bedside table. There was no rousing her."

Alice shook her head. "She's grieving hard for her man, but she can't keep turning to drink for comfort. I know she don't like therapists, but she needs to see one. Buster's passing is too much for her to handle on her own."

I groaned inwardly. How were we going to get our mother to agree to professional help?

"But first things first," Alice continued. "Vi, go over to your momma's, try to get her up and help her get dressed and bring her over here as soon as you can. Rose needs to see her, otherwise she'll think . . . well, she'll be worried. Maggie, Jim and I put ten fresh cut-up chickens in the meat refrigerator, so you might want some extra prep time before the staff arrives."

My head was spinning. Alice gave Vi the keys to her car so I could have the truck to get over to the restaurant later. Alice and I went in to see Gran. She was still sleeping, but I saw the sweetest smile on Alice's face when she laid eyes on her old friend. "She looks much better without that big tube in her mouth."

"I agree. I'll be right back. I'm going to check in with Jim."

In the hallway, I clicked my phone on and heard the chime of a new email. It was from Chef Jamie. Glad he'd finally replied, I opened the email.

Maggie, In light of recent events, we have decided to end your employment with us effective immediately. You are no longer required at work. Best, Chef Jamie.

My heart stopped. I started to sweat, the back of my neck got hot, and I felt as if the hallway was spinning. I read the email again, and then another time to make sure I'd read it correctly. I had. I'd been fired.

Chapter 17
Magnolia

I needed to breathe. I walked into the waiting room, oblivious to everyone around me. *Chef had fired me.* After all this time, all my work . . . had been for nothing. Oh, my God. What was I going to do? I wondered who already knew. I wondered if Ronny knew. *Shit.*

I bit my lip to hold back the hardening in my throat and the tears that were threatening to spill out. I bit down harder and closed my eyes. *Stop it, Maggie! Get it together!* When I opened my eyes, I saw a couple of people gazing at me sympathetically. Thank God, Gran had awakened and was getting better. That's what mattered, not losing my job. But it did matter. That job meant a lot to me! One day I was up for a promotion, and the next week it was over.

I forwarded the email to Jim. Within moments, he

replied, and said he'd call me later. He also included some very colorful language not worth repeating. I took a trip to the bathroom to pull myself together. I was so angry, but I was also stunned. I didn't think this would happen. I mean, I supposed I'd feared it would happen if I made a horrendous mistake in the kitchen, but I never thought he'd drop the hammer on me like this. All I'd done was ask for—not demand—a little more time off for a family emergency.

I needed to be strong for Gran. I knew she would sense my distress and get worried. Thank goodness she was still asleep when I reentered her room. I told Alice I needed to do a few errands before heading over to the Lantern. She and I would talk later. I kissed Gran gently on the forehead and I did the same to Alice. She was the living, breathing definition of a great friend.

When I climbed into the truck, I started to take apart the minimal email. Chef had started with the phrase, "In light of recent events" and signed off with "Best"? I didn't understand. It just seemed so cold to end my years of employment with a two-sentence email. I had spent hours in his kitchen, learning, cooking. We'd spent so much time together, working only inches apart. Not all my memories of Bar JP were bad. Even Chef Jamie could be funny sometimes. I just couldn't believe it was all over. No, I wouldn't let all the time and heartfelt effort I'd put into my job go into the trash.

I took a deep breath and typed a reply.

Dear Chef Jamie,

I want to thank you for the opportunity to work alongside you and the team at Bar JP. Over the last two years, I learned so much from you, and truly believe that who I am as a cook is mostly to your credit. Thank you for taking the time to mentor me and mold me. My grandmother is on the mend, and I will return to New York City soon. With that in mind, I hope you will still consider recommending me for the next available position at Jean Paul's. I have worked very hard for you and I am loyal. I want to work there more than anything. Best, Maggie.

I swallowed my pride. I hit send. I immediately forwarded my email reply to Jim. Two seconds later, I was thinking, *Oh, man, what did I just do?*

On the drive home, I calmed down and started to feel proud of myself. I just didn't want to lose it all. I didn't want to think I'd sacrificed everything I had worked for to be with my family. *Fine, cut me out of Bar JP, Chef, but it's not fine not to consider me for the position I've been working toward forever!*

It occurred to me that I'd probably had the courage to send that email because Gran had woken up. I was no longer terrified that she would die. Gran was my source of strength, my lighthouse. If her light went dark, I wouldn't know in which direction to sail.

After I pulled into the driveway, I sat in the truck for a moment, realizing that I had driven the entire way home without turning on the radio. I'd just been listening to the voice inside my head. I rubbed my face, pressing my palms into my eyes. I realized that I had unintentionally blown off Sam for coffee. I grabbed my phone and sent him a text.

Hey! So sorry! I had to run. Rain check on that coffee?

I hoped he wasn't upset. I wanted to see him, but right now I felt the career side of myself pulling ahead of everything else. This was probably why the relationship with Ronny had gone on as long as it had— convenience. I wondered then what else I had let slide for the sake of my career. My family? I thought the answer was yes. I felt selfish, but I had to keep moving. I had a lot to do.

One of those things was my mom. She needed professional help, and I needed to figure out a way to present that option to her without causing another blowup.

I got out of the truck and walked into Gran's garden. Sam had given me those beautiful beets; maybe there were some vegetables here I could use for service, too. I was fairly confident Nancy Meyers could have gotten her inspiration for her kitchen gardens from Gran's. The white picket trellis was covered in climbing vines, and the soft, brown weedless soil was covered with winter squash peeking out from underneath velvety dark-green leaves. The island breeze carried the scent of Gran's rosemary plants. I went into the potting shed, grabbed the scissors, and snipped a bunch of rosemary. I could use it in the butter for the mashed potatoes that would be served with the fried chicken. I looked around at her herbs and listened to the tinkle of the wind chimes' sand dollars. I snipped some parsley and thyme. Those herbs would add depth or brightness to any dish. I also plucked a half-dozen bright-yellow lemons to add to the fish dishes. Gran liked to sing to her garden, so I started humming just to let the plants know their momma would be okay.

The garden was so peaceful and quiet but alive and busy at the same time. I was startled by the buzz of my phone in my pocket. It was a text from Sam.

Hey! No worries! I hope everything is ok? Wanna meet this Saturday for lunch at my farm? I'd love to show you around. 12:30?

I was glad I hadn't blown it with Sam and replied that I would see him then, and he sent back a smile. I couldn't wait to see him, but I had an ocean of issues to swim through before Saturday. Buster's funeral was looming, I had a restaurant to run, my mom, and Gran's health situation. I had to think about how we would hopefully transition her home. Not to mention my career looming in limbo. The screen door slammed shut and I turned around to find Jim.

"Hey, girl! I just got your email! I am just so proud, but oh, man, am I dying to know what he'll say! I bet he spit out his espresso when he read that email!" Jim shouted over to me. "You going over to the Lantern?"

"Yeah, in about thirty. Jimmy, I told you the bad news, but not the good news. Our girl is going to be okay! Gran woke up!"

"No! Oh, that's fantastic! Thank God!" Jim said.

"Yeah, she still isn't out of the woods, but it's a big step in the right direction," I said, smiling wide.

"Whatever! I'll take it! Forward is better than backward!" Then he waved me over and wiped some dirt off my face.

"I gotta talk to you. I've got a couple of situations," I said.

"More? How many situations do we have? Good Lord," Jim said and gestured for me to join him on the porch swing. "I'm getting whiplash!"

"Well, several." I kicked off my shoes and joined him.

Jim threw his arm behind me, and I kicked off a porch post. My heartbeat moved to the rhythm of the swing. I heard the chain catch and release with each click and push.

"All right, Magnolia, what we got now?" Jim said.

"I'm glad you liked my reply to Chef's email . . ."

"Liked it? I loved it. I was so impressed. You were professional yet strong and self-assertive to that jerk!"

"Right. But honestly, I feel shattered. I've never been fired from anything in my life! I don't want to tell my family about it, so for now I'm going to say I'm getting a week's vacation."

"So you're not going back to New York with me this weekend?"

I shook my head. "Gran's just starting to recover, my mother's in no condition to take care of her, and Vi's losing her mind because Chris is leaving town. She can't handle the restaurant on her own."

Jim inhaled deeply and bit his lip. "Got it. What else?"

"Lily," I said.

"Oh, man. So, what are you thinking?"

"I think she needs help, Jimmy. Professional help, right away. Help that includes a plan of action. And I need to present it to her without causing another blowup," I said.

"Hmm, like another rehab facility? Hasn't she gone to all of them?" he said.

"Basically, yes. And the most she got out of any of them was a boyfriend or two, never lasting sobriety. She needs something different! I wish I knew where we could get her the right kind of help," I said.

We swung for a moment, and I listened to the birds. The breeze was picking up, and it started to feel like maybe a storm was coming.

"I might have a solution," Jim said.

"Go on," I prompted.

"Well, whenever I don't know where to turn for expert help, I ask Auntie Belle. She knows the best doctors, lawyers, shrinks, trainers, hairdressers, tailors, et cetera. She may know of some new kind of rehab program. I'll give her a call. We better get moving. We have a lot to do for dinner, don't we?" Jim said as he got up.

"Yes, we do. Feel free to tell Belle anything, I don't mind. I'm gonna go wash my face, change my clothes, and I'll meet you out here in fifteen?" I asked. He nodded and pulled out his phone.

I went inside and made fast work of getting ready. Jim was waiting for me at the bottom of the stairs with a smile on his face.

"Belle's got a plan, and lucky for us she is in town. She feels terrible for Lily—suddenly losing the love of her life. She wants to take us—you, me, Vi, and Lily—to lunch or dinner someplace special like 82 Queen downtown—that's her fave. She thinks that would be the best way to broach a plan to get Lily some help. Friday after Buster's funeral or tomorrow, Thursday, for lunch. Which works?" Jim asked.

"Probably tomorrow for lunch. I'm not sure what condition my mom will be in after the funeral," I said.

"Yeah, you're right. Friday could be messy. But let's hope it isn't. Maybe I can find Miss Lily some Xanax," Jim said, half joking.

"Please! Slip it into her coffee," I joked back, feeling slightly guilty.

"Maybe I should find some Xanax coffee for all of us. We're gonna need it."

After a couple more phone calls—mine to Violet, who was with our mother at the hospital and managed to cajole Mom into accepting Annabelle's invitation, and Jim's to Belle to confirm—we were set for lunch tomorrow at 12:15. I was looking forward to it. Spending time with Annabelle at one of the loveliest restaurants in Charleston would surely lift anyone's spirits, even my mother's for a little while. Despite the cataclysmic email from Chef, I felt more in control of my world as I drove us to the Lantern.

When we got to the restaurant, Jim set his shopping

bag down on the bar. "You get into the kitchen and get to work, girl. I'm working the bar again."

"Oh, Lord, well, the locals best get ready for ya!" I said, shooting him a wink.

"Umm, excuse me, I'm doing it because someone needs a little supervision as far as the locals are concerned. Wouldn't want another Victoria's Secret demi-cup slingshot situation tonight. I have to keep my blue eyes on ya," he said. "Any update from the sexy, sandy farmer?"

"Oh, yes, sir, lunch and a farm tour on Saturday."

"For a roll in the hay?"

"Shut up!"

"If I find hay in your braids, so help me, Magnolia, I'll call Father Gregory so fast!"

"Don't worry, I'll give you all the details!" I said.

"Don't you dare leave out one word!" he said, pinching my arm.

I got into the kitchen and buckled down. I pulled my notebook out of my backpack and jotted down the changes I would be making to the menu. Aside from dressing up the fried seafood platter with homemade tartar sauce instead of using the bottled stuff, I wasn't changing much. Basically, I was sticking to what the Lantern was already doing but adding a special new entrée—Great-Grandmother Daisy's fried chicken with rosemary mashed potatoes—and a new beet salad. We still had plenty of mac and cheese to work with, and maybe we could make some chicken fingers from scratch for the kids. I wished I'd thought about ordering more than chicken last night. But thanks to Sam's thoughtfulness—I smiled as I remembered how thoughtful he'd been last night in the bar—we could offer more than an insipid garden salad to our customers.

I saw Ben in the corner sharpening a knife. He blushed when he saw me watching him. I had a young, inexperienced crew to work with, but at least they weren't standing around smoking cigarettes and eating fries, as they'd done when Nate was in charge.

I went into the office to find the supplies ledger so I could order sweet potatoes from the produce supplier for a sweet potato bisque I wanted to make tomorrow. I also needed to find a better supplier of dairy products. The eggs I'd used last night were okay, but they had small, pale-yellow yolks. Good chickens provided eggs with huge orange yolks that were the same color as the inside of a mango.

I pushed aside a few dirty dishes and coffee cups on the large wooden desk that had belonged to Daisy and shuffled through the messy piles of papers, some of which were stuck together. I saw bills from the previous months—had they been paid?—scrawled handwritten notes that I couldn't decipher, and brochures from several frozen-food suppliers. When I opened the file drawer, all I found were pads of order tickets that the waitstaff used. I noticed that the left foot of the desk was propped up on a yellowed phone book, and the desk chair's cushion was held together with a thick strip of duct tape. A sour smell was coming from the trash can. I decided to take the trash out. I'd get around to cleaning the desk later.

Violet burst through the back door. "Hey, Mags. Listen, everyone, staff meeting in the dining room in five, okay?" Violet said a little too loudly. She looked stressed. She pulled me toward her and said more softly, "I am so thrilled that Annabelle is going to find Mom some help. She really needs it. But it was so sweet to see Mom with Gran—"

"Vi, Mom didn't say anything about Buster to Gran, did she?"

"Well, I told her to steer clear of any upsetting topics of conversation, but Mom just broke down at one point and it all came pouring out."

I felt my face grow hot.

"But, Maggie, it's okay. Gran's okay. She didn't faint, her heart rate didn't spike. She just patted Mom's hand and comforted her. It was like old times. Gran's really getting better."

"I hope so."

"Come on, Mags. Into the dining room. I have a couple announcements to make."

Violet looked all business. She was wearing a black patterned skirt and a dark-purple silk blouse, gold French knot earrings and her pearls. Her dark-brown hair was pulled back in a ponytail, and she was holding a clipboard.

"All right, I know y'all might have heard some rumors about what's going on, and I'm sorry to have to tell you that Buster passed away yesterday," Violet said.

The room fell silent for a moment. Then Frankie burst into tears. Dark rivers of mascara were rolling down her cheeks.

To my surprise a few of the other servers were crying, and the male members of the staff looked sad. I shot Jim a look of disbelief. It became obvious to us that we hadn't realized how much the staff liked Buster. Clearly, I'd missed that memo. I felt the back of my neck get hot. I was embarrassed and angry at myself for making a negative snap judgment. These people who had worked with him had known him much better than I had. As I looked around the room, I saw staff members looking shocked and hurt. I heard people saying, "How did this happen?" "Poor Lily. They were so in love," and genuine expressions of concern for my mom. I felt a pang in my heart for her.

Violet told the staff about Buster's funeral on Friday

morning and that they were all welcome to attend. It occurred to me that it would be a good idea for me to go to the funeral. Not just for my mom, but for the staff. Maybe it would be a good move, politically. I couldn't believe how upset they all were, but eventually they calmed down.

Violet reached over to a tote bag she'd put on a chair and tossed it to me.

I unzipped the bag and found a white chef's coat inside.

"Violet? What's this?"

"It's Gran's old chef's coat. I want you to wear it. It's been a wild few days for the Adams family."

I held up the coat and saw that *Maggie* had been embroidered, no doubt by Gran, on the front panel. And on the shoulder, she had stitched a small white-and-green magnolia blossom. This coat was a tangible piece of evidence that Gran knew all. She knew that I'd be cooking here eventually. It made me smile as I ran my fingers along the embroidery.

"Everyone, my sister, Maggie will oversee the kitchen. Nate has moved on, so she will be making changes to the menu and keeping us afloat in the back until we can hire a new chef. She is taking time off from her job in New York to help us out, so let's all help her get up to speed and be successful."

Ben and Miller didn't look surprised by the news, and I guessed that Ben had told Miller. Word traveled fast. But they both looked so . . . clean. Odd thing to notice, but they were both clean-shaven. They also had real chef's coats on. They must have been scared or impressed. I was hoping it was both.

"Maggie, would you like to address the team?" Violet said, smiling.

"Uh, yeah, sure. Hey, y'all. For those of you I haven't met yet, I look forward to working with you. This is a weird situation for all of us, but I am happy to jump in. I've got some ideas to make the menu stronger, but please know, I'm here mostly to help, not to reinvent the wheel.

"I have loved this restaurant all my life. It's why I became a chef. Love of food and hospitality has been in my blood for as long as I can remember. This restaurant is my second home, that kitchen is basically my living room. What I mean to say is that the Magic Lantern is my heart. I hope that we can all work together to make it wonderful . . . even better than it already is!"

I hoped that my message was well received by the staff. I realized that I might have come off as controlling, and I wanted them to like me. We couldn't afford to lose any more employees.

Violet smiled at me. "Thanks, Maggie! Questions, anyone?" Violet asked.

Miller raised his hand.

"Yes, Miller?" Violet said.

"Yeah, I was wondering what kind of changes Chef Maggie is thinking of making? We're so used to doing the same thing every night, I just want to get on the right page."

"Maggie?" Violet nodded in my direction.

"Hey, Miller. First, don't worry about calling me Chef. Although I appreciate that, Maggie is fine. And, I'm glad you asked. I've been thinking about the history of this restaurant and how it's changed over the years. I thought it might be fun to bring back some of the classic dishes and remind our customers about what made us who we are, but not to do a huge overhaul of the menu . . . right away." I smiled at Ben but muffled a laugh.

"Like a greatest-hits menu?" Miller asked.

"Exactly! I want to keep the seafood platter, but maybe try it as a tower, adding in some raw options like oysters and clams. As well as maybe some . . ."

"Crab claws? Or lobster? Maybe even some tuna tartare?" Ben blurted.

"Sure!" I was shocked that these guys were so open to change. "In fact, today we're bringing back the original recipe for my great-grandmother Daisy's fried chicken. It's what started this place. Maybe we could offer two sides and some corn bread with it. Y'all ever hear of a blue-plate special, a lower-priced meal that changes daily?"

"Oh, cool! Kickin' it old school, Maggie? I like it!" Miller said.

"Yes! And I'm thinking of doing most things in house. I know that means a little more prep . . . and actually cooking, but I'm confident y'all can do more than defrost frozen food. Also, I'm open to new ideas— maybe a fantastic recipe for tomato pie or pimento cheese for a fun app. Those recipes that come from y'all's families, not cookbooks. Feel free to share."

I saw the cooks and even some of the servers nodding with approval, and I was thrilled that my ideas seemed to be going over well. I knew that even in my family's restaurant, there might be some pushback. There always was, but it seemed as if some of the staff were getting . . . dare I say it . . . inspired? I looked over at Violet, who was beaming at me.

Frankie came up to Violet and me at the end of the meeting and offered to help us organize a reception after Buster's funeral—bartending, flower arrangements, whatever we needed. Violet thanked her and said she'd check with Mom and Buster's daughters. It was really sweet of Frankie. I was sure we'd need an extra set of hands. God, there was nothing crazier than a Southern funeral. I wondered how many people would show up . . . and who.

I put on my new chef's coat and went back into the kitchen to do a quick inventory with Ben. He walked me through the mess of dry storage, as well as the freezer and walk-in refrigerator. We pulled out dozens of eggs, flour, salt and pepper, and some cayenne. Ben found me a few dredging trays and called Miller over.

"Okay, y'all, I'm assuming y'all's Southern mommas didn't grow no fools, and y'all know how to fry chicken, but I wanna show y'all how *I* fry chicken, and how I want it done in this kitchen," I said, noticing that I was slipping back into my Southern accent.

"Oh, so like, we don't just take the chicken out of the freezer and throw it in the fryer?" Miller said, smirking.

"Oh, no, we do not! It's a four-step process. First you want to take your portioned pieces of chicken and cover them with . . . wait, what is this?" I said, noticing that the salt I had asked for was fine-grain salt and the pepper was preground.

"Umm, it's salt and pepper," Ben said, looking at me as if I had lost my mind.

"No, boys, we don't use this kind of salt unless we're salting water. It's iodized salt. It has a metallic tang and makes the food taste too salty. Do we have kosher salt?

Also, don't y'all have a pepper grinder in y'all's knife kits?" I said, arching an eyebrow.

"I think there *might* be a box of kosher salt in dry storage," Ben said.

"Okay, go grab it, and while you're there, check for whole black peppercorns," I said.

Ben came back with a box of kosher salt and a giant plastic bottle of whole black peppercorns. Miller filled his old pepper grinder with peppercorns.

"All right, let's start by preparing the dredging pans." I watched as Ben and Miller followed my instructions.

"Parmesan cheese?" Miller said. "We're not cooking Italian food."

I rolled my eyes. "Yes, keep grating it, and when you're done, whisk it into those eggs. Now you know the secret ingredient of our fried chicken."

Once the dredging pans were ready, I showed the young cooks through the four steps. They watched me closely, Ben, sweet baby—bless him—wrote everything down. The first step was to dry the chicken pieces with a paper towel, so they were tacky but not wet. This would enable the seasoning to stick to them. The secret here was not to salt too far in advance, because although salt helped enhance flavor, it also dried out meat. The second step was to dredge it in the flour mixed with cayenne pepper. After you shook off the excess flour, you put it into the mixture of eggs and grated Parmesan cheese. Finally, you dunked it into a second flour mixture that contained enough freshly ground black pepper to turn the mixture gray. This chicken was, as the kids say, fire, meaning it was so good. Its heat was balanced with the Parmesan cheese.

Miller showed me the fryer, which I noticed had been scrubbed so well it shone. I was pleased. The oil in the fryer, however, was old and smelled bad. I told the boys that fried chicken needed clean oil. They would have to change the oil after every three batches they fried. I also instructed them to prepare and fry all the chicken tonight. What we didn't use we could freeze.

"I thought you hated frozen food, Maggie," Ben said.

"I do hate commercially produced frozen food and food that's been frozen for a long time, but the freezer is a great place to hold freshly made foods, like fried chicken and house-made pasta, to make them last a few days longer," I said.

"I'd love to learn how to make pasta one day," Miller added.

"Didn't they teach you that at cooking school?" I asked.

"I dropped out," Miller mumbled.

Hoping enthusiasm could compensate for limited

training, I said, "On Saturday we can run a special. Wanna come in and help me?"

"Oh, hell, yeah! We're both in," Ben said.

"Cool," I said and smiled at their excitement. Maybe this would be fun.

After Miller switched out the oil, I showed them how to fry the chicken and to test the meat's internal temp to make sure it wasn't over- or underdone. Soon enough the kitchen smelled damn good. I let the boys sample the finished product.

The minute Miller took a bite he started dancing, and Ben joined in.

"Oh, God, Maggie! This is freaking good!" Miller said.

"Damn, girl, you fry chicken better than my grandma!" Ben said. Then, getting serious, he added, "Please, don't tell her I said that!"

"I won't." I laughed. "But all the credit goes to my great-grandmother Daisy."

Later I showed Ben and Miller how to make one of the mother sauces, béchamel, and how when you add cheese, it becomes Mornay, the perfect sauce for mac and cheese, which we then added as a side to the fried chicken.I brought over the bag of beets Sam had dropped off last night and told them how to prepare them for a new salad we'd be offering tonight, demonstrating knife skills when needed and giving compliments. I wanted them to enjoy working here, and I wanted them to want to learn.

Soon enough the kitchen was smelling the way it should. Ben asked if we could put on music, and I said it would be okay as long as we stayed on task. It wasn't long before people were smiling and sharing tastes of the dishes they were preparing.

"Here, try this!"

"Oh, man! That's slap-your-momma good!"

Alice showed up about an hour before service would start.

"Mmm, mmm, girl! Woo-wee, this kitchen smells good!" She was smiling from ear to ear.

"Well, you know, I'm dropping some of your knowledge on these kids! What are you carrying, Alice?" I said, pointing to the giant bag in her arms.

"Violet called me and said you were thinking of selling some oysters. I asked my cousin to pick up a bushel for y'all." She handed the bag to me.

"Oh, wow! Thank you, Alice! What do I owe you?"

"Just your life. I got some pies in my truck and another bushel. Can you spare some hands to help me unload?"

The cooks went outside to Alice's truck and brought in six pies, a crate of veggies, and a bushel of fresh crabs. I was beside myself with excitement.

We took out large hotel pans, filled them with ice, and poured the oysters and crabs on them to keep them fresh. It was a beautiful sight.

Her veggie basket also included the juiciest grapefruits I'd ever seen. I decided to serve them alongside the beautiful crab. My mind was going crazy with different ways to combine all these fresh ingredients. In New York we had wonderful seafood and produce, but most of it was imported. According to my palate, though, no crab was tastier than one that had been swimming a hundred yards from your table earlier in the day.

Jim showed up and grabbed a few of the grapefruits for another signature cocktail. I just loved that everyone felt so inspired. Maybe this revamping of the Lantern could work. Violet came in with a blackboard and decided to write all the new offerings on it, calling them blackboard specials until we could print out a new menu.

After service started, the tickets poured in fast! I couldn't believe it at first, and then I learned that Jim had posted the blackboard specials on his social media and Violet had put them on the Magic Lantern's Facebook page. Evidently, locals heard the news and brought their neighbors. I noticed fewer tourists than before. We were so busy filling orders of the fried chicken, I was literally sweating, but I was smiling, too, and so were the other cooks. We were enjoying this! What a different vibe from last night.

I should have known that it was a little too good to be true. At 7:00 p.m. Frankie came into the kitchen in tears.

"Oh, my God, y'all, the biggest B's I've ever met are out there, and they hate just about everything and are making the stupidest demands. I'm gonna lose my Jesus, y'all. I'm serious!" Frankie slammed down a few plates.

"Whoa, Frankie, are those their plates? What's wrong with them?" I asked.

"Maggie, nothing's wrong with them. Every single person in this restaurant has been basically licking their plate, but not these two. Maybe they're disappointed that it's not made of gold? Hell, I don't know! I think they just wanted to complain and make me miserable. Well, mission accomplished!"

I shot the cooks a look.

"Who are these women? Are they regulars?" I asked.

"I don't know, they obviously crawled straight out of hell," Frankie said.

"Okay, Frankie, take a beat. Let me see what's going on," I said. "Go grab a water."

After asking the boys if they had a hold on it, and

they said they did—most of the tickets were for burgers and fried chicken, which was something I was confident they could handle—I took off my apron, pushed open the saloon doors that led to the dining room, and looked for Violet.

I found her behind the bar slinging cocktails with Jim. Her silk blouse was stained, and Jim wasn't even looking up or sassing anyone. It was as busy out here as it was in the kitchen. I decided not to bother them and just see if I could find the obnoxious customers myself. It didn't take long. There in the middle of the dining room were the two meanest-looking girls I'd ever seen. Now, I lived in New York City, where resting bitch face is a real thing, but this was different. One of them looked as if she was smelling something offensive and the other just looked plain bored and unimpressed. I wondered if anything had impressed this woman in her entire life.

One of them had curly blond-on-blond hair that was pushed back from her face with a pink headband that matched her pink Lilly Pulitzer dress, milky-pink manicure, and pink Jack Rogers sandals. She was tanned and toned and rocked an enormous diamond on her left hand. Ugh, I'd grown up with girls like this. The other one had long, glossy brown hair, straight as an arrow, and was wearing a lime-green sweater set, with the cardigan caped over her shoulders, and gold

Jack Rogers sandals. She, too, had a door-knocker ring. Why were they complaining about the food? Lord, this was up to me. I straightened my back, took a deep breath, and moved toward their table.

The girls glared at me through their fake eyelashes and perfect liquid eyeliner. The glossy brunette's lip curled up higher than Elvis's ever had. They must have seen that I was looking at them and heading in their direction, because their snarls quickly melted into smirks. The blonde gave me a once-over and looked appalled by my shirt, black leggings, and clogs.

I made my way up to the table, putting on my Southern armor, my smile.

"Hey, y'all, I heard there was a problem with the food? I'm the chef, how can I help?"

The blonde shot the brunette a look and giggled behind her dainty hand.

"Oh, darlin', we know who you are! The food is absolutely delicious! I just wanted to play a little joke, now that we share a restaurant! I'm Dixie and this is my sister, Caroline." The brunette, obviously the dominant one, stretched out her hand to shake mine. Her hand was limp and freezing cold. I wondered if she had any blood in her.

"I'm sorry, what? How do we share a restaurant?" I asked, confused.

"Oh, you sweetheart, you didn't know? Our father, Buster, owned fifty percent of the Magic Lantern!" Dixie said, and they both made a dramatic sign of the cross.

"Yes, sugar! Bless my poor daddy!" the blond one, Caroline, said in a grating, high-pitched voice.

"I'm sure you are mistaken. My grandmother Rose Adams, owns this restaurant," I said, starting to feel the room spin.

"Oh, sweet girl, you're out of the loop! Your momma got your grandmother to sign over half of the restaurant when Daddy covered the renovations . . . although this menu looks nothing like the fun fish shack Daddy described."

I felt my cheeks get hot and my heart start to race. Could this be real? Were these chicks telling me the truth? Violet appeared at my side and looked stressed.

"Well, hey, there, Miss Violet, you look like someone rode ya hard and put you up wet!" Dixie said with a laugh.

"Oh, well, it's been sort of busy here tonight," Violet said, straightening out her skirt and noticing the stain on her blouse. She blushed. "So nice of y'all to stop by. I didn't see you come in. How are y'all doing?"

"Actually, Magnolia and Violet, we're both so upset about Daddy . . . like your momma. Spoke to her this afternoon. I'm super happy now, though, to see y'all. I suppose we should be prepared for a shared future together, even without the wedding. Guess we are family now in business! Oh, and we have some suggestions we want to pass along for this place."

"Oh, yeah, we do! We could have a real-live business meeting! Does tomorrow work?" Caroline asked. The sisters grabbed each other's hands in excitement.

"Umm, no, we have too much going on tomorrow as it is," I managed to squeak out. I felt like I was going to faint. Trying to imagine sharing anything with these two women was painful.

"Sorry, y'all!" Violet said through a smile that looked more like a grimace.

The sisters didn't look happy. "Well, I'll just drop off our list tomorrow!" Dixie said. They both pushed back their chairs and stood up, not even bothering to push their chairs in.

"I'm assuming this is on the house, right, partner?" Caroline said, pointing her finger at the table.

The women laughed, slid their expensive bags into the crooks of their elbows, and walked out, sashaying like cats wagging their tails.

Chapter 18
Magnolia

When the girls left the dining room, I stood there taking deep breaths. I looked over at the bar, which was crazy busy. Jim was clearly getting slammed with his signature drinks but took a moment to shoot me a look. I just couldn't wrap my head around it. How did this happen? I saw that Violet was avoiding my gaze. I grabbed her elbow and led her directly into the office.

The restaurant was still busy, but dinner was slowing down. I poked my head in the kitchen to check on the tickets and make sure that there weren't too many orders flying in and that the cooks could handle it. I took a breath.

"Talk to me right now, Violet," I said, using my big-sister voice.

I searched her face. She was looking at her feet and tugging at her skirt. A curl had escaped from her ponytail, and she tucked it behind her ear.

"We didn't want to tell you, Maggie. We didn't see a need to tell you. You were up in New York and didn't have anything to do with the Magic Lantern." She saw the expression of disbelief on my face. "I know we should have," she said almost inaudibly.

"Uhh, yes, you should have! What were y'all thinking? Gran can't know."

"No, Gran knows. She wasn't happy about it. We were concerned about losing the restaurant, Mags. It got really bad last year. Mom was running things into the ground—"

"Wait a minute! When I got here Sunday night, you told me Mom was doing so well running the restaurant," I said.

"She was after Buster stepped in. While he clearly doesn't have the best taste, he had a better head for business than Mom, and he did have some deep pockets and a dream of running a restaurant," Violet said, a little defensively.

"Good Lord, Violet." I shook my head. "So, what's the damage? How much money do we owe these monsters?"

"Oh, a hundred thousand dollars . . ." she said.

"One hundred thousand dollars?" I gasped.

She nodded. "Which is probably why they consider themselves our partners."

"Violet! What in the world? The restaurant looks so cheap!" I was shocked.

"Well, Maggie, money is a strange thing. Price has nothing to do with taste."

"That's the truth," I grumbled.

"I didn't know Buster had told his daughters about his investment in the restaurant. I figured the girls wouldn't find out and this might . . . just go away."

"Are you high?" I asked, only slightly joking.

"No, I am not. Goodness, Maggie!" Violet said indignantly, gesturing to her stomach.

"What about Gran?"

"She wanted to keep the restaurant, no matter what. Her hands were tied, and she made me promise not to tell you, or worry you," she said.

"That doesn't sound like her," I said.

"Well, she never really said not to tell you, but when Mom and I realized that she hadn't told you, we assumed . . ."

"Omitting the truth is also lying. Jesus, this family!" I tried to sort all this out. First thing I did was whip out my phone. "Time for a quick little social-media stalking session."

"Now, Maggie, what is that going to solve?" Violet said.

I rolled my eyes at her and typed in Dixie's name, but then realized I didn't know her or her sister's last names. *Okay,* I thought, *use your skills.*

"What's Dixie's last name, Vi?"

"Oh, Maggie, give me your damn phone," she said. She tapped for a minute, then said, "Foster."

"That was fast!" I said.

"Amateur! I just went through the only account I knew, Buster's. I switched out of Instagram and changed over to Facebook. Let's be honest, people of a certain age are more active on Facebook than Instagram."

"You really are wasting your talents here. I think the FBI is recruiting," I said.

"Please," she said.

I watched her scroll through Buster's profile and found pictures of both of his daughters. There was one of him on Sullivan's Island with his arms around both of them, a cigar in his mouth. The girls were in bikinis, looking like Playboy bunnies, which was odd, as they were his daughters. We searched a little deeper and found out that Dixie was married to a man named Chip Foster who was a successful cosmetic dentist.

"Good God, this chick's teeth are so white they are almost blue!" Violet said.

They were as bright as snow on a sunny day. I looked at Dixie's teeth more closely; they looked a little too good. Oh, Lord, the woman was Botoxed, pulled, and was sporting fake teeth! I wondered if you would have to worry about cavities with fake teeth.

"Let's find the other one," I said to Violet, very impressed with her skills.

"Here she is!" Violet said.

Caroline was about as orange as a clementine. *Somebody needed to lay off the spray tan,* I thought. One of the photos posted showed Caroline stretched out in a chaise longue on a big electric-green lawn. She had married the owner of a landscaping business in North Carolina.

I was worried. From the intel we were gathering I saw that Buster's daughters had plenty of money, no jobs, and tons of free time to fight a battle with us. Not to mention enough bad taste to do serious damage to the Lantern if they got involved.

We were in deep trouble. "Violet, we have to figure this out," I said.

"How? We have zero extra funds," she said. "But wait! Buster loaned us the money about seven months ago, and Mom was confident it would be repaid quickly from the Lantern's higher profits. We need to check the accounting ledgers. Maybe the money's been paid back, and Dixie and Caroline don't really have a claim on the restaurant," Violet said hopefully.

I looked down at the messy desk and my stomach turned queasy. "Okay, you'll have to show me where Mom and Buster kept the books. There has to be some paperwork or agreement or something. And don't say anything to anyone, not even Jimmy, about our supposed new partners. What if they are just trying to scare us? Maybe they don't actually have any intention of getting involved!"

"Those girls looked giddy about being more than silent investors, Maggie. Didn't you hear them? They have ideas!" Violet said.

I pushed her out the door into the dining room and hopped back on the line intending to finish service, but the incoming orders had slowed down. At a quarter to ten I decided to start the closing routine. One of the things I wanted to show the team was the proper way to store and organize food, so I filled them in on the new procedure for breaking down their stations and properly cleaning them. No one would leave until we were all done. I knew that would make everyone work faster. As we rage-cleaned the kitchen, I got really worried. I had no idea how deep our mother had gotten us. Why had the restaurant been in this kind of financial trouble? I hoped it wasn't as bad as it seemed. I also thought that talking to Gran would be helpful, if I could figure out the words.

When the kitchen was clean, the tickets were done, and the food was wrapped up and put away, I did a quick inventory of the produce. In addition to the beets, I also found a long butternut squash in the box of gifts from the garden. Laughing at myself because its suggestive shape brought a few erotic images to mind, I put it back into the crate. I was looking forward to seeing Sam again. Okay, Maggie, stay on task. Time to track down Violet and take a look at the restaurant's books. How did we wind up in bed with Buster's daughters? *Oh, bed*, I thought. Stop thinking about Sam!

After checking in with Alice, who told me Gran was sleeping and the nurses were pleased with her progress, I decided to hold off on visiting her until tomorrow morning, when she would be awake and perhaps even talking. I gave Jim a big hug of thanks for all his great work at the bar and told him to head home and relax while Vi and I "straightened up a few things in the office." After a half hour of sifting through the piles of paper on the desk and examining an accounts ledger that wasn't up to date, very little had been straightened up or straightened out in my mind about the Magic Lantern's financial position. I agreed with Violet that the best course of action would be to wait until after the funeral to bring Mom in to show us her record-keeping systems and procedures.

"Our top priority is to get Mom to that lunch tomorrow so Belle can convince her to get professional help," Vi said. "I'll pick her up, and we'll meet you at 82 Queen."

Feeling discouraged, I walked home alone after locking up the restaurant. I reminded myself that Gran was awake and getting better. She'd know how to handle this problem. The cold wet air hugged me and I could hear the ocean waves rolling in and crashing on the shore. Making my way down Middle Street, passing the huge light-blue water tower and the Island Gamble on my left, I looked up to see Miss Maggie and her husband on the porch swing. Their niece Beth was out there, too, drinking a glass of wine with them, laughing. I'd always loved that family, I didn't know them well, but Beth's momma, Susan, and Susan's husband, Simon, used to come into the restaurant often. They were so in love, everyone could tell, and I secretly hoped to grow up to be like Susan.

I turned the corner on Station Twenty-Eight and looked behind me to locate the lighthouse. I loved its weird shape, and its fading black and white paint. There was something about lighthouses that always made me feel secure. Maybe because their beacons had once led people home. It made me dream about Sam a little, too. Charleston is a major port city, so there are always container ships passing by the island. Their fog horns had provided the music I'd fallen asleep to when I was growing up.

When I arrived home, I didn't see Jim but heard him talking on the phone in his room. I washed the day off in the shower, got into bed, and drifted off to the sound of my favorite music.

The next morning I raided Violet's closet for something to wear to lunch. I chose an outfit that my mom would approve of. It was one of Violet's many Lilly Pulitzer dresses. This one was solid black except for a gold ribbon around the V neck. I paired it with gold flats and went over to the mirror. I looked like I was in a uniform. I unzipped the dress and returned it to the closet. That wasn't me back when I'd lived in the South, and it wasn't me now. I went back into my room to see if there was something in the armload of clothes that Jimmy had packed that I could wear to the lunch. I found a floral blouse hanging in the closet that must have been Violet's. I put it on and was surprised that it not only fit but was super comfortable in a favorite-blouse kind of way. Then I found my skinny jeans, and my pearl necklace, a high school graduation present from Gran. I felt put together enough to please both my mother and my grandmother. After I put on some rose-colored lip gloss and mascara, I didn't look half bad! This outfit felt more like me, more casual. I slipped into my flat brown leather strappy sandals and was out the door. While I felt a certain amount of trepidation about the lunch with my mother and Belle, I couldn't wait to see Gran.

Jim was already outside standing by the truck, looking as if he'd stepped right out of a Gucci advertisement. He was wearing a very posh sweater, tailored slacks, no socks, and loafers, and a pair of thick black-framed glasses that were purely cosmetic.

"Well, well, well, James. You look nothing short of fabulous!"

"Thank you, Maggie! I was going for editorial," he said. "Not too bad yourself. Very modern Southern. I approve."

I drove us off the island, down the causeway, through Mount Pleasant.

"Hey, love, why don't you tell me all about the two nasty Nancys that waltzed in and ruined y'all's good mood."

"Jimmy, we've got another problem, but I really don't know how we're going to get out of this one," I said.

"Well, we are just lousy with problems over here. And we thought New York was hard?" he said.

I explained that Buster's daughters considered themselves my family's partners in the Magic Lantern because their father had apparently invested over a hundred thousand dollars in the restaurant.

"Good Lord. So what do we do? We obviously have to buy them out!" Jim said.

"Yeah, but we can't afford it," I said.

"Well, I'm sure I could ask Belle for a loan," Jim said softly.

"I am so in love with you for offering, but no, babe. I can't let you do that. I need to figure out another way. Thank God Gran woke up. When she gets stronger, I'll tell her what's going on. Maybe she'll have some ideas," I said.

After we went over the Ravenel Bridge, it wasn't long before I pulled into the MUSC parking lot. We stopped in the gift shop and bought a pretty vase of flowers for Gran. When we entered her room, my heart soared. She was sitting up in bed without the oxygen mask.

"Gran! No mask! I am so happy to see your beautiful face!" I gave her a hug and a kiss on the forehead.

Smiling, she put her hand on her throat. "I'm still a little hoarse, but I'm so happy you're here, Magnolia. And Jimmy, you, too."

Jim came over to Gran's bedside. "Mrs. Adams, you made the sunshine brighter when you woke up yesterday. We are so relieved that you're getting better." He set down the vase of flowers on the table by the window, so they'd be in Gran's direct line of sight.

"Thank you for the lovely flowers," Gran said. "Can't wait to get back into my garden."

"Just give it a little time, Gran," I said. "I can't wait to join you there. Your herbs are doing great. I took some rosemary, thyme, and parsley to the Lantern for dinner service last night. Oh, my gosh, Gran, I love the chef's coat. You embroidered my name and that beautiful magnolia? Violet gave it to me yesterday."

The mischievous smile on Gran's face as she winked at me lifted my heart. She seemed like her old self. "I knew you'd be cooking at the Magic Lantern one day, Magnolia. I know you're just helping your mother until she regains her bearings, and I so appreciate that, but I don't want this to interfere with your career in New York."

"Don't worry, Gran. I'm able to take some time off from my job." I smiled even though I was lying to my grandmother.

After Jim excused himself to get some coffee for us, I pulled a chair up to Gran's bed and took her hand. "How do you feel, Gran? Is anything bothering you?"

"My throat's sore and I'm still feeling a little sleepy, but I'm more concerned about Lily than I am about myself. I was so relieved when I saw with my own eyes that she didn't get hurt in the car accident. But I could tell something was wrong, and then she told me about Buster." Gran shook her head. "Unbelievable. Your mother has suffered so many losses."

"Gran, I don't want you to worry about Mom. You have to focus on your own health. Please, we need you, we love you. Violet and I are here for Mom, ready to help her in any way possible. Annabelle is taking all of us to lunch at 82 Queen today. When Jimmy told her about Buster's sudden death, she wanted to do something for Mom, try to lift her spirits. And you know Annabelle has lost a couple of husbands, so we're hoping she can give Mom some advice on coping with her grief." *No need to burden Gran.*

"That is so thoughtful of Annabelle. She is a fine woman. And I know you and Violet will help your mother. She couldn't ask for better daughters, and I couldn't ask for better granddaughters." Gran frowned. "There's something I wanted to tell you and Violet— it's important—but I just can't think of it right now."

I patted her hand. "It'll come to you. You suffered a pretty bad bump to the head, lady. I'm just glad you're not calling me Violet or Lily!"

"Caffeine at last!" Jim said, walking in. He handed me a cup, pulled up a chair, and joined us.

As Jim regaled Gran with the news of his latest audition for a doctor's role in *ICU New York*, I wondered if the "something important" Gran wanted to tell me and Violet concerned the money Buster had invested in the Lantern and what it had entitled him to. I was wary, though, of bringing up anything that would make her anxious. Clearly, she was already concerned about my mother.

I saw Gran close her eyes, and I looked at Jim, who raised his eyebrows. "Don't worry, you're still a scintillating conversationalist, it's just that the sedation still hasn't worn off. Maybe we should let her rest." I stood and kissed Gran on the cheek, and Jim and I walked out to the nurses' station, where I was assured by one of the nurses that Gran was doing fine and that Dr. King would stop by to see her this afternoon.

It was only eleven thirty, so Jim and I decided to head downtown and walk around the historic district where 82 Queen was located. Gran's old truck struggled down some of the one-way cobblestone streets, but we got lucky and found a parking spot a few blocks away from the restaurant. As we walked down to the Battery at the tip of the Charleston peninsula, I once again felt grateful for Charlestonians' sacred allegiance to land-

MY MAGNOLIA SUMMER • 301

marks and anything old. That's what made Charleston one of the most beautiful cities in the country. The Old City had a low skyline of buildings with tile roofs and quaint chimneys and a cobblestoned streetscape with gas lanterns hanging from wrought-iron poles. It was called the Holy City for many reasons, one being that until recently, no building could be built higher than the tallest church steeple. I couldn't resist doing a few dance steps on the checkerboard sidewalk in front of the John Rutledge House on Broad Street. It dated back to the late eighteenth century—Rutledge had been a signer of the Constitution—and I loved the front entrance's romantic ornate wrought-iron fencing.

"What a vista!" Jim said as we reached the Battery, where the Cooper River on the east side of the peninsula and the Ashley River on the west side flowed into the harbor. We walked through the waterfront park, which was filled with war memorials, cannons, and statues. "You can keep New York Harbor, Magnolia. Charleston Harbor is still the top to me."

I laughed because when we were in high school Jim had constantly talked about moving to New York City, and how much bigger and better in every way it was than Charleston. Now he was proclaiming the superiority of Charleston's harbor. But I knew what he meant. While both harbors were impressive, Charleston's Battery was more charming and quaint—and cleaner—with its White Point Garden. We strolled around the Battery, stopping so Jim could pay his respects at the monument where the eighteenth-century pirate Stede Bonnet was hanged. I heard the first chime of the bells of St. Michael's. "Come on, we better start walking back. It's twelve o'clock."

"Bells to remind us of our date with Auntie Belle!" Jim said, although he seemed reluctant to turn his back on the glorious view of the harbor, where sunbeams danced over the water. "You know, St. Michael's bells were removed from the steeple twice. First, by the British, as punishment to the rebels during the Revolutionary War, and then by city officials who took them to Columbia for safekeeping during the Civil War. Only one was left behind to ring an alarm for Charlestonians still in the city. When the Yankees took the city in 1865, the bell rang dutifully until it cracked."

"You are such a history nerd, Jimmy. Very impressive."

"Well, Charleston is in my blood. Yours, too, Magnolia."

The sight of the pale-yellow façade of 82 Queen with the large golden numerals on the small black awning over the narrow entrance always made me smile. It was one of the grand dames of the Charleston restaurant scene. Opened in 1982 and comprised of three adjoining eighteenth-century town houses and a courtyard, it was the first restaurant to combine the local African, French, Caribbean, and Anglo-Saxon tastes to create a new culinary genre known as Low-country cuisine. Anytime I had a meal there it made me feel like I was eating my heritage. My family had celebrated more than a few special occasions there.

The maître d' led us into the famous ivy-covered courtyard, where Annabelle was sitting in one of the butterfly-back white wrought-iron chairs at an umbrella-covered table. The air outside suddenly became lighter. It was like Christmas morning for me, I was so excited to see her, and I instantly felt as if everything would be okay. She stood and gave me a hug. "Oh, my girl, Maggie, it's so good to see you!" She turned to give Jim a hug. "Jimmy, darlin', you look like a movie star!"

"Look who's talking, Auntie Belle," Jim replied, blushing.

"It's a tad chilly for April, but you know Charleston. I figured this was okay under the heat lamps?"

Annabelle looked beautiful and elegant, as always, with her lustrous brown shoulder-length hair and big hazel eyes enhanced by the exact right amount of makeup, but she wasn't in her usual flashy garb. Today she wore fitted charcoal-gray trousers, black leather kitten-heel ankle boots, and a pale-blue pashmina shawl over a cream-colored silk blouse. Her wrist held the most iconic Charleston bracelet from Croghan's Jewel Box on King Street, the club bracelet. It was a thick gold rope with small diamonds down the center that lit up her wrist with every expression she made. Surprisingly conservative attire for a lady who favored leopard-print everything.

Jim held his aunt's chair for her and then did the same for me. When all three of us were seated, Annabelle got right down to business. Giving my hand a gentle squeeze, she said, "I was so relieved yesterday when Jimmy told me your gran regained consciousness and is on the mend. But I'm sorry you all had to experience so much anxiety and worry. And now, your mother is dealing with her fiancé dropping dead? Good Lord! Now, tell me before Lily and Violet arrive, how bad is it?"

Jim and I looked at each other, and he nodded at me encouragingly. "Bad," I said. "Momma's not at her best. She's hurt, angry, and she's drinking heavily. Even before Buster had the attack, she fell off the wagon and I caught them smoking weed at the restaurant." Belle looked concerned and nodded supportively, but didn't say anything, so I kept going. "I believe my mother loved Buster, but I think she also viewed him as her ticket out of Charleston to the life she wants and claims she deserves."

Annabelle arched an eyebrow. "And I imagine she is taking her anger out on you?" She had known our family a long time and was aware that I was my mother's scapegoat.

I didn't say anything, but Jim chimed in, "You got it. And Lily's been drinking until she drops. She needs help in the worst way, Auntie Belle."

Annabelle tapped a finger against her chin. I couldn't help admiring her fuchsia nail polish. "I see, a three-pronged problem—grief, addiction, and hopelessness due to thwarted dreams. Didn't Lily want to be a dancer when she was young?" No sooner did she say that than she stood, smiling and spreading her arms wide. "Here are my other Garden Girls!" I looked over my shoulder and saw my mother and Violet walking into the courtyard. *Garden Girls* was a nickname Belle had given our family. It would have been cheesy coming from anyone else, but I'd always felt flattered by the genuine affection the special name denoted.

My mother was dressed all in black—a tight-fitting, long-sleeved top, leggings, and large black sunglasses that covered almost half of her face. She looked like she was hiding from the paparazzi. She was so thin the sun shone through the gap between her thighs. Violet

looked like the perfect Southern belle in a green patterned shift dress with a matching cardigan draped
over her shoulders. But there was a special radiance
about her; I supposed it was that pregnancy glow. I
smiled widely at her and rose along with Jim as she and
my mother approached.

Once the hugs and greetings were finished, Jim said,
"Miss Lily, please take this seat." He stepped back
from the chair he'd been sitting in and held it for my
mother. "You and Aunt Belle so rarely get a chance to
catch up." He moved around the table and took a seat
next to Vi.

"Hey, Momma, you look so chic!" I said, knowing
my mother always responded well to compliments.

"Yes, you sure do, Miss Lily, you look très French!
Sending me some major Audrey vibes," Jim said.

No response from my mother, and with the sunglasses covering most of her face, all I could see was the
grim set of her mouth.

Annabelle directed a gentle smile at her. "Lily,
darlin', it's so good to see you and your fabulous daughters and my brilliant nephew. Now I don't feel so bad
about being dragged away from my pool in Palm Beach
to attend a board meeting for the Charleston Symphony. Jim filled me in on what's happened when we
spoke yesterday. When it rains it pours, does it not?

First your momma's car accident and now your fiancé's sudden . . . departure." Belle shook her head. "I don't know how you're holding yourself together."

"It's been a tough few days. I don't even know . . ." My mom's voice cracked, and she grabbed a tissue from her purse and slipped it behind her sunglasses to dab her eyes.

Annabelle placed her hand over Lily's. "Well, I'm so glad y'all could join me for lunch today. You need some pampering. Jimmy, call the waiter. Lily, honey, you're so thin, we need to put some meat on your bones. You don't want to lose your curves," Belle gently chided.

I saw my mom smile, and I blessed Aunt Belle. How did she manage to do that? Jim winked at me.

A young female waiter came over to our table. "Hey, Mrs. Williams, so nice to see you," she said, giving Belle and the rest of us a big smile as she handed out menus. "Welcome to 82 Queen! Is this y'all's first time dining with us?"

"Oh, no, we've practically been asked to pay rent!" Jim said.

"Welcome back! I'm Liz. I'll be taking care of you today. Here's some pimento cheese to snack on while y'all peruse our menu. How about drinks?" Liz set down a dish of crackers and the restaurant's delicious cheese spread, a staple of every Lowcountry home.

After my mother and Annabelle ordered sweet tea and the rest of us Diet Cokes, responding to his aunt's subtle gesture, Jim said, "Oh, I don't think we need the menus. I'll order for everyone. Let me see if I can remember everything. Maggie is easy, she would like the tomato pie. Aunt Belle will have the queen's salad, and she would like me to ask you to put the dressing on the side, but don't do that, because then she can make a big deal about having tried to avoid the calories and enjoy eating the creamy buttermilk-herb dressing anyways," Jim said, winking at his aunt.

"Violet would like to order a rare burger—ahem, please make it medium so she will not have to send it back—with French fries and a side of mayo, and Lily would like a cup of she-crab soup with absolutely no crackers or bread whatsoever. And I'll have the Carolina crab cakes."

"How'd I do, ladies?" Jimmy said, knowing that he had everyone's order right and was proud of himself.

"Well done, Jimmy," cooed my mother.

"I'm impressed!" Liz said. "I'll be right back with your drinks."

"You know I just want to take care of y'all, especially you, Miss Lily, you're like another momma to me," Jim said.

That comment must have hit my mother right in

the heartstrings, because she started to smile, but then she tightened her jaw. "Why do I all of a sudden feel like this is a setup?" she said, arching her eyebrow at Annabelle.

Annabelle looked at my mother with all the generous Southern honey she could muster. "Lily, this lunch is only about friends helping friends." Belle gently kicked me under the table, giving me my cue to strike up a side conversation with Vi and Jim.

"So, Jim, what's going on with the *ICU New York* audition? Pretty convenient that if you get the job— and I'm sure you will—you'll be working a few miles from home," I said.

"Oh, no! I'll be California bound. They shoot the series in LA."

"What?!" Violet and I said simultaneously.

As Jim explained the rationale for filming on a set in LA, I tried to keep track of two conversations, straining my ears to hear what Annabelle, who had leaned closer to my mother, was saying.

"I know what it's like because when John died, I went to pieces," Belle admitted. "And I know you've been through this before when you lost Scott."

"No, no, that was different. It didn't seem real," my mom said softly.

"What do you mean? Because it was so long ago?"

"Not just that. I did some foolish things with him, and my head was muddled. But he didn't love me." My mother was practically whispering, and it was almost painful to strive to hear what she was saying. ". . . all about the kids . . . especially Maggie. He only had eyes for his baby girl, gave all his love to her, it's as if I wasn't there, except for . . ." *What?!* "But with Buster, it's different. He really loved me, and we had so many plans to travel around the world after he franchised the Lantern—"

"Franchise your family's restaurant?" Annabelle looked aghast.

"Buster was a brilliant businessman. He picked out sites along the Carolina coast where we could open Magic Lanterns, you know, fish shacks for tourists, and make a fortune. Momma . . ."

I could have strangled Vi when she interrupted my eavesdropping. "Maggie! Maggie, are we going to visit Jim in Hollywood?"

My mother looked at me suspiciously and stopped talking. Thank goodness, Liz distracted everyone when she appeared with another server, carrying our entrées. "Hey, y'all, ready for some Lowcountry grub?"

Even though I was reeling from what my mother had said about my father, and her and Buster's plans for the restaurant, I didn't want her to know I'd overheard anything, so after the first bite of tomato pie, I said to Vi the first thing that came into my mind, which, admittedly, was kind of dumb. "Of course I want to visit Jim, but is it safe for pregnant women to take long flights, go through all those airport security machines?"

Violet crossed her eyes, as she'd done as a kid. "Duh, Maggie. Look at Angelina Jolie, she's always pregnant and flying around to save the world!"

Jim gently pointed out that half of the Jolie-Pitt kids were adopted, but he was sure air travel was safe for pregnant women.

"You look beautiful, Violet." Mom seemed relieved to change the subject.

"Thanks, Momma. We've got a lot to look forward to, Grandmomma!" Violet said, rubbing her belly.

"Lily, Violet is right. With so much to look forward to, you must take care of yourself and get some professional help at this difficult time. I did both times, when Thomas and John passed, and it worked."

Annabelle had let the bullet out of the gun, and we all took bites of our food, except my mother, who hadn't even picked up her spoon. My stomach was in knots as I waited for her counterattack, but Violet preempted it, saying, "Momma, we're gonna have a lot of fun with my daughter."

"Violet, you don't know that it's a girl yet," I said, not able to stop myself.

"Maggie, I can just tell," Violet insisted.

"Well, it probably is! I mean, y'all don't have boys, it seems," Jimmy said.

"Y'all are crazy and overreacting as usual," my mother said. "If you think I'm letting anyone call me grandmomma, you're out of your damn mind. I'll go by Mimi or Lovey."

My mother's counterattack wasn't as bad as I'd expected, and she picked up her spoon and started eating her soup. Jim arched his brow at me. Annabelle just smiled before taking another bite of her salad.

"Lily, do you know Carol Goodwin? She's a big fundraiser for Spoleto, has great style, never seen her out of a Chanel tweed. Well, she got a little carried away with food and drink after her husband died. Very sad. Poor thing couldn't even fit behind the wheel of her Mercedes convertible, but one day she did squeeze herself in and got stopped for DWI. Enough strings were pulled that she wasn't charged, and she decided that it was time for a little change of scenery. She booked herself on a monthlong wellness cruise that operates out of Charleston. When she came home, she was twenty-five pounds lighter and the only thing she drinks to excess is green tea. She told me she had a great time getting healthy. Now she goes back every few months for a little refresher."

"What do you mean 'refresher'?" Jim said.

"Well, Jim, while it's a luxury cruise, a good part of the luxury is the experts they hire to help passengers cope with stresses—loss of a loved one, loss of a job, plain-old aging, other life challenges—that lead to, shall we say, less than optimal behavior patterns. It's basically a rehab program on the sea! But you wouldn't know it by looking at the brochure. I took a peek at it, and let me tell you, that Ritz-Carlton cruise ship I was on last year probably got their interior design from this!"

"Wait, Annabelle, you're saying that your friend goes willingly on a rehab cruise?" I said, trying to back her up.

"Yes, ma'am! Carol gets to travel the world and work on herself! They have everything there! Spa, yoga, hair salon, and amazing food. I guess they want you to tackle one demon at a time, because they serve food by Michelin-star chefs!"

"What's it called?" Violet asked, pulling out her phone.

"Serenity Cruise. Google it, Violetta," Belle said.

"Oh, I'm on it. Wow! Look at this! A Kate Hudson look-alike leads the yoga retreat!" Violet said, showing us the drop-dead-gorgeous web page on her phone.

"Hold on, I've heard about this cruise!" Jimmy said. "I think a ton of celebrities have gone. I'm sure Lindsay Lohan has."

"Y'all just wait one dang-gum minute. There is no way I could ever afford a cruise like that! Besides, I don't have a problem! I can't leave the restaurant!" Lily said.

"Momma, you could leave it with us. Maggie is taking some time off from her job in New York, so she can help us out while you—"

My mother cut her off as she laser-focused on me. "This is why you came back after so long, isn't it? Momma's accident was a good excuse, and Buster's incident makes it even sweeter. With me wrecked emotionally, you can be the savior of the Magic Lantern, and I bet Momma supports it!"

"That's not true!" I protested.

My mother shook her head as she opened her purse and lit a cigarette.

"Lily, you can't smoke in the—" Jim said.

"Please!" Lily said, tossing the cigarette on the courtyard pavers. "I'm done with y'all and your crazy ideas. Did you beg Annabelle to come up here and dangle a ridiculous fantasy in front of me that can never happen? My life isn't a Lifetime movie, if you haven't noticed, and y'all aren't scriptwriters! Nothing in my life ends with a nice little bow on it. I can't afford a trip like that, and I don't need one!"

"Mom, please settle down, we are only trying to help," Violet said.

"Help? More like entertaining yourselves at my expense and also clearing the way for Maggie to take everything away from me again!"

Was my mother really saying this in front of other people?

"Lily!" Annabelle said. "You're not making sense."

Lily rubbed her eyes. Annabelle had disarmed her. She might hate me, but she respected Annabelle.

"Lily," Annabelle said more softly, "if you agree that going on the Serenity Cruise is a good idea, I'll pay for it."

"No. I can't take this. I'm outta here."

"Mom, please stay." Trying to stave off disaster, I grabbed her hand, but she snatched it away from me.

My mom stalked out, leaving us all sitting there shattered.

Chapter 19
Magnolia

Later that night I was thankful that service wasn't crazy busy. It was paced evenly, with the order tickets coming in steadily. Violet had set us up with an app called Resy that took a lot of the stress out of taking reservations. When I was in middle school, my "job" was to take down reservation requests on the old aqua Princess phone that had been in the restaurant for as long as I could remember. Now people did everything on their cell phones. In a way I was nostalgic for the old way, but this was simpler.

And tonight, I was especially grateful that Ben and Miller were quick studies, so the three of us could handle the orders without a lot of drama, because, to be honest, I was still going over in my head what I'd overheard at lunch. But I remembered that my mother had gone in and out of the hospital a few times after Dad had left us, and one of those times had been right after he'd died in the motorcycle accident. Gran had gently explained that she needed more "rest" because she was so upset about Dad. Vi and I had always assumed that her heartbreak had been more than she could handle.

After my mother had abruptly left the restaurant today, Violet had run after her to make sure she was okay and to give her a lift home.

As I prepped, I remembered the conversation.

"Maggie, I'm sorry I wasn't more helpful," Annabelle said.

I was still too dazed to respond, so Jim jumped in. "But you were helpful, Auntie Belle. You told Lily about the Serenity Cruise, and you even offered to pay her way."

"Of course you helped, and your offer to pay for her trip was so generous of you." I paused to take a couple of deep breaths. "I'm sorry if I seem out of it, but I'm shocked by what my mother said about her and Buster intending to franchise the Magic Lantern and her not feeling my father's death was real, and feeling worse about Buster's dying, and my father's not loving her and loving me more than her and Violet . . ."

Jim's eyes widened. "What are you talking about? When did Lily say all this?"

"While you and Vi were talking."

Annabelle reached over and took my hand. "Maggie, I'm sorry you heard all that. And it's probably best not to repeat it, because who knows if any of it is true? Your momma's hurting bad. She seems very mixed up. I think the best way for her to regain some perspective and learn healthier coping skills would be to go on the wellness cruise and get away from Charleston, which she seems to view as the land of broken dreams, for a while. Give me her email address and I will send her a brochure for the cruise and call her tomorrow to encourage her to go."

I knew Belle was a bighearted woman, but at that moment I understood why Jim considered her a fairy godmother.

The next morning Violet and I drove over to our mom's place. It was around eight thirty, and I wasn't sure if she'd even be awake yet. When we got to the door of her apartment, Violet didn't knock; she had a key and let us in. The place was an absolute mess, a drastic change from what I'd seen before. There were takeout boxes all over the counters, used glasses everywhere, and the place *stank*.

"Should we find Mom?" I asked.

"Maggie, I know where she is, she's asleep, and trust me, you don't want to wake her. Clearly, she's hurting."

It was better not to bicker. Violet started fluffing the

pillows and arranging magazines on the coffee table, then Mom came out of her room.

"Nice of y'all to drop by. I didn't know you were coming. I would have made something to eat or cleaned up a bit," Lily said and threw back a drink.

Uh-oh, I thought, and Violet must have thought the same thing by the look on her face. Violet put down a pillow and headed toward Mom.

"Violet, what did you expect?" Mom said with a shrug.

"Momma, nobody expects anything of you right now, we're just here to keep you company, and get you ready for what's ahead. This has got to be just awful for you," she said, giving her a hug.

My mother wrapped one arm limply around Violet, and with the other took a swig of her drink. Swaying on her feet, she lost her balance, and Violet almost caught her, but down Mom went on her butt, spilling her drink all over the carpet.

"Oh, no! Mom, are you okay?" I said, tossing Violet the paper towel roll so I could help our mother up.

"Mom?" Violet went to her, and my mother burst into tears.

"I'm so *not* ooooookkkkkaaaaaayyyyy!" she wailed.

"Mom, let us clean this up and maybe a quick shower?" Violet suggested.

Mom nodded, and Violet left the room. I heard her crank the shower on.

"Come on, Momma," I said softly.

"Don't you pity me, Magnolia. I'm fine. I can handle anything. I handled *you*, I can handle this."

"Mom, let's not fight, okay?" I said.

"You're not the parent here. I am. Okay?" She got up and swiftly moved to the little acrylic bar cart across the room, refreshing her drink.

I bent down and cleaned up her spill.

"I'm going to go get some doughnuts, be right back," Violet said and left.

I stood there in the apartment taking it all in, and then I heard the sound of glass shattering against a wall, then the same sound again. Tiny explosions, one after the other.

"Mom?" I called out. "What are you doing in there?" I realized my mom was throwing things in her bedroom, and I didn't want to get a perfume bottle or picture frame thrown at my face, so I decided to knock.

"Momma?" The noise stopped.

"Leave me alone, Magnolia," my mom said.

"I can't do that, Mom." I tried to open the door, but it was locked. I waited and nothing happened. "Mom, please, I want to help."

"God damn it, Maggie. Leave. Me. Alone." My

mom was now pounding her hands against the door. "You can't be here right now. I need to be alone. I need, I need . . ."

I stepped back from the door, which was shaking with every pound of her fist, and I thought of my sister when she was little and throwing a tantrum. My mom would just hold her until she calmed down. She would tell Violet, "It's okay. I'm here. I love you." I could hear my mom sobbing. She was literally wearing herself out. I heard her slide down the door to the floor. I decided to join her by sitting down on the floor on the other side of the door.

"Mom, it's okay. I'm here. I love you," I said, just like she used to say to my sister.

I heard her sobbing again. She sniffed and sighed deeply. She blew her nose. "I keep dreaming of him," she said. I pressed my ear against the door. "I dreamed that this was a misunderstanding, and that the empty space next to me in my tangled sheets was still warm from his body. I could see him smile in his sleep and even hear a little laugh. He threw his arms around me, pulling me close, opening his eyes, and saying, 'I love you, my angel' before drifting off to sleep again. I used to look at his face when he slept and wondered if his mother had seen the same sweet, peaceful expression on his face. When I opened my eyes, I realized I was waking up to my new life, my awful new life without him. Why does my subconscious play this awful game with me?"

"I'm so sorry, Mom," I said, feeling her heartbreak.

"Buster wasn't a complicated man. He was warm, and straightforward, and unapologetically himself. Whoever he loved, he loved fully. It was a world of black and white for him, not a mess of gray, like it is for me. He just loved me, period. He didn't want anything except to make me happy. I'd never experienced that before. Love for me always came with a price, and his love only came with a feeling of always."

"Mom, I had no idea . . ." I said.

"I know, Maggie. I don't think anyone . . . I really loved him." She started to cry softly again. "I'm such a mess."

As I sat on the other side of the door from her, listening to her cry, I realized I *hadn't* really known Buster and I had made some unfair judgments about him, my mother, and their relationship. My mom could be poetic. I had forgotten about that. She was a creative person, a dancer, she'd dabbled in painting and had been pretty good. When she spoke her heart, it was shattering.

I heard her get up and unlock the door. I took that as a signal that it would be all right if I entered, so I did. I saw her hugging a pillow and getting into bed.

I lay down next to her but was careful not to touch her.

She squeezed the pillow as she sobbed into it. She'd lost another man she loved and her hopes and dreams for the future. I was crying hard, too. I wanted my mom to know she was not alone. I don't know where all the tears came from, but it was like a waterfall of childhood trauma and current heartbreak. I cried for my mother, for myself, for my sister, for Gran.

My mother got up on her knees and started punching the padded headboard, seeming to enjoy the pain she must have felt in her knuckles. She just needed to hit something. She picked up the pillow and threw it as hard as she could across the room. It landed on the dresser, knocking perfume bottles to the floor. Glass shattered. I took a deep breath and let out a scream. My mom jerked up and looked me dead in the face and then yelled with me. She jumped off the bed yelling like a crazy person. I followed her. She spun around, went over to the dresser, and yanked open the drawers; one came all the way out and broke when it fell to the floor. I jumped out of the way and landed on a shard of glass that sliced my heel. She pulled clothes out of the fallen drawer and tore a few of Buster's shirts.

I grabbed what was left on the floor and helped her tear it up further. She threw a tiny vase, picked up a perfume bottle, and handed me one to smash.

We were wild together, destroying everything, making way for a new reality, I supposed. One I was unsure of, and one my mother didn't want to face.

I caught a glimpse of myself in the mirror over the dresser. My hair was in wild disarray, my eyes were red and swollen, and my makeup, left over from last night, was smeared around my eyes and on my cheeks. My reflection made me laugh. I looked insane. My mom looked at me, shocked at first, but then saw her own reflection and started giggling.

Suddenly I was aware of the pain in my heel and looked down at my foot. My mom was out of breath, but she looked at me, saw the blood on the floor, and grabbed me, pulling me into her bony embrace. We hugged for a long time. Then we stood there looking at each other.

My mom grabbed my hand, led me to the bathroom, and inspected my foot. She washed the cut and put a Band-Aid on it. I plugged the sink, filled it with warm water, and dunked my face in it. I patted my face dry with a cloth.

"I have to face this day, even if all I want to do is go back to sleep," my mom said.

I found my mom's broom and dustpan and swept up our mess, dumping all the broken glass and ripped clothes into another black garbage bag. One of the lessons my mother had taught me was never to try to save money on paper towels or garbage bags. Life's messes required the good stuff. When my mom came out of the bathroom, she went to her closet. She took out a few black dresses and laid them on the bed.

My mom chose a black linen sheath dress and put on her pearls like a good Southern girl. I found a cardigan and some red lipstick and tossed them over to her. She shot me a smile and nodded toward the bed. I looked at the dresses and chose one that was on the larger side. Even so, I barely managed to squeeze into it. I snagged a pair of kitten heels. At least we wore the same shoe size. When I was all put together, she gave me a smile of approval. She took a small gold locket necklace out of her jewelry box and placed it around my neck.

"Maggie May, my girl, I'm sorry. I'm so sorry, I'm so . . ." She started to get a little emotional again.

"I love you, Mom. I really do. I want you to know that." The words came directly from the childhood corner of my heart.

"I love you, too, Maggie. I'm such a bitch," she said into my hair as she gave me a hug.

"Yes. But I am, too," I said, and we started laughing again. "I know this has got to be unbearably hard."

"Yes. I need a cup of coffee," my mom said.

Just then Violet came in with a box of Annie's

Hot Donuts in one arm and three giant coffees in the other. To my surprise, my mother ate two doughnuts! It wouldn't have been polite to let her eat alone, so I had a couple, too. And let's be honest, doughnuts were always better warm.

Funerals in Charleston usually took place at McAlister's funeral home, a large yellow building with white columns in West Ashley. The funeral director, Darryl Young, was the kindest man, and he was known around Charleston for being a true professional who always went the extra mile to make sure that your saddest days went as smoothly as possible. When we walked in, there was a vase of fresh white lilies on the large round table in the center of the spacious foyer. A tiny smile ran across my mom's face. She walked up to the arrangement and read the small card that lay next to the lilies. "From Belle and Jimmy," she said. It was a nice nod to my mom, and I think for a moment the fragrance of the flowers gave her strength. She pulled a pretty red scarf out of her bag and wrapped it around her shoulders.

Darryl came over to greet us. "While I'm sorry you're here, Lily, it's always nice to see you. My deepest condolences to you and your daughters." He smiled sadly.

"Thank you, Darryl, for everything you've done to

make this day come together," my mom said, clenching her jaw and struggling to keep her composure.

We had met Darryl before. We Catholic families had so many family members and friends we considered family that funerals were not infrequent events, and they sometimes felt like family reunions. But I was reminded that this wasn't one of those occasions when Darryl led us to the chapel where Buster was laid out and I saw Dixie and Caroline. They were surrounded by people who I assumed were family and friends of theirs and Buster's. The sisters broke away and made a beeline for my mother.

"Oh, Miss Lily, thank goodness you arrived," said Dixie, who was wearing a low-cut black spandex dress, before pulling my mom into a bear hug.

Caroline, dressed more demurely in a long-sleeved black lace dress, carefully dabbed her eyes with a matching black lace handkerchief. "I need a hug, too. Then let's go say hello to Daddy."

Neither of the sisters had acknowledged me or Violet, but we dutifully followed the three sobbing women to the casket, the top half of which was open. True to form, Buster was dressed in a Hawaiian shirt with a gold chain around his neck. The mortician had deepened his tan, and he looked like he did the last time I'd seen him, maybe just more at peace. It was no wonder that after gazing at the love of her life for a few seconds, my mother sank down on the kneeler and sobbed loudly. Violet and I rushed forward to support her, but Dixie and Caroline blocked our way. They joined Mom on the kneeler, propping her up and sobbing along with her. I looked over my shoulder and saw that people had stopped talking and were looking with concern at my mother and Buster's daughters. Two worried-looking men in business suits were hovering nearby, appearing not to know what to do. The sisters' husbands, I figured. Then I saw Darryl enter the chapel with a priest dressed in a cassock and carrying a Bible. As they quickly walked to the casket, the two husbands stepped forward and helped their wives to their feet. Darryl softly said something to our mom and did the same for her.

"Miss Lily, you sit up here with us while Father Gregory says some prayers for our dear daddy's soul," Dixie said, gesturing to the front row of chairs.

There was no room in the front row for me and Violet, so we walked as inconspicuously as possible to the back of the crowded chapel. Just as the priest started to say a few words about Buster, Jim walked in, appropriately attired, as usual, in a dark-blue suit, pale-blue shirt, and Hermès tie. How did he manage to do that? I was 99 percent certain he hadn't brought a suit from New York. He leaned over and squeezed my and Violet's hands.

As I half listened to the priest, I couldn't help but wonder how I would broach the subject of Buster's loan. *By the way, Mom, did Buster really invest a hundred grand in the restaurant? And where could Vi and I find a record of this loan and any repayments in your disorganized account books?* I felt guilty for thinking of mercenary matters at a time like this, but the loan and the exact amount of it was weighing on my mind. I was also anxious about Caroline and Dixie's presence and participation at the Lantern.

After the priest finished the prayers for Buster and offered words of solace to all who loved him, Dixie and Caroline stood and invited everyone to join them in the reception room to give their daddy the kind of send-off he'd like, "with a glass of beer, something good to eat, and plenty of corny jokes."

Buster's family exited the chapel first, my mom with them. Among the last to leave the chapel, Violet, Jim, and I entered the sunny reception room, where the din of conversation was quite loud, ladies were filling luncheon plates at buffet tables, and men congregated around the bar at the far side of the room.

As I looked around for my mom, an elegantly dressed young woman gave me a hug. I didn't realize it was Frankie, the waitress, until she stepped back and gave Violet a hug, too. "I'm so sorry, y'all. Buster was a good man. His time came too soon. I have to go find your momma. I'll see you later at the Lantern."

Ben, Miller, and a few other Magic Lantern employees were with Frankie and offered their condolences, too. It was so thoughtful of them to come. I was startled to see the guys with their shirts tucked in. A couple of them had even shaved.

"I heard Hamby is catering," Violet said. "Let's take a look at the food."

Buster's daughters certainly hadn't spared any expense, and, surprisingly, had chosen the perfect dishes—ham biscuits, maple ham slices with artichoke relish, golden pimento mac and cheese, and a tray of salad. Not a morsel of frozen seafood in sight! Of course, I gave all the credit to the caterer, one of the best in Charleston. I was impressed by the beautiful blend of lettuces, Bibb, frisée, and red oak. I wondered out loud where they got ahold of such gorgeous bright lettuce, and a member of the Hamby team, who was filling the beverage canisters with sweet tea and lemonade, told me the produce came from Sunflower Farms. It took me about three seconds to realize that it was Sam's family's farm she was talking about. Goodness, he seemed to be everywhere.

While Jim filled a plate for himself, Violet and I made our way across the room to where Mom was seated beside Caroline and Dixie, who were holding court, accepting condolences, and chatting with Buster's family and friends. As I watched her, I got the impression that she was finding some comfort in being considered part of Buster's family. When Dixie caught sight of me and Violet, she raised her hand, palm out, to the next couple that was approaching. "Hold up, Emmy. We need to talk to Lily's daughters."

Violet leaned down and gave our mom a hug. "Oh, Momma, I admire you. You're doing so well. That was a beautiful funeral service, Dixie and Caroline. There wasn't a dry eye in the room."

I nodded and smiled. The sisters beamed at Violet but didn't even look at me. "Thank you, Violet, so glad you came. Look, y'all might have heard Daddy requested cremation rather than burial. So, we're taking a boat out in a few days to scatter his ashes at his favorite fishing grounds up near Myrtle Beach, and your momma is coming with us."

I saw my mother bite her lip and start to cry. "Momma, are you sure you're up for that? I'll go with you, we both will. You don't have to go if you don't want to—"

Caroline cut in, "She already told us she wants to

go. Daddy would have wanted her to go. Miss Lily told us you two will hold down the fort at the Lantern until she, me, and Dixie are up and runnin' again."

I felt my stomach clench. My mother had never told me or Violet that Buster's daughters would be running the restaurant, and now she wasn't disputing Caroline's claim that they'd be doing exactly that. I gave my mom a questioning look, but she ignored it, directing her response to Dixie and Caroline. "I'm so glad you girls are taking an interest in the Magic Lantern. Your daddy put so much into it."

"Yes, he did." Dixie nodded. "A hundred thousand dollars, in fact. I have the canceled check you cashed last September, Miss Lily. Caroline and I can't guarantee that we'll fill our father's huge shoes as your business partner"—she paused, blinking her eyes in a show of fighting back tears—"but we will certainly try."

Chapter 20
Violet

It had to be tonight. I couldn't wait any longer to tell Chris about the baby. Mainly for the sake of my own anxiety. Holding a huge secret like that from him was dang near impossible; especially with all the nausea, he would get worried and suggest that I visit a doctor. I wasn't drinking my usual gallon of coffee, took naps frequently, and on more than one occasion, put my keys in the freezer. But none of this seemed to spark any questions or suspicion from him yet. I knew he was super stressed out with work, so I was hoping a nice dinner would not only feel good in his tummy, but also remind him that home was where he could unwind. Momma always said that the secret to keeping a man was making sure the six-inch radius around his belly button was happy, so the kitchen and the bedroom were spotless and ready for some action.

Chris had always talked about wanting children, so I expected him to be thrilled. Sure, it wasn't the *best* timing, but when *was* the best time to have a child? I was getting excited about my little bean, and I had already planned Pinterest boards with all things baby-related. I wanted to give this child the childhood I never had. Besides, I had mentally started a baby book, had it monogrammed and everything. I was sure it was a girl, and I'd always known what she'd be named.

I pulled out all the stops that night and was making his favorite, Mississippi Roast. Now, don't judge me, y'all, but I found some good recipes on Pinterest, and this was one of them. You just needed a giant roast, a stick of butter, a packet of dry ranch seasoning, a packet of au jus seasoning, a jar of pepperoncini, a slow cooker, and you were good to go. I inhaled its delicious smell. I wasn't a chef like my sister, but I could work a Crock-Pot.

I grabbed a linen tablecloth, napkins, and some of the silverware that I got while antiquing one Sunday with Gran. It was plated, but with a quick dip in a silver bath, it looked good enough for Buckingham Palace. Setting the table was something we Southern ladies took very seriously. I'd had to thrift-find some china and just told everyone it was my great-grandmother's, and I told the same fib about the cut-crystal vase in the center of the table that I got for twenty bucks on sale at Marshalls. I added a grocery-store bouquet to it and said a tiny prayer that it was enough.

I turned on some light jazz music and smiled at myself for remembering to put a bottle of nonalcoholic wine in the fridge. I thought that I should have fun with this; if I was going to announce it, I might as well be creative. When the roast was done, I took it out to rest and threw some baby carrots in a fry pan and glazed them with honey and orange juice. Then I preheated the oven for some baby quiches that I got from Costco. I also had roasted some baby potatoes with the roast; hopefully Chris would catch on to the joke . . . he would have to get it when I served the baby spinach salad with goat cheese and strawberry vinaigrette.

The front door opened just as I was slicing the meat into tiny baby portions. I giggled as I licked the delicious gravy off my fingers and placed the dinner under foil at our seats. I heard his keys hit the dish by the door, and then heard him moan as he inhaled the smell of the roast and also as he slid off his uncomfortable shoes.

"Hey, babe, is that what I think it is?" Chris asked.

"Yes, sir, thought you might need a treat." I giggled again, holding back my excitement.

"I do, because I've got some news," he said as he walked into the kitchen. "Did you get your hair done or something?"

"No, sugar, I just did it myself. You like?"

Chris gave me a sheepish smile and eyed the baby quiches. I poured two glasses of the nonalcoholic wine, but didn't let him know what I was pouring. I set the glasses out.

"So, what's the news?" I arched an eyebrow.

"Uhh, well . . ." He drifted off, popped a baby quiche in his mouth, and loosened his tie. "Yum. I haven't had one of these since a wedding or something. Is it a special day? Did I forget . . . shit, what day is it?" He blushed a deep crimson.

"No, don't sweat it, baby, it isn't our anniversary for another month." I laughed.

"Phew. Well, I'm starving," he said as he took a sip of the wine and scrunched his face.

We did a little chitchatting and then moved to the dining room, where he sat down, pulled off the foil, and stared right at me.

"What is this, Violet?" he said.

"What do you mean?" I let out a little nervous laugh.

"Are you putting me on a diet or something?" He took a bite. "Is this some sort of new trend? Am I fat, or . . ." He looked upset.

"Not quite, Chris. I've got some news, too," I said, a little disappointed that he wasn't catching on.

"Yeah? Who's getting married now? Are we so broke now that you have to portion this food so small? What did you buy now?" he said.

"What was your news?" I said.

"You go first," he said. He got up for seconds and returned with more of everything. "If you aren't telling me yours, it's probably expensive." He laughed at himself.

"Well, as a matter of fact, it will be," I said.

"Okay, I'll go first," he said. "You're not going to like this."

"Well, is it about me? The house? Your mother?" I asked.

"No, it's about work," he said.

"That can wait, honey. How do you like your *baby* potatoes?" I shot him a wink.

"They're good, as usual, Violet. Go great with the meat. Why did you say 'baby' like that? Oh, God," Chris said and stared at his plate.

"What?" I asked in a Pollyanna voice.

"Violet, please tell me this is a joke?"

"Umm, nope. Not a joke . . ." I heard my voice get very small as I saw dark clouds fog up his eyes. His face had an expression I'd never seen before, or at least not directed at me. His hands clenched into fists and he pounded the table.

"God damn it, Vi!" he growled. "How did you know?"

"I took a test at the hospital . . . I . . . I fainted when Maggie got into town, and the nurses made me take a test." I stammered slightly, worried he was about to start yelling.

"No, not how do you know . . . how did you know . . . about my case?" he said.

I got cold all at once and felt sick. I started to sweat under my arms, and the backs of my legs stuck to the plastic my mother insisted I put on our dining room chairs. I could feel myself start to panic. What case was he talking about? Did I forget that someone mentioned something to me?

"Chris, I don't know what you mean!" I struggled to find my words.

"I'm going to Japan!" he blurted. "You must have known! You must have gone through my phone or something. Well, you haven't trapped me, Violet. Pregnant or not, this isn't my problem, because *we* aren't ready, and I'm leaving the country!"

"Not *your* problem?" I said slowly. I couldn't believe what was coming out of Chris's mouth. I felt myself get good and mad. "What are you accusing me of exactly?

Trapping you? Going through your phone? Damn it, Chris, my head is spinning!"

"Yes, trapping! You and that sick mother of yours. Always scheming to get me to do more than I'm comfortable with. Hell, our pillows in our bedroom are monogrammed! I don't know how many times I have to tell you that I'm not ready. That *we* are not ready!"

I stared at him. Christopher. My Christopher, who I've loved for as long as I can remember. My laid-back, easygoing, fun, good Southern gentleman. This wasn't him. This wasn't like the man I loved at all. My mind raced to all the quick excuses for him, and then I realized it. Maybe he was just telling me the truth. He wasn't ready, but he was only half right, because I was ready.

Sometimes life gives you moments like that one, where you can pause for a second because you know better. I knew that I needed to be smart. His hump was up, and it was because he viewed me as putting him against a wall, but I hadn't. I had a choice. I could fire back, have a huge fight, and say a bunch of things I didn't mean, or I could gather myself and get some advice. I had to lower the temperature of the room and save my next move for when things were less hot. However, he had accused me of two really terrible things. But trapping him into parenthood was another thing altogether. I wasn't just Violet anymore, I was Violet and this baby's momma. I had to stand up for her.

"Christopher, do you think this is perfect timing for me? With all that's going on with my family, you think this will be easy for me? You're about to go to Japan! Give me some credit." I saw him squirm in his seat and take a long drink of the fake wine.

"So there's no booze in this, is there? Damn it. Guess I can't blame my temper on it then." He looked up at me. "Violet, I'm sorry. I shouldn't have said that. I'm so stressed out with work, and I've been so nervous about telling you this . . . I have so many questions." His eyes cleared to a lighter blue and I could tell the storm had passed.

"This is not how I envisioned this evening going," I said.

"I know . . . me, either. Well, I expected a fight," he said, getting up to go into the kitchen.

I sat there for a moment and took a tiny sip of water, then heard him rattle around in the fridge for a can of beer. When I heard it crack open, I relaxed a little, but then felt a giant wave of fear rush through me. Japan. A job. He was leaving. To another country, halfway around the world, and I was carrying his child. I'd have to do this basically alone.

Chris returned with a second can of beer in his hand,

his belt undone, and missing his necktie. He rubbed his forehead and plopped back into his chair. I just looked at him.

"No, Violet, I can't not go," he said, reading my mind. "It won't be forever. Two or three months tops."

"Okay," I said and started to cry. I couldn't help it. I was just so sad. I was scared that he was leaving, and I was upset over what I thought would be a sweet evening. He was being a jerk. I had expected a little shock, maybe even a little resistance or disbelief, but not this.

"Oh, Violet. Baby, please don't cry. I'm so sorry," he said.

"I even did baby carrots!" I sobbed.

"I know, and baby spinach, and baby quiches. I get it. I'm an idiot. How . . . Can we do this over?" he said.

"Do what over?" I asked, feeling sick.

"This evening? I fucked it up."

"Langu— Yes, you did." I pouted and sniffed.

"Okay. Go stand in the kitchen. I'm going to come through the door again . . ."

"Chris, stop it." I fought off a smile.

We finished up dinner. He pulled his chair next to me instead of across from me. He apologized again, and I decided to forgive him. I needed to talk to my family. Alice and Maggie would know what to do. After the dishes were cleaned and the kitchen was sparkling, I took a long, hot shower. I slipped into my favorite night-gown and then in between the sheets next to Chris.

"How are we going to do this if I'm in Japan?" he asked.

"I don't know. But I guess families do it all the time, right? With war and stuff?" I said.

"I should tell you I am going because of you," he said. "It's an unbelievable opportunity and a giant chal-lenge. It would really give me a leg up for a promotion. We are expanding our international affairs and the fact that I'm even being considered is a big deal. I have to do it, Violet, for our future."

And that made my heart full. At least he was consid-ering a future with us. I felt a little lighter.

The next morning, Chris left without waking me up. I rolled over to grab my phone and called Maggie, who picked up on the third ring.

"Hey, Violet, what's up? What time is it?" she asked, sounding groggy.

"It's eight fifteen. Maggie, I'm freaking out," I said.

"Why? What's wrong? Is it Gran? Mom?" she said, jolting herself into the day.

"No, no! Sorry to scare you. No, it's Chris."

"Chris? Jesus. Okay, what happened?" she said.

"Ugh, it's bad news. He got a case in Japan, and he's

going to take it because it means a big promotion for him. It's only for a few months . . . or so he says, but I know these cases can run on and on. How am I going to do this alone? Ugh, we had a huge fight . . . but now I don't know what to do. He's accused me of pressuring him, and . . . all this just seemed to come out of no-where, after I told him about the baby," I said, choking back a sob.

"Wait, you told him about the baby? You didn't tell me that!" she said.

"Yeah, I told him last night. The response was under-whelming . . . then he just left for work. He's leaving on Tuesday." I gave in to the tears.

"Okay, Violet, I am going to ask you a scary ques-tion and I need you to be honest with me, okay?"

"Okay, what?" I said.

"Do you really, truly want to marry Chris? Like, is he the one?"

"Yes. I'm in love with him, Maggie, and I'm carry-ing his child. I think it's obvious I want to be his wife."

"Okay, then we need a plan of attack."

"You sound like Mom," I thought out loud.

"Rude, but probably accurate. Anyway, what I think we need here is a little psychological warfare," she said.

"Warfare? I like the sound of that," I said. I felt myself calming down.

"Okay, here's what I'm thinking. He feels pressured, right?"

"Right."

"Does he want the baby?" she asked.

"Don't know, but I can't imagine he'll leave me high and dry. He's a good guy, but . . ."

"Has some cold feet. Okay," she said, and I could hear her pacing. "But we want him on your side, right?"

"Right."

"Well, if we want him on your side, but he's running in the opposite direction, maybe what he needs is to think you love him and want to support him more than anything. Maybe you should throw him a going-away party!"

"Maggie . . . that's genius! If I do that, I'll look super supportive, and so easy breezy!"

"Yes . . . and maybe we disguise it as a baby shower, like a couples' thing? It'll get him excited for the baby!" she said.

"Oh, that's a great idea, but it's too early. I'm like five minutes pregnant. Maybe I should invite his parents and leave the pregnancy test out," I suggested.

"Now who sounds like Mom?"

"Well, if they know, and he knows, and they know that he . . .

"All right, I'll leave that up to you . . . but you should know that your manipulative side scares me, girl," she said.

"Yeah, I know. This is a really good idea. I'm scrolling Pinterest now. What do you know about Japanese food? Wanna cater?" I asked.

"Oh, Lord, Violet, Sunday? The restaurant's closed and you'll have the day off."

"Yes, and surprise him!" I said, giggling and borderline squealing.

"Let's do some fun Asian-inspired food!" she suggested.

"Is it too soon to do this tomorrow? Thank you, Maggie, this is perfect."

Chapter 21
Magnolia

It was warm for late April, but it was one of those days when you could feel summer poking its head up but realizing it had arrived too early by the time evening rolled around. When I looked out my bedroom window this morning, the sun's rays cut through the clouds, spilling golden light on everything below. There was electricity in the air and butterflies in my stomach as I tried to decide what to wear for my lunch date with Sam. A date. A real date, with someone who truly thrilled me.

I was warm and jumpy, but also relaxed. It was strange to simultaneously feel anticipation and ease, but I wanted to be in Sam's arms again, that much was for sure. Oh, those gorgeous tan arms that felt as strong as the roots of a cypress tree. Woo! Yes, I was so ready for this.

I looked at the clothes in my closet, some left over from high school and some belonging to Violet, and wondered what would be the most flattering. It was almost May, getting warmer by the minute; the jasmine was starting to bloom. So, I could ditch a sweater, and maybe even show off a little skin. I paused, wondering if it was a bad sign that I was already thinking about that. Whatever, this would be fun. I was going back to New York, but I could live in the moment for once, right? I could allow myself to escape the problems of my family and the restaurant and all the stress that surrounded me for a few hours, right? Time off for good behavior? I thought so. In the back of my closet, I saw a pink wrap dress that was hopelessly Southern. Pale pink, with little flutter sleeves all in a Swiss-dot fabric that you could see through if you held it up to the light. I would need nude undergarments, which I was sure I had. My mom always told me never to wear wild undies, you never knew who'd see them! What if I got in a car wreck?

I pulled my hair up and allowed a few red curls to fall out of a messy bun at the nape of my neck. I slipped the dress on and gave my lips a quick swipe of gloss.

I chose small gold hoop earrings that had belonged to Gran at one time and stepped into a pair of gold flip-flops. I looked at myself in the mirror and reminded myself I was going to a farm.

Jim walked in. "Ready for the big . . . Oh, my God, Magnolia!"

"What? Too much?" I said, grimacing.

"Good God, no! You look absolutely perfect! You look like a mouth-watering pink confection! A true Southern Magnolia! I love it!" Jim said.

"Really? I'm going to a farm. Maybe I should just throw on some jeans."

"No, ma'am, you wear that exact outfit. Here, wear these," Jim said, handing me strappy sandals with a little heel. His sincerity was shocking. I decided to wear the dress. It wasn't like I would be *working* on the farm. I'd been invited to lunch.

"Okay. I'm off," I said and gave him a quick kiss on his cheek.

"Go have fun, Maggie," Jim said. "Kiss him good."

"Counting on it."

I ran down the stairs and snagged the key to Gran's truck. As I put the key in the ignition and rolled the windows down, letting the humidity curl my hair further, I took a deep breath, inhaling the scent of honeysuckle from Gran's garden, letting excitement radiate around me. I got out my phone to text Sam that I was on the way, and he replied with a smiley face. I pulled out of the driveway, the gravel crunching under the truck's old tires, and left Sullivan's Island, driving down the causeway, looking at the bright-red oleander bushes and palm trees. I turned on the radio and listened to some old beach music, humming along to the tunes and taking in the scenery around me.

I loved driving over the ocean, watching all the shrimp boats and the seagulls flying around them looking for a snack. Many people find them annoying, but I'd always been struck by the beauty of their white wings gently flapping against the bright-blue sky. It was low tide now, and I could see the sandpipers pecking around the oyster shells that dotted the marshlands, hoping to get lucky. It was a privilege to coexist with these wild creatures in their natural habitat. I felt a pang of sadness for taking all this for granted for so many years. When I was a teenager, I'd wanted so badly to run away from the Lowcountry, but in running away from my childhood and my family I'd lost this. I shook my head, trying to banish my regrets and second-guessing, trying not to think about my mom and how hurt I'd felt yesterday when she'd preferred Dixie and Caroline's company over mine and hadn't straightened them out about their role at the restaurant. Later, Vi had told me to chill. Of course, Mom wanted to be with Buster's family at this sad time. They all loved him; it was good for them to grieve together. I knew she was right, and I wasn't going to let my mother's problems ruin my day. I turned up the tunes.

Before I knew it, I was on Johns Island, in another world entirely, and had to pull out my phone again to use my GPS. A large part of Johns Island was rural and wild compared to Charleston and its surrounding barrier islands. Johns Island was home to Angel Oak, the most stunning tree I'd ever seen. Sixty-six feet high, with a circumference of twenty-eight feet, it was supposedly the oldest living thing east of the Mississippi River—hundreds, perhaps a thousand years old. I had to bring Violet out here, I bet she could take some great pictures of it. Carefully keeping my eyes on the road while holding my phone at the same time to punch in the address of Sam's farm, I bumped down winding dirt roads, finally finding a long white fence with a giant sign that read SUNFLOWER FARMS THE SMART CHOICE SINCE 1935. I smiled and pulled in the driveway through the open gate bordered by two stone sunflower planters. The long dirt road ahead of me was lined with giant oaks dripping with curly gray Spanish moss. I drove past rows and rows of orchids on either side of the main driveway, which led to a drop-dead antebellum white house, complete with an enormous wraparound porch and a huge front doorway with an equally huge transom window and leaded-glass side windows. Considering its age, the house was very well kept.

The red-brick base of the house was lined with trimmed rosebushes, which dotted the white house with hot pink blossoms. I pulled around to the side, where there was a small paved area and another car was parked. When I walked up the few steps to the front porch, I saw the front door was open behind a screen door with a sunflower-shaped door knocker. I tapped the knocker and looked around at the haint-blue porch ceiling, the pristine white rocking chairs, and the long dark-green joggling boards lining the windows. This house was fancy, smelled of generations of money. I was thankful I hadn't thrown on my jeans. I swallowed hard, just a tiny bit nervous.

I heard the clack of heels approaching the front door and I straightened my posture. A woman who couldn't have been more than five feet tall appeared at the door. She was wearing a pink shift dress, the exact same color as the flowers out front, with a butter-yellow cashmere cardigan hung over her shoulders. I could tell that it was super soft without even touching it. Around her neck hung a triple-string graduated-pearl necklace, which shone against her tan skin, and I saw diamond studs sparkling out of her perfect blond bob. When she brought her eyes up to meet mine, I realized they were the same shade of yellow-brown as Sam's eyes. This must be his momma. Oh, boy.

"Hey, there! I'm Magnolia, I'm here to see Sam," I said.

"Oh, hey, honey! I'm Mary Katherine Smart, but everyone calls me Bunny. I'm his momma! It's so nice to meet you!" She opened the door and welcomed me inside.

The foyer was just as impressive as the exterior. I stood on an antique rug that was brightly colored with royal blue, cream, and various shades of yellow. The massive round marble-topped knotted-mahogany table in the center of the room held a sprinkling of silver picture frames and a flower arrangement that was taller than Bunny. The fragrance of lilies hit me right away.

"Oh, my gosh, your home is so beautiful! The flowers smell—"

"Just divine, right? I adore lilies," Bunny said, inhaling theatrically. "It took a lot of renovation, but I'm so very proud of our family home." She gestured to the space with a perfectly French-manicured hand. "Not too bad for a farmer's wife, huh?" She gave me a wink.

"Not at all! Goodness, it's exquisite!" I said, noticing the very large sweeping staircase with sunflowers carved in the newel post and balusters.

"Yes! The stairway, well, it is our opening number and makes quite a first impression! If you look closely, you can spot different fruits that this land provided our family. It was custom made, by hand. I have a cousin who's a woodworker, and he's really very talented." She beamed.

"Wow, well, I love a good story. I grew up on Sullivan's Island in the same house my great-grandparents built," I said.

"Is that right? Well, I love Sullivan's Island. Sam used to date a girl out there. I thought she was great. Oh, well," Bunny said. "Sam told me he wanted to show a friend of his the farm. He told me you were a cook?" she said.

"A chef, yes, I am. My family owns the Magic Lantern on Sullivan's Island, and I'm in town for a little while." I saw a look of confusion on her face. "Oh, do you know it?"

"You said your name is Magnolia, right? Are you Rose's girl?" Bunny asked.

"Yes, Rose is my grandmother!"

"Wow. I mean, oh, my goodness! I knew you looked familiar." Bunny looked me up and down then. "We have a long shared history together. How is Rose? Sam told me she was in a car accident. I was so sorry to hear that."

"She's hanging in there. We're all so relieved that she's improving," I said, noticing her looking increasingly uncomfortable.

"Well, I will make sure to pray for her and your family. It's nice to meet you, Magnolia. Let me go get my Sam. Wait right here." She turned and walked away.

As her heels quickly clicked down the black-and-white-marble hallway, I wondered what I had said to make her speed away. I tried not to dwell on it and took a peek at the framed pictures on the center table. The frames were so perfectly polished I didn't want to touch them and leave fingerprint smudges on the frames. But I smiled as I looked at a picture of a small boy, missing a tooth, running on a dock, swinging a freshly caught fish on a line. He was so adorable, I hoped it was Sam. There was another of a few people pulling in a crab pot, and a few family Christmas-card pictures. I thought about what it must have been like growing up in a house like this. I imagined magnolia-leaf wreaths and garlands at Christmastime, tied up with big bright-red bows winding around the staircase and hanging in perfect swags. I bet they had color-coordinated ornaments, not handmade ones like ours. I was sure that Bunny pulled out all the traditions, never failing to make her great-grandmother's fruitcake. I bet she soaked hers in aged rum for thirty days, too. We just got the hard log version from the Piggly Wiggly and called it a day. We were always too tired to make one.

Lost in my comparisons of holiday festivities, I didn't hear Sam enter the room.

"Hey, girl," he said, his voice as low as thunder, sending an electrical charge through me.

I spun around and faced him. He seemed taller in this room, but totally comfortable. He was wearing a Carolina-blue button-down shirt, jeans, and brown leather Sperry boat shoes. He looked at me as if we had known each other our whole lives. It was easy, and warm. He was biting his bottom lip, drinking me in as I stood in his home.

"Hey, yourself. Nice digs, Sam," I said.

"I'm still just a boy digging in the dirt, Maggie." He moved closer to me.

"Yeah, in a white coat and silver frames," I said.

"Yeah, I know it can be a little overwhelming. Let's go look at my dirt."

"Okay," I said, taking his outstretched hand. Feeling his fingers wrap around mine made me forget about the nagging feeling of not being good enough for my surroundings.

He led me down a wallpapered hallway hung with oil paintings of people dressed in nineteenth-century garb, passing tastefully decorated rooms. The French doors at the back opened to a brick patio lined with pale-pink mature camellias, as soft and demure as a fainting debutante. We faced a landscape of wild oaks all knotted and twisted with time and dripping with Spanish moss, like the ones lining the driveway. Looking at their thick trunks, I wondered how old they were and what stories they would tell if they could talk. Their branches swayed in the breeze, which I felt ruffling my skirt. I looked over to my right and saw that the Intercoastal Waterway lined the property. The Smart family's farm was perfectly situated for shipping their produce to market. I noticed Sam looking at me.

"It's beautiful here," I said. "Show me more, Sam."

He smiled and led me to a dark-green tractor.

I raised an eyebrow. "Oh, you can't be serious."

"Come on, city girl. I'll keep you safe, plus we gotta get away from Momma." He picked me up and plopped me down on the tractor like a rag doll.

"Lots to unpack there, Sam," I said, rolling my eyes but at the same time feeling like I was in high school again. "Are you planning on kissing me behind a haystack or something?"

"Oh, I plan on a lot worse, Maggie." He threw the

tractor into gear, and it bumped down a long stretch of land, going faster than I thought a tractor could go. He took a hard left, and we came to a clearing bordered by a white fence, beyond which were rows and rows of what appeared to be soybean, corn, and other plants. The soft dark-brown earth was giving way to bright-green new life. I spied a few plots of empty land.

"What's growing over there?" I asked.

"Nothing at the moment. A crop failed, so now we have a vacancy."

He stopped the tractor, jumped down, and came around to my side. "This way, Maggie." He grabbed me under my arms, picked me up off the tractor, and set me down on the grass. I felt my heels sink into the earth. I bent down and took off my sandals.

"Oh, we're going shoeless?" he said, laughing at me.

"Yeah, I can't do heels here," I said. "I want to feel this earth."

"I get it." He chuckled. "Okay, so I made us lunch." He gestured to a picnic table with benches at the edge of the clearing. The table was draped with a white table-cloth. As we walked over to it, I could see two plates and a covered dish in the center of the table and what I thought was fresh bread wrapped in a napkin snuggled into a sweetgrass basket. A small etched-glass butter bell filled with bright-yellow butter and two wineglasses with the same etched pattern were also on the table. In a wooden salad bowl, I saw fresh veggies. He had even included some wildflowers in a vase. He had thought this out.

"Well, well, well, Dr. Smart. You didn't do this for little ole me, did ya?" I teased in a Southern drawl.

"Oh, it's just a little something I threw together. It was nothing, really," he said, mimicking a proper Southern hostess who I imagined was his mother. "Okay, I had a little help from the housekeeper."

"It's beautiful." I sat down as he plated me a lunch that smelled as good as it looked. He uncovered the dish, revealing a golden puff pastry crust with brightly colored vegetables underneath, oozing with herbed goat cheese. It was so fragrant that my mouth started watering.

"Yeah, it's as good as it looks . . . and smells. Just some simple vegetables. Try this." Sam held up a forkful of the hot casserole and blew on it, and after a few moments, he fed it to me.

"Good, huh?" he asked.

"Good Lord, Sam, this is fantastic!" I said, licking my lips. "More, please."

He continued to feed me, and when the cheese got drippy, licked his thumb and dragged it across my lip. I caught it and gave his finger a playful bite.

"Oh, you want to play like that, huh?" He gave me a teasing smile. "I think the fresh air might be making you a little wild."

"I am feeling a little primal," I said. "Is that wine I see?"

Sam nodded and pulled a bottle out of the basket. With the ease of an experienced server, he pulled a wine key out of his pocket, uncorked the bottle, wrapped it in a linen napkin, and poured a perfect glass for each of us, making sure to tilt and turn the bottle so that not a drop fell on the tablecloth. He raised his glass, and I did the same.

"To nature's bounty, to what we can do with it, and to us," he said, and we clinked our glasses.

"The earth provided for us today. Man, that squash is out of this world! What kind is it? It's so sweet!" I asked.

"Oh, you noticed. Of course, you did, Chef! Kabocha squash. It's a new crop. I'm glad you like it." He smiled.

"Yeah, it would make an amazing soup with butternut squash, I think . . . maybe a little bacon and fried sage," I mused.

"Oh, God, yeah. Thick and velvety. But it also makes an amazing soufflé, too."

"A new crop? Do y'all often try new vegetables? Seems like this place is so traditional," I said.

Sam gave me a look. "Oh, are you referring to Bunny? Yeah, well, she grew up on this farm, so she's kind of set in her ways. But Momma started a new line of business for Sunflower Farms. She started our online heirloom CSA program and our grow boxes for people all over the country."

"What's a grow box?" I asked.

"It's like a subscription for plants that you can use for container gardening or whatever you like. It's pretty cool, and it's very popular."

"Wow, I didn't realize," I said, taking a deep sip of wine.

The weather was bright and sunny, with a cool breeze that kept lifting the little wisps of hair off my neck and ruffling Sam's. I shivered, but the wine and hot food were so cozy I didn't mind. I took in the scenery around me, realizing that the farm was way bigger than I had originally thought.

"So, Sam, what do y'all grow out here besides experimental squash?" I asked.

"Well, we grow just about everything, all year round. Everything but pumpkins and watermelon, because they take up too much space."

"Could you show me some of the fields?" I asked.

"Sure can. Right this way." Sam took my hand and

helped me off the bench. Not letting my hand go, he led me to the field in front of us, which was full of tall plants and people working the land. He waved to some of them and they smiled back. Everyone seemed happy here. All orderly and perfect. The soil felt cool beneath my feet as I walked, but occasionally I hit a few patches warmed by the sun. I was walking behind him, letting him lead me, and then suddenly he stopped and turned to face me.

"Maggie, I can't stop thinking about you."

"Oh," I said, not knowing how to respond, but feeling the back of my neck get hot, and suddenly becoming aware of my breathing.

"You are one of the most beautiful women I've ever met, and there's something about you that . . . I just . . ." He took me down a path away from the public eye and looked at me then, and a slice of sunshine hit his tan face, illuminating his golden eyes. I reached up and tucked a lock of his sandy hair behind his ear. He kissed my hand, and I cupped the side of his face. He leaned his face into the palm of my hand. Then his lips moved down to my wrist. They were soft and cool. My skin started to burn from the inside out. He kissed the inside of my elbow and I shivered. He stopped and looked at me, and I couldn't help but think he looked like he was pleading with me. I leaned forward and he looped his other arm around my waist, pulling me into a deep kiss.

I went almost limp in his arms as we kissed, and it felt wonderful. Every part of me was smoldering and yearning for more. My legs almost gave out when I felt myself go on my tiptoes to press harder into him. He pulled away.

"Whoa," he said.

"Yeah, whoa," I returned, my chest now heaving as I tried to breathe.

He smirked and took a step back, taking me in, but continued to hold my hand.

"Come, follow me, Maggie."

"Right now? I'd probably follow you anywhere."

He started to jog, and I followed him, keeping up as we went down more and more rows of plants. Soon we came to a line of wild oaks, like the ones lining the driveway and behind the house, but these were close to the water, the marshlands. I was guessing we were at the edge of the property, because there wasn't a soul around. I caught a glimpse of a dock not too far away, but we were secluded by the trees' low branches and Spanish moss. Laughing, we collapsed under the oaks and sat there. Sam gave me that look again.

"I have to have you, Maggie," he said, breathing

hard, and something told me it wasn't because of our jog through the rows of crops. The look in his eyes seemed to reflect the heat that I felt in every cell of my body. We were both starving for each other. I could see he wanted me as much as I wanted him, something I hadn't ever experienced before, and it gave me a new sense of confidence. I knew then that I was about to become even more primal than I had planned.

"That's good, Sam, because I want you, too," I said.

He inched closer to me and took the clip out of my hair, letting my wild curls fall down all around my shoulders. He took a curl and brushed it off my neck, planting kisses along my collarbone. I felt myself go weak again, and I let out a giggle. Was I really going to do this outside? In public? Yes, yes, I was. I needed to have a little romance, and life was short! Why not allow myself to give in to desire? He used just the slightest nudge of his nose to slide the strap of my dress off my shoulder. I let it fall. He unzipped my dress in the back and slowly untied the bow that wrapped it around me.

"Oh, my God," he said just under his breath.

"Now you," I said as I let the dress drop onto the grass.

He undid his shirt and I stared at his tan chest, covered with a light dusting of golden hair. He reminded me of a lion, and I felt like a lioness, proud and ready. His belt was off so fast, it clunked when it hit the ground, and he stepped out of his jeans. I was almost blinded by my desire for him then. It was like the edges of my vision were blurred. I reached out to him, and he pulled me close, unhooking my bra and tossing it on the pile of tangled clothes on the grass, and then pressing me against him again. His chest was so warm against my skin that it only made me burn hotter. I looked up at him and he bent down to kiss me again, one warm hand against my waist and the other at the nape of my neck. The cool Lowcountry breeze wrapped around me, and I smiled through the kissing. This was fantastic.

I could barely hold myself up any longer, and I almost tripped over my own feet. He laughed and grabbed his shirt, spread it on the ground, and laid me down on it. He lay down beside me on the grass.

"You are so unbelievably beautiful, Maggie," he said, and I felt truly beautiful and adored at that moment.

"God, Maggie, do you know what you do to me? You are so, so sexy." He moaned.

I let out a giggle and slid off my remaining clothing and pulled him to me.

He hung over me for a moment, and we continued kissing, and I heard the water from the marsh gently slosh up against the dock behind us. The weather was picking up and the wind was getting stronger, but I didn't care. Sam was keeping me warm. He plucked a long piece of grass and ran it down my body, sending shivers through me. I gasped, and he continued.

"Come to me, Sam, please."

"Not yet. Not . . . just . . . yet," he teased.

The blade of grass grazed my ankle, my calf, up my leg, and then up inside my thigh, skipping what needed the most attention, and tickling my stomach. He ran it over my breasts and across my neck and then I totally lost my sense of time and space.

We made love then, under the trees, near the bank of the marsh sprinkled with snow-white egrets. I held him to me, and I looked up at the sky, thinking that this moment must be what absolute perfection was like. It felt as if we were melding together in a timeless kind of bliss. When we were both satiated, Sam shielded me from the breeze with his big body, keeping his arms around me, and I curled into his nook, closing my eyes. Every part of me tingled with pleasure and satisfaction. I had never felt like that before.

I opened my eyes sometime later, realizing I'd fallen asleep, feeling startled by where I was and remembering that I had a dinner service to run that evening. I sat up.

"Well, as lovely as this afternoon has been, Dr. Smart, real life calls. I have to get myself to the restaurant," I said, getting dressed.

"It was lovely, sure you have to go so soon?" He grinned.

"Yes, I am sure. I do feel better, though. I guess this was what the doctor ordered."

"I surely didn't order it then, but can I order it now?" he said, trying to pull me back down to him.

"No! Stop it, you bad boy, I have to get to work. But I'm taking your shirt as hostage, till we can do this again. It's getting chilly. How do we get back?" I asked.

"All right, all right, fine." He smiled. "You know what they say about Charleston, if you don't like the weather just wait ten minutes. This way, Maggie May."

Please, no nicknames. But I let it slide. He wasn't Ronny. "Hey, what are you doing tomorrow?" I asked.

"Nothing as of right now. Why, what's going on?"

He led me back through the crop rows to the picnic table.

"My sister and I are throwing a going-away party for her boyfriend, who's going on a long business trip to Japan," I said. "It's at their house in Mount Pleasant, around six. Can I help you bring this stuff back to the house?"

"No, don't worry about it. I got it, Maggie."

The table was so beautiful, and I loved that he had thought of just about everything, or at least his housekeeper had. It was a beautiful gesture. I snagged a heel of bread and got a thought.

"I wonder . . ." I started.

"What's going on behind those green eyes, Maggie?"

I felt myself blush. "Well, I was thinking about family history, and ours particularly . . ."

"Maggie, I was going to tell you, I swear, there just wasn't time . . ."

"What? I was going to ask about our grandparents. What are you talking about?"

"Our grandparents? Go on," he said quickly.

My blood ran cold. I started to experience very familiar feelings of distrust, suspicion. "No, Sam, *you* go on." I heard an edge in my voice. "What were you going to tell me?"

It was his turn to blush. "Maggie . . ." he started. "There's no good way now to tell you, but I promise I was going to. Things between us just kind of . . . escalated."

"Oh, my God, Sam, spit it out!"

"Violet and I used to be in a relationship. It was short, it didn't work out, and we parted as friends," he blurted.

My heart started to pound in my ears, and I felt my stomach drop and my pulse quicken. I took a deep breath. He was talking, but I couldn't really hear him.

"Wait, what? You *dated my sister*?"

"Uh, yes, but it never . . . went anywhere," he said.

I picked up the basket and casually pelted him with a piece of bread.

"Maggie, nothing really ever happened with us!" he protested.

"Oh, Lord, was she the girl you moved back for?" I asked, and his blush deepened.

"Well, yeah. But, like I said, I didn't . . . we didn't ever . . . you know, there just was no juice."

"Ugh! Why didn't you tell me, Sam? There were plenty of opportunities!" I pelted him with another piece of bread.

"Maggie! When could I have done that? When you were bashing the bumper of my truck, when we were ripping each other's clothes off at the restaurant? At the hospital where you and your whole family have been coping with a crisis?" he said.

"Well, I'm going to go with right in between the car accident and us ripping each other's clothes off. Right about there!"

"I wasn't thinking about your *sister*, Maggie, I was thinking about you . . . and your red hair, and your wild eyes."

"Oh, just stop it!"

"Maggie, come on! It isn't like that!" Sam said, holding his hands up.

"Yeah? Then how is it?"

"You can ask your sister, I swear she won't tell you anything different."

"Oh, I will ask her, bubba!" I said.

Why hadn't she said anything?

"Nice to hear your Southern accent coming back," he said, teasing me.

"It comes out when I'm mad." I put down my basket of ammo, took off his shirt and threw it at him, and stormed off toward Gran's truck.

"Come on, Maggie! I'm sorry, I swear! Let me make it up to you," he called as he followed me.

"Stay away from me, Sam Smart! I'm all set with dudes making it up to me!" I called over my shoulder, now running, hoping I could find my way back to the truck. I was out of breath when I got there, but I jumped inside, threw it into drive, and left a cloud of dust in my wake. I couldn't get away fast enough.

Chapter 22
Magnolia

As I drove back to Gran's, I felt myself spiraling. What I had liked about Sam was his honesty, and now, I felt like such a fool. I took a deep breath as I pulled into Gran's dirt driveway, wishing she were on the porch. I missed her ability to take one look at me and know exactly what was bothering me and how to fix it. I suddenly felt the full weight of her absence and doubted my ability to navigate my romantic life. How could something feel so right and be so wrong? How could Sam let it go on to the point it did . . . twice? Why were men so selfish? He wanted something, so he took it. They were all the same.

I went straight upstairs to give myself a hot baptism. I needed it. I was glad to find the house empty. But as I cranked the hotter-than-hell water on, tears spilled out of my eyes. My judgment was horrible.

I heard the bathroom door open. "So how was the lunch?" Jim shouted over the sound of the running water.

"Jim, just give me a second, okay? I'll be out in a moment." I sniffed, trying to wrap up my mini melt-down. I didn't want to get caught crying over a guy again. That was all I needed, and, honestly, I didn't want Jim's tough love right now, I just wanted to forget about Sam Smart.

"Magnolia Adams hiding the dirt from her best friend? Not acceptable. Give it to me, girl, but quickly. It's getting late, and we must get to service," Jim said.

"Jim, lunch was really nothing to rave about. You're right, though, we gotta move!" I said, hoping he would drop it.

"Maggie, I see a crumpled wrap dress over there hanging over the side of the hamper with grass stains on it. You better tell me what happened, you bad girl," Jim teased.

I was in no mood for Jim's banter. "Give me five minutes."

"Uh-oh. Okay, but just so you know, my Paperless Post has been going wild! Almost everyone has already

RSVPed. I had Violet's friend Amelia throw together a baby registry, and thanks to the power of the internet and Amazon, it's almost completely filled!" Jim said, now serious. I heard the bathroom door close.

After drying myself with a towel and quickly combing my wet hair, I headed for my bedroom. I was glad that Violet would have people excited for the baby, and the party would be fun, but I was still too mad to think about it. I looked at the clock on the bedside table and hurriedly dug around to find some clean clothes to wear to work. After I pulled on black leggings and a white tank top, I twisted my hair up into a messy bun and quickly slathered on some moisturizer. Even on a bad day I couldn't let my skin suffer.

I heard a knock on the door, and Jim poked his head in, looking worried. "Can I come in?"

"Is there something wrong with me, Jim?" I asked.

"What do you mean?"

"Like, maybe a giant sign on my face that I can't see but reads, 'I'll believe anything'?"

"Jesus, not again," Jim said.

"Yup, again," I said, nodding. "I'll keep this short because I know we're cutting it close, but basically, I had the most fun I've ever had, only to find out that guess who used to date Sam. And guess who didn't tell me!"

Jim frowned as he thought. "Well, you're not close to any of your high school friends who still live around here, so they wouldn't matter . . ." I saw the lightbulb go on in his head. "No, ma'am! Not our Vi?" Jim's mouth hung open.

"Jim, I'm so pissed," I said.

"Well, I can see that, and I don't blame you." I rolled my eyes for thinking I could hide anything from Jim. "But you're not a fool, Maggie! There's nothing really wrong with this situation besides the fact that both Sam and Vi weren't exactly forthcoming. Think of it as their lying on their résumés."

"It's a little worse than that, Jim, please! Violet saw me talking to Sam at the hospital and they pretended not to know each other. She guessed that he was the guy I'd fooled around with the night before and even teased me about marrying a doctor. I'm a joke to my sister!" I said, cramming my feet into my chef's clogs.

"Now, Maggie, you might be overreacting—"

"And what about him? The night I hit his truck I told him I was Rose Adams's granddaughter, i.e., Violet's sister. And the next day when I ran into him at the hospital, he gave me this sad story about how he moved back here for a girl, but it didn't work out, and he felt bad for hurting her. He was talking about my sister!"

"Hold on a second," Jim said. "That doesn't make any

sense. I don't remember Vi being heartbroken in the last few years, she's only been thrilled because Chris started paying attention to her. Wait! Maybe Vi ditched Sam for Chris, and maybe Sam was the one who got hurt."

"Oh, God!" I wailed. "That's even worse. Sam might still be in love with her, which is why he jumped on me. If he can't have Vi, any Adams woman will do!"

"No, Maggie, that's not right, that's not what I meant." Jim waved his arms like an umpire calling a runner safe. He sank down on my bed. "But wow, how the tables have turned!"

I grabbed a tissue and wiped the tears off my well-moisturized face. "How have the tables turned?"

"Maggie, how is this any different from Violet's dating—well, more than dating Chris?" Jim asked.

"Oh, those turning tables. Well, it's totally different because—"

"You're in the uncomfortable position now?" Jim interrupted.

"No, it's different because a lot of time passed between my breakup with Chris and Violet's starting to date him. Also, I never lied or hid facts," I said. "Also, I feel so used!"

"Maggie, don't go crazy here. You're acting like the first woman who ever had a guy stretch the truth to you to get under your chef's coat," Jim said.

"You are the only one who can talk to me like this without me killing you," I said.

"I know." Jim smiled. "Sugar, you didn't want Chris, and Violet didn't want Sam. Sounds the same to me! Maybe now you understand why Violet's so touchy when she sees you and Chris together. Oh, girl, this is very 'As the Magnolia Turns.'" He laughed.

"Jimmy, this isn't funny! My feelings are hurt, and I'm mad as hell!" I protested.

"I'm sure you are! He pulled a fast one . . . but tell me, princess, how was it?" he asked.

"Jim! Please!"

"That good, huh?"

"I can't believe Violet didn't tell me! Maybe she thought it was funny," I said, making a face.

"Violet isn't malicious, Maggie," Jim said.

"Damn it, Jimmy! He's so cute, and I really liked him, I can't help it, and that makes me even madder," I said. "There was just a different vibe with him, I don't know how to explain it."

"Electric," Jim said.

"Yes, exactly, he touches me and it's like I light up. God, what a waste," I said.

"How is it a waste?" Jim asked.

"Well, I can't see him anymore!"

"Why is that? Violet knows, he knows, now you

know. I mean, at this point the damage has been done, might as well have a good time. Come on, let's go to work," Jim said, throwing his arm around me and leading me downstairs.

"I have to talk to Violet." I grumbled all the way to the front door, then stopped when I saw Jim's travel bag. "I forgot you're going back to New York tonight!" Now I felt even more downhearted, if that was possible.

"Big audition on Monday! But I'll put in a few hours behind the bar at the Lantern. The taxi isn't coming until eight to take me to the airport."

I entered the restaurant through the front door instead of the kitchen door, hoping to find Violet at the reservations desk, but she wasn't there. I said hello to the few servers that were in the dining room, rolling silverware, wiping down menus, and sweeping. I went to the back and found her there seated at the old desk, sifting through papers and various folders.

"Hey, Vi, I need to talk to you."

"Now is not the best time, Maggie, I've got my hands full. I can't find last month's bills anywhere."

"Violet, it's important," I said.

"Can it please wait till later? I really need to finish this before the bank closes."

"What do you mean?" I asked.

"Well, one of the things Mom did, or told me she did, was prepare a spreadsheet of all our costs, and another one for the bills. I got an unpleasant call from Berkeley Electric earlier saying we are behind on payments. Anyway, I've spent the better part of this afternoon looking for those spreadsheets and any other proof of payment, and I can't find them. Sorry, I'm a little frustrated and I'm thinking Mom might not have paid . . . for a few months."

"How is that possible? Well, look at this office, it's a total mess, no wonder you can't find anything. I'm sure it's somewhere . . ."

"Well, if we can't prove that we've paid our electric bill for the past ninety days, the woman over at Berkeley said they can turn off the power at any time. I think I worked a little bit of a grace period, but—"

"Yikes, Violet! We can't lose power in the middle of service! What would that say about us?"

"Nothing good!" Violet took out her phone.

"Okay, let me know if I can help, but I do want to talk later."

She stared at me for a moment. "Maggie, are you upset?"

"Yeah, but it can wait. We'll talk after service. One emergency at a time."

"No, I think I know what this is about," Violet said.

"Do you?" I arched an eyebrow.

"Yeah, it's about Sam."

"Yeah, Violet. You should have told me! I feel like a total idiot!" I said.

"Oh, come on, Maggie, it's not a big deal! It didn't work out with me and him, and honestly, nothing physical, well, nothing major, ever happened!"

"Is that supposed to make me feel better, Vi? He *moved back* here for you!" I said. "Clearly y'all had a relationship that was important even if it was just emotional, and that kind of makes me feel worse!"

"No, girl, that's not exactly how it happened. Remember, he's from here! He applied to several residency programs, and when he got into MUSC, his mother went crazy! She put a lot of pressure on him, kept pushing and pushing him to come home, and he caved. It wasn't about me. Once he got here, we realized there was just no—"

"Juice. Yeah, he told me, and I can totally see Bunny doing that," I mumbled.

"Oh, so you've already met her?" Violet said.

"I've done a lot more than just meet his momma, Violet! I wouldn't have if I had known y'all were involved," I said.

"Maggie, listen, you don't even know how long you're going to be here! I figured why not let you have some fun after that Ronny drama. It was obvious after you told me about your escapade on the bar that you and Sam were on fire for each other! I'm in a strange way happy for y'all! I mean, how serious could it get, and to be honest, I'm a little preoccupied right now with this dang pregnancy and Chris leaving!" She looked back down at the papers on the desk.

"Violet, neither of y'all said one word. It hurts my feelings! Like the two of you knew something and didn't tell me, and you know I have trust issues!"

"Maggie! Oh, my God, you are so overreacting!" She looked me in the face. "Oh, shit, girl, you like him, don't you?"

"I'm trying really hard not to like another liar!"

"Maggie, can you blame the guy?"

"Yes, I totally can!" I said a little too loudly.

"And you think I'm the drama queen? You're starting to piss me off, Maggie. I could be a real brat about this, because God knows we've been here before," Violet said.

"Oh, you mean with Chris? Yeah, that wasn't the same thing! A lot of time had passed when you started seeing him, and I *never* lied to you about my relationship with him."

"I didn't *lie* to you, either, I just didn't give you all the details. Calm down. Also, it's been about two years."

"Oh, God, Violet, stop being so self-righteous, you're so like Mom!" I said.

Well, that did it. Violet slammed the folder she was holding on the desk and stood up. "Magnolia, get over yourself! It isn't always about you, and your moods, and your heartbreak, and your professional struggles! You're creating unnecessary drama! Gran's in the hospital, the restaurant is failing, my child's father is leaving for another country . . . those are *real* problems! Not your stupid manufactured melodrama!" she yelled.

Jim and Alice walked into the office, just in time.

"Hey, hey, now, girls!" Alice said. "What's going on over here? I'm here to drop off these paper lanterns for the party, didn't know I would get an episode of *Jerry Springer*!"

"Girls! Goodness, y'all are acting like cats! What in the world?" Jim said, pretending to be shocked when he knew damn well what was happening.

"Oh, please, Jim!" I said.

"Is this about Doctor Farmer? Maggie, I don't think it's a good idea to get your sister so upset, darling." He motioned to his belly.

"It isn't like she's going to give birth here and now!"

"Maggie!" Alice said in her mom voice, which immediately stopped me. All of a sudden, I was ten years old again, and I was in trouble for cutting all the hair off Violet's Barbies. So, I did what any little girl would do when she got caught for misbehaving, I left the office. I went directly into the walk-in fridge, where I could literally cool off. The kitchen staff probably saw me, or at the very least, heard me, because not a soul came in there.

I felt embarrassed now, because this whole fight was my fault, and Violet was pregnant, and she was correct, and I shouldn't be upsetting her like this.

I heard a light knock at the door before Violet came in holding a mug of hot coffee. She walked over to the giant crate of tomatoes I was sitting on and sat down next to me, silently giving me the coffee.

I didn't look her in the eye, but I drank the coffee. It was so good, and I was such a jerk.

"Violet, I'm sorry. You're right. I'm the worst," I said.

"You aren't the *worst*." She nudged my shoulder. "It's okay, and I'm sorry, too. I should have told you. It wasn't right."

"I'm sorry if I'm acting like a bad big sister. I shouldn't be upsetting you right now, and I know you didn't mean to hurt me," I said.

"Maggie, I'm not fragile, and, of course, I would never hurt you intentionally. Let's just move past this.

I promise to tell you everything from now on. I didn't mean to make you feel like a joke or anything. I didn't think my history with Sam would ever be an issue, I just assumed that you would go back to New York and, like . . . what would be the point. I was trying to avoid . . ."

"This," I said.

"Yup. I didn't want another blowup. It's been quite a week! I love you, Maggie."

"I love you, too, Vi." I drained my cup. "Let's get out of here."

I entered the kitchen to find two very large crates of kale that I hadn't ordered. They were from exactly where I thought they were from. Sam's farm. I guessed one man's roses were another man's kale. It was nice to see him make an apology, but I'd need more than some good produce to get over this. Still, I might as well make good use of the kale . . . it wasn't the kale's fault.

"Wow! Look at all this, Chef! It's beautiful!" Ben said.

"It sure is," I said, picking up a bunch of the kale. The waxy leaves were a perfect dark hunter green, curled like a Southern belle's petticoat. They still smelled of earth. It reminded me of this afternoon, and I pushed away the memory. I needed to focus.

I thought through different dishes that featured kale. It was similar to collard greens, which were popular throughout the South. I thought about braising the kale in some bacon fat, maybe adding a cheese sauce and bread crumbs, and baking it . . . but then I thought about the chilly weather that had blown in this afternoon and realized that soup was the best solution. I couldn't make heartbreak soup, although I had thought about that, too, because then Violet would know I was still upset, and I'd probably cry into it. I had done enough of that.

"How do you feel about a Tuscan kale and white bean soup?" I asked the kitchen.

"Sounds good to me! We actually have a ton of canned white beans in dry storage," Miller said.

"Perfect, let's use it. Zero cost. I like it. How about potatoes and lemons?" I asked. "Do we have enough chicken stock?"

Ben spoke up. "We still have tons from the other day. We had some leftover bones, and I just thought why not use all the scraps and make some extra. We can freeze extra, right?"

"Yes, absolutely, but don't worry about that, we'll use it. A good stock is the spine of most recipes. I'm really impressed by your initiative, man! Go grab a gallon of stock, some potatoes, lemons, red pepper flakes, and the beans, and let's give this a whirl," I said.

"What about adding some sausage? We've got a ton of it, and we need to use it," Miller said.

"Good call, I like how you think!" I said, and he returned my smile. We needed to use everything we had. Keeping costs low was more important than ever, and I was grateful for the kale, but still too mad to use my manners to thank Sam. I'd get there . . . but not yet.

An hour later, the cooks gathered around a large bowl that I had topped with bacon and a little Parmesan cheese. I gave everyone a spoon and told them to try it. I made up another bowl and had the waitstaff try it as well. If they didn't try it, they wouldn't know how to sell it or recommend it.

"Chef Maggie, this is de-lish! Oh, my goodness, I don't think I've ever had anything like this! Yummy!" Frankie approved. "I'm gonna sell the ever-loving God out of this tonight!"

"Awesome! All right, y'all, we're calling this Slightly Spicy Tuscan Kale, Sausage, and White Bean Soup," I said.

Violet walked in and shot me a smile, grabbed a spoon, and dug in. "I love it, Maggie, it's the perfect thing for this weather."

"Everything okay?" I asked.

"Yeah, the electric company gave us a grace period. We're okay till Friday."

"Well, that's good!"

"I guess. Now to find the money," Violet whispered to me.

At ten minutes to eight, I slipped out of the kitchen and joined Jim and Violet at the bar. She was going to take over after he left.

"Jimmy, I want you to get that role in *ICU New York*, but you better come back to Sullivan's Island ASAP," Violet said as she gave him a big hug.

"No need to worry about that, little momma. The role I want most is fairy godfather to that baby." He kissed her head, then pointed to a piece of paper on the bar. "Here's the recipe for a Midori cocktail I came up with for your Asian-themed party. Hope Chris likes it!" Violet gave him an even bigger hug.

I walked out to the porch with him, feeling glum about his departure. He put his bag down, and we put our arms around each other. We looked out at Middle Street. I could faintly hear the music from the bar across the street. I turned to Jim. "How can I thank you for everything you did for me and my family?"

He squeezed my shoulder. "Magnolia, you know we're in this together."

"I'm going to miss you so much." I hugged him tightly. "But I'll be back in New York in a couple weeks."

Jim pushed me away from him, holding on to my shoulders and giving me an incredulous look. "Uh, yeah, okay. Violet's having a baby and her boyfriend is deserting her, Lily is borderline losing it, and Gran's fresh out of a coma . . . great idea, Maggie, let me help you pack! You're not going anywhere, toots. Might as well cozy up with the farmer and fight for your family's business," he said.

"You mean just give up on New York?" I looked at him as if he were crazy, and he shot me a look.

"I don't know where that sass is coming from, Maggie. You cannot abandon your family, and why? Because you couldn't live with yourself knowing that everything fell apart because you put your own ambitions first . . . and who said you can't go back to New York once you've straightened out your family's business?"

I took a long, hard look at him and almost immediately felt myself soften. He had a point. It wasn't as if anyone in New York was clamoring for my return. I let out a breath I didn't realize I was holding in.

"Fine. Maybe it will take a little longer than two weeks to untangle the Magic Lantern's problems."

"Fine," Jim said, meeting my eyes, and we both started laughing. "I know you, girl. You aren't selfish . . . or as tough as you want us all to think you are. You don't walk out on the people you love when they need you."

"Ugh, I know, Jimmy. It's just a lot," I said.

A taxi pulled up in front of the restaurant.

Jim picked up his bag. "Yes, girl, it is a lot. Everything that's worth a lot requires a lot of effort. You can't grow while you're comfortable, y'eh?" Jimmy said, using a Gullah phrase for "You hear."

"Just go, already!" I said and gave him a quick kiss on the cheek. "And call me after the audition on Monday!"

Back in the kitchen, Ben and Miller told me a lot of orders were coming in for the Slightly Spicy Tuscan Kale, Sausage, and White Bean Soup. By the end of the night, we had, in fact, sold the ever-loving God out of the soup. Down to the last bowl. Once the kitchen had been cleaned, I went to find Violet. We had a party to finish planning.

Chapter 23
Magnolia

I planned on arriving at Violet and Chris's house the next day around noon to start setting up the party. I was excited to do something nice for my sister, and I loved surprises. Nothing like a fun project to bind us back together. Also, I was curious to see their house and how she had decorated it. They'd bought the house a year ago, and Violet had told me it was small but in a good school district. Talk about planning ahead.

I woke up a little early and saw that I had a missed call from Alice. Figuring that she probably just had some last-minute questions, I decided to rest a little longer and get up in five minutes and call her back. As it turned out, I fell back asleep. The problem with that is that I tend to sleep harder the second time around and dream more vividly than usual.

I dreamed of my father, something I hadn't done in years. I was on the back of his motorcycle driving down the causeway on our way to Mount Pleasant to get some ice cream. I sat in his lap. Mom never let me ride on his bike, but she was with Violet somewhere, so we were getting away with it. I could feel the wind whipping my braids behind my head. I was shrieking with delight. He gave the top of my head a kiss, and I could see his dark-brown eyes, the black stubble on his sharp jawline, his crooked front tooth. I inhaled the scent of his dark-brown leather jacket.

My ringing phone woke me up. I didn't want to leave my dream, but I couldn't hold on to it with all the noise.

"Hey, Alice, what time is it?" I answered hazily after seeing her name shoot across the screen of my phone.

"It's ten a.m., child, and I've got some bad news. Where are you? Are you alone right now?" Alice said, sounding very serious.

"I'm at home, and yeah, I'm alone. Jim flew back to New York last night. What's going on?" I said, getting scared.

"Your gran had a series of strokes last night. We are all lucky she was here at the hospital, but she's not responding very well to the tests. She's unable to move her legs and feet. Might be permanent," Alice said.

"Oh, my God. Is Gran awake, does she know what's going on?" I asked, feeling my throat tighten.

"Yes. She is awake, but she's disoriented. At best, Maggie, we are looking at a long stretch of physical therapy. We've got a long road ahead of us, girl."

"Does Violet know?" I asked.

"Oh, yeah. She's here. Got here early, when I called y'all. Your momma's here, too," Alice said, sounding overwhelmed.

"Alice, I'm sorry I didn't pick up the phone. I'll be there in a half hour."

"Maggie, there's nothing you can do for your gran here. I know that sounds harsh, but Rose is heavily medicated. They're monitoring her closely and don't expect a change in her condition anytime soon. Violet asked me to ask you to go to her house. She's got her hands full with your mother, and Chris is running around doing all kinds of errands before he leaves. My cousin Livy is going to get sushi from the restaurant she used to work at, so it's the good stuff. She's going to swing by later to drop it off. I already paid her, and you and Vi and I can square up later. You can start working on the decorations. Violet said she'd meet you at her house after she takes Lily home and gets her settled. If I was you, that's what I'd do. I can stay here and call if there's any changes. A distraction, in my opinion, is the best thing, because all we can really do now is wait," Alice said.

I didn't like the idea of not being with Gran, but if my sitting at her bedside wasn't going to help her, I could help Violet, who had fifty people coming over to her house that evening. In addition to food prep, I was sure the house needed to be cleaned. I mean, it probably was clean by my standards, but not by Violet's. I had a lot of pillow-fluffing in my future.

"Okay, Alice. Tell Vi I'll get over to her house right away. Thank you for being such a good friend."

"Friend? Girl, Rose is my sister. Key is under the mat at Vi and Chris's place," Alice said.

"Got it." I clicked off and went to wash my face. My poor gran. Why did she have a stroke when she was coming along so well? Was she going to be all right? Would she be able to walk again, talk again? As I dried my face, I shut my eyes and prayed silently for her recovery.

Alice was right, a distraction was exactly what I needed. If I set my mind to prepping out a party and decorating Violet's house, I wouldn't be worrying about Gran every minute. Gran always said worrying was useless, it was paying the toll twice. I grabbed a dress Jim had packed for me and a pair of stacked heels. I snagged my headphones and iPhone, too. I had a lot of work to do, and music would help me move faster.

I threw all my gear into Gran's truck and made my way to Violet's house, crossing all the bridges. My favorite was the West Ashley connector, because it reminded me of the bridges in Paris and I loved looking at all the white boats in the marina. Charleston was so gorgeous. The sunshine gave everything a golden glow, and I caught sight of myself in the mirrors when I moved into the fast lane to pass a truck. I didn't look terrible. The sunlight in my hair made it look as if it were on fire. I rolled the windows down and let the Lowcountry do its worst on my hair.

I easily found Violet's midcentury brick cottage. It looked more charming than it had in the photos she had sent me. To the left of the house stood a giant old knotted magnolia with waxy hunter-green leaves. I was sure Violet had used her clippers on it to make garlands and wreaths. She was the crafty one in the family. I used the knocker on the light-blue door to announce my arrival in case Chris was at home. When no one answered, I knocked again. Still no response. Figuring he was out, even though there was a shiny new pickup truck in the driveway, I grabbed the key

MY MAGNOLIA SUMMER · 393

under the monogrammed doormat and let myself in. On a side table, I saw a white ceramic bowl with the word "keys" painted on it. Okay, that's where the keys go. An oval mirror hung above the table. Surrounding the mirror was a collection of wooden frames containing photos, sayings, and both photos and sayings. One read "Laughter is the best medicine," and it contained a photo of Violet and Chris at the beach with him splashing her in the ocean. Another frame read, "Home is wherever I am with you," and had a key glued beneath the words. I assumed it was a memento of the day they'd moved in. There was another wooden sign with a Bible verse and yet another with the motivational quote, "Have as much fun as you possibly can!" Good Lord. Violet, come on.

There was a gallery wall leading upstairs that was full of her photographs. That felt more like her. The pictures were of various farms and animals. There were even some pictures of basket weavers downtown working on their sweetgrass baskets. Those baskets were some of the most beautiful creations I've ever seen, and the craft had been passed down for hundreds of years in the Gullah culture. Sweetgrass baskets were a Lowcountry staple.

I went into the living room. It looked like a grown woman's home, decorated to a T, with neutral tones predominating. The walls were painted sea-glass green, except for one bright-white shiplap accent wall where the saying "You and me by the sea" had been stenciled in gold. There were two white slipcovered couches with large burlap throw pillows, one of which had "Welcome to our Nest" embroidered on it, and a pale-blue-and-white buffalo-check armchair. The area rug was fluffy, and I immediately removed my shoes and walked across it with my bare feet. It felt heavenly! There was a large wooden coffee table in the center of the room that looked right out of HGTV. Two very large Georgia Bulldogs flanked the TV, which was on a shelf above a gaming console. *That* was absolutely not Violet. But the expensive Diptyque scented candles on the end tables absolutely were. I inhaled one called Mimosa. It was amazing. I considered slipping it into my bag. Payback for all the dresses of mine she'd stolen in high school. Ha! Sister karma.

I needed to see the kitchen. It looked like a movie set, and had a serious lemon-yellow theme going on. The knives were hung in size order on a magnetic strip on a white subway-tiled wall. A little anal, if you asked me, but still precious. I took one off the strip and checked its blade. Razor sharp. I was impressed. The cooking genes were in there somewhere. After replacing the knife, I was drawn to the double-door stainless steel LG refrigerator. That thing must have cost a pretty penny. When I opened the doors, I found the shelves spotless, with everything organized by color, size, and use. It looked like the refrigerator case of an upscale grocery store.

I decided to take advantage of the empty house to do a little recon on my younger sister. I snooped full force in her bedroom, which was dominated by a queen-size bed with a giant beige velvet tufted headboard. Three monogrammed, starched, and ironed Euro square pillows rested against it. I noted that the monogram included both of their names. That struck me as weird. It broke the Southern code of decorum. You never did a joint monogram unless you were married. I rolled my eyes at Violet for jumping the gun. It looked like they were already married to me. I thought about that for a moment. Was Violet pushing Chris into a life he wasn't ready for? First a house, now a baby. Man, she had her claws in deep.

This perfectly decorated house reinforced the impression I'd gotten when I'd seen Chris at Gran's earlier in the week that he was an entirely different person from the boy I'd dated in high school. He used to be a bit of a country boy wannabe. I'd never thought he'd become a lawyer. But that brief encounter hadn't given us a lot of time to catch up, especially with Violet's prickly reaction to seeing us together. I wondered if he still listened to country music, still loved to hunt, fish, and go mudding. He had always been a blast. I looked around their shared bedroom, spotting the bedside tables, and, deciding to be an adult, I did not open the top drawer of either of them.

On the bed were two giant shopping bags from Party City, containing what I correctly guessed were party decorations. I couldn't help but giggle at the paper lanterns and chopsticks. Yeah, Chris was going to Japan, but did we have to make it so corny and like borderline racist? This wasn't New York, so I supposed I could relax and not worry about being so cool and cosmopolitan all the time. I had to give it to Violet, she always threw a good party and knew how to have fun. I took the bags down to the living room to assemble the decorations, but before I could get started the doorbell rang. I looked at a clock. It was noon already. That had to be Alice's cousin with the sushi.

"Hey, you Magnolia?" a tall woman in skinny jeans and a red spandex top asked when I opened the door. I nodded, and she shoved a covered aluminum dish at me. "Here, put this in the kitchen, and come out to the car and help me bring in the rest of the stuff."

As we unloaded the car, Livy introduced herself as Alice's "younger, more stylish cousin." With her ease at issuing orders, organizational skills, and high energy, she was as much a force of nature as Alice. "Look here," she said, pointing to the labels on the trays as we put them in the fridge. "Tuna sushi rolls, California rolls, yellowtail and salmon sashimi, seaweed in case you want to make your own rolls, and condiments. Plus a few bags of groceries Alice figured you would need."

"Thank you so much! You and Alice thought of everything."

"Alice gets the credit, I'm just the deliverywoman. Sorry about your gran. We're all praying for her. And, Magnolia, don't you let your troubles keep you from throwing a great party and enjoying yourself. Keep your spirits up! Alice told me this party is important to your sister. Good luck, baby!"

Livy was out the door before I could thank her again. Wow, she and Alice really had given me everything I needed, not just the food but something just as important: permission not to feel guilty about prepping for a frivolous party—okay, maybe not so frivolous to Vi—when my grandmother lay in a hospital bed recovering from a stroke.

I dug out my headphones, cranked up the volume, and got to work.

First, I assembled decorations, inserting fishing wire into the lanterns so we could hang them, then I removed a stack of travel-bingo games and a word search for things like "wasabi" and "futon." I spotted an air fryer and decided to make some healthy egg rolls. I couldn't find good last-minute Japanese food, so I went for my favorite Asian food. I roasted some chicken and made a peanut satay. I threw together some dumplings . . . okay, I found a box of frozen ones from Costco—they were the best. With the oven and the burners going, it got hot in the kitchen. I took off my sweater and rocked out, dancing around in my headphones as I cooked.

I had my iPhone on shuffle, and I blame Apple for the next series of events.

Time to be honest: some songs just unleashed me, and during an emotionally turbulent time such as the one I'd been experiencing the last week, music helped me forget my troubles and power through. Ariana Grande did it for me. I was straight up dancing to the music, shaking my butt, and doing little spins. The food was cooking, doing fine on its own, so I used my spoon as a microphone. It felt great to just move and sing. I added a few air punches and hair flips. I was deep into my own choreographed number for one of her singles when I stirred the duck sauce a little too hard and I splashed sauce all over my shirt.

I turned the volume down and went into Violet's laundry room, intending to throw my shirt into the washer and raid her closet for an old T-shirt. But as I yanked off my shirt, an amazing Latin pop song came on, and I started dancing again, hips swaying, deep bends, and booty circles. I couldn't help it. I twirled myself around the little room and knocked right into sweaty, half-naked Chris, who was standing in the doorway, watching me. He slipped his arm around my waist to steady me. I hadn't heard him come in! Damn! I froze and dropped the plastic fabric softener bottle I'd been using as a maraca.

"Oh, hi, there, Chris. I, uh, didn't see you there." I was totally mortified and felt my face turning red as I stepped back from him. He was stifling a smile.

"Hey, there, yourself, Maggie! Here a little early for the party, eh?" A smile broke across his face.

"Oh, uh, I'm setting up, and I spilled duck sauce on my shirt. It's in the wash." I was looking directly into his blue eyes.

He still had his hand on my waist and his arm around me, which was noticeably more muscular than it had been in high school. God, his body was . . . solid.

"Nice moves, Mags," he said with a laugh.

"Shut up, I'm so embarrassed." I felt the heat in

my cheeks, and I pulled away, realizing we were both half-naked . . . and he was looking.

"Shit." He rifled through a laundry basket and threw me one of his T-shirts. I pulled it on and took inventory of his six-pack. Good Lord, he sure wasn't a skinny teenager anymore! Whew!

"Sorry, Maggie, I didn't . . . mean to startle you. I was out for a run. But you do look good dancing around my laundry room, maybe you want to show me more of those moves at the party tonight? Do people dance at going-away parties?" He was teasing me, but it made me uncomfortable.

"Chris, stop it. Have you heard from Violet?" I said, quickly redirecting the conversation to my sister.

"Yeah, she's on her way home now. The house smells amazing!"

"Good. We're going to have fun tonight, but I thought this would be a surprise party?"

"Nah, Violet can't hide anything from me. She gets so excited. Can't keep a secret."

"Oh, okay," I said, thinking that was probably a good thing.

"Well, it should be a good time. I'm going to go shower, and then you can tell me what I can do to help." He walked out of the laundry room.

I tried to get it together and went back into the kitchen. What had just happened? Was Chris flirting with me? No, he was just teasing me, and I was being oversensitive.

I got back to work, and before long I had the dumplings thawed and ready to steam. Then, I threw together a delicious plum dipping sauce. The egg rolls were assembled, lined up like little soldiers on a baking tray, ready to fry. The fried rice was done and could be reheated, and the sushi stations were set up, ready to go in the fridge.

I went into the garage, hoping to find a ladder so I could hang up the paper lanterns. Instead, I found shelves loaded with plastic labeled containers for every single holiday, including Valentine's Day. Who decorated for Valentine's Day? This house was so organized, even the garage looked like an Instagram picture. Sheesh! I decided to take advantage of the situation, and after digging around for a while, I found some Christmas lights. Those were always fun and festive. Then I took my time putting everything back exactly as I'd found it. I didn't need Martha Stewart lecturing me.

I headed back to the kitchen and was surprised to hear music—the driving rhythms of the sixties instrumental music that Chris had grown up to because his

father was a fan of surf culture—and even more surprised to see Chris, looking very put together in khakis
and a blue-and-white-striped button-down shirt, working at the island. He was throwing together tiny little
wonton wrappers full of crab, and what appeared to be a
whipped chive-and-cream-cheese stuffing. He was slicing and dicing like a professional! Those sharp knives
belonged to him, not my sister. Rocking the brightly
polished Global knife through a handful of green onions,
he looked up and shot me a wink.

"Hey, Maggie, I was thinking . . . who is Gran's
power of attorney?"

"What? What is a power of attorney?" I asked.

"It's someone who can make decisions on your
behalf should you be unable to make them yourself.
Like, if Gran slips into a coma again, who has the legal
authority to make a medical decision for her or access
her bank account to pay her bills?"

"I guess my mom?" I shrugged. "That would make
sense, right?"

"No, not necessarily. It can be anyone. It doesn't
have to be a relative. We should find out, especially if
Lily decides to go on that rehab cruise," he said.

"I'll ask Violet," I said.

Not wanting to think about things like that, I went
over to inspect his work and saw that the green scal-

lions were sliced at a perfect half-inch cut, all uniform, on a diagonal. I arched an eyebrow at him. He smirked and did a little spin, dipping a spoon into a pot of what looked like some sort of custard on the stove. He fed me a bite and my mouth exploded with happiness.

"Chris, is that jasmine I detect . . . and mango? What the . . . where did you learn how to . . ." I stammered.

"Cook like this? Well, Maggie, I've changed a lot since high school. In my spare time I like to take lessons at Charleston Cooks downtown. Sometimes even Violet tags along. We have this great instructor, Liz Vena. She taught me almost everything I know. I can braise short ribs with the best of them, thanks to her. Impressed?" he said, and I took another taste of the custard.

"Chris, I am impressed. This is delicious! Last time I saw you cook anything we had to call the fire department!" I teased.

"I've come a long way, babe," he said.

"Yes, you have, and I'm sure Violet loves this! Do y'all cook together a lot?" I asked, shifting the conversation to her.

"Yeah, we do. I'm happy I can do more than grill a steak like most guys."

"That's the right answer in my book, obviously," I said. "How often do you take the classes?"

"Well, not as often as I'd like to. I'm always working. That sister of yours likes a certain lifestyle. I'll never be as good a cook as you, Maggie, but I can try," he said, mocking me.

"Oh, please, Chris," I said and tossed a towel at him, which he quickly grabbed, twisted, and snapped at my butt.

"Ouch! Ugh, I walked right into that one." I started to laugh. I dunked my hands in a bowl of water in the sink and flicked water at him.

"Stop, Maggie! You'll ruin the expensive grass wallpaper! Can't get it wet!" he said.

"Stop, Maggie!" I sang, mimicking him. "I'm a professional food fighter, Christopher, you don't want to start a war with me!" We were both laughing. I thought it was so easy to fall back into a friendship with him. I'd like having him as a brother-in-law.

Then it got a little out of hand.

"Oh, I think I'm a match for you, Maggie," he said as he started to put the food away.

"Oh, yeah, because you got bigger and better since high school, I know, I know. Gone are the guns, ducks, camo, and fishing poles. You're a big-time lawyer now who takes gourmet cooking lessons. My, you've grown up!"

"Oh, you're asking for it now," he said, lowering the heat on the custard.

A full-scale water-flicking fight broke out, and we were acting like a couple of kids, with him chasing me around the kitchen island and me shrieking. There was water all over the floor and I went sliding. Chris caught me and I felt his strong arms around my waist again, and in the interest of full disclosure, I couldn't help noticing how *good* he smelled.

This was too much. I mean, it was a little too easy to fall into the playful rhythms of our high school years. But he hadn't looked *this* good when I was dating him. Ugh, this line of thought was trouble with a capital T.

"Hey, Chris, you know what I just realized? We don't have enough ice! We need some for drinks, and I want to put the sushi on beds of ice."

"I can go grab a few pounds at the gas station down the road," he said.

"That would be great, thanks!"

"I'll get out of the way and give y'all the space to decorate. Girl stuff," he mumbled, and I rolled my eyes.

"Good idea. I can do a little magic on this place, plus, Violet might want to do a grand review and all," I said.

"Yeah, you're right, she's so into that. Maybe I'll call Gage and see if he wants to grab a beer before the party. Kill some time, catch the end of the game."

"Gage?" I asked.

"Yeah, my buddy. He's another associate at the firm. He'll be here tonight with his wife, Kathleen. They're fun. He's going to Japan, too."

"Can't wait to meet them! Yeah, now's the time to take advantage of a chance to hang out with the boys," I said with a laugh.

"Yeah, I guess Violet and I will probably be spending more nights at home, not going out so much, after I get back," he said.

"Are you excited about it?" I said.

"Yeah! I can't wait to see Japan! I've always wanted to go, the culture is amazing. Not to mention, this is a fantastic career opportunity for me!" he said quickly.

"No, Chris, I mean about the baby," I said.

"Oh, right. Well, I'm going to head out, I'll be back with the ice before the party starts."

O-kay, I thought, he didn't want to talk about the baby. Made sense, he was still processing the big news of a big responsibility coming at him months down the road. Chris was way more sophisticated these days, more worldly, and that was a good thing for my sister. He'd gotten a law degree, learned to use a razor, thrown away his camo fatigues, and taken cooking classes. He could almost pass for a gentleman now. I wondered if he worked on Broad Street downtown. He sure looked the part.

I got to work and started to hang the lanterns and set out some paper flowers. Before I knew it, it was time to get in the shower. I helped myself to Violet's products. She always had the best-smelling stuff. After scrubbing myself with her lavender bodywash I felt like a new woman. I grabbed one of Violet's fluffy white towels and dried off, found a blow-dryer and a round brush. I worked some magic on myself, and my red hair tumbled down around my shoulders in voluminous waves.

I'd packed my own makeup, but as the sister of a Sephora VIP member, I decided to open up Violet's drawers and sample the latest trends. I found an eye shadow palette by someone called Natasha Denona. I chose a color for my lids that looked like liquid copper. It made my eyes pop, and when I lined them with black liquid liner, I felt like Cleopatra. I used some bronzer that made me look as if I had a healthy relationship with the sun, and some mascara that made my lashes so long they felt like awnings. I took a picture of the products I'd used so I could buy them for myself.

I changed into my dress and stacked heels. I looked

in the mirror and realized it had been years since I had, one, been to a real party for real, and two, liked my reflection. The dress had a high hemline and a low neckline and hugged my hips in a way that was, dare I say, sexy? I felt good. This wasn't a traditional baby shower; it was at night and served cocktails. I added a pair of gold hoop earrings and walked into the kitchen. There I found Violet going over a checklist.

"Hey, Maggie! Thank you for jumping in early!" She gave me a half smile.

"Sure, no problem. How's Gran?" I asked.

"She's stable, but it's scary, Maggie. She goes in and out of consciousness and is very confused about where she is. I know she's got to be scared, too."

"Do the doctors know what caused the stroke?" I asked.

"They don't really know. It could be a side effect of the trauma of the accident, or of the surgery."

"Oh, my God. How can this be happening? Where's Mom? Is *she* okay?" I asked.

"She's not great, Maggie. She was upset about Gran taking a turn for the worse. I smelled alcohol on her breath at the hospital this morning. Thank God, she took a car service to the hospital. I had to take her home. This is just a lot," she said, and then got sick in the sink. "It's too much, Maggie. How am I ever going to . . . handle all of this?" Violet blotted her mouth with a paper towel.

"Violet, you're handling it amazingly well. We have each other and we have Alice, it's going to be okay." I looked at her tummy. "Rotten kid. Be nicer to my sister." I shot her a wink. "Want something to drink?"

"Yeah, there's ginger ale in the fridge, can you grab me one?" She smiled.

"Sure thing." I cracked one open.

"I'm only able to deal with this because I have help. Thank God you're here, Maggie. I do have some good news, though. Mom has decided to go on the rehab cruise. She leaves on Tuesday," Violet said.

"Well, that's great! What changed her mind?"

"Since our lunch on Thursday, Annabelle's been emailing her info about the cruise, and late this morning she called Mom. I think it was the allure of escape and travel. Mom said yes, and with a click of a mouse, Annabelle bought her a ticket," she said.

"Man, Aunt Belle is a lifesaver!" *For Mom.* "Let's hope the therapy sticks this time."

"Maggie, come on, we have to be positive."

"I know, I'm sorry, I'll be supportive, it's just . . ."

"Not our first time at the rodeo. Got it." She sipped the ginger ale. "You look so good, Maggie! You sure do clean up nice! Is that my makeup?" Violet said.

"Big-sister tax," I joked. "I was a little on the fence about this dress, it's so tight."

"In all the right places. If I could wear a dress like that right now I would! I hate everything in my closet. Literally anything with a waistband makes me want to hurl," Violet said, and I was glad the mood was lightening up. We had gotten good over the years at putting bad things in tiny compartments under our beds. "Have you seen Chris?"

"Yes, he popped in for a little while and then went out to get ice and have a beer with a friend before the party. By the way, he asked me earlier if we know who Gran's power of attorney is. I assume it's Mom, and if she's going on the cruise, we need to make legal arrangements in case . . . something else happens to Gran while Mom's away."

"So like Chris. Can't stop thinking like a lawyer." She rolled her eyes.

"Well, it is a good point," I said. "We had a good chat. I think he's really excited about Japan."

"Wish he was as excited about the baby. I imagine he'll have a great time with all those beautiful Asian women while his baby momma stays at home getting fat," Violet said.

"Okay, first of all, you aren't getting fat, you're

pregnant. Second, you are gorgeous, Violet! Everyone knows that," I said.

"I feel like a messy blob, Maggie. Can't wait for that pregnancy glow to show up! I don't feel like I can compete with another woman, especially one in another time zone who comes without strings. I'm not engaged, remember? I have zero ownership of him."

"Ownership? Have you lost your mind? You and Chris own this house together. That's a huge sign of his commitment. This house is decorated like a television show! You have a closet full of designer clothes! Chris provides for you, and maybe that's the way he shows his love. I'm sure he's going to miss you and his wonderful life here. Let the man live, Violet! This also is an opportunity for growth in his career, that's important for him. When he comes back from his business trip, he's going to take on a completely different role—being a daddy. So, cool it with the other-women anxieties," I said.

"You have no idea how hard this is, Maggie. I'm going to hop in the shower. When I get out let's go over the food stations. I'm nervous because I invited some people from Chris's firm. I want everything to be perfect. Can you set up the bar?"

Violet emerged forty minutes later looking like

a new woman. She had curled her hair and styled it charmingly, with half of it up in a ponytail and the rest falling to the bottom of her neck. She wore a bright-red dress that swished when she moved. Her lipstick matched the hue of the dress perfectly. She looked comfortable and unstressed. She dashed around the house, straightening up little things here and there, and put on a perfectly curated playlist for the evening. She rehung some of the paper lanterns. I'd thought the lanterns looked fine before, but with Violet's attention to detail and her superior sense of interior design, they now cast a magical glow in the foyer and the living room. Chris came back and, after depositing the ice in the freezer, gave Violet a kiss on her cheek and complimented her dress. She shone. He poured me a delicious glass of red wine, and one for himself. Around six, guests started to arrive.

The first people to show up were two couples from Chris's firm. A senior partner, who greeted my chest first, helped himself to a drink at the bar, while his wife looked around the living room, turning over a decorative china plate and checking the tags on a few of the throw pillows. The senior partner had brought Violet and Chris a bottle of sake as a hostess gift and demanded that they "start taking shots" as soon as possible to get the party started. The other couple was Chris's friend Gage and his wife, Kathleen. Chris greeted them with hugs and poured each of them a glass of wine. They were as warm as the Lowcountry sunshine, and I immediately felt like I had known them my whole life. Kathleen was a recent graduate of the College of Charleston, with a master's in creative writing and an undergraduate degree in Russian lit. Initially I was intimidated by her surfer-girl good looks and her résumé, but once we started talking and she dropped a Harry Potter reference, I relaxed and realized she was super laid back. If I ever moved back to Charleston, I would want to live next door to her. She and her husband had two small children and were relishing an evening away. Because Gage was following Chris to Japan, Kathleen and Violet were organizing a support group for the mates left behind. I felt a pang of jealousy, wishing I could be a part of that.

More and more people arrived, and I recognized a few from school. It was nice to catch up with some of our old friends. There were a few other associates from the firm as well as paralegals in attendance, and I realized I was having a great time. It was one of those parties where you found yourself enjoying the whole vibe. The music, the food, the company, everything just lined up, and people were laughing. Violet stood near the front door, chatting with people, so she could greet guests, and still managed to be at Chris's side whenever his drink needed refilling. She was the best hostess.

I went up to her to see if she needed anything and when she said, "a drink," we both laughed, and I grabbed a cold Diet Coke for her. As she took her first sip, a couple came up to us.

"Violet, I cannot believe this house! You sure are a diamond to Chris! I bet he thinks marrying you was the best decision he made in his life!" said a blonde, who couldn't have weighed more than a hundred pounds, holding on to the arm of her suited lawyer husband.

"Uh, well, we aren't married. I'm his girlfriend," Violet said.

"Oh, honey! I think that's so romantic and unconventional. It's very, uh, modern! Anyways, y'all have a lovely home," she said, trying to recover. "Where's the bathroom?"

Violet showed her the way, with the blonde's husband trailing behind them. When Violet returned, I could see she was uncomfortable, but she shook it off and we went to check up on Chris.

"Hey, baby, you need anything?" Violet purred to Chris in front of a few work friends.

"No, sugar, I'm all right, just chatting here with Jay and his wife, Christina, about Japan." Chris gave her a squeeze and introduced me. "This is my high school sweetheart Magnolia, Violet's sister! She's a New York City chef nowadays and the brains behind this whole party and even made us those sushi rolling stations over there. She's so creative."

I blushed. "Well, Violet is the brains of the operation, I just helped a little," I said, trying to shrug it off.

"Wait, are you telling me you dated both of these gorgeous women, Christopher?" Jay, a partner, said. "Way to go, son!" He clapped him on the back and my stomach roiled. Stupid boys' club. It existed here as well as in the kitchens of New York. I looked at Violet.

"Yeah, ha, ha. Well, we are in the South, best to keep it in the family!" Violet said, making a joke that fell flat. "Uh, let me go refresh y'all's drinks."

"I got it, Violet, you stay," I said.

"You've got such a pretty girl, Chris, when are you going to make it official?" Christina said, through bleached veneers and way-too-thick false lashes. She was at least fifty, but her body looked twenty.

"Oh, I don't know, we just want to enjoy this stage in life together for a while," Chris said, emptying his drink.

Good Lord, the pressure was *on*. I went into the kitchen and poured myself a shot of sake to take the edge off. Picking up a fresh plate of hors d'oeuvres and a bottle of wine, I returned to Violet, who was chatting with three women who, I swear to God, were wearing the exact same Lilly Pulitzer shift, but in different colors. Forcing myself not to roll my eyes, I passed around the shrimp dumplings.

"Oh, my God, this looks de-vine! Violet, you're so lucky to have a chef as a sister! We should have a dinner party soon! Wouldn't that be so *fun*? While our husbands are all in Japan! Well, your boyfriend, Violet, our husbands. Listen, I think we need to come up with a plan to get you that ring, girl! Enough is *enough!*" The brunette gave Violet's hand a little squeeze.

My poor sister. I was sure this was not helping her nausea. I decided to turn up the music and get people dancing. How many more times could Violet and Chris shrug off questions about their relationship? I went over to Violet's iPhone and found a playlist called "Get Up and Dance!" I turned it on. Quickly, the mood lightened up. The music was perfect, and the wine, the sake, and Jim's Midori cocktails were flowing. I grabbed my sister away from the women and spun her around. She giggled and joined in, seeming grateful for an escape. Before long, everyone was dancing. The party was on fire, everyone was laughing, even the senior partner spun his wife around a few times. Chris pushed back the furniture and the older guys decided to show us younger people how to shag. It was a true Lowcountry dance only the locals knew well.

I took a break to grab water for some people, myself included. At one point Chris was moving across the dance floor to Michael Jackson's "Thriller," which was hilarious! I'd forgotten how much fun dancing is. Sometimes I think the lack of social dancing is what's wrong with my generation. Back in the day, people would go to sock hops or supper clubs and dance the night away together, releasing tension and having fun. Now if you want to go dancing in a nice-girl type of way, you have to wait for a milestone like a wedding or a birthday.

After I rehydrated the dancers, there was a break in the music, and I heard the doorbell. Violet answered the door and standing there, under Violet's porch light, was Sam Smart. Six feet tall, sandy haired, and holding a bouquet of flowers and a bottle of wine. Dang it. He smiled at Violet, gave her a hug, and caught my eye, shooting me a pout. I turned on my heel and went back into the kitchen, but I smiled to myself. After refreshing the sushi stations into little plates and pulling Chris's dessert out of the fridge, I poured myself a glass of wine and drained it quickly. I chased it with another and set out with the plates of sushi. I didn't see Chris or Sam or Violet as I set them down on the buffet table, so I returned to the kitchen. As I was washing a few dishes, I felt someone press up against me. Oh, God. He wrapped his hands around my hips and pressed his thumbs into my lower back, pulling my butt into his pelvis. I spun around and Chris laid a big fat kiss on my mouth. "God, I've missed you, Maggie."

I froze for a moment. Out of the corner of my eye I spied a tacky frame labeled "Sisters," and inside it was a picture of me and Violet. I shoved him off me so hard he took a step back.

"What in the hell do you think you're doing, Chris?" I yelled.

"What's going on in here, y'all? Oh, my God, Chris! Maggie? What happened?" Violet cried. Sam was right behind her.

"Nothing!" Chris said. "I slipped and lost my balance . . ."

"Chris, you're bleeding!" Violet said.

"Oh, man." Chris looked down at his bare feet. He must have removed his shoes while dancing and stepped on some broken glass in the kitchen.

"Let me take a look at that, buddy," Sam said. "I'm a doctor."

"Chris, are you okay?" Violet said.

"Yeah, baby, I'm good," he said, looking at me.

Ashamed. *Good*, I thought. At least he had the good sense to be embarrassed.

"I'm going to take out the garbage." I grabbed the huge bag that was full of empty wine bottles. I needed some air.

I went out the side door into the alleyway by the garage and tossed the bag into the garbage can. Before going back into the house, I checked my phone and saw a text from B-Rad. It read:

Hey, girl! Man, we miss you. I heard what happened. Dumb move on Chef's part, but guess what? Remember Chef Michelle who used to be chef de cuisine before Chef? Well, she's opening a restaurant and needs a right-hand man . . . or woman. Hit me back and I'll put you guys in touch. Miss you, Red.

I was shaken! Chef Michelle! A promotion! A chance to work with a world-class chef, and she had been rumored to be doing an all-female team. How cool would that be? Now I had a reason to go back to New York, but many more reasons to stay in Charleston.

Just then Sam appeared.

"Hey, there, killer," Sam said through a smile.

"Hey, yourself," I mumbled. "Killer?"

"Maggie, clearly we walked in on an incident."

"Does he need stitches?" I asked.

"Nope."

"Too bad."

"I'm sure you had your reasons," Sam said.

"Well, I had one good one."

"Hmm."

"Yeah, hmm."

"Maggie, I'm sorry, I should have told you the full story. I will never lie to you again," Sam said.

I looked at him, waiting for more. "That's it?"

"Yep, that's it. When one is truly sorry, the only words that matter are the apology, identifying what exactly the apology is for, and a promise to not do it again. You don't need an explanation. I was wrong, and I'm sorry I hurt you."

"Oh," I said.

"'Oh'? You look disappointed."

"No, I'm actually relieved. I don't need a lengthy explanation. You should have told me. So should Violet, but . . . I guess it is what it is," I said.

"Okay. Maybe let out a good ole holler?"

"What?"

"Just a good ole yell. You need to send off the emotion."

So, I yelled. Then I yelled again, and to be honest, I felt better. Then I started laughing.

"Come here." Sam pulled me into a bear hug, kissed the top of my head.

I let out a huge sigh. "Shit. I think I forgive you."

"Truce?" he said. "Friends?"

"Friends," I said, then mumbled into his chest, "Chris kissed me in there."

"Lucky guy," he said. I looked at him, pulling away. He held up his hands. "Bad joke."

"Yeah! Jesus, is he out of his damn mind?" I said.

"He's drunk, has cold feet, and is about to move to the other side of the world for at least eight weeks to work at a job that's giving him a major case of impostor syndrome," Sam said.

"How do you know all of that?" I asked.

"People tell me things, and I know Chris's family. He's the first to graduate college, let alone law school. This house is full of Violet's decorating style. There isn't an ounce of him in here. He loves her, but isn't ready to get married, and now they're having a baby? Everything's coming to a head and he's getting locked into a life he isn't ready for. He'll come around, though."

"You think he'll come around?" I said.

"Well, I don't know one hundred percent, but I'm willing to put my money on it. He's a good guy. Violet has great taste in men." He wiggled his eyebrows at me.

"All right, that's funny," I conceded with a giggle.

"Can I kiss you now?" he said.

"I want to say yes, I'll admit, since we're in this

honesty bubble, but I think we need to cool it, Sam. I need to get my head on straight. I can't even see clearly. Between my mom, Gran, Chris, and Violet, I've got a full plate. Plus, a job opportunity in New York just came up, and I want to consider that. I need to think about an exit strategy. I don't want to lead you on," I said.

"Well, that sure is honest. I'll be missing you till you change your mind, friend."

"Friends. At least till I get it together," I said.

He gave me a longing look and bit his lower lip.

"Focus! I'm serious, Sam," I warned.

"Focus, okay, I can do that. You throw a mean hook," he said.

"Shut up. Let's go inside."

Chapter 24
Violet

Thankfully, the next morning I woke up to find a small pile of hostess gifts by the door next to the key bowl. Chris was in the kitchen making us coffee, so I decided to bring them to him and we could open them together. Who knows, maybe there was a cool surprise among the wine and candles.

"Chris? Look, honey, your friends brought us little gifts!" I said.

"Oh, that's nice. Open it up. I'm allowing you one cup today, so I'm making it a twelve-ouncer," he said.

"I know I need to cut back on the caffeine. But it's bad enough I couldn't even try the sushi from last night. Tell me it was horrible." I pouted.

"We decided not to lie to each other, Vi," Chris said.

"Ugh, you're right. Okay fine. Soon enough," I said

as I ripped the wrapping paper, revealing a fancy bar of soap. "Well, this smells fantastic!"

"Here's your coffee." Chris slid over a blue-and-white mug.

"Thanks, baby. Why don't you open up the next one?" I passed him a small green wrapped box.

While he opened it, I went over to the cabinet over the coffee maker to get a little more sugar. This child had a sweet tooth, and I couldn't help but add an extra packet of sweetener to my coffee.

"Oh, great," Chris said flatly.

"What's the matter?" I turned around to find him shaking his head, holding a onesie with the company's logo across it. "Aww, that's cute!"

"Is it?" he said and put it down on the counter. "I literally just told Steve at work. I need to get some air." He started to go into the living room.

"Chris? What's the matter, it's just a onesie!" I said.

"It's not just a onesie, Vi, there's going to be a human in that onesie one day soon!"

"Yeah, in about eight months. That's how these things work, generally," I said.

Chris just looked at me and then at his feet. Then up at me again with this look like he was begging or searching for a way out. I knew that look. I knew he wanted me to let him off the hook. Somehow tell him this was all a joke. I felt a pit in my stomach that had nothing to do with the baby. He wasn't ready and wouldn't be anytime soon.

I started to pace. Then I stopped, put my hands on my hips, and said, "You want out, don't you?"

"I don't know, I just . . ."

"You just what, Chris?"

"I'm not ready, Violet. This is all so fast!"

"Well, sorry, buster, I can't exactly slow things down."

"I know. I know. I'm sorry."

I looked at him then and something inside me snapped. I decided that I had had it with him not being ready. I felt like I was always pushing him. I pushed him to move in, to buy a house, to get serious. He had dragged his feet at every life-changing event. It was exhausting. I didn't want a man who had to be convinced about me or this life we had built together. If he didn't want to be a part of it, fine. I could deal with him shortchanging me, but not me and the baby growing inside of me. It was clear at that point that I wasn't making decisions for myself anymore. It was for both of us. Me and the baby.

"You know what, Chris? I'm done," I blurted.

"What do you mean you're done?" he said.

"I'm done with you! This is over," I said.

"How can you say that, Violet? We love each other!"

"Yes, we do. But love isn't enough, Chris. We need commitment. Full commitment. I am pregnant and I need you on board right now . . . and you're not there. It was one thing about marriage, but now it's marriage and a baby, and you will be away for months! I'm tired, Chris. I don't want to be with someone I have to keep convincing to stay and move on to the next level. I want to build a life with you, but it's time we stop pretending that that's what you want, too."

"I do want that . . . just not now."

"Well, what am I meant to do with that? We can't undo this!" I gestured to my stomach.

"Violet."

"Don't you dare suggest . . ."

"I wasn't! I wasn't! Oh, God, no, Violet. I just . . . I need more time, and I know that's impossible. Maybe when I get back we could . . ."

"So, you want me to wait here for a few months while I grow a human being and wait even longer for you to decide? No, sir. No, thank you. No more. It's over, you're off the hook."

We stood there for what seemed like ages staring at each other, waiting for the other to hit the undo button or say something to go back to the peaceful morning we were having before the onesie. But that was it. Truth is like that. Once all parties involved know it, you can't take it back. In that moment I had drawn a line in the sand. I was for the family, and he was for himself. It wasn't fair to my unborn child to have a half-in, half-out dad. He or she deserved more than that, and to be honest, people voted with their feet. He didn't want this, he wanted an escape, and I needed to give it to him. He was too much of a coward to ask for one himself.

"Violet, I'm sorry," he said. He was no longer protesting.

"Yeah, me, too, Chris," I said.

He went upstairs and started to pack. He was probably packing for his trip, but it felt like he was packing up to leave-leave. I looked at myself in the hall mirror and for the first time in a long time, I liked what I saw. I stepped back and saw a slight swell in my tummy area. I rubbed my hand across it. "It's just you and me, kid." I smiled at my reflection, feeling protective over this little life and feeling oddly confident in myself. I had made the right decision, even if it hurt . . . and I knew it because I didn't need to cry. I felt capable. I could be a momma, and a good one, too. I had just conquered the first of what was sure to be many tough decisions in the realm of parenthood. Maybe violets don't have thorns like roses, or heavy fragrances like lilies or magnolias, but they are just as strong.

Chapter 25
Magnolia

A few days after the party, I woke up in the blue-gray light of a sunrise. Tossing and turning for a few minutes, tangled in my soft, cool sheets, I knew I wouldn't fall back to sleep. There was too much on my mind, too much to do, so I rolled out of my squeaky bed and went downstairs to the kitchen. I made a huge pot of coffee. While I waited for it to brew, I thought about everything that was going to happen in the next couple of days. I had sent an inquiry about the job with Chef Michelle, we had a Zoom meeting scheduled for this afternoon, today my mom was leaving on the wellness cruise, and in a few hours Chris would be flying to Japan.

The ding of the coffee maker along with the delicious, nutty aroma announced that the coffee was ready.

I poured some into my favorite mug and went outside to the porch swing. I loved early mornings when I had the chance to enjoy them. Usually, in New York City, I was rushing off to work, but occasionally I got up early enough to leisurely sip a cup of coffee with the quiet world around me. I was grateful I had the opportunity to center myself today.

I had some time to spend with Gran and tell her about everything going on, and my mind was a little overwhelmed with all the medical information about stroke rehab and recovery that the doctors and nurses had given me. I looked at the sky, which was turning a shade of periwinkle blue. A slice of moon was still visible, and I spied a beautiful white heron in flight. The birds in the palmetto trees were greeting each other. I sighed. When I was a child, this morning ritual used to include Gran. She used to "get me up with the birds," and I'd usually follow her into her garden, where we'd check on the plants. I missed her, and truth be told, I didn't feel completely comfortable in this house without her, maybe because she was such a big part of what "home" meant to me.

Her recovery would not necessarily follow a straight line. While her speech was much better, almost perfect, her movements were still strained. When the doctors felt she'd progressed enough to continue her recovery at home, she would need a full-time aide and a ton of therapy. Gran wouldn't like that. She hated to be dependent on anyone. I was also worried about the cost. With the financial condition of the restaurant and our dependency on it, I wondered how far Gran's medical insurance would go in covering the cost of her rehab. I impatiently wanted the doctors to give me the exact date when she'd be fully recovered and back to normal. But, of course, that was impossible, and we were in limbo, waiting to see what would happen.

I sipped my coffee. The only upside of feeling so worried about Gran was that it made my problems seem less significant. The Sam situation would just have to wait. I had bigger fish to fry, both literally and figuratively. We clearly were attracted to each other. And what was wrong with that? With all the responsibilities I had, I needed to keep my wits about me, and when I was in his arms, I was so consumed by lust it impaired my ability to think.

I leaped off the swing. It was getting too hot for my long pajama pants, time to get changed and moving. The sun had risen, the clock was ticking.

A half hour later I was showered and dressed in a tank top and some cutoff jean shorts. It was going to get too hot for anything else. I slipped on some old flip-flops. Summer was here in the Lowcountry, and she doesn't play. We were officially in the time of year when the afternoon microburst storms would break the heat, but then cause humidity so thick you could swim through it. I was headed to the hospital first, to check in with Gran. The temperature was climbing, and I was sure it would reach triple digits.

When I got to her room she was up, deep in a tabloid about her soap operas.

"Good morning, Gran! I see you are busy rotting your brain!" I teased.

"Oh, hey, Magnolia! Oh, hush. What brings you in here so early?"

"You, of course! I needed to lay my eyes on ya before you are released into the wild."

"Thank God that's happening soon. I need to get my hair done, and I'm desperate for a pedicure!"

"I see your priorities are in line."

"Oh, stop. Haven't I taught you since you were a child that hair is fifty percent of a woman's looks? A deep conditioning wouldn't hurt you, Miss Thing."

"Gran, I am an islander these days. I can't concern myself with frivolous things like beauty products. Plus, that's what hats are for." I dug around in my bag for an old Yankees cap and put it on.

"Girl, take that off! We can't let anyone see that you're a convert!" she joked.

"Okay, okay." I tied my hair into a messy bun.

"Well, now you just look like a pineapple. God, I've missed you, girl. Come give me a smooch." She gestured to give her a hug and I did. It was healing just to be in her embrace.

"Heard someone threw a great party. Violet called me yesterday," she said. "Maggie, what's wrong?"

"Nothing. Alice's cousin Livy hooked us up with the best sushi. The party was fun. Violet is a great hostess, and it was nice to meet some of her friends and see her gorgeous house."

"What's happened, Maggie?"

"Gran, a lot."

"Are you going to tell me, or do I have to guess? Don't you know by now you can't . . . I see you got your coat shined."

"What in the . . . well, yeah, that's part of it."

"What's going on in New York? Let's start there. We'll get to the heartthrob later. Save the juice till the end."

"Lord, Gran."

"What? I can't have a little entertainment at my age? I've been in a hospital bed forever and ever. I'm in need of a little thrill."

"Just don't ground me."

"One of the perks of raising your granddaughter. I don't have to give you a time-out for having fun." She giggled, and I felt myself relax. "All right precious, tell Gran what's going on, hmm? Your job in New York?" She arched an eyebrow waiting for me to fill in the rest.

"I was let go because I asked for a week of vacation. I couldn't go back to work after a couple days when Chef wanted me to. Not with your condition being so serious and all the other stuff that needs attention, like Buster, and Mom, and hello, Violet!"

"No, you couldn't, and what kind of person doesn't understand that?" Gran asked, but when she saw my face, she seemed to realize I had, and that it hadn't made a difference.

"I just feel like I am being pulled between two different lives with entirely different responsibilities and expectations of me. I've got drama on both islands, Manhattan and Sullivan's! Both are important to me. I feel like a jerk for even thinking about going back to New York, but there's an opportunity for me there."

"Is it a good opportunity?" she asked.

"Yeah, it's to work for an amazing rock-star female chef who's opening a new restaurant," I said.

"Do you want it?"

I thought about my answer for a moment. I looked deep into my heart and let out what had been bubbling up. "Yes, I do, and I feel terribly guilty about wanting it."

"You should go get it, then, or at least try! Your life is in New York, even if your heart is here. I don't want you waiting around on my account, and neither would Violet. Your mother is headed off on a cruise. What are you going to do there? Hire a rowboat and keep an eye on her? If you ask me, the choice is already made," Gran said.

"Gran, what about the Lantern? We owe a lot of money. Yes, I know."

"Violet told me she spilled the beans."

"Gran, how could y'all not tell me?"

"Because, Maggie, I don't now, and I didn't then, want anything holding you back from reaching your full potential. As your grandmother, it's all I want to see. I want to see my chicks fly!"

"Well, that's very sweet, and thank you, but Gran . . ."

"But what? As soon as I get out of here I'll figure something out, Maggie. Don't worry. Go be the best version of Maggie, don't worry about us."

"But what about Violet? How is she going to run the restaurant and do photography while pregnant? With

Mom gone? With you needing help? I know you don't want to talk about that, but it is a real situation."

"Magnolia, we will figure it out. I have a few people who I can call to help out at the restaurant, and Violet will prioritize her work. I worked my entire pregnancy. Adams women are tough."

"Gran, is that the best line of thinking?"

"Maggie."

"I can't just go."

"Well, do you have the job yet?"

"I have an interview today."

"Why don't you just have the interview, and we'll talk about this afterward?"

"Okay."

"Oh, I can't wait for another baby!"

"I know, it's very exciting!"

"Violet's going to be a great mother, watch," Gran said and smoothed out the blanket on her bed.

"We have to buy the sisters out. But first we should talk to a lawyer."

Gran didn't say anything for a moment. "Put that issue on the back burner. Right now, we should look to hire a new head cook and a front-of-house manager—and an accountant. I bet Alice's niece Charlotte would do the accounting. Does mine, and I think she does hers for her store. I'm sure she'd give you the family discount."

"And you?" I said.

"What's to be done, Maggie? You and I aren't doctors or God, and it's in his hands right now. When I'm home I'll have a nurse or an aide to help me. It'll work out, and besides cooking meals, doing laundry, and keeping me company, what can you do? FaceTime me once a day. I'll take care of myself, plus, you know Alice won't let me go hungry."

"Are there any problems you can't solve?" I asked.

"Just one."

"What's that?"

"Why you feel it's your responsibility to fix everything," Gran said.

"I think I need to get a grip. Maybe if I talk to Buster's daughters, they will throw in some money to hire an experienced head cook and a manager. I mean, they did show some interest in the restaurant. Maybe they aren't so terrible," I said hopefully.

"Well, don't get ahead of yourself, but I do think that getting close to the enemy isn't a terrible move. If you let them feel like they have some say in the business, they might back off," she said.

"We really do need a good manager. Violet doesn't really want to run the restaurant."

"I think you should talk to Buster's daughters as soon as possible."

"You're right, if Dixie and Caroline want to be involved, I should let them help me—with the financial side of things."

"It's wonderful, Maggie, that your momma is going on that fancy wellness cruise. She and Violet told me about it when they were at the hospital on Sunday. Your momma is a good woman. She needs to smile again," Gran said.

"Man, when it rains it pours. Timing here is terrible," I grumbled.

"Well, look, I don't know if there ever is a good time to be pregnant, or recovering from a car accident, or rehabilitating yourself from an addiction, but here we are. We are going to have to rise to the occasion, deal with our troubles as best we can, and go on with our lives, Maggie," Gran said.

"It just seems like a lot," I whispered.

"Because it *is* a lot. We will get through this. Girl, you are young and at the top of your game. Hire some good people to run the Lantern, then go grab that opportunity in New York. We all want that for you, and so do you. You don't need anyone's permission to take the wheel to your own life. Drive on, girl. Don't look back, we'll manage."

I felt I had a new lease on life. Gran was a sensible woman. If she didn't think I'd be abandoning them by pursuing the job in New York, then I'd feel a lot better about that interview with Chef Michelle.

After giving Gran a big hug, and thanking her for the reality check, I drove to my mom's to get her ready to take her to the ship. Even though it was hot, I rolled down the window so I could take in the Lowcountry air. I was going to miss it when I got back to New York. I started making a list in my head of everything I had to do to exit responsibly. As soon as I could, I needed to call Dixie and Caroline and ask if they'd foot the bill to hire a manager and a head cook. Of course, I'd say this more diplomatically. It would be a godsend if we found someone who could do both jobs. But first I'd talk to Violet to make sure she approved of involving the evil stepsisters. And before or maybe right after that, I'd have to tell her that I would be going back to New York.

When I arrived at my mom's apartment, I was surprised to see her smiling. She was wearing a kimono and had hot curlers in her hair.

"Hey, love! Come here and give your ole momma a smooch!"

"Uhh, okay, Mom." I pecked her on the cheek.

"Oh, that was so sweet, give me another!" She turned her head so I could kiss her other cheek.

I sniffed. "Mom, are you—"

"Drunk? No, honey, just relieved and excited to be leaving Charleston! Thank you, Maggie. I really appreciate you helping me. I only wish I had asked you to do one more tiny favor for me, and now it's too late."

"Maybe not. What do you need, Mom?"

"I wish I'd asked you to make me some biscuits. I wanted to take a batch with me on the cruise. Good way to make friends," she said.

"Mom, that's so sweet! I wish you had remembered. I could have whipped some up. But they aren't that great . . ."

"Are you insane? They're the most delicious comfort food, worth every single carb. They're crusty and flaky. Put some salted butter on a hot one? Heaven!" she gushed.

"I just tweaked Great-Grandmother Daisy's recipe. I use White Lily flour and add a teaspoon of vanilla extract," I said with a shrug. "I'll write down the recipe, and maybe you can get one of the cooks on the cruise to make them."

"I'd love that. Thanks, sweetheart!"

I quickly wrote down the recipe and gave it to her. She stuck it in her wallet. I was surprised that she wanted anything from me, but honestly, my heart softened then. My mom was glowing, and I secretly said a prayer that this time would do the trick. It would be so nice to have her sober. It would be so nice to have more sweet moments like this.

"Okay, Maggie May, I think it's time! Let's get a move on! I don't wanna be late! Violet's meeting us there, right?" she said as she wheeled her suitcase to the door. She didn't go any farther. She turned around and gazed at her apartment. Her buoyant mood seemed to deflate, and she looked sad. I thought she might cry. She squeezed her eyes shut. "Too many memories here. I can't keep thinking about him." She opened her eyes and nodded. "Let's go."

We drove across the Ravenel Bridge to the port in downtown Charleston. It was raining lightly, and my mom, being my mom, tied a scarf around her hair. She looked like a movie star from another era.

"Mom, this is going to be so great for you," I said as we parked.

"I'm nervous, Maggie," she said quietly, looking at her lap.

"I'm sure. Most people get a little nervous when they're about to embark on an adventure," I said.

"Yes, I suppose."

"Mom, you are one of the bravest people I know. We can do scary in this family, God knows we've had enough experience with it."

"I feel . . . a little selfish, Maggie. I shouldn't be leaving my mother at a time like this."

"Momma, you can't pour from an empty cup. You can't be of help to anyone if you aren't helping yourself. Okay? I'll keep an eye on Gran. And if there's an emergency, you can disembark at a port of call and fly back to Charleston. Annabelle told me that. I'll even email you every day so you can still feel connected to us."

"I don't think I can get email there . . . or I'm not supposed to read it all the time, or something. I don't remember what the director said." She was sounding confused and foggy now. I saw her pull out a flask.

"Mom," I said.

She handed me the flask. "You're right. Here. Throw this out."

I gave her a hug. "Let's go."

Violet rapped on the window with her usual perfect timing. She was jumping up and down with a homemade sign that read BON VOYAGE, MOMMA! I bit my lip to hold back a laugh. Violet was so silly sometimes, but I was glad of it now. She'd made sure this moment would be light and fun, not dark and dreary.

We walked into the bustling terminal and headed for the Serenity Cruise sign. When we entered a small glassed-in office decorated in soothing shades of pale blue, an attractive middle-aged woman with blond-streaked hair and perfect makeup greeted us. Mom hesitantly gave her name.

"A pleasure to meet you, Mrs. Adams. I'm Jane. I can check you in. Please have a seat." She smiled at me and Violet. "You, too, ladies. Mrs. Adams, am I correct in assuming these are your relatives?"

"Yes, my daughters, Magnolia and Violet."

"Really?! I thought they were your sisters or cousins."

Mom seemed to relax. She loved this kind of reaction—when people assumed she wasn't old enough to be our mother.

As Jane inspected Mom's passport and typed into her computer, I asked, "How many people will be going on the cruise?"

Jane looked up. "We'll be sailing with sixty guests."

"That's all?"

"Our wellness experts have found that to be the op-timal number. But including professional staff and op-erations, about two hundred twenty-five people will be on board." Violet, Mom, and I looked at one another. It certainly was exclusive. "Yes," Jane continued, "*Seren-*

ity Gem truly is a gem of a ship. It can accommodate everyone comfortably. All staterooms have queen beds and ocean views. There are two dining rooms, one with a dance floor and another for more casual meals, an indoor-outdoor pool, a fitness center, a dance studio, a yoga studio . . ." Jane paused, as if to think. "Oh, yes, and of course a spa and a library."

I was impressed—and thrilled when Jane said Violet and I could take a tour of the ship, but only a quick one because the safety briefing would start in twenty minutes.

The three of us were agog as we walked up the gangway. *Serenity Gem* wasn't one of those big hulking cruise ships I so often saw in Charleston Harbor, it was a sleek luxury yacht. Captain Henderson, a handsome guy who couldn't have been older than forty, greeted us and introduced us to Helen Sanders, the cruise coordinator, who handed off Mom's luggage to a porter. "We'll put these in your stateroom, Ms. Adams. Visitors are not permitted in the staterooms," Helen said apologetically. "But please feel free to walk around the *Gem* with your friends and join us in the Azure Room in fifteen minutes for the safety briefing."

As we walked along the pristine teak decks, I wondered if they kept visitors out of the staterooms to prevent anyone from smuggling aboard booze or illegal substances. No doubt, they searched the guests' luggage at some point. I didn't dwell on that for long because I was bowled over by the ship's beautiful interiors. We peeked into the elegant dining room. Its décor matched that of any of Charleston's four-star restaurants. A wall of floor-to-ceiling glass doors opened to the deck. The fitness center was filled with shiny exercise machines, and the impressively stocked library had comfy sofas and a few desks. As we looked around, we passed other guests of all ages who were saying goodbye to their loved ones.

"Oh, Momma, I'm excited for you!" Violet said, tearing up, as she hugged our mom. "This is going to be so amazing. I'm just worried you're going to get used to all this luxury and not want to come home!"

The three of us laughed.

A voice with a British accent came over the loudspeaker, gently reminding people that the briefing would begin in five minutes.

"I have to go to the ladies' to comb my hair!" Mom said, looking panicked.

"Mom, you look beautiful, as always," I said.

She looked at me for a moment, then hugged me tightly. It felt so good I didn't want it to end. But it did when she turned to Violet and hugged her, too. "Thank you, girls. Thank you for looking after Gran and the Magic Lantern while I'm away."

There might have been tears in her eyes, but I couldn't be sure because she quickly turned and walked away.

Out on the pier, Violet and I watched the crew and the dockworkers prepare *Serenity Gem* for departure. There was so much uncertainty and stress swirling around in my head, I wished I could sail away on that beautiful boat, too.

"Mags, I've got something for you." My sister pulled a folder out of her bag and handed it to me. "I called Gran's lawyer, and it turns out you're Gran's power of attorney. In the event she is incapacitated, you're in charge of everything—her health care, her finances, and the restaurant."

"Oh, my God. Does Mom know?" I asked.

"Nope, nobody did. Now we do. I guess Gran didn't think she'd wind up in the hospital or whatever. At least she planned ahead, just in case."

"Yeah." I felt kind of stunned as I looked down at the folder. *Why did Gran lay all this on me?*

I looked up at my sister. Her eyes were glassy with tears. "Vi, don't feel bad. Gran probably chose me because I'm older."

"I don't care about that! I broke up with Chris."

"Oh, Violet. Oh, my God! How are you not a total mess right now?" I put my arm around her.

"Because I was just done, you know? I'm tired of it. I had to. I just couldn't take him dragging his feet anymore. It wasn't good for me or for him. I have bigger problems that require my attention than trying to convince someone to stay." She put her hand on her stomach. "I'll be all alone, Maggie."

"You're not alone, Violet," I said, hugging her tight.

Back at Gran's house on Sullivan's I prepared myself for my Zoom meeting with Chef Michelle. It was a new world, post–COVID-19, and the world was working differently. Typically, I would interview at a new kitchen by doing what was called a stage. It was a period of time, usually one or two full shifts in a kitchen dinner service, where the leadership could observe how I used my skills and how I interacted with the existing staff in their kitchen. But now, I was being interviewed this way. I liked that Chef Michelle wanted to get a feel for who I was first, before she let me into her kitchen. I was there at three thirty sharp in the virtual waiting room.

Chef Michelle appeared in her office, which I imagined was inside a kitchen. The table behind her was painted hot pink, and that made me smile. She was very polished in her crisply ironed and starched white chef's coat, which looked even cleaner against her olive skin. Her ink-black hair was pulled tight in a neat bun, and she had a small nose piercing that made her approachable.

"Hey, there!" I said.

"Hello, Maggie!" said Chef Michelle. "It's so good to see you. Thank you for taking the time to chat with me today!"

She sounded genuinely thankful. Which was a clear left turn in vibes. I liked her immediately.

"Oh, gosh, I'm just so thrilled by this potential opportunity!" I responded. "I have to say I am a huge admirer of yours. I've watched your career closely. You are a major inspiration for us girls on the line!"

"Oh, stop, you're going to make me blush! Maggie, your own reputation is impressive. You have come highly recommended."

"I have? I mean, awesome, but curious to ask who—"

"Chef Jamie. He adores you!" Chef Michelle let out a small chuckle, as if she was surprised to see that I was surprised by her comment.

"Wow. I mean, that's great to hear . . ."

"Ah, it's news to you, huh?"

"Well, I mean, I worked my butt off for the guy . . .

sorry, I'm nervous, I shouldn't have said 'butt' in an interview . . ."

"Ha! Maggie, I get it. Jamie and I go way back. He really leaned into the old-world way of kitchens. You should know right now that my kitchens are *nothing* like that. We are all on the same side. I don't subscribe to all that crap. Sure, we have order and roles in our kitchen, but everyone gets the same amount of respect."

"Well, that's refreshing."

"Look, it's long hours, I'm not going to pretend like it isn't. Working in a kitchen is working in a kitchen, but you spend all those long hours with your team. If you create a negative environment, I believe it poisons the entire experience, accidents happen, and people get sick . . . not to mention quit. You will spend more hours with us than you will with your own family. I want to create a space that you are proud of and like to come to."

"Well, that sounds amazing! Almost too good to be true."

"Well, I mean, it's still a kitchen."

Chef Michelle and I shared a laugh at that, and I realized that I would really like to work for her.

"So what is the job exactly?" I asked. "What are you looking for?"

"Well, Maggie, I am looking for someone who is

passionate, who still wants to learn but is also able to maintain the standards that I put into place. Officially the job is for a sous-chef, but it's really more like you need to be me when I'm not there. It's a large team, and I simply can't be everywhere at once. There is also an opportunity for growth into a chef de cuisine position. I've got another project in the works in the next two years."

"Wow. So, like, my dream job. How many people?"

"About twenty cooks would be under you, probably more. That doesn't include dishwashers."

"Okay."

"Construction finishes up this week. I'm very excited. It's an all-female team."

"All female?"

"Yep. Something I have always wanted to do."

"I've never worked in that environment."

"Well, no one will be upset if you have to cry in the walk-in!"

We both caught the giggles then.

"Oh, man," I said. "I've been there too many times."

"Same, girl."

"When can I come stage?"

"No, that's not necessary. I'll just have you start. If you're awful, I'll just fire you. The job's yours, Maggie, if you want it."

It was like the world stopped for a moment. I had to take a beat to think. Whoa, silver platter in front of me, my dream job. Holy crap.

"Wow, I mean . . . can I think about it?"

"Of course . . . but don't take too long."

"Thank you. Good Lord, this is so exciting. I just need a little time to get my mind around this."

"Speak then, take care."

And she signed off.

Chapter 26
Magnolia

It was mid-June, and feeling like full-blown summer. The air was so thick you could cut it. It was the kind of weather that made you want to find a vent and sit on it. There was nothing you could do to escape. It was hotter than anywhere else on the planet, and my hair was wild. There wasn't a scrunchie this side of the Mason-Dixon Line that could keep it under control. But I almost didn't care, even as I looked over at Violet, with her straight-as-a-pin hair, in Gran's truck as we drove around finishing some last-minute errands for Gran because . . . she was coming home!

"Maggie, this is wild!" Violet said, looking up from her phone. "I got an email from Grandpa Earle!"

I looked over at her, and the truck almost swerved off the road. She had to be joking. "Violet, what are you talking about?! We haven't heard from our paternal grandparents in close to twenty years!"

"I didn't tell you, but I wrote to them earlier in the spring because my obstetrician asked me for a family medical history, and I knew nothing about health issues on Dad's side of the family. I used the return address on the last birthday card they sent me—"

"Violet, you saved that card and envelope all these years?"

"I save everything. I'm sentimental. But I didn't hear back from them until now! Grandpa Earle says here he moved from California to Oregon a couple of years ago, and it took the postal service a while to forward the letter. Oh, no! He says he moved because Grandma Kate died of a heart attack, and he wanted to be closer to some friends."

"Violet, would you just read me the email?"

"Okay. 'Dear Violet, it does my heart good to hear from you and that you are going to have a baby. Losing touch with you and Maggie has been a constant source of sorrow for me and your grandma, but the past years have not been easy, and we didn't want to burden you girls. Kate had coronary bypass surgery ten years ago. It helped for a while, but she needed another operation and was not the same after that.'

"How sad! Then he says, 'So heart problems are

the only health issue you should watch out for. I'm sorry Rose was hurt in a car accident. While Kate was bitter till the end, I forgave Rose. Please tell her I don't blame her for what happened, and let me know when my great-grandchild arrives. No reliable internet or cell service out on the ranch, but I'll be sure to get back into town in the fall. God bless you, Grandpa Earle.'"

Neither of us said anything for a moment, then Violet said exactly what I was thinking: "What does he mean he forgave Gran and doesn't blame her for what happened?"

I shook my head, not wanting to dredge up dreary old memories. "I guess he blames Gran for Mom divorcing Dad, convincing her to do it, and maybe he and Grandma Kate believe that drove Dad over the edge into more drugs and more reckless behavior."

"I'm going to email him back and ask him—and thank him for getting back to me," Violet said.

"Did he send you his phone number, or his address, or say where in Oregon the ranch is located? He implied he doesn't use email very often. I don't think he really wants to be in touch with you or me."

"No, he didn't send any contact info other than the email address, and I don't think it's his own— Vicky@Vickysbarandgrill," Violet said quietly.

A bitter laugh came out of me. "Violet, we've done fine without the Parkers all these years."

"I know, but family history is important. I'll tell Dr. Vick," she said and put her phone away. "So have you made your decision about Chef Michelle?"

"Yes. Violet, I want to take it."

"Are you asking my permission?"

"No. Kind of? I don't know."

"Take the job, Maggie." I looked over at her and she was smiling.

"Really? Are you sure?"

"Yes, just maybe help me find a replacement?"

"Oh, my God." I felt elated. "Violet, this is really happening!"

"Maggie, this is what you've wanted your entire life! How could this not happen?"

After we ran in and out of Publix, filled the tank with gas, and even got Gran's truck washed, we finally arrived home. Violet and I ran around the house to make sure everything was in order.

"Ready to go!"

I ran down the stairs, stopping briefly to straighten the photo of Great-Grandmother Daisy. *Why couldn't that frame hang straight?!* The living room looked perfect—sparkling clean and elegant. We'd cut some fresh magnolia blossoms and floated them in the giant cut-crystal bowl Gran kept on the coffee table. It really was a beautiful house, and it was in tip-top shape for Gran's return. It was Sunday, and the restaurant was closed for Sundays and Mondays now. It was a choice that was difficult to make, but it helped lighten the load not just on Violet, but on the whole staff.

The table was set with Gran's best china, and I was putting the finishing touches on the ginger carrot soup, glad I'd put on one of Gran's old-fashioned frilly aprons, so I wouldn't spill anything on the tangerine-and-white Lilly P. I'd borrowed from Vi's closet, along with a pair of high-heeled sandals. I'd thought the colors might clash with my red hair, but they didn't. I looked like a cross between a sunbeam and a flame—bright and cheerful. I almost spilled a box of kosher salt into the soup when I heard the whining of a power saw coming from the front porch.

"Vi, what's going on?" She didn't hear me.

Alice had gone to the hospital to pick up Gran and her home-care aide. Someone was attacking our house, and I had to defend it myself. I turned down the flame beneath the pot of soup and ran out front.

"What do you think you're doing?!" I shouted at the two men who were dismantling part of the porch railing. After they'd carefully placed the railing on the ground, the taller man turned toward me. "Sam?"

"Hey, Maggie. Whatever you're cooking in there is quite enticing. And you don't look so bad yourself!" His gaze roamed over me appreciatively.

I ignored that. "Why are you ruining our porch?"

Sam tipped back his cowboy hat and shook his head. "First, you didn't think I knew how to replace the taillight on my truck, now you think I can't handle carpentry. You know, I did an orthopedic surgery rotation, which requires sawing bones, during my residency." He laughed and gestured to the other man. "Meet master carpenter Luis Gutierrez, who does some work for us at the farm." Luis doffed his hat and smiled. "We're installing the ramp for Gran's wheelchair. How were you going to get her into the house?"

I felt like kicking myself. We hadn't thought about that. "Well, I figured we could help her up the stairs, a few of us could carry her if necessary."

Sam raised his eyebrows. Luis chuckled. "Didn't Violet tell you? She was sitting on the porch when I stole away from the hospital yesterday and came here to take measurements, and—"

"You were here yesterday? No, she didn't tell me!"

"I asked her if I could install a ramp, and she said it would be okay."

"Why didn't you ask me?"

Sam just rolled his eyes at me. "Women."

The two men laughed and went over to their truck, opened the bed, and took out the shiny, white wooden ramp and carefully set it down by the porch where the railing had been removed. It fit perfectly. I ran down the porch steps, almost twisting my ankle in the high heels, and threw my arms around Sam's neck. "I can't believe you did this! Thank you, Sam Smart, man of many talents!" It felt so good when he put his hands around my waist and pulled me close. I peeked over his shoulder and said, "Thank you, Luis!" But the man had already walked back to the truck to give us some privacy.

"You are very welcome," Sam said.

"Sam, I have to tell you something. I got a job offer in New York, and I'm going to take it," I said. I wasn't planning on telling him that moment, but I knew that eventually it would have to come out, and seeing his generosity made me feel obligated to be honest with him.

He then mimed being stabbed in the heart.

"Stop, Sam!" I whined.

"I knew it, you were just too good to be true, Maggie. No, I'm just teasing you. I knew this would happen, and honestly, I'm really proud of you. What's the job?"

"It's for a big-time chef up in the city. It's an all-female crew and I'd be her number two. There is also a chance for growth within the company. It's good money, too. I've really been working for this my whole life," I spilled.

"Well, then, you have to go," he said a little more seriously.

"Yeah, I do. I have to give it a shot." Something tugged at my heart and I felt my breath catch a little. What was the matter with me? "I'll be here a lot, though. I'll want to be around the baby and all. I mean, I'll be here more . . . than before."

"Well, if you ever need a farm tour . . . you'll know where to find me."

"Sam, why do I feel like we're breaking up?" I joked, but that's totally what it felt like.

"How can we break up? You were never mine," Sam said wistfully.

"Sam."

"Maggie."

"They're here, Maggie! They're here!" Violet squealed excitedly, breaking the tension.

I ran down the front steps to Alice's minivan. Jim jumped out of the front passenger seat, smiling from ear to ear, and moved to the back of the van. "Guess who's coming to dinner?!"

"Hold up a minute, I have to activate the ramp," Alice called.

Jim opened the back door and turned to me and Violet. "Watch this! Alice's new van is like the Batmobile."

"Jim! Oh, my God, what a surprise! I thought you had—"

"Filming, yes, I'm very famous now. There's a writers' strike. They should wrap it up in a week . . . till then I'm with my flower girls!"

With a whirring sound, a metal ramp unfolded, and Gran, looking beautiful in navy slacks and a silky blue-print blouse, and of course her pearl necklace, made her grand entrance, working the controls on her wheelchair and rolling down to the driveway at a stately pace.

"Gran, welcome home!" Violet and I said in unison before we smothered her with hugs. "You look beautiful!" Vi added. "It's so good to have you here, back where you belong!" I said.

Jim started singing "Hello, Dolly!" and we all laughed and cried.

"Oh, my girls. It's so good . . . to see you . . . and to be home!" I basked in my grandmother's adoring gaze as she said this. She looked at the house. The multicolored balloon bouquet Violet had tied to the porch railing was fluttering in the breeze. "Whose birthday is it?" Gran asked, grinning. We all laughed, and she turned her wheelchair to inspect the yard. "Azaleas look good, so do the rhododendrons."

"So who's going to introduce me to this tall glass of water?" Gran scooted right up to Sam and gave him the once-over. "I'd rather have you than a bunch of balloons!"

"Gran!" Violet said. Sam blushed. Gran had clearly forgotten Sam from when he dated Violet. Maybe her memory was affected. I got nervous, but Sam played into it perfectly.

"Well, anyone would be so lucky. I'm Sam Smart. It's nice to make your acquaintance." He shook her hand, gave it a kiss, and then took a dramatic bow. Gran was tickled.

"Well, ladies, it's time I move on to the next project," Sam said. "See you around." While he picked up his tools and left, Gran took a quick tour of the garden.

I heard a car door open and saw a petite woman in a white pantsuit step out of the van's back seat.

"Maggie and Violet, this nice lady is Mrs. Nicole Lloyd, your grandmother's home-care aide," Jim said. "She's going to be helping you twenty-four seven for the next two weeks."

Violet and I shook hands with Mrs. Lloyd, who smiled at us and said, "Please call me Nicole."

"Welcome to our home, Nicole," Violet said warmly. "We're delighted that you'll be staying with us."

"What is that heavenly aroma I smell?" Jim asked. "Time for lunch, no?"

Nicole pushed Gran's wheelchair toward the ramp. "How smart of you to install a ramp. It will be much easier for your grandmother to go out and about!"

"Smart, indeed! Sam did a great job, didn't he, Maggie?" Violet said as she led the way up the ramp.

"Yes, it was quite a surprise, Violet," I answered sharply.

"Is there anything Sam Smart can't do?" Jim said as he and I walked up the porch stairs. "Farmer, cowboy, doctor, carpenter. Quite a guy!" He winked at me.

"Sam Smart?" Gran said. "Oh, goodness, I totally forgot him! Embarrassing! But he was sweet to play along. Wait, I remember he was sweet on you, Violet, and felt so bad when you took up with Chris. How nice of him to do this."

Gran's gaze shifted from Violet to me, and she smiled. "Oh . . . oh, I see. Let's go inside, and you girls can bring me up to date."

The ginger carrot soup was a big hit. Gran pronounced it the best meal she'd had in weeks. "Is this on the Lantern's new menu?" she asked. When I shook my head, she said, "Why not?"

"Good idea, Rose," Alice said. Even she praised the seasoning, astutely picking up on the pinch of nutmeg I'd added.

I was happy that Gran thought the soup was good enough to serve at the restaurant, but I felt sad, and tried not to show it, as I watched my "Wonder Woman" grandmother struggle to raise the soupspoon to her mouth with her left hand. She was still working to regain the use of the muscles on the right side of her body. Nicole, seated next to Gran, tactfully helped her toward the end of the meal. Violet, Jim, and I kept up a steady stream of cheerful chatter, pretending we didn't notice. As we moved on to dessert, an apple pie Alice had brought over, I filled Gran in on my first run-in with Sam, which made her laugh, and our budding "romantic friendship," which was how I described our relationship. Gran asked Violet a few questions about her pregnancy, careful not to ask about Chris, and then we discussed the new menu items at the Magic Lantern, but we kept everything light and positive, steering clear of Buster's daughters' interference and the financial problems.

After Violet, Jim, and I did the dishes, Jim went upstairs to call a couple of New York friends and Nicole unpacked in the smaller room, which had been Gran's office, next to the one where Gran would be sleeping.

Violet and I joined Gran and Alice on the screened porch.

"Thank you, girls, that was the nicest welcome home you could have given me." Gran smiled, then took a deep breath. "I just wish Lily were here, too."

Alice patted Gran's hand. "Rose, that girl is off doing what she needs to do. I'm so proud of her, and I know you are, too. She's setting herself straight."

"We just got a postcard from her when she was in Jamaica. The cruise is heading down to Aruba next, I think," Violet said. "She said the toughest part of her day is trying to stay out of the sun. So like Mom to worry about sun wrinkles!"

Gran looked confused. "Postcard, yes, I want . . . the postcards."

"Mom sent you one, too, Gran," I said. "I saw it on the table in your hospital room. Do you want me to ask Nicole where she put it?"

Gran shook her head. "Maggie, get me my stationery box, please. The postcards are in there. Bottom drawer of my . . . my dresser."

Violet gave me a puzzled look and Alice frowned, but I said, "Of course, Gran. I'll be right back."

When I got back to the porch and placed the polished mahogany box on Gran's lap, she opened it and immediately started emptying it of the stacks of monogrammed stationery. Violet helped her. When she got to the bottom of the box, she pulled out a handful of old postcards. "Here they are," Gran said, sounding relieved.

I took the box off her lap so she could spread out the postcards. The one on top had a picture of the Eiffel Tower.

Gran held it up and smiled. "From Momma when she took her first trip to France. A . . . a few years after Eddie and I went." Gran set it aside and picked up another one and laughed. "This was from Lily when she went to Washington, D.C., on her seventh-grade trip." It was a postcard with a photo of the U.S. Capitol. "Eddie went as one of the chaperones. I couldn't go, I couldn't leave the restaurant."

We sat there for half an hour as Gran reminisced and showed us postcards from family and friends. "There must be another box," she said tiredly when she got to the end of the stack. "I have more. Where did I put them? My jewelry box, the button box?"

Alice walked into the house and returned with Nicole.

"Mrs. Adams, how about taking a little rest before we do your evening exercises?" Nicole suggested. "Maybe we can go outside later."

"No." Gran shook her head, looking worried and lost. "I have to find those postcards."

Not liking to see my grandmother so troubled, I quickly said, "Gran, I'll look for those boxes and bring them down to your room, and you can look through them later."

"Big day and all! You must be a little tired," Violet chimed in.

Gran's eyes were heavy. Nicole smiled at us and wheeled Gran away. Alice followed them.

Violet grabbed my hand and pulled me to the front of the house. "What was all that with the postcards?"

"I don't know, Vi. I'm worried, too," I said. "But we knew she wasn't going to be her old self when she came home. We have to give it time."

Chapter 27
Magnolia

Two weeks later

I had made the decision to go back to New York. I accepted the job with Chef Michelle, and got permission from everyone that it was okay to go. I kept things cool with Sam. That last part was the worst part, and was giving me pangs before I fell asleep at night. I scolded myself because it was just unrealistic. How could I be two places at once? Life was the longest thing any of us did, who knows what would happen with us . . . maybe one day. In my bedroom there was a window that had a partial view of the ocean. It was just a slice, but it was still the ocean. I opened it, letting in the salty air that within moments combated the air-conditioning. I would miss the smell of the salt water, but part of me was excited about returning to a life where I just belonged to myself.

The next day, I touched down at LaGuardia. It was a bit of a culture shock, but somehow it felt just as hot here, just a whole lot less romantic. The city was like an oven, all that concrete trapping the hot air. I heard the roaring of the M15 bus instead of the ocean, and I wished I was back on Sullivan's Island. Violet called me when I was in the cab on the way to the apartment and I picked up on the first ring.

"Hey, girl, you are not going to believe what has happened!" Violet squealed.

"What? Is everyone okay?"

"Yes! Sister, the most attractive . . . I mean capable man is now working at the Magic Lantern!"

"What? Who? What do you mean?"

"This guy, his name is Adam Foreman, and he is just a marvel! He can do literally anything. He cooks, he is tech savvy, he can make a mean martini. He's literally a gift. But the best part? His favorite thing to do, besides run a wine program, is to run the front of the house! He has a degree in restaurant management from the New York Culinary Institute! What are the chances?"

"Wait a sec, why in the world does a guy like that

want to work at the Lantern? I mean, sure, I love the place, but that résumé sounds like it's a better fit at, like, Fig or Husk or one of the big dogs downtown," I said.

"Well, I thought the same thing, but he actually went to the College of Charleston and fell in love with the area, and always wanted to come back. His aunt has a house on Sullivan's, and she is actually a regular here. Do you remember Ms. Foreman? She's amazing! Anyways, she heard the other night that we needed help with you leaving, and suggested that Adam come and take a look, and . . . gosh, he's so polite, too, he brings me a green tea every morning . . . and not to mention the guy can dress!" She whistled.

"Are you okay, Violet?" I giggled, because she clearly was crushing on this guy. "I think it's a conflict of interest to date an employee."

"Oh, hush. I do not have a crush . . . although last time I checked, we don't have an employee rule book, so . . ."

"Good Lord, you're pregnant with another man's child, Violet!" I said in a drawn-out Southern accent, to let her know I was joking, not scolding her.

"Chris who? A girl can dream!" she returned in a perfect Southern belle impression.

"Well, joking aside, that sounds too good to be true. Can we afford him?"

"Yes, we can," she said.

"Well, then, perfect! What about cooking? Who's going to run the kitchen?" I said and for some reason felt very uncomfortable asking about that.

"Well, Alice is helping out, and Adam is also doing a few shifts. Miller has really stepped up, and honestly, we are all just kind of making it work until we find the right person."

"Okay, I mean . . ."

"We are going to open at four thirty for dinner, too, to help out the early birds."

"Okay." I sighed.

"We'll be fine, Maggie."

"Okay," I said again.

"Maggie, also, can I tell you something? I'm having a girl!"

"What? You've been saying that all along."

"I had an ultrasound this morning. I was right!" She squealed again.

"You were right! What are you naming her? I was thinking maybe Charlotte. I love that name . . ."

"Poppy. She has to be a flower, Maggie," Violet said.

"Oh, well, that's precious and perfect and of course she does! Oh, I hope she has red hair like me!" I was squealing, too, but I felt a pang of sadness. I missed not being able to hug her and jump up and down and maybe go shopping right then and there for little pink dresses. I took a breath.

I made this decision. It's okay. This is what I want.

I hung up with my sister, paid the cabdriver, said hello to the doorman, and went up the elevator to our apartment. I opened the door, and even though Jimmy was back in LA (the writers' strike had ended and filming had resumed), I had expected to see him. The apartment felt empty, and despite the scorching temp the space felt cold and lifeless. I set my mind on unpacking, and turned on my Alexa with some fun music. I needed to shake that feeling and change the empty vibes pronto.

After unpacking, I went about getting ready for work with Chef Michelle. My chef's coats were ready to go in my closet. I unpacked my knife roll and decided to give my knives a good sharpening session. As I wet my sharpening stone and moved my knives up and down it, a love song came on and I started singing along. Then I found myself missing Sam.

You were never mine.

He had said that sad sentence, and I couldn't get it out of my mind. Belonging to someone. Something I had always secretly wanted. My father was AWOL, my mom, forget it. I couldn't be with Gran or my sister . . . but I thought . . . no, I made the right decision. I just wanted to belong to myself. That was good, right? I mean, the most important relationship anyone has is with themselves . . . and yet. Nope! I wasn't going to go there. I was a dream chaser, and my destiny was calling! Ha! Time to change the station.

I was pleased when my phone rang, further changing the vibe. It was Jimmy.

"Welcome home, princess! Sorry I couldn't be there."

"God, me, too. I'm trying very hard not to be lonely, which I think is a feeling I am not too familiar with! All that family time . . ."

"I bet the apartment feels empty," he said.

"Huge."

"Hey, we haven't talked about the sexy farmer-doctor-cowboy yet. How could you leave him?"

"I didn't leave *him*! I left Charleston."

"Same thing, sugar. When is he coming up to visit you?"

"Not sure."

"When are you going to visit him?"

"Stop, Jim."

"No, lady, you stop and think about how long a farmer can go without taking a hayride!"

"Oh. My. God. Stop!" I said.

"When does the new gig start?"

"Tomorrow, actually. I'm sharpening my knives. Hey, thanks for getting my coats cleaned!"

"One less thing you have to worry about," he said. "Look, I gotta run. Call me later, okay?"

We hung up and I was left thinking about hayrides.

A week later I was falling into the rhythm of my new job nicely, and I was feeling less homesick. Chez Michelle featured fine but unfussy French food with a Big Apple spin. They did between 350 and 400 covers a day, whereas Bar JP did 500. While Chef Michelle was intense, passionate, and strict about meticulous food prep, she was not histrionic and didn't play games like Chef Jamie. It was a lot easier to maintain and run the day-in and day-outs, and thankfully, we didn't serve brunch. No one likes to be on a brunch shift. Showing up in the kitchen at 2:00 p.m. and leaving Chez Michelle at 10:30 p.m. gave me the opportunity to establish a little bit of a personal life. I took up yoga at Pure Yoga and was quickly getting into the best shape of my life. I was learning, too. I was picking up new techniques from Chef Michelle and my co-workers, who were far more buttoned down than my friends at Bar JP, but often I had to bite my tongue when I thought a different seasoning would improve a sauce's flavor, or a more delectable pairing of vegetable and meat or fish occurred to me. I kept reminding myself that this was Michelle's restaurant, not mine . . . or my family's.

Mom had finished her program but had decided to do another round. She had struck up a great relationship with the staff on the ship and had impressed them with her dance moves. They wound up offering her a job as an assistant dance instructor, which offered a significant discount on the cost. She was happy, and getting healthier, and everyone was relieved to be seeing some progress from her.

August had almost arrived in New York, and I found myself daydreaming about the beach. Work was beginning to feel normal, but I couldn't help it. It would be nice to just run into the ocean after dinner service, which I had done earlier that summer at the Magic Lantern. Chez Michelle was awesome, to be sure, and it was becoming one of the hardest reservations to snag, but I wasn't escaping the vibe of the city.

Chef Michelle was gearing up for a wine dinner. She was asking for everyone's input, but honestly, she didn't take any of our advice. It was more than frustrating, but I decided to go home and really get my creative juices flowing. Maybe I could come up with something that would impress her and have it featured on the menu. That would be extra wonderful, because I knew that the dinner was getting featured in a few magazines and, of course, reviewed by the *New York Times*. It would have to be something soulful and creative, something that would pair well with the wine, too, of course, but something that would really charm the critics. What could I do? I also noticed that a dessert had not been chosen. Chef Michelle was gifted in pastry as well as savory and really favored having a hand in each selection. We had a pastry chef, but she was called sous, just like me.

The week went by slowly. I had made several suggestions and had every single one shot down. The other cooks had given up. Chef Michelle needed a meat course, and had ruled out my idea of a pie or tart for the dessert; she went with a lemon pot de crème. Fine. Boring, if you ask me. The wines were mixed from California, and honestly would have paired really well with some of the dishes I had created for the Lantern, so finally on Friday I knocked on her office door with a plate of my grandmother's fried chicken and a glass of chardonnay that matched it perfectly. I even threw in my gran's collard greens for good measure. I thought that this simple approach maybe wasn't breaking any culinary ceilings, but it was really good, really solid, flavorful food. Also, who didn't like fried chicken?

"Chef?" I knocked, waiting on her response.

"Yes, Maggie, come in!" she said.

I opened the door to find her hair in tangles around her shoulders. She was sipping the last of an iced coffee. There were only ice cubes left, and she swirled them around again and again, sipping every so often, as if each swirl would generate more coffee or something.

"What's that? Family meal?" she said, looking at her watch.

"Umm, no, Chef. I had a little inspiration from home." I placed the dish down next to her and set the glass of wine by it.

She looked up at me and made a face. But then she raised her eyebrows and gestured for me to hand her the fork and knife I had in my hand. She cut herself a bite, closed her eyes, and took a long sip of wine. She held them together in her mouth and nodded. I had won!

"Just as I thought. It's good, but I'm sorry, Maggie. We are French. There is nothing French about fried chicken." She handed me the plate back but kept the wine.

I was crushed.

"Okay, Chef, but maybe there's a way we could bend the rules for this? I mean, fried chicken is great with chardonnay, and . . ."

"Maggie, darling, this isn't the Magic Pot back in the Outer Banks of North Carolina. This is Chez Michelle in New York City. Here we want innovative! I thought you knew that. Sweet idea, though. Try again, I suppose! This is so hard." She pouted her lower lip.

"Okay. Back to the drawing board," I said and left with basically a full plate in my hands.

I went outside into the alley behind the restaurant next to a dumpster and ate the rest of the chicken myself. It was damn good. It was perfectly fried and moist. You could taste the gentle hints of thyme and cayenne pepper I had used in the buttermilk last night to brine it. It was perfectly seasoned and crunched with every bite. The collards that she totally ignored were tender and rich with vinegar and bacon. I felt like my gran was hugging me from the inside. I was let down, but mostly because back at the, ahem, Magic Lantern, not pot, this would have caused a riot. We would sell out in minutes. I wondered how the Lantern was doing.

Then I got to thinking, a lot of the food in the Low-country, and the food I grew up with, was heavily influenced by the Creole cultures that were a result of the horrors of slave times, but also settlers coming from all different parts of Europe. There had to be something that was French and Lowcountry that would inspire Chef Michelle and pair well with a white wine? Think, Maggie!

Then it hit me. Grits. There is nothing more Southern than grits! We could easily sub in some grits for polenta! I could whip up a fish dish, maybe trout almondine, and place it over grits! I went to work as fast as possible. In the kitchen, I had to work with what I had, and sadly, within minutes I realized I didn't have trout. Okay, what was in the walk-in? I raced inside to try and pull together something fast and easy, and staring at me were some beautiful pork cutlets. I took one and pounded it within an inch of its life, tossed it in some flour, a quick egg bath, and then in some panko. I got together some grits. I had a small sack of them that I had brought in the first week for family meal. I made them the right way, low and slow, and added a handful of Parmesan cheese and heavy cream. They were perfect and tasted like velvet. I lightly fried the cutlet and placed it over a nice creamy portion of grits, but topped it off with some fresh peppery arugula with a bright lemon vinaigrette. Okay, so this wasn't entirely French, and it had my sneaky Southern element, but I thought it would be perfect for Chef. It was my play on chicken paillard.

I plated it and brought it to Chef, who moaned with the first bite.

"Okay, Maggie. I see what your game is." She laughed.

"What game, Chef?" I said.

"You know that we are being reviewed, and you

thought you could pull an original recipe of your own to steal the thunder?" She was smiling, but none of her was joking.

"No, Chef! I just thought this might be different but still French," I said. "I was trying to help."

She got up and handed me a binder.

"What's this?" I asked.

"It is an archive of my recipes. Find something in there. When you have your own restaurant, put this dish on your own menu. But as long as you cook in my kitchen, you will cook my dishes."

"I'm sorry, Chef," I said, a little shocked.

"No harm done. Now we are clear. This was delicious, though. Time to do lineup for service!" She handed me the plate.

I went through service with a sense of defeat. She was right, this was her gig. I wasn't trying to undermine her, exactly, but I was doing what I thought was harmless self-promotion. I didn't mean it to be disrespectful, but I was out of line. I had to do some adjusting, I wasn't the chef, I was a chef among many but under someone. Before, what I said went. Now I had to answer to someone else, and honestly, it was aggravating. I missed the freedom I had at the Magic Lantern, but it wasn't here. It wasn't a big-league restaurant. The *New York Times* would never review a restaurant on Sullivan's Island.

Or would it?

Sullivan's Island was changing every time I turned around. Gone were those old beach cottages, demolished to be replaced by multimillion-dollar showstoppers by famous architects like Beau Clowney. Everything that man touched was a Hollywood dream! He had turned fleabag shacks into giant white seaside mansions. Even the old restaurants were being replaced by chic bars and shops. You used to be lucky to find a burger on the island, and now you could choose between places to get an organic pressed juice or a crudo. Charleston had been voted the most desirable city in the world! I don't know how it beat Paris, but okay. It wasn't the place where I grew up anymore, but it was getting more beautiful by the day.

I needed to clear my head. I decided to text B-Rad, my buddy from Bar JP. He quickly responded that he was meeting the guys at our old haunt uptown and to come meet them. I was getting excited to go. Even if Ronny was there, I wasn't nervous. It would be nice to swap some stories and see how they had been.

"Red! Red! Red!" they cheered when I walked in.

B-Rad whistled. "Red! You look different! But good different! Did you cut your hair or something?"

"I've missed you!" BJ embraced me in a bone-crushing hug.

Everyone laughed, and I felt comfortable with them. I told them about Vi's pregnancy, and my mom, and the whole drama with the restaurant. I told them about the Lantern's history, how it was started by my great-grandmother and how it was passed to my gran. I told them about how she had added a bakery and made it French. I then went into how Lily had changed everything to a fish shack, and how gross that fish tank was in the front of the restaurant. Also, about how gorgeous it was to be next to the ocean and how beautiful the island was, the air filled with sea salt and jasmine. I got excited when I told them how I had spent the summer trying to restore it to its former glory. I got the chance to put my own spin on my grandmother's classics, and the best part, about how well the restaurant's changes, my changes, were being received.

Ronny was scrutinizing me, and it made me uncomfortable. "What's up, Red? Why are you in New York?"

I forced a smile to my face. "Ha, ha! I told you I was coming back. Here I am! Just started at Chez Michelle, thanks for the tip. By the way, it's great to see you guys."

All three appeared taken aback, surprised, stunned, and were looking at me as if I were crazy.

"Why do you want to be an overworked, underpaid, unappreciated line cook in a New York restaurant when you can run a cool place like the Magic Lantern in the enchanting Lowcountry?" BJ asked.

B-Rad said, "Yeah, what about all that Southern tradition and family legacy stuff?"

I opened my mouth to explain and then closed it. All I could mutter out was, "Well, I got a promotion to sous-chef?"

"Oh, man, cool," Ronny said sarcastically. "I'm sure you are finding out like I did that sous-chef isn't that fun."

"Yeah, it's not exactly what I expected."

I filled the guys in about the whole wine-and-food saga, and the boys all were shaking their heads.

"Red, I know you've got this idea that New York City is it, but you're telling me you were practically given a restaurant to run, and be the head chef of, and basically make it what you want, and you're here? Uh, right by the beach, too?" BJ said.

"I sure would like to jump in an ocean after a long, hot shift. Today it must have been three hundred degrees," B-Rad said.

"I think you should rethink this, Red," Ronny said. "Even though you look good."

B-Rad kicked him under the table and mouthed, "Stop it."

"All right, all right!" Ronny said and held up his hands.

"Y'all, it's not exactly that simple. The restaurant is in a financial situation. My mom went into business with her boyfriend, later turned into her fiancé. But then he suddenly died, leaving us with the problem of his daughters, who both fancy themselves restaurateurs. So now we have to deal with them and the amount of money my mom got from Buster, her fiancé."

"Red, I would give my left . . . uh, eye, to work in that place. Imagine all the potential. Also, I've seen like a million James Beard nominations in Charleston. It's kind of a hotspot!" BJ said.

"Well, we need a chef, and if you're not up to that, at least a good line cook," I said, smiling.

"Who's better than me?" BJ said, and we all laughed.

Ronny went over to the bar and came back with a tray of drinks—three shots of bourbon and a glass of bourbon with two ice cubes. I smiled. He remembered how I liked it.

He raised his glass. "A toast to the return of our Southern Magnolia!"

I took a sip and looked around the table. Ronny, B-Rad, and BJ hadn't changed. That was reassuring. It felt good to be back with my old friends, but I felt somehow removed or out of place. I decided to pick up the next round of drinks, so I made my way to the bar.

"What can I get you, little lady?" The bartender, with jet-black hair and ice-blue eyes, said with a deep Southern accent.

"Where are you from?" I asked.

"The Deep South, darlin'," he said.

"Where's that, because I'm from the South, too."

"I knew I caught a whiff of an accent, but I bet you're more coastal. I'm from Louisiana."

"I'm from South Carolina," I said.

"Near Charleston?" he asked.

"Yeah, very close. On one of its barrier islands. Sullivan's Island?"

"No way! My family owns High Thyme! My cousins, but still family!"

"Oh, my God! What a small world!" I said.

We chatted for a few minutes about his childhood summers spent on the island when he visited his family. He knew a lot of the same people I knew, and when he brought up the tragic loss of the Piggly Wiggly, I felt that familiar tug on my heartstrings of homesickness.

I went back to the guys with the drinks. Ronny feigned jealousy over me and the bartender and BJ gave him a face. I didn't feel anything for Ronny other than friendship; besides, a leopard can't change his spots. Ronny would always be a flirt, but the line was there, and we both knew it. The conversation wound down and it was getting late. Ronny insisted on accompanying me on the subway. I allowed it, swearing on Gran's pearls, to the other boys, I wouldn't let him cross said line.

"It's good to have you home, Red," Ronny said.

"Yeah, it feels nice. But home feels different now," I said.

"What do you mean?" he asked.

"I don't know . . . just different. I feel a little out of place here since coming back."

"Well, you had a crazy summer."

"I did. But . . ."

"But what?" Ronny grabbed me as the train swayed and I almost lost my balance. He pulled me into him, and I looked up at his face.

"I feel . . . like something is unfinished," I said, realizing that was exactly what had been bothering me.

"I'm so glad you said that, Red," he said, and he leaned down to kiss me.

"Oh! Yuck!" I said and pushed him off me.

"Yuck?" He looked hurt.

"No! Sorry! No, not 'yuck,' just . . ." We stared at each other. "Ronny, not yuck. Just not anymore."

"Oh. I thought . . ."

"Yeah, I know, I know what you thought. I am unfinished with Sullivan's Island. My business is unfinished, and it's still haunting me here in New York."

"Okay . . ."

"I know, I'm probably not making sense, but I think I need to go back. Also, I think I'm in love with Sam."

"What? Who's Sam?"

"My doctor farmer."

"What? Maggie . . . wait."

"Nope, this is my stop. Good night, Ronny!"

And I hopped off the train.

Chapter 28
Magnolia

I don't know why I have never been a good listener. Everyone in the world could have told me I would be here, and maybe everyone knew it, but for some reason I would never admit that I belonged right here on this island, where the women before me had carved out their own lives. When I took a moment to really evaluate what my true goal was, it was to make something my own. I wanted something in my own right, in my own shape and my own truth. It took me too long to realize that all of those things were linked to the rites, shapes, and truths of my family, and there was something, actually, everything beautiful about that. I found myself at home. I never needed to go away to learn that, but I'm glad I did, because it made the homecoming that much sweeter.

It was just after Labor Day, and the summer tourists on the island were finally thinning out. Gone was the insane midweek beach traffic, and here was the new pace, which was still a lot busier than it ever was on my old Sullivan's Island. I parked Gran's new golf cart in the spot behind the restaurant and dropped my jaw at not one but two Ferraris passing down Middle Street. What in the world? The money had discovered Sullivan's Island, that was for sure. Well, I guess that meant I could upcharge the fried chicken.

Violet was now six months pregnant. Gran was now walking around with a cane, using it as an accessory to any point she was making, and my mother was now on her third cruise. I hadn't heard from Sam, but I was too busy to text or call him. Okay, honestly, I was hiding in work and avoiding him. I didn't know what to say, and I felt guilty for ever leaving him and a chance at a future with him. Did I even deserve it anymore? I did have my hands full with the restaurant.

The Magic Lantern had gone through a makeover in the last month. We had a series of uncomfortable conversations with Dixie and Caroline about the finances, and I realized that I would just have to deal with them for the near future. I had brainstormed a few ideas, and after Gran got involved and called their momma down for some lunch, we all decided that they would stay involved, but as silent partners. Emphasis on the silent. Dixie was pregnant with her third baby, and she was in no mood to drive back and forth; Caroline would just as soon collect a check. All this "restaurant stuff" was getting in the way of her very busy schedule. What her schedule included beyond watching garbage TV, I could only guess.

Their mother, Mary-Ann, to my absolute surprise, was actually hilarious. She was super supportive of my idea of restoring the Magic Lantern to its original glory. She even helped us convince her daughters to let us repaint the whole place a bright candy-apple red. She gave us various tips on music, which we appreciated. Unlike her daughters, she was laid back and easy. She begged me for the fried chicken recipe and actually helped us prep for our big reopening night. It was fun to have her in the restaurant, I'll admit. I could feel a friendship budding, and I didn't hate it.

Adam Foreman made it his absolute mission to be the best, most well-rounded, polite, funny, helpful employee ever known . . . and also to make sure Violet was paying attention, and boy, was she ever. He was so sweet, it made me giggle, and we had a banter between us that was organic and refreshing. We closed down service on more than one occasion laughing till my sides hurt. Violet just rolled her eyes at us, knowing and loving the fact that he was entirely hers. He had my vote, but no one was asking.

The new menu included all the greatest hits from the Lantern's glory days, as promised, but it also included some of my new creations. The tables now had paper tablecloths, brown paper of course; on every table there was a small mason jar full of crayons, and bud vases filled with wildflowers collected from the island. All the art on the walls came from our home. The older posters were reframed, some beautiful food prints that Violet had were blown up and set in places of honor, but my favorite wall was the one outside the kitchen that came directly from my bedroom. I took all of my family's recipes and hung them.

"Maggie! Aren't you worried that someone will steal them?" Alice asked.

"Nope. I have made your pie crust three hundred times and it still doesn't taste like yours," I said.

"True enough." She smiled.

Alice had been hired as our pastry chef. She baked her pies in the morning, or off site, and brought them in as needed. They were beautiful, and let's be honest, the world needed some of her magic pies. Pecan, peach, strawberry rhubarb, lemon chiffon, chess, chocolate pudding . . . the list went on. She even made a root beer pie. It was incredible. BJ from New York decided he wanted to check out Charleston and came and joined our team. It was awesome to have him, because I trusted him and could actually have a night off. He happily served as my sous-chef. He was also desperately in love with Frankie the waitress and sweet tea, respectively. I caught him saying "y'all" and knew he was a lifer.

The big night was set for September 12. Everyone was rushing around, even Gran. We had closed for a week before the grand reopening to get all the prep done and get the place in tip-top shape. Not to mention to alert the press. We wanted it covered everywhere. We were lucky, because one of Jim's high school friends worked for *Eater* and owed him a favor. So we were counting on them showing up. Speaking of Jim, he was there for opening week, promising to teach the new girl all his tricks when it came to cocktails. He kept an eye on my budding friendship with Adam, making sure to say over and over that I was *his* best friend.

It would have been warm for September anywhere else but here. The kids might have been back to school, and the stores might have already been pushing the pumpkin spice, but it was still summer in the Lowcountry. I cranked the air-conditioning and lit the gas lantern in the front. The mood was celebratory. Jim poured out a ton of champagne in chilled glasses, free for everyone on arrival. It felt more than great to be there. I finally felt like I belonged.

The night went faster than I had imagined because we were so busy. It was wild how many tickets we did. I don't think the machine stopped. One ticket after another just cranking away. Around nine it slowed down, and I couldn't believe it had been that long. We were quite literally out of food. Alice called me into the dining room around nine forty-five saying we had a problem. Just as everything was going well.

I pushed open the saloon doors to a dark dining room. The lights were turned out, but about a million tiny votive candles were lit, and there in the center of the room was a giant chocolate cake with a huge magnolia in the center. The entire dining room burst into very loud applause, and I felt tears run down my cheeks as I laughed at the same time. Gran came over and handed me a knife.

"Congratulations, Maggie, on a huge, successful opening. You're home."

I was home.

I cut the cake and we gave everyone a slice. Everyone licked their plates and sucked the icing from their fingertips. I was sure I could feel my butt grow past all that yoga hard work. Oh, well. It was worth it.

Around midnight I was locking up when I heard a

knock at the front door. I went to open it, and there in the doorway was my Sam.

"Hey, girl."

"Hey, yourself. Sam, I'm . . ."

"Home."

"Yes, I'm home, and I'm yours if you'll have me."

"Oh, hell, yeah!" He grabbed me and we kissed. As I pulled away I noticed something.

"Is that chocolate?"

"I wasn't about to miss out on cake."

Author's Note

Dear Reader,

This book took me forever and a day to write. It taught me how to write a novel, and I have to say it was a rough road . . . until I got a good editor who shined a light on how freaking long it was. The original manuscript was over seven hundred pages, and I quickly realized absolutely no one wanted to take a huge encyclopedia to the beach!

I am sure that you have some questions, like whatever happened to those postcards that Gran wanted to show the girls? What's going to happen to the restaurant? Will Chris ever get it together for Violet? I have fallen in love with these characters and feel they aren't done yet.

They have more to tell you! I just want you to know that I've decided to save those answers for my next Lowcountry tale. Stay tuned, and thanks again for picking up my story. I hope it made you smile.

Love,
Victoria

Acknowledgments

First and foremost, I need to thank every single person who has encouraged me along the way. This was a really hard thing, y'all, like, really hard. It's one thing to say you're going to write a novel, but another thing entirely to actually do it. When I printed it out, my husband took one look and went, "Whoa, all that came from your brain." Yep, babe. It did. Also throw in two children under five years old, one born during this process, a global pandemic, and losing my soul mate and best friend, my momma. I've got one fabulous pair of Manolo Blahniks to fill! Now, very humbly, I am attempting to carry on her legacy. It is a privilege and an honor, and I mean that with all of my guts. That's what my son, Teddy, says when he really, really means something. With all of my guts, I wrote this book.

I wrote this book because I wanted to read this book. An early writing lesson given to me from the great Dot: *Write what you know and write what you'd want to read.* I also wrote about the professional cooking world because for a while, that's what I did. I left to have a family and attempt writing, and I miss it, so this was my way to work through that breakup. It's okay, though; now I cook for those I love! It's much more fun, even though my regulars really only want chicken nuggets and mac and cheese. Oh, well.

I need to thank three people first. Suzanne Gluck, my agent, who I owe my left arm to. She is a fairy godmother and a dream maker. The very best in the biz, and I couldn't believe my ears when she decided to represent me! Without her I would not have this chance at all, so thanks to her from the bottom of my heart. Suzanne, you are the best!

Carrie Feron, my beloved editor, you are a life changer. Rolling the dice on me was a huge leap of faith, I am sure, and boy, am I glad you did! You have become family to me, and I trust your brain more than my own. Not only are you beyond brilliant, but you are damn funny, great to be around, and have the best commentary on my pages. You gave me faith in my writing and made me truly feel like this dream isn't a dream anymore. It's a reality, and I owe that to you.

Let's write fifty books together! I promise to not write any more cleaning scenes . . . well, maybe to limit them. You know I can't help myself.

Liate Stehlik, thank you for taking a chance on me. You were so loved by my mother, and I cannot thank you enough for adopting me, too. I feel so supported here. You made me an author! Thank you, thank you, thank you!

Thanks also to the publishing team, Kelly Rudolph and Jennifer Hart, and to Asanté Simons, Carrie's assistant and one of the first to read my book. Thank you for believing in me!

To my perfect family: Carmino, the love of my life, and Teddy and Thea, my wildlings. Thank you for being my why. For loving and supporting me so I could chase and catch this dream of mine, Carm; I love you to pieces, and I am so proud of you! I hope this inspires you to read. Pick up your dang socks. Teddy and Thea, I hope one day when you can read, y'all see this and know that through very hard work and determination you can do anything. Your momma loves you more than every star in the sky, every grain of sand on every beach, and more than an ice-cold Diet Coke in the can with a slice of lemon. Y'all are the best kids. Both of you are already beyond my wildest dreams! I love you down to your last freckle . . .You, too, Carm, thank you for tolerating me locking myself in the office like a weirdo for the past few years!

To Liz Dorsey, aka "Liz Thank God," our wonderful nanny, who's been keeping my children out of my office so I could write. Thank you for making sure the house doesn't burn down, and for taking the matches out of Thea's hand. Ha!

To Roberta and Brian, who read my pages early on and have encouraged and cheered me on through lots of FaceTimes. Both of y'all should have been my brother and sister, but I'm okay with this setup, too. Move to Charleston already!

Also to my real brother, William, who is the most brilliant man alive for marrying Maddie, and they just added another female Frank to the world, Miss Hanna! Will, you should probably get started on another kiddo, I will ruin this one!

To Maggie Crawford, my early-on editor. Thank you for all your guidance. You taught me how to write a book. Your help was priceless, and I so appreciate you!

To Adriana, the best older sister in the world. Without your friendship I don't know where I'd be. After my mom went to the big cocktail party in the sky, you took me under your wing, and I just . . . thank God I'm not handwriting this, my liquid eyeliner would be all over the page! Having someone who's in the trenches with me is priceless. That would be the marriage trenches, the motherhood trenches, and the writing trenches. God, I devour your advice and count the moments till our next phone call where we cackle like witches. It's soul medicine.

To my best friends, Adam, Liz, and Lauren. Good Lord, the three of y'all hold me up. It is all due to y'all being the three smartest and funniest people I know that I ever made it through 2019, 2020, 2021, and 2022 . . . well, just thanks for keeping me afloat. Thank you for standing by me and being generals in my army. Same goes to Poodle, Charlotte, Amber, Catherine, Seth, Claire, Kat, and her amazing hubby, Gage . . . I am so lucky in friendship, so if your name isn't here I'm sorry, forgive me, I love you and owe you a beer.

Daddy, you and I lost our sun. We went through hell and back together and were left holding each other's hand. There is no one I trust more, respect more, or am more inspired by. Your strength is where I got mine, and being your daughter is one of my highest honors. I love you the most any daughter has ever loved her dad. You are my lighthouse. Your faith in me and your support of this process is why this book is in existence. Does this make me an eagle? Thank you so very, very much.

Momma, how can someone thank someone for a lifetime? I finally did it! I finally finished my f***ing book! I will spend the rest of my life honoring your memory in any way I can. Be it through my love for my children, respect for myself, or words on a page. I miss you with every breath I take. You gave me everything. Thank you for making me the woman I am. Thank you for planting the seed in my heart to be a storyteller. I hope from heaven that this makes you proud.

And, finally, to the readers. Both new and old. Thank you for being an entire army of support for me when I lost my mom, for the countless comments, messages, posts encouraging me to keep going. Thank you for loving my family, my mom, and me, too. I hope this book makes y'all proud! Especially those super DBF fans! (Ginger, I'm looking at you.) Consider yourself cousins to me.

I hope this book makes y'all laugh, and if you bring this book to the beach, which is exactly where it should be read, just know it is an honor to be in your beach bag.

Thank you for buying this book and supporting me. May you never get another head cold.

Thank you,
Victoria

Heartbreak Soup

2 cups coarsely torn, bite-size pieces of day-old
sourdough bread

I use a garlic loaf from Publix bakery.

Extra-virgin olive oil

Kosher salt and freshly cracked peppercorns

For the love of God, don't use preground pepper.

1 pound sweet or mild Italian sausage, casings removed

½ cup dry white wine

1 to 2 yellow onions, finely diced

3 medium carrots, finely diced

3 celery stalks, finely chopped

3 to 4 large garlic cloves, minced

*If you use preminced garlic, I will never speak
to you again. Get a whole head of garlic, peel the
cloves, and please, God, press them through a
garlic press. It makes a difference!*

Red pepper flakes, to taste

I use about 2 teaspoons, but I like it spicy.

1 to 2 bay leaves

1 (15-ounce) can diced tomatoes, drained

*It's easier if you use the petite diced ones from
Hunt's.*

1 (15-ounce) can cannellini beans, rinsed and drained

4 to 6 cups low-sodium chicken broth

1 to 2 tablespoons red wine vinegar

4 ounces grated Parmesan cheese

1. Preheat the oven to 400°F. Toss the bread pieces with olive oil, salt, and cracked pepper. Lay them out on a rimmed baking sheet. Toast them until golden brown and very crunchy, 15 to 18 minutes. (If you are using fresh bread, toast the croutons further.) Let them cool.

2. In a large Dutch oven, add about 3 to 4 tablespoons of olive oil and heat over medium heat. Cook the sausage and brown it, breaking it up with a wooden spoon.

3. Add the white wine all at once and cook it down until it's almost gone. Add the onion, carrots, and celery. Cook for about 8 minutes. Add the garlic, red pepper flakes, a pinch of salt, and a crank of pepper. Stir them together until the vegetables are soft, about 20 minutes. Add the bay leaf, tomatoes, beans, and broth and bring to a boil. Reduce the heat and simmer for about an hour, stirring occasionally.

4. Add about three-quarters of the croutons to the soup. Just before serving, add the vinegar. Season with salt and pepper if needed. Serve, garnishing with the remaining croutons and the Parmesan cheese.